the
RAVISHING

USA TODAY BESTSELLING AUTHORS

AVA HARRISON
VANESSA FEWINGS

Editor: Jenny Sims
Proofreader: Jaime Ryter, Deborah Kuhn
Cover Design: Hang Le
Cover Photo: Wong Sim
Cover Model: Lucas Bloms
Formatted by: Champagne Book Design

For those looking for an escape…

We wrote this one for you.

Enjoy the ride.

"Hell is empty, and all the devils are here."
—William Shakespeare

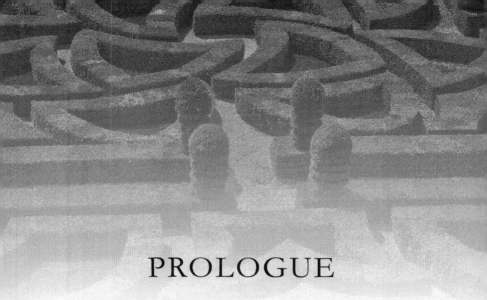

PROLOGUE

Cassius, 14

UNEASINESS SLITHERED IN THE SHADOWS.

It manipulated the air into something heavy and strangely tangible. The sunlight that streaked into the chapel shrank, dimming the once-bright colors of the stained glass windows above.

Something's wrong.

I tried to draw in a deep, wary breath, but it felt like the oxygen I inhaled was stabbing me inside my chest like shards of needles cut too deep.

He's coming for us. . .

Just like he promised.

Sensing him before I saw him, I moved from my position at the end of the pew and glanced around sharply, fighting this visceral feeling.

But nothing was out of place. Nothing was wrong.

Despite the evidence that this feeling was unwarranted, my mind dragged me back to that Louisiana swamp where Stephen Glassman had taken me today to prove a point to my father.

There, in that desolate marsh, he had delivered his brutal warning. His threat was full of loathing for my family. The words poured from his ugly mouth. Vicious words I was ordered to carry back to my father.

Stephen Glassman was coming for us.

You're being irrational.

I clenched my fists, angry at myself for feeling this way. Weak against the wisdom that nothing could touch us. We were Calvetti. A respected family of old money that even now flowed like a river, marking us as descendants of Italian aristocracy. Heirs to a vast fortune who had settled a century ago in the outer district of New Orleans.

Untouchable.

And for the first time in my life, I doubted my father's insistence that no one could harm us.

The fallout of today refused to lift. Sweat snaked down my spine as if I were back there with him. With Glassman. Getting in his car at gunpoint. Letting him take me out on the green murky waters in that small motorboat. Deep into the marsh, where the trees swallowed the sun.

Glassman had made his point to my father.

He could get to us.

Any of us.

At any time.

My father's enemy had let me live today. But he'd left me with the scent of stale swamp lingering in my nostrils, the mixture of saltwater and decomposition not letting go.

Mr. Montebello had told me my fear was irrational.

That Stephen's threats were vapid.

But I couldn't shake this feeling. Still, hours later, it unnerved me. The way the sound of those insects from the swamp continued to resonate in my ears, coaxing me back to them. To that untamed place. They begged me to undo what had been unleashed.

"I'm handling it." Mr. Montebello had stretched his arm around

me, and though he was my father's lifelong attorney, he'd done nothing to reassure me.

Because he hadn't seen the look in that man's eyes.

Within the chapel, head bowed in reverence, I prayed for peace. Prayed for courage. Asked God to show me how to live with this fear.

I had homework. A dinner to look forward to. Friends to see later.

Instead, I was in here. As if it would help.

St. Mary Magdalene lauded over the chapel from her stone pedestal. Her outstretched arms bestowed a blessing, reassuring everyone who entered they would be protected. Even the worst sinners.

But would she keep our enemy at bay?

Pulling my gaze away, I walked to the exit, it was time to head back to the house.

I stepped out and breathed in the thick air, noticing that, at my presence, hundreds of birds scattered in the sky.

Their wings flapped with fury. The air seemed to suck up their panic.

The swarm echoed, getting stronger. Louder. Forcing me to shield my face as if the slipstream of their dread could reach me.

I tracked their flight, and my eyes didn't leave the birds as they soared in the sky.

They were escaping.

But from what?

I shifted my gaze downward. It sent me off balance, like seeing through a tunnel with everything rushing me at once.

In the distance, my mother and sister sliced through the path. Their faces contorted in horror.

Everything moved too fast and too slow. They closed the space between us, but my feet stuck to the ground, rigid as they rushed toward me. Like gasoline poured over a spark, a flash of terror struck within. Fear erupted around us and in us, spreading like wildfire as they moved faster, driven by something unseen.

They staggered and wrapped their arms around each other,

willing one another on. Their strides were disjointed, slowing, and sluggish.

I forced myself out of slow-motion and sprinted toward them, desperate to reach where they'd faltered.

My flesh chilled to ice when I saw it—a bright red stain on my mother's blouse.

A stark contrast to the white fabric. It reminded me of spilled merlot soaking her chest. Wine spreading like streaking vines, tracing across the material. *If only it was that.*

I tore across the lawn trying to reach them, drenched in sweat, feet sluggish.

My mother tumbled to the ground. My sister's arms gave out as she fell with Mom. Both of them crashed to the grass, and their wails formed a haunting anguish.

"Cas—" A cough rattled from Mom's lips, cutting off my name with the horrific sound.

I watched, frozen in place while she tried to finish her words, as she tried to say my name. But nothing came out. She was too weak to speak. Her mouth opened again. Another failed attempt. Her frail arms lifted to grasp me.

"Help her, Cassius." My sister's voice cracked, cutting through the fog and making me look toward her. Her eyes, normally lit with happiness, had dulled. Replaced by a haunted expression, as if their light had extinguished. "Please," she pleaded with me.

It took a minute to understand what was happening. The remnants of shock lingered far too long, but then I moved into action.

My hands reached out, trying desperately to scoop up my mother. Trying to bring her to safety. But she was too heavy. Too resistant to move. She settled in my arms, her chest rising and falling fast. I watched her struggle to breathe, each inhalation drawn out and painful.

Her breaths came out ragged.

She was choking.

Scarlet seeped out the sides of her mouth as she swallowed and gagged, gasping for life.

Caught in a flash flood of panic, I dropped beside her, staying with her. Blood coated my hands. Its metallic scent saturated everything. The bright red from her mouth darkened, and a fresh crimson followed in its place.

She isn't going to make it.

"Stay awake!" I pleaded. "Stay with us."

"So tired." Her eyelids fluttered.

"Don't close your eyes. Don't give up."

Hoisting up her blouse, my hands scrambled beneath the sopping wet silk. My fingers tangled with my sister's as we struggled to stem the flow of red. I applied pressure to the puckered wound, trying to stop the flow, pressing my palm hard against the gape. I fought against the oozing. It came out thick, fast, and endless around my hand. Blood ebbed against my fingers for a few seconds, then seeped through in a strong current with no dam.

"Who shot her?" I asked Sofia. The sound of Mom's wheezing echoed around us, but Sofia didn't need to answer. *I knew.* "Who?" My voice strained, ragged and hoarse. Unfamiliar. No longer my own. It belonged to a boy about to lose everything.

"Tell me," I pleaded with Mom.

Tell me who did this!

"Glass—" She coughed a spray. Red rivulets trickled out between her lips and soaked her chin, her throat, down and onward until it met the dirt, pooling there. Her complexion had turned pale. A dusky hue.

Glassman.

My own chest tightened knowing it was my fault. I hadn't prevented this.

I wiped away the stain of blood that soaked her face and trailed her jaw.

"Get help!" I yelled at my sister, pointing toward the house.

She shook her head, frantic. "We can't go that way."

Mom's hand grasped my sleeve. "Cas."

She was bleeding out, dying in my arms, and there was nothing I could do about it.

"I'll go," I told my sister.

"No." Mom's grip held me fast.

"Mom, we have to move you." My voice was firm. Commanding.

"Can't." Her gaze tore into me.

I placed my hands behind Mom's back, and moved her upright to try to keep her awake. I needed to keep her alive until my father or one of his men came to help us.

Mom's eyelids flickered open and squinted. Failing to see. She took a breath as if she was summoning the last of her strength to speak to me. "T-take your sister. K-keep her safe."

"I'm keeping you both safe," I bit out through gritted teeth.

"No." She shook her head. "T-there isn't time."

"I won't leave you."

"It's too late for me. . ." she wheezed. "Your father. . ."

My eyes darted to look at Sofia. What was she saying? Mom was delirious. That was what this was. . .confusion from the blood loss.

Mouth bone-dry, I asked, "Where's Dad?"

Sofia shook her head. Unable to speak. Unable to say what I knew in my gut.

"Please. . ." Mom implored. "Save"—she swallowed hard—"your sister."

"Mom, please!" Sofia begged. Her face was ashen.

"Go," Mom pleaded. "They-they will find—" Her voice broke on a cough.

"Mom, I'm going to carry you to the chapel." But as I spoke those words, I knew she couldn't bear it.

Refusing to believe this bitter truth, I tried to lift her again. She cried out.

I couldn't bear the agony in her voice. The pain.

No, I won't say goodbye. Not like this. Not here in the dirt. Not when it was just my sister and me. She needed the best care, and she deserved the best doctors. She deserved to live. She deserved for us to fight.

"Mom. . ."

Her eyes fluttered open, and when she stared at me with that knowing look, I lost my will to speak. She grasped my hand with a strength I didn't know she had left in her.

"P-protect y-your sister." She tried to force a smile, but winced. Hers closed on a deep inhale. "She's all you have now."

An icy breeze swept past us. An omen.

And then it happened.

The glacier froze over.

Mom's eyes went wide and stilled, staring at nothing and at everything all at the same time. As if seeing the world anew. I lowered her to the ground, feeling unworthy of holding her in this state of stillness.

"Mom?" Sophia begged.

I raised my hand to quiet her.

A gunshot rang out.

Ignoring my sister's scream, I pressed a finger to Mom's carotid to check for a pulse but felt nothing.

"Mom's dead," I told her, forcing her up onto her feet. "We have to go." I stared at my sister. "Are you hurt?"

Tears streamed down Sofia's cheeks. "No."

"We need a phone," I said.

Raw emotions swelled and roiled, and I forced myself to endure them.

Be strong for Sofia.

Crack. Crack. Crack.

The bullets spewed in endless streams.

Springing to my feet, I grabbed the back collar of my sister's shirt, trying to drag her with me but feeling her resistance.

Dazed, she moved her feet slowly at first, reluctantly following.

With Sofia's hand in mine, following like a rag doll behind the power of my hold, we scurried across the lawn toward the chapel, back the way I'd come.

A shadow appeared in the doorway, cutting us off.

"This way." I yanked Sofia's arm left, frantically pulling her in the opposite direction. Everything in my gut told me this was the only way toward that shelter, exposed but known. Off across the sprawling lawn, voices carried in the darkness behind us.

Yelling.

Closing in fast.

Those first hedges of the maze stretched wide, threatening to swallow us whole as we disappeared within its sprawling walls. Enveloped by its darkness, both of us had long memorized the pathways, the turns, and the corners.

The leaves drowned out the noise of our footsteps.

Our pursuers followed us in, desecrating the maze with each step.

Looking for us.

Hunting for us.

Their voices carried over the height of the hedges. They were right on the other side of the greenery, so close they could reach through the shrubs and touch us if they knew we were there. They stormed through, searching every crevice, every angle, every conceivable space they expected to find us.

Leaning low, we continued on, weaving this way and that, avoiding contact, following familiar pathways, trusting what only we intimately knew—this place and all its secrets. As well as we knew each other.

We crouched inside our four-walled leafy hideout, cowering in the center, my hand cupped over her frightened mouth.

Shielded by familiar lush greenery, the foliage encased us like a womb. With my arm wrapped around her to comfort and protect her, I drew Sofia even closer against me to shield her with my body.

I should leave my sister here, safely camouflaged where she wouldn't be found.

I should go out there and face off with those men. Fight them with my bare hands. At least try for what they'd done.

"Protect your sister." Mom's haunting last words sabotaged my plan.

My fury formed a shape.

Claws.

They ripped me apart, shredding my nerves.

Gnawing into my flesh. Their marks absorbed bone-deep, marrow-deep, leaving a new me in their wake. Invisible talons reshaped my essence, forging something malevolent, dark, and disruptive. A craving so real, I felt my cells mutating, sculpted into the purest vengeance.

Adrenaline surged through blistering veins, bringing clarity.

Bringing death.

I would kill him.

But before that, I would dismantle his life piece by piece.

And once that was done, I would find the one thing he loved most . . .

And destroy it.

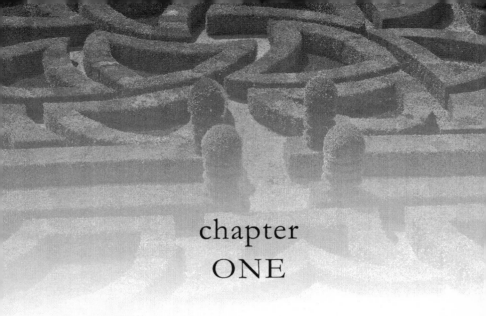

chapter
ONE

14 Years Later . . .
Anya, 18

A FLURRY OF NERVOUSNESS RUSHED THROUGH ME.
I knew I had to move, but my feet felt weighted to the ground, refusing to go down there and mix with all those people I didn't know.

Peering out and down at the lawn from behind my bedroom window, I watched a group of teenagers trampling over our well-tended garden.

Some of them explored the bouncy castle. Some hungrily shoved cake into their mouths.

Others were watching a nightmarish clown whip up balloons in the shape of weird-looking animals.

I hate clowns.

I didn't recognize a single face.

And I suspected neither did my brother.

They were all strangers. All invited over from happy homes to come and make it look like this was one, too.

A show for the neighbors.

Another demonstration of how fucked up our world really was.

All of this is to celebrate my birthday.

The big eighteen.

But the funny thing was, I didn't know any of them. The only person I knew was my brother.

The brother who rarely spoke to me and preferred his privacy. His video games were far more entertaining than talking with me. I was just his boring big sister.

We usually passed each other in the hallways of this mansion— two children ushered here and there by our strict nannies and, as we got older, private tutors.

They had fired the last one for letting me use her iPad to scour the Internet. We were still interviewing for a new one for Archie. Sucks, because I liked Elizabeth. She was kind and patient, always sneaking in books for me to read and comics for Archie.

That time I'd downed too much of my dad's gin, she had pretended the bottle broke. Then made sure I had enough water to drink and painkillers to hide my hangover. She'd hug us in the kitchen while making cookies. She was funny and made us laugh, brightening this place.

We really liked her, and that, apparently, put a target on her head, and she had to go.

We didn't do fun in this house.

I made my own entertainment. Devouring every book I got my hands on, including all the ones Elizabeth had snuck in. She had given me everything from the classics to modern-day fantasies, novels by Jane Austen to Sarah J. Maas.

Late in the evening, after my parents were in bed and the house was silent, I'd sneak into the poorly stocked library and take whatever caught my interest, bringing it back to my room and reading late into the night.

When I was feeling brave and was sure my parents were out, I'd sit in the living room and watch old movies. Sometimes, Archie would join me; sometimes we'd even talk.

Now that we were older, you'd think my brother and I would be close, but we weren't.

I hated to admit it to myself, but I had no one.

This loneliness was again messing with my brain because those nightmares were back. The same ones that haunted me years ago. Elizabeth said it was stress-induced, but from what?

Sending a burst of breath onto the windowpane, I ran a finger through the condensation to spell Anya in cursive across the glass.

Walking hand in hand with someone the same age—I'm four, I think. My socks soaked from the snow. We made our way along a river. Peering over a snowcapped railing into the distance at ornate towers that lauded over a city.

It was always the same dream.

Later, while using Elizabeth's iPad, I had recognized the spiked towers of the Kremlin.

Now, what the hell did that mean?

I'd never lived in a place where it snowed. Yet, I could swear I knew the coldness of snow between my fingers, the way it melted to the touch and pooled in my palm.

Elizabeth had told me it was probably something I picked up from a TV show I had watched. That it was probably because a part of me was yearning to go somewhere. As far away as Russia, apparently.

Peering down some more, I marveled at the spectacle my parents had conjured up of suburbia. We assimilated with the neighborhood as if what happened within these walls was ordinary. Even though my parents were hardly here.

The reality of my life made me sad.

The same routine. Same confinement. Same meals.

This feeling I didn't belong.

That something was off.

Maybe it was the fact that I knew our family was in shambles. That they left Archie and me too many nights to sleep in this big house alone. If that wasn't weird enough, they also wouldn't allow me to mention it—forbade me to discuss what happened in this house with anyone.

They wanted everyone to believe we were happy and perfect, trying desperately to portray us as a white-picket-fence family. Even our teachers who homeschooled us didn't see the truth. They'd never known what occurred in this house when the door shut behind them and they left to live their own lives.

They didn't know that my parents were rarely home. That when they were, they didn't speak to us. And if we confronted them about their neglect, they would punish us. Either locked in our rooms, all luxuries removed, or worse, by my father's hand.

One day, I hoped to get away, but I knew the scars would linger for a long time.

My memories were too rich and too real.

The strictness overflowed. Yet the love you'd expect from a family who seemed to have everything didn't.

Escaping the compound was impossible. Fleur de Lis-shaped spikes decorated the iron fence surrounding the front of the house. I could see it from here. It looked pretty but deadly. Along the sides and back of the property, ivy stretched the length of the high brick walls, creeping its way as if masking what those walls really meant.

The gate in the garden only opened for deliveries. The one at the front was merely for people my parents deemed worthy. That slim door to the side wall secured with a large padlock and reserved only for god knows what. No one used that one.

I never understood it. Why the security? I knew my father was a powerful man, but this made no sense.

Often, I sat at my bedroom window, looking out at the world and wondering if I'd ever escape. It's ironic since most people would dream of living like this. The luxury around me was reserved for fantasies, not nightmares. But even the velvet drapes and lavish marble couldn't hold back the echoes of solitude.

All I had to do was buy that plane ticket and make my dream of escaping a reality.

It wouldn't be easy to leave, considering they monitored our every move. Guards were always present. They wouldn't even let us go to school, instead, they homeschooled us.

Our parents knew how to fake affection.

It made me wonder why they'd wanted me.

Stephen—as my brother liked to call him—was always busy, and Mom was just as distracted with her social life. Too involved with her committees and parties. Often having to go away on business of her own.

The truth is, my parents were strangers to me. They didn't feel like parents.

Through the window, I saw my mother looking over the crowd, and I knew without a doubt that she was searching for me, wanting to introduce me to her friends as her beloved daughter. Showing a brightness off to them that came off as creepy if you knew the truth—that she was one way with me in public and another when alone.

My avoidance had been discovered, and if I didn't appear soon, there'd be hell to pay.

It's time to get fake.

I took a deep breath, squared my shoulders, and headed out of the sanctuary of my room. The only place I could let my dreams run wild and believe in more. In a life where I could run wild and free.

Where I could visit coffee shops or head out to the movies with friends or alone. Maybe even dare to go to a club.

In my dreams, there would be a Billie Eilish concert to see. Maybe see Harry Styles live. And if I was really lost in my thoughts, I would go to dinner without my parents, maybe even visit Café Du Monde in the French Market and eat my weight in beignets and drink enough coffee to keep me up for a week.

When I stepped outside onto the lawn, I glanced around to decide what path to take, where I could hide and not have to play the game and pretend that we all liked each other.

I didn't look like them and didn't feel like them. Hell, I didn't even sound like these interlopers.

Another thing drilled into me from an early age was to perfect my accent, so I sounded uber posh, like one of those Ivy League students. The ones who got to make decisions for themselves.

I was raised to be perfect. Poised, polished, and precisely elegant.

No southern accents. No hair out of place and, most importantly, no personality—in case I was ever noticed.

It was exhausting, to be honest.

What was it all for?

Perhaps for this precise moment, when I could make an appearance and smile and wave at strangers as Glassman's daughter. Giving credence to the web of lies they'd spun about my brother and me existing happily in this place. One happy family that could make the neighbors think they were the outliers.

Across the lawn, surrounded by Archie's fake friends who he didn't even know, my brother stopped talking just long enough to stare up at me with the same emotionless expression. That silent warning to prevent me from coming over. He didn't want me embarrassing him in front of these people he hoped would be his friends.

There was no affection here.

Not even in his eyes.

It didn't take him long to make his way over to me. We might not be close, but we both agreed this place sucked.

The one thing that tethered us together.

He stood beside me. Neither of us spoke. Both of us watched the crowd as if we were waiting for something to happen. As though someone might point out what we were so good at hiding.

I'd filled in the spaces between the mystery—imagined my dad was an American spy, and that was why he kept us safe in Louisiana. Or maybe he advised senior political figures with his foreign business insight, which warranted the impenetrable-iron-gates kind of protection.

Archie looked miserable. Both of us just looking out at his fake friends, who seemed to be having fun, as we waited for the curtain to rise on our ruse.

"Where is he?" I finally asked.

Archie turned to face me, cocking his head in a question. "Who?"

I shook my head at his silence. "Dad. Who else?"

"Oh. . ." He trailed off for emphasis. "You really think he'd be out here for this?"

I let out a long, drawn-out sigh. "Yes." I shouldn't have hoped, but somewhere inside me, I'd convinced myself I deserved it. "He told me he would be."

"Wow, Anya. You actually believe that shit." No matter how much he disappointed me in the past, I did.

"He didn't attend mine."

"You weren't turning eighteen."

"True. He was out of the country on business on my sixteenth birthday, remember?"

I nudged his arm playfully. "You know he loves you in his own twisted way."

Archie smirked, but then his eyes filled with sadness. For him or me, it was hard to tell.

Regardless of how I wanted to protest, I knew he was right. They treated us equally. A fair dose of shit for us both.

Still, for some reason, I thought today would be different. I had this false belief my father would come through today on my eighteenth birthday. That he'd leave the sanctity of his office and make an appearance.

I was wrong.

So painfully wrong.

"I know you want out." Archie sidled closer. "You'll be able to leave soon."

His voice cut through my inner rambling, and I looked up at him, up into his big eyes that were filled with hope and jealousy all mixed into one. We always spoke of this day, when we were legal and what would happen.

"Technically, I can go, but the question is will he let me," I muttered under my breath.

"Can he stop you?"

"Yes."

"Mom wouldn't want you to go."

I gave him a look he deserved. He gave me a knowing nod of agreement back, confirming what we both knew. She'd hardly notice.

This cage was not just fortified with towering walls, my parents also etched it in fear. Fear of the unknown, of the world outside my bubble.

Someone must have known why we were forced to live like this.

A grandparent, maybe? An aunt or uncle? Someone held the answers, and the knot twisting in my stomach demanded I find them.

I walked away.

From behind me, I heard his question. "Where are you going?"

I didn't answer. Refused to have him stop me.

If Dad wasn't coming out here, I'd go to him.

Walking through the throngs of people without slowing my pace, I headed inside. With each stride more resolute, I would ask him why he didn't think me important enough to show up.

I pushed down the butterflies swarming in my belly.

The closer I got, the worse it felt, as if they were frantically flapping their wings in a panic, trying to dissuade me. Terrified I'd pass out from nerves, I turned the corner and faced that sprawling hallway and saw the open door to his office.

He was standing there.

Imposing.

Leaning on the doorjamb, he was seemingly deep in thought. Half in his office, half out, as though unsure.

And he was never unsure.

Larger than life, his shoulders filled the space, his eyes dark with an intensity that shook everyone they fell upon—as though looks really could kill.

His mind clearly on anything other than the celebrations outside.

Our gazes caught, and his eyes narrowed in displeasure. I opened my mouth to speak, to say something that would garner his affection and remind him what today was, but before my words came spilling out, he gave me a look that rocked me to the core. It looked a lot like disappointment.

He shut the door—shutting me out, leaving me standing in the hallway.

chapter
TWO

Cassius

SOFIA WAS THE ONLY GOOD THING LEFT IN THIS WORLD, AND seeing her free of worry was like breathing in the freshest air for the first time in decades. It was everything.

She was everything.

Beneath the archway of freshly plucked flowers, I watched my sister have the first dance with her new husband, Jake Powel.

I wasn't the only one either.

Hundreds of guests sat at the surrounding tables, and they were equally enamored by them.

Normally, I wasn't much for details, but even I could see the beauty around me.

The cream-and-silver-themed décor was an understated touch, but it reflected my sister's personality to perfection. She'd never gone for showy. Sofia was as humble as she was beautiful.

And tonight, she looked stunning in her wedding gown. She hadn't wanted to spend a fortune, but when she saw the Tom Ford gown, the smile that spread across her face was enough for me to hand her my black card and demand she buy it.

She'd gushed that it was made from the finest lace, but as an older brother, all I saw was a plunging V-neckline. One that my mother would have loved, but my father would have raised his eyebrow at.

Regardless of my protective nature, she looked gorgeous, and seeing her dance was enough to make me form a real and genuine smile.

She could have asked for extinct animals to be reanimated for today, and I would have done everything in my power to make it a reality. I only wished Mom could've been here. Instead of me walking Sofia down the aisle, it should have been Dad.

Mom had asked me to promise to look after her, and after all these years, I could honestly say I had done just that.

I loosened my tie. I preferred jeans and T-shirts to this black tuxedo. Predictably, I had gotten wary looks from some guests who'd caught my tattoos. The ones that showed on my hands and fingers.

Good thing I didn't give a fuck about other people's opinions.

I was too busy ensuring my father's empire continued to thrive.

Wealth also gave me the resources to protect her—protect this newly married couple and any children they might have.

Ridley Montebello crossed the edge of the dance floor to reach me. I gestured a welcome not only to a good friend but also my trusted attorney. That black tuxedo made him fit into the crowd like all this finery was easy for him, and in so many ways, it was.

Ridley and I had gone to boarding school together. Both raised far from home, we had bonded instantly. That and the fact that his father and my father had been long-time business associates and friends as well. He'd taken over his late father's law firm right out of Harvard. None of this decadence would faze him. Nor the impressive guests who'd flown in from Italy. The Venice crowd was made up of distant cousins and other relatives I tried to keep track of. A few nobles were thrown in to make things interesting.

Lowering his voice, Ridley muttered under his breath, "Someone tried to infiltrate the wedding."

The hairs on my nape prickled as my hands balled into fists.

"Bad time?" His words rose over the music.

"Yes." I was happy for a brief moment. But now, thanks to Ridley, all sentimentality was fading. "Talk."

"One man. He's alone. He's contained, obviously."

"Where?"

"Boathouse. Want me to call the police?"

I felt a rush of frustration that one of my favorite places at my sister's French Provincial mansion in the bayou was about to become a crime scene. Though I would see to it that no one reported anything that went on in here. No one needed to know what happened in the boathouse.

"He works for Glassman." It wasn't a question. I didn't need a gut check to figure that out.

"We're getting that gist from him, yes."

"He sent an amateur."

"I'll have him arrested for trespassing."

"Not yet." I made it sound casual.

Because the man was no doubt here to do so much more than step onto private property.

Keeping my eyes on the dance floor, I asked, "His name?"

"We're working on it."

Keeping my tone even, I asked, "Does he have a message from Glassman?"

Though having one of Glassman's men here to ruin all of this finery could be construed as the message.

Ridley raised his hand in a gesture of defense. "Remember, I'm your attorney, so don't say anything that will implicate me."

"Do we have him well-guarded?"

"Of course." Ridley turned to face me. "Don't do anything you'll regret."

Even now, Ridley had no idea of the extent of evil I'd wielded over the years. He remained blissfully unaware of the men I'd dealt with to maintain our survival. At twenty-eight, he still romanticized the world. As my friend, continuing to shield him was a priority. I'd always sensed he knew of my misgivings but was wise enough not to go there.

I raised my hand to keep him from saying anything else. Not when my sister joyfully waltzed around the dance floor in the arms of her groom. And certainly not when that view of her devastating happiness deserved a respectful silence.

Sofia glanced over at me with sheer love in her eyes. Her bright cheeks flushed with contentment.

This moment wouldn't be tainted by *their* name.

They'd already taken enough.

"Sofia looks beautiful," said Ridley.

My sister looked more than beautiful. She was stunning in the same way our mother was. The mirror image of a piece of our past before the nightmares unfolded, and we were orphaned during that balmy night all those years ago—though it could have been yesterday.

Nearby, a burst of wings took flight. I turned my eyes skyward to follow the flock of sparrows scattering the sky.

The weight of my mother heavy in my arms as she slipped away, that scarlet curse of blood merging with tears.

The rest was blurry.

"Cassius."

I came back to the moment, furious with myself that Stephen was stealing this evening from us, too.

"Just talk to the guy," Ridley said, warily. "Then kick him off the property."

Stephen Glassman might have fulfilled his promise to destroy our family, but he'd failed to kill me that day, and that was where he'd made a fatal mistake.

Anyway, today wasn't about him. It was about family.

I was proud of Sofia for making a good life for herself despite our past. In all fairness to Jake, no man would be good enough to marry my sister. Even a high-powered banker like himself. Though he had the money and sense to know keeping her safe was a priority.

A few weeks after their honeymoon, they'd be living in England because that was the best place for her. He'd gotten a job at the

London Stock Exchange, so there'd be more than enough money. Though she never needed to worry about that.

And if Jake faltered in any way, I'd crush him financially. So there was that. From the way he behaved around me, he knew it, too. Now that Sofia was married and would soon start a family of her own, I'd be sharing the responsibility with him of keeping her safe. That look he threw my way proved he'd honor his word to shield her.

A knowing respect for me as the patriarch of the Calvetti family.

Frank Sinatra's "The Way You Look Tonight" rose out of the surround-sound speakers.

It was no surprise when Sofia broke away from Jake and gestured for me to join her for the second dance. I stepped foot onto the dance floor and walked toward her.

To some, I'd appear rough around the edges or to the more discerning guests on the groom's side, dangerous even. We'd survived too many years with only each other for support for either of us to care about the opinions of strangers.

Approaching Sofia, I gave a small bow as Jake stepped aside. With a motion of gratitude, I led my sister away, and we began a slow dance together. I pulled her into my body in an affectionate hug, and she wrapped an arm around my neck, the other holding me close.

"Isn't all of this perfect?" She looked up at me.

"It really is."

"You're the best brother a girl can have."

"You didn't always think that." My brow arched.

"When I was five and you wouldn't let me play with your toys."

"You mean my miniature Italian car collection?" I winked.

"Do you still have it?"

Trying to hold a fake smile, I feigned it was somewhere. She didn't need to be reminded it was in the attic of our old home. The home that had brought her so much grief. The one she rarely visited. Yet, I had stayed there as though afraid my promise to myself all those years ago might never be realized—when I was ready—on my terms.

And not after I'd let the Glassmans have an eternity of knowing

I was coming for them. Maybe tonight. Maybe in another decade. When they'd spent even more years watching their backs and jumping at shadows.

"You like Jake, don't you?" She'd broken my melancholia.

"He makes you happy."

She rolled her eyes.

"Seems decent."

"I love him."

"Him loving you more is what matters to me."

"He does."

"You're a great couple," I said to reassure her with a wry smile.

It seemed to work as she rested her head against my chest and relaxed into the slow dance.

Time would tell. Jake had married into the Calvetti family, and that meant he was aware our father had built one of the greatest shipping empires in the world. Maybe Dad had also dabbled on the edge of the underworld, but it had been me who'd finally taken us right into its center.

It hadn't always been this way.

As a young man, I was shipped off to boarding school and lived amongst the upper crust of New York society until I graduated. Foolishly, I'd believed it would always be like this.

Privileged and safe.

Until that evening.

That short visit home to New Orleans.

The future I envisioned for myself changed in the blink of an eye.

I had seen the worst of what men can do. I'd been unprepared for the slaughter that ensued, taking our parents from us, and I had been forced to become a man before I was supposed to.

Forced to put myself second and my sister first. I'd done it gladly. I'd do anything for her.

"You've given me the best wedding." Her eyes watered with emotion.

Pulling her closer, I said, "Shhh."

"This will be you one day."

"Focus on you," I said firmly. "This day is yours."

Me having a lover meant that she would be vulnerable to the whim of a man who would take his revenge out on her. Loving anyone left me vulnerable, and I needed to remain vigilant. Needed to be constantly poised to take down that family.

But only when I was ready.

There was a glimmer of affection left for my sister. The Glassmans had stolen the rest.

All that remained was hate.

That was what they'd done to me. Replaced my soul with an endless void after murdering our parents. The unseen scars were a testament to their attack that day.

I had failed.

I wasn't able to protect them.

Unable to save Mom.

The memories of that house in the woods marked what those people were capable of. At fourteen, that event left more than an indelible impression. It had carved out a monster.

Forever changed.

Though I did what I could to protect Sofia from my darkness.

"Mom would be so proud," I whispered close to her ear.

She closed her eyes as she sank into Sinatra's dulcet tones and sighed as though letting the memory of our parents wash over her. I held onto this thought of Mom, bringing her into this moment, even as I endured the loss of her, so she could be with us in her own way. Dad, too, would have loved every second of this wedding.

Glassman had stolen that from us.

And I would repay him by delivering him to hell.

The bad blood between families would never cease until that entire family was wiped from the earth.

I'd start with his children.

That was what I had told Glassman three weeks after he'd killed my parents. He'd laughed in my face, but something told me my words had rattled him.

Even with our security tight, I'd suspected one of Glassman's men would attempt to make a show of it this evening.

A counter-threat.

Which proved he still thought of me as a hazard. I was flattered, to be honest. Knowing he was still scared gave me a warm feeling all over. Like downing a Macallan Old Double Cask Whisky and letting the liquor flow through your bloodstream.

It's time.

Ridley didn't need to know the details of what was to happen next.

After this dance, I'd head off to the boathouse to become acquainted with our trespasser.

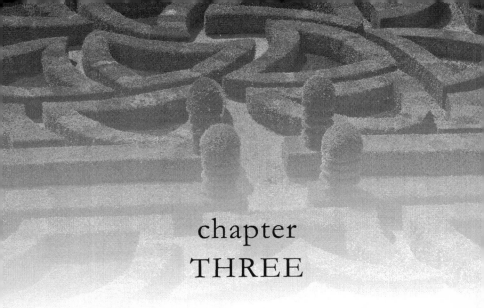

chapter
THREE

Anya

CONSUMED WITH DREAD, I STOOD IN ARCHIE'S BEDROOM staring at his bruised and swollen left eye. "What happened?" He sat in his swivel chair and turned away from me. Sliding his headphones back on his head. . .

I hated seeing him hurting.

Archie gripped his controller and went back to playing *Fortnite*. The video game fired-up on his monitor before him—plunging his character into mayhem.

I took a step closer. "Archie, was it Dad? What happened?"

"Leave me alone."

"Not until you tell me."

He threw down his controller and yanked off his headphones. "Dad found me in his office."

"Why were you in there?"

"Go away."

"Talk to me—"

"Leave me alone!"

I left him for a few minutes to calm down, brought back a bag of frozen peas from the freezer, and placed it over his bruised eye, just like I'd seen in movies. His expression softened as he sat back on the edge of his bed.

I sat beside him. "Please."

Archie slid the make-shift icepack of frozen peas down his bruised cheek. "Ever wondered why we aren't allowed in his office?"

"He doesn't like when we move things." I shrugged.

"It's more than that," he grimaced.

My back stiffened. "What do you mean? Did you find something?"

"Yeah." He nodded. "I'd have to show you. You won't believe me otherwise." He threw the defrosted bag of peas onto his desk.

We left his room.

He led me down the hall, pausing before my parents' room. His index finger rested on his lips, gesturing for me to remain quiet. They weren't home, but a stray staff member could see us, and maybe even report back to them that we'd been in here.

Archie turned the handle and went in.

Curiosity made me follow him.

Stopping before a painting—a boring green valley with lush trees that drew little attention—he reached up to remove it from the wall and revealed a safe hidden behind it.

With the ease of someone who'd memorized the code, he punched away at a series of digits on the numbered pad. A beep and a click and it opened.

"I watched Dad," he answered my unspoken question. "Promise me they'll never know I showed you this."

"Promise." Looking beyond his hand, I watched as he reached into the gaping safe filled with papers.

Archie removed a leather binder and flung it open to the first page.

"What's this?" I asked nervously.

He rested his hand over one of the photos. "Promise you'll never ask Mom or Dad about it."

"Show me."

Sliding his palm away, Archie pointed at a photo of a small girl about four or so. She could have been me when I was that age. We were similar in that both of us had brown hair and her eyes, like my own, were a deep shade of blue. But she wasn't me. That birthmark on her wrist proved it.

"Who's that?"

A deep swallow rolled down Archie's throat. "Her name was Anya."

My stomach roiled as though my name was poison, and it was threading its way into my blood and constricting my veins. "That's not me."

A wave of emotion flashed over him. "I know."

My thoughts swirled in confusion as I tried to grasp what he was saying. I struggled to take in a deep breath, but the air failed to reach the bottom of my lungs.

"Are you okay?" he whispered.

"We had a sister?"

The shock was evident in my voice.

Archie flipped over the page and pointed at another photo. "That's what it looks like."

With a dry mouth, I managed, "Why didn't they tell us?"

"Don't know. When I asked about them having other children before us, Dad took off his belt. . ." His face revealed what he'd done with it.

"They had other children," I repeated, trying to make sense of it.

He swallowed hard at that.

I frowned at him. "When did you find this out?"

The room was spinning.

He looked full of shame. "A month ago."

"I don't believe you."

"Look at the photo with Mom holding a little girl."

"It could be a friend's baby."

"It's not. I'm sorry to be the one to tell you."

"Tell me what?"

"There's an adoption certificate." His face went pale. "Your parents' names have been removed."

"My parents?" My fingers felt numb. "Not Mom and Dad?"

"There's a black strip across all the important details."

Watching him unfold it, I peered over his arm to read the doctored document that revealed so little—yet so much. Did it really hide my birth mother's name?

A lump lodged in my throat.

He tucked it away as quickly as he'd unraveled it, sliding it back into the album.

The room closed in.

My body chilled to zero degrees, or so it felt. "How come I didn't know? Wasn't told?"

"Hopefully, this explains a lot."

"What else haven't you told me?"

Why hadn't they told me?

"I got a ladder and went up to the attic. There were dolls up there you've never played with," he said, his voice distant.

"Maybe you just don't remember me having them." He was younger than me, after all.

"I'd remember. There are more photos of that same girl with Mom and Dad."

"Show me."

He stared at me for the longest time. "The ladder's gone."

"We can't get up there anymore?" A slither of disbelief. "You should have shown me."

I always believed our parents were merely eccentric. The only comparison I had was with the families who occasionally came over. Which wasn't saying much.

Archie reached out and grabbed my arm. "It's not just you."

"What?"

He turned a few pages in the album and pointed at a photo of another baby dressed in blue.

"Is that you?"

"No." His fingers curled on the page. "His name was Archie."

His words resonated with the same burden. "Wait. You are adopted too?"

"I think so."

"Why didn't you tell me?" I asked solemnly.

"Because they never talk to us about anything, and I knew they would never talk to us about this."

Heady, I reached out to touch the wall, but it was too far away.

"You're the first person I've told," he admitted.

"We have to ask them about it."

Archie looked horrified. "Dad gets violent around anything to do with this."

A memory popped in my brain—*running down a dimly lit hallway, someone calling me back.*

Russian.

Someone was speaking Russian.

I reached into my thoughts for more, but it dissolved like ice in the sun before I could touch it.

They weren't dreams. They were memories.

"I hate that they have the same names."

Sadness shimmered in his eyes. "One day, I'm going to find out who my real parents are."

"Maybe you're wrong."

"I'm not. There's bound to be more stuff about us in Dad's office. That's why I was in there." He slid the album back into the safe, closed the door on it, and punched a series of numbers to lock the mechanism.

Unsettled, I caressed my chest. "You should have told me."

"I was scared you would go to Dad."

"I wouldn't. You should have trusted me. I might not be your blood but—"

"You'll always be my sister," he cut me off. His flash of kindness confused me, but I welcomed it.

In this home, after what we had been through, I needed it.

"Maybe this is why they homeschooled us?" I said more to

myself than him. "They didn't want us talking with our teachers or friends? They don't want anyone to know?"

"They control what we do on the Internet. And now we know why."

Memories scattered like fireflies in the night as I felt the agony of a stolen past.

I had never belonged here.

I cleared my thoughts. "We could leave together."

"Unlike you, I'm not done with school. I still have my exams. Anyway, there's no money for us to take. We'd never survive."

In a daze, I strolled over to the bed and sat on the edge as all this sunk in.

"Careful, they'll know we were in here."

I sprang up and turned to smooth the duvet.

"You can't tell anyone." He came closer. "You know that, right?"

I pivoted to face him. "We just go on pretending?"

"Yes."

As my flesh chilled, I couldn't bear to look at him because, for me, that wasn't something I could do.

Not anymore.

I pointed to his swollen eye. "Can I get you anything else?"

"Just want to play *Fortnite* and forget I exist."

I was too shaken to say anything else.

Too rung out with shock.

After we left our parents' room, we went our separate ways.

I watched Archie returning to his bedroom, feeling sick at what Dad had done to him.

Standing there at the top of the staircase, I looked around at what was meant to be our home but now felt foreign.

My world was unraveling.

Everything I knew to be true was a lie.

Learning I was adopted had come with a price. Dad had punished Archie for looking for clues about his family. Archie had been brave and he deserved me to be just as courageous for him.

This house might be one of the most beautiful properties in

the Garden District, but inside its high gates and fancy walls, it festered with lies.

I couldn't remember the exact moment I saw my parents as cold-hearted and cruel. Perhaps when I'd observed our neighbors from a distance being playful with their children in contrast to our parents' behavior. It started when we were so young that we'd gotten so used to it.

The faces of those children in the photos he'd shown me would haunt my days and become my nightmares—adding to the older, more mysterious dreams I had.

Morbid thoughts of what had happened to them spiraled in my imagination. Finding out felt like an obsession—a catalyst for me going downstairs.

Heading for that one room we were forbidden to enter.

Our parents were clearly unstable.

This house was more like a prison than a home.

Once inside the forbidden zone, I opened drawers and rummaged through papers in Dad's desk. If he caught me in his office, I knew I would have a bruised eye like Archie.

Inside the bottom drawer of my father's oak desk was a piece of paper caught in the drawer. My curiosity spiked, and I tugged it gently so as not to rip it. Easing out the yellowing paper, I saw it was a document—a copy of a deed for a cemetery plot in Lafayette Cemetery.

It might not be the clue Archie had been searching for, but it was sketchy.

Heart thrumming, I slid the drawer closed.

Within minutes, I was throwing on my flats and sneaking out the back of the house. I should have changed out of my dress, and grabbed a coat, but I couldn't risk someone catching me.

The last time I'd risked leaving here was when I went to see the float Mom had decorated for Mardi Gras. I'd gotten away with it that time, though no such luck the following winter. They'd caught me before I even left the house.

It was easy to punch in the numbers now since I memorized the code and once I did, I snuck out.

This wasn't about being defiant. This was about finding answers. Finding the truth.

Taking the same risks that my brother had. I was doing this as much for him as I was me. Up Third, turning onto Prytania Street and along Washington Avenue, I made my way toward Lafayette Cemetery. I'd often peeked out the window and watched the crowds amble by the front of our house on their walking tours. Now, in the dead of night, the streets were empty.

A rush of adrenaline surged through me from being outside—a forbidden trek along the path, hurrying by intriguing multicolored houses with their cast-iron fences and lush foliage that complemented their well-tended gardens.

Making it to Lafayette Cemetery quickly, I found the gate open and went on through

I pulled out the map of the burial plot and walked carefully upon the rubble pathway that ran alongside a stone wall, recalling Archie telling me this cemetery dated back to the eighteenth century.

Each weathered above-ground tomb differed from the next, and many were in states of decay. It made me sad to think that the relatives had either moved away or had died and could no longer tend to them.

As I hurried along the outer wall and took a sharp left into the center of the graveyard, I marveled at the stillness—as if even the wildlife knew to be respectful.

And there it was, the generously sized Glassman tomb.

I felt a jolt of intrigue when I climbed the short three steps of the structure, vast compared to those that flanked it on either side.

Whoever had visited recently hadn't secured the door properly because a padlock hung open. It wasn't like I could go back home and warn Dad. The thing would have to stay this way. I wondered if Mom ever came here. Maybe it was her who'd left it open.

Thoughts of who my birth family were swirled around my mind—I pushed them away.

I nudged open the door and stepped inside, the sound of my soles echoing on the stone floor. Heart pounding, I held my breath as though being here might offend the dead.

My eyes adjusted to the dimness.

Running my fingers across each long marble tomb, I estimated about ten of my relatives were buried here. If I was adopted, maybe not. Maybe I was only related by name.

What the fuck?

My throat tightened—Archie Stephen Glassman was inscribed on the far side of a marble coffin. Nausea welled as I moved to peer down at the one beside it. My focus blurred when I read the neatly engraved name of Anya Helena Glassman. They'd even given my middle name to her—no, wait, it was me who had been given hers.

This was where they'd ended up.

A sob formed for an unknown child who bore my name. If not for being shown those photos by Archie, I didn't know what I'd have done. If it wasn't for Archie, I'd just slip away from the Garden District and never look back.

The hairs pricked on my forearms, and I knew, knew with every cell of my being that I wasn't alone.

Someone was standing at the door.

The air thickened, and dust danced within the rays of the moon flooding in. Light reflected off minute particles like a hex had been cast on this place.

The walls of the crypt felt like they were closing in.

I looked into those dark eyes that were glaring back at me.

The thought of what he'd done to Archie rushed through my brain.

"Hello, Anya."

"What happened to them?" I asked weakly.

My father stepped in, his suede shoes crunching on the unswept ground as he faced the resting places of his lost children.

"Dad?" I coaxed.

"We were trying to protect you from this."

"From what?"

"It's complicated." He gave an unnerving smile, meant to comfort, I suppose.

"They have our names?" Emotion made my words heavy.

"We wanted to recreate the family we'd lost."

I observed him.

Reminded of the spirited punishments he'd delivered in the past, I put some distance between us.

He noticed me stepping back and gave a careful nod.

"Your mother and I love you dearly, Anya. You know that. We've wrapped you in cotton and done our best to keep you safe. It hasn't been easy on you." His eyes darkened. "Or us."

"How did they die?" My question echoed in the lonely chamber.

"Don't worry about that now." He shook his head thoughtfully.

I studied my namesake's tomb, and a shudder swirled up my spine. I tried to shake the thought that one day I might lie within one of these.

"Did something bad happen to them?" I needed him to say it.

"How did you find out about them?" He eyed me. "From Archie?"

My thoughts flashed to what Dad had already done to him. Dread welled, and my belly ached.

"Found the receipt for the plot in your drawer." I fixed my stare on him to convey Archie had nothing to do with this. "Bet when you were my age, you had a similar curiosity, Daddy." I threw in.

"My office? You're not allowed in there. But you already know that, don't you?"

"I'm sorry."

"Let's go home, sweetheart." He closed the gap between us.

His closeness sent a chill up my spine, but I walked with him toward the door, feigning compliance.

He threw an arm around my shoulders to guide me back the way I had come. What a rarity this was, him showing any kind of patience. But I knew the truth. It was a lie.

He was waiting until we got home.

There was something more going on here, and as we left the cemetery, it hit me.

He wanted me to find that tomb. Or that's how it felt.

His Mercedes was parked outside Lafayette Cemetery. He drove us back to Fifth Street in silence—the distance short. My fingernails dug into my palms all the way there.

I tried to cope with the consequences of what I'd done.

Once home, dad guided me toward his office. That look in his eyes told me to prepare for his impending violence.

As we were about to enter his office, a loud bang echoed from outside the front door.

Then a blood-curdling scream carried from somewhere in the house.

"He's here!"

Dad grabbed my hand and pulled me along. "Hurry." He dragged me behind him.

The sound of spraying bullets ricocheted, and I ducked as though it would help. A scream built in my throat, and I was too terror-stricken to release my grip on Dad's hand.

We made it to the foot of the stairs.

"Up!" Following his direction and not letting go, I ascended two at a time. My shoulder was yanked painfully as he pulled me up behind him, and I regretted my earlier adventure as though I alone had brought mayhem with my rebellion.

Mom dashed out of their bedroom and gestured for us to follow her inside.

"No," said Dad.

"I can't." She sounded terrified. "Not like this."

"We agreed."

"Please, Stephen—"

"Not now!" Spittle escaped his mouth as he yelled it.

"I won't!" she bit out.

"We talked about this, remember?" His voice was calm, it almost sounded rational.

She cowered against his anger, stepping back into the room.

Dad turned to me. "Get your brother and meet us here," he snapped.

He was right—I'd be faster.

Already taking flight, I sprinted along the hallway toward Archie's room. When I made it through his door, I couldn't see him. Just his unmade bed. I flung myself toward his bathroom and found it empty.

Turning sharply, I headed back to my parents' bedroom and stopped abruptly inside.

Where the hell had they gone?

Bolting out to look for them along the hallway, I glanced through the banisters. My stomach clenched when I saw the men ascending the stairs. All of them wearing combat gear.

Jesus Christ, they were wielding military-grade weapons. A dark stranger shouted an order from behind them. In seconds, they'd be on the balcony, and they'd see me.

Pivoting, I bolted toward my bedroom. Glancing one last time through the banister at the tall man in a black suit—

His sinister dark brown eyes found me.

I leaped back, but it was too late.

He'd stripped me bare with the intensity of his scrutiny. The kind of look that tore through a soul with unforgiving darkness.

He took the stairs two at a time to reach me.

I crashed into my bedroom and slammed the door shut behind me. Then I turned the lock.

My heart beat violently in my chest.

A ringing sounded in my ears.

It was hard to breathe.

Each inhale of oxygen felt like sharp stabs in my chest.

Fear blinded me as I staggered across the room.

Once inside the closet, I tripped over my feet as I shut myself in and crouched, hiding beneath a row of clothes as though they would shield me.

Behind me, a shoebox crushed beneath my weight. Then the sound of more boxes tumbling over filled the space.

I cursed each one, hugging my knees tight to my chest as my heart battered against my rib cage.

They've got the wrong house.

Once they realized their mistake, they would go.

Stay hidden.

Drawing in quick breaths, I replayed these thoughts, listening for any sound to indicate they found Archie or my parents. Even after everything, I still couldn't bear for anything to happen to them. Thank God the staff wasn't here yet.

A drawn-out silence highlighted my ragged breaths.

SLAM.

My bedroom door was breached.

With a hand over my mouth to prevent a scream, I peered through the slats at the blur of movement on the other side.

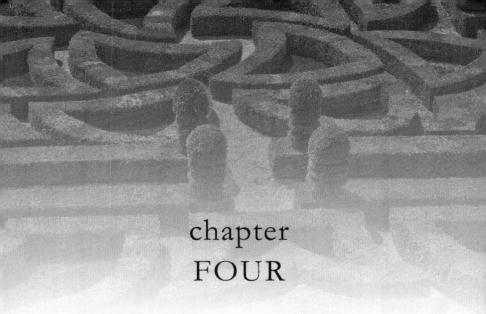

chapter
FOUR

Anya

THE CLOSET DOOR FLUNG OPEN.

The silhouette of a man towered above me.

A sliver of light flooded in and danced across his striking face. He was thirtyish, maybe younger, with devastating features that formed a handsome man. For a fleeting second, his deep-brown eyes reflected kindness as they held mine.

Right up until his full mouth tightened with hate. The same stranger I'd glimpsed from the balcony was staring down at me. His suit clashed with the others. The tie around his neck loosened with a studied casualness.

He focused his attention as though equally fascinated. The stark contradiction of sexy yet rugged. Tattoos marked his hands to reveal so much more about him—things I never wanted to know.

If I survived, remembering his face was crucial because questions would be asked later. A rendering of him would be marked in pencil by someone trying to stir my memory. It made me wonder if they'd believe the sketched phantasm I came up with.

A description considered unreal—because his allure was too captivating. His features were too attractive for a mere mortal.

Men poured into the room behind him. They stood back a little.

One of them braved to step up. "Want me to check that she's unarmed?"

"She's unarmed," he replied, not keeping his eyes off me as he knelt. "Unless she's strapped a pistol to her thigh." He smirked. "Have you?"

I shook my head.

Intrigue marred his face as he reached out to pry my hand off my mouth. "Anya?"

"Don't hurt me."

His brow furrowed. "I'm not promising anything I can't deliver."

I exhaled sharply. "You've got the wrong house."

Swiftly, he ran his hand along my stomach. His fingers trailed upward and swept beneath each armpit.

Along my chest.

Beneath my breasts.

I couldn't breathe as he explored me.

It was only when his hands moved to my back, and he withdrew them from my spine, that I let out my breath.

He cupped my cheek. "I've been looking forward to this for a very long time."

"What do you want?"

His smirk was menacing. "To savor every second."

Me, he's talking about me.

There, beneath his left cuff, was the hint of a red tattoo. Half in a daze, I reached for the edge of his wrist and eased his cuff up a little to reveal an intricately inked design of the sun. His eyelids became heavy as though with contemplation, watching my intrigue wilt.

Then he removed his hand from my face and reached for my hem.

I flinched as he continued his search up my dress, and found my inner thigh.

His fingers moved fast, traveling upward with quick, detached professionalism.

I snapped my thighs closed, trapping his palm between them to stop him from going higher.

"Don't fight me."

"What are you doing?" I bit out, refusing to relent or give in to this stranger.

"Open," he said huskily. "Don't ask dumb questions."

Keeping my eyes on his, I eased open my thighs as though hypnotized by his severity. His hand swept along my inner thighs as he continued to frisk me. "She's good."

"Is it her?" asked someone from behind him.

He gave a sharp nod.

My head crashed back against the clothes behind me as this heady danger morphed into confusion.

He was evil.

Like a dangerous animal you see inside a cage.

One you can't take your eyes off.

One you would consider touching for a brief second before you remember, you'd lose a hand.

Victory danced over his expression. "Where is he?"

"Who?"

"Again with questions we both know you know the answer to . . ." he trailed off. "Your father."

"Don't know."

"Your mom?"

Shaking my head, I conveyed I had no idea.

He lowered his gaze. I felt relief he had taken his scrutiny off me for a few seconds. I'd never met a man this merciless, even if his eyes were a contradiction of what first made him appear sophisticated.

He moved with measured calculation.

Now, close up, he had shown who he truly was. A jagged soul who spoke with a raw cruelty, and for some reason, hated me.

A scar-faced man stepped up behind him. "Cassius, want me to do it?"

I replayed his name in my mind. *Cassius* was too elegant for a monster like him.

He rose to his feet and stepped out of the closet. "Take her. But don't hurt her. No one gets the pleasure of hurting a Glassman but me." His lips tipped up into a smirk.

With a gesture of command, two of Cassius's men hurried forward and yanked me up. They dragged me out, and I went with them, moving fast, unable to resist. I was shoved forward across my bedroom, and my feet barely kept up with being hauled along.

They manhandled me down the stairs to the ground floor. When we reached the kitchen, I was shoved onto my knees, bruising them.

Cassius's commanding presence made the other men straighten up around him. When his attention zeroed in on me again, it sent a chill down my spine. He came closer with an air of arrogance.

One of the men gave a nod of authority. "House is clear, sir. Only her."

He shook his head. "They're here. Somewhere. Find them."

"We could burn it down when we leave," said Scarface.

Panic lodged in my chest, and I shook my head in dread. Not with Archie hiding out here. Not when my parents had somehow found a place to shelter.

"I'm begging you, don't," I said.

"Want to show us where they're hiding then?" said Scarface.

"I don't know." I hoped they'd believe me and not go looking for Archie.

Cassius gave me a look someone would give when considering their next move. His subtle cologne contradicted his fierceness with the hint of a balmy breeze.

He stood there, hands in pockets, tall and dashing like he'd stepped out of a successful business meeting and wasn't in the middle of a home invasion. Like a man whose reputation was flawless. That strong jawline and seductive presence all added up to someone else. The tattoos on his hands were the only clue he didn't follow the rules.

"Your parents threw you to the wolves, Anya." His eyes flashed with revelry. "For which we're grateful."

His words snapped me back to that moment when Dad had sent me off to look for Archie. *The look of horror in Mom's eyes.* They'd disappeared and hadn't waited. I shouldn't be surprised.

Cassius's eyelids flickered with interest. "They were in this house when we arrived. Where are they?"

Had these men been watching our home?

"They left." I tried to sound convincing. The truth was that my parents had vanished into thin air in the seconds it took to get to my brother's room and back.

"I don't know anything," I snapped.

From behind, a foot kicked my spine, sending a shock of pain into my back.

"Do that again," Cassius sneered at the one who'd kicked me, "and I will acquaint your brain with a bullet."

I matched Cassius glare for glare. "If it's the silver you want, take it."

He gave a ghost of a smile to mock me.

"She's lying?" asked Scarface.

Cassius motioned to me with a flick of his hand. "Up."

Obediently pushing to my feet, I faced off with Cassius with a jaw taut with rebellion.

"Where's your brother?" he asked.

"Out."

He dragged his teeth over his bottom lip. "Don't lie, Anya."

"He's at basketball."

"Where?"

"College."

"Which one?"

I hesitated. . .

"Your brother doesn't go to college. Neither do you. You *were* homeschooled. He still is." He towered over me with a threatening stance. "Care to revise that?"

Struggling to refill my lungs, I burst out, "I can't think."

"Do you know who I am?"

I shook my head while glancing at the others as though that might reveal it.

"Your father never warned you about me?"

"No."

He looked amused. "Though we really can't trust anything a Glassman says."

"We have an alarm."

"Disarmed," said Scarface.

Cassius glared at him, and the man fell silent again.

"My dad would have called the police." I braced for a strike from Cassius.

"Trust me." He looked defiant. "Your father wouldn't want to bring them here. Want to know why?"

"He would do anything to protect us." Though even as those words spilled out, my eyes must have reflected the truth.

Cassius reached out and pressed his thumb against my lips, gently rubbing the plump skin. My face burned with shame. No man had ever touched me like this. I'd never shared an intimate moment with anyone, and it felt like my being was being stormed by fire. At the same time, sensations were stirring in places I never touched, tingles alighting and bringing a heady rush.

"You like that?" he said.

I bit down on his thumb.

"I've killed for less, Anya." His words hit their intended mark.

My jaw slacked, and I eased my bite.

He slid his thumb out and grabbed my jaw with an ironclad hold, fingers digging in painfully. "Glad we understand each other."

I trembled, especially when the strap of my dress slipped off my shoulder.

He let go and brushed a strand of hair out of my eyes. "I'll ask you again." Cassius lifted the strap back up my arm. "Where's your dad?"

His touch lingered on my upper arm and sent a shiver that

traversed into my fingers. This man was molten lava and arctic ice mingled in a dangerous formula.

His beautiful face was a lie. A trick of nature to make a person believe his decency. But forced into being this close to him, I saw the devil in Cassius.

"We found his office," barked one of his men.

Cassius looked thoughtful as though mulling over a decision. "Show me."

Steadying my gait, I regained my balance.

Cassius led the way toward the back of the house. "Bring her."

His men shuffled me behind him into Stephen's office.

A swivel chair sat crooked behind the desk. The room was filled with items that made our family look normal. Or maybe these men would see through this ruse, too.

Our parents didn't hide their enjoyment of the finer things like the lavish vacations they'd taken in far-off destinations. A trip to Egypt where they'd posed before a pyramid. In another framed image, a shot of our family in Hawaii on a boat—all of us smiling as though happy to be there. Then there was one of Dad golfing with friends. *Friends we had never met.*

One of the frames was lifted off a shelf and examined more closely by Cassius —the one taken of Mom and Dad at a party. They looked like a couple without a care in the world.

Cassius threw it onto the desk with disgust.

Guilt swarmed around me as I realized why Dad had been so strict—because of this. He'd tried to protect us from *this.* These men. From Cassius, whoever he was. Waves of anguish crushed me. I had been so foolish, so spoiled, and so naïve.

Men moved about the room. Opening drawers. Removing frames off the walls. Exploring his desk drawers. Scattering papers. Throwing items here and there to get to what they were looking for.

Cassius pivoted to face me. "Where's the main safe?"

"I don't know."

"It's very obvious you want to die today."

Raising my chin, I tried to sound convincing. "He never tells us anything."

I flinched when he stomped his foot. Continuing to strike the carpet with his heel as he moved about the office, he tested the floor with his sole. A hollow thump sounded with another crash of his foot.

Cassius gave a knowing nod to his men.

They got to work, ripping up carpet at the edges and peeling it back. Far enough to reveal a wooden door set in the floor.

Cassius turned his focus to me. "Want to know what happens when you lie?"

Frantically, I shook my head. "I didn't know about it."

"You get one chance with me." From his arrogant glare, I'd used up any further chances with him, too.

A sledgehammer was brought in. One of the men used it to pound the secret wooden door set in the flooring.

Remaining in the corner, with perspiration spotting my brow, I watched the strikes that splintered and spliced through hardwood. Then I counted the steps toward the door, considering making a run for it.

"Don't even think about it," snapped Cassius.

Any man that had to steal, clearly didn't possess the brains to earn what was hidden in that hole. Yet, he came off educated, which clashed with the way he looked—menacing and rough and surprisingly sophisticated in a cold-blooded way.

"Any idea what's in there?" he asked, though he kept his sights on the gaping floor.

"I don't know."

He tilted his head as though assessing if I was telling the truth. "I suppose we'll know soon."

The lid was wedged open with the sledgehammer. A glinting came from within the deep cavern. Rows of stacked gold bars. Why would Stephen have this? I didn't know this man at all. The businessman who was my father. The man who'd left me vulnerable to these thugs. So many more secrets.

One of the men lifted out a gold bar. "Sir?"

"Someone had a contingency plan." Cassius raised his glare to the one with the scarred face. "Bring it back with us."

The scarred man asked, "What about her?"

Cassius didn't look my way. "She's mine."

My back hit the wall as I tried to decipher what he meant.

His to kill.

Or to keep.

chapter
FIVE

Anya

VIOLENTLY, THEY DRAGGED ME TOWARD THE FRONT DOOR like a rag doll. It felt like I was being swept along by an invisible undertow. With each inch they pulled me, I fought against the impossible strength of these men as their grips burrowed into my flesh.

Cassius followed as though merely going for an evening stroll. But I knew, knew he was taking me with him.

How many times had I wanted to get out of the Garden District? Escape this house. Leave behind this life. Find my way to someplace I belonged.

I'd stayed for Archie's sake, and now I was leaving without him.

I hoped they hadn't found him. If anyone hurt my brother, they'd have to contend with me. I was done playing nice. Being good never got me anywhere.

His men were brash enough to use the front door. Even with the long driveway, they could be seen by staff or even a gardener. Or maybe a crowd on a walking tour who'd stumbled upon this crime. I was shoved into the back of an SUV before I had time to call out for help.

I was angry with myself for wanting more. Wanting something else. I'd never even considered things could get worse.

This was a fucking nightmare.

The one they'd called Cassius tugged on his sleeves to neaten them. The way he wielded power over the men proved he was the one to watch out for. From the back seat, I watched him heading my way. He glanced back, sweeping his gaze across the windows.

Then he climbed in beside me.

He filled the space in the passenger seat with his threatening presence, sending an invisible wave that hit me like the shock of an electric eel. His charismatic power carried on his filthy glare, reaching my soul and shattering my sense of self. Because I was nothing to him. What I wanted or needed didn't count.

Looking past him, I stared up at the windows for any sign of my family, praying my father would burst out of the door wielding his gun and come save me.

"I'm not going with you," I chided.

Cassius raised his hand to quieten me as though annoyed to be this close.

I kicked him. "Are you listening?"

It happened quickly, him asking for rope from one of his men who sat in the front seat. Cassius snatched it from him. With his strong hands on my shoulders, he moved me, so my back was turned to him. Using the rope to bind my hands behind me, he tugged on the knot to send jarring discomfort into my wrists.

"You misunderstand, Anya. You no longer have a say in what happens to you." His stare burned into me like a fire. Combustible and barely contained.

Struggling was useless. He was too strong. Overpowering. That show of aggression, a glimpse of what he was capable of. My wrists burned like fire from the rope. I slumped back into the seat, defeated.

"Drive," he ordered.

The car navigated down the driveway and pulled out onto the road, picking up speed as we approached the end of Prytania Street.

My heart was thudding so hard I feared I'd pass out. Struggling with these binds, I was sure if I kept wriggling my wrists, I'd get free.

Cassius focused on his phone. His expression was calm. What kind of a man wasn't fazed by kidnapping a girl?

A ruthless one.

One I needed to fear.

What had gone wrong with my father and him that would lead to him taking me?

A business dealing, maybe?

It didn't matter. The only thing that mattered was my father failed to protect me from this monster.

The worst part was he would probably blame me.

The SUV picked up speed, and we weaved around other cars to make it out of the city. Familiar homes and stores and buildings flew by. How far were we going?

I inhaled sharply. "Who are you?"

He didn't look up from his phone.

This man was abhorrent. Didn't even try to make this easier. Didn't try to reassure me. Which could only mean one thing. . .

He's going to kill me.

"They'll come for me," I said.

"I hope they do."

"You disgust me."

"Divider up." Cassius gestured for it to be done.

The glass glided upward and sealed us in the back.

He turned to face me, his voice formidable. "My men don't like to hear others disrespecting me." He shrugged. "They can be trigger happy."

"Maybe it's you they hate," I said bitterly.

He looked right through me. He went to say something but changed his mind and leaned back to watch the world fly by.

Trembling, I fought against the binds burning my wrists. I refused to give up trying to escape them.

It sparked a curious reaction from him. "Bravo for trying. But what's the plan for after? You going to kill me, little girl?"

I let out a long, drawn-out huff, well aware he was right. Even if I managed to get the rope off, what then? "What did I do wrong?"

"You're a Glassman."

"Please. Take me back. I won't tell them anything."

"No."

"You can't kidnap me."

He looked amused. "And yet . . . I *did*."

"Let me out!" I screamed it.

"By all means, make a scene but don't expect to arrive alive."

Tears stung my eyes when I glanced left and saw the freeway. I tried to keep my mouth shut and not have a panic attack.

Cassius snapped his phone to his ear. "We're on our way. I have one of them. She's—" He glanced my way. "—a handful, so strip the room of all sharp objects."

He was making sure I didn't use them on him, too. I was sure of it. Because he could see it in my eyes. When I got to where he was taking me, I was going to stab someone, if that's what it took to escape.

chapter
SIX

Cassius

WINDING DOWN THE WINDOW, I LET THE COLD AIR DRAG across my face, cleansing me from *that* house. I pulled off my loose tie before tucking it away in a pocket. *This.*

This was the moment I had waited for.

The moment I had imagined—though disappointingly lacking in carnage.

That fucker had hidden like a coward. I would have sold my soul to get to Glassman. I suppose, in many ways, I had.

Though the adrenaline was lessening, it still brought a heady warmth. Similar to one of my five-mile runs, blood surged through veins and brought an addictive aliveness.

The mission could be considered a failure if not for *her*. Nothing had prepared me for the satisfaction of capturing Anya. Her terror was raw and real and vibrant. Fear shimmered in her eyes. I drank it in. Drank in her visceral terror like she was an extension of him.

She slid all the way over to the other side of the seat. It would be easy to reach out and touch her. Run my hand over her perspiring body to lessen my starvation for retribution.

I was taking a piece of them with me.

Glassman would probably come for her himself. With an army of men. It would be on my turf, and I'd be ready. He could hide for a while, but at some point, he'd have to extricate himself if he wanted Anya to live.

She looked my way. "Please, I'll do anything."

Her panic caused my pulse to quicken.

"If you insist on talking," I sharpened the words like a blade, "then by all means." I left the rest unsaid.

She was close to tears. Seemingly holding on to her dignity as if such a thing was possible.

Maybe she'd experience the same futility I had endured when I was around her age. Though I'd tracked their ages, I calculated that she was eighteen, so a few years older than me when her father had stormed my home.

She was a toxic pleasure running through my veins as my imagination set to work on how much suffering I'd inflict. Of all the spoils of war, she was the ultimate reward.

"I have to go back!" she said, panicked.

Shoving my phone back into my pocket, I turned to face her, and then gestured for her silence when she went to speak again. Demanded Anya remain quiet so the return to the house would be tolerable. This girl was the devil's spawn. The child of a psychopath. I wondered which traits she'd inherited. With her long brunette hair, large blue eyes, and plump lips, she clearly resembled the Glassman's lineage. Slender with disarming features that hid what lay within—a tainted soul.

The blood running through her veins was pure poison. She was dangerous, no doubt. A hazard needing to be contained. A captive requiring observation. A careful handling. Like a trapped lioness whose bite would scar.

Anya Glassman had just become the ultimate bait. I would use her to draw them out. Stephen Glassman would be frantic once he realized his daughter was gone. He'd experience the same agony he'd put me through when he destroyed my family.

What the hell had they been thinking to leave Anya vulnerable? We could have killed her on sight.

Just like I'd promised him.

Lifting my focus from the freeway and returning my attention back to her, I savored the way she trembled. With her wrists bound behind her back, it pushed her chest out and emphasized her pert breasts. Her nipples pebbled from the chill of the late-night air that blew in through the open window. Locks of hair falling over her delicate face. She was pretty, with her wide-set blue eyes and surprisingly angelic features. The kind of depth in her gaze I'd not expect from someone of her lineage. No doubt a throwback to an ancestor who had more decency than her father. Nature's way of trying to dilute the Glassman ancestry, but she was still her father's daughter.

Her terror stirred my diabolical side. The side that man had carved out of a teenage boy. Like Victor Frankenstein, who'd created a monster he could no longer contain. Only that was fiction, and I. . .I was all too real.

The darker side of life.

That's what held a vivid fascination for me now.

Seeing her wither in confidence brought a visceral satisfaction. I'd wreak boundless devastation to her life. I reeled with the possibilities of what having her under the same roof would bring.

Today, karma was wielding a sledgehammer.

She was mine.

Anya zeroed in on my inked hands, seemingly fascinated. I imagined her trying to fathom what kind of man I was. Confused over the reason I'd invaded her home. I wasn't here to appease her, merely use her.

She was strikingly exotic, ethereal really. If allowed to blossom, I imagined she'd break hearts. I'd spare those foolish boys their infantile mistakes. Those youthful lovers too naïve to see she was venom. I wondered what kind of dreams she'd once had for her future. The life she imagined for herself.

She let out a long exhale as though unable to tolerate the danger. With each shallow breath, she sank into the seat as if trying to disappear.

"My father will unleash hell if you don't let me go."

Gliding over to her side, I grabbed a lock of Anya's hair and pulled her head back. "Hell?" My lips moved in close to hers. "That's where I'm taking you."

She winced. "Fuck off."

Grabbing her chin, I squeezed hard until she whimpered. "What did you just say to me?"

Her short breaths hit my lips. Breaking my glare, she turned her head submissively.

I let go of her chin.

I'd take my time to get to know her likes and dislikes. Then use this to play with her. Discover her fears. Then torment her with them. Psychological suffering was just as important as her physical pain. There was wisdom in taking my time to analyze her weaknesses. Use the knowledge to break her down. Wrecking her was going to be the finest entertainment.

"We have money," she whispered. "Let me call my dad."

I curled my fingers along her cheek. "I have your father's gold."

Realizing her ability to bargain was lost, she withdrew into the corner again. "Where are you taking me?"

Glancing at my watch, I estimated we'd be there in less than half an hour.

"Cassius, please."

My name left her lips like a goddamn prayer. Reaching a part of me that lay dormant. I shivered off the effect. She could seduce a lesser man. Someone naïve to who she was.

The way her tongue darted to wet her lips was dangerously evocative. I'd captured an exquisite creature, and there was nothing crueler than to have her believe this was her fate.

"He'll come after the gold," she whispered.

"I have the only thing he'll miss."

With windswept futility, she turned her focus to the window.

Studying her reaction, I added, "I'm sure he's willing to die for you."

Anya's expression went from disillusioned to something else as though an epiphany struck her. "He knew you'd come for us?"

"Yes."

"Did you hurt his other—"

"His other what?"

She held my stare and then turned away. "I wasn't sure if you'd done this before?"

"I'm a patient man." My breath hitched. "I'm surprised your father didn't warn you."

"He was trying to protect us."

"Clearly, he failed."

"Why are you doing this?"

Reaching out to touch her, I tucked a strand of hair behind her ear and felt a pang of sadness for her, that she'd lived under the same roof all these years with a psychopath. "Exactly how much grief have I caused your family?"

She continued to stare out the window. "You've ruined my life. I've not been allowed to do anything. Go anywhere. A prisoner in my own home."

"Sorry to hear that," I lied.

Satisfaction settled in my gut that they'd been living in terror for a decade because of me.

chapter
SEVEN

Anya

CASSIUS DIDN'T KNOW ABOUT THE OTHER CHILDREN. OR maybe he was bluffing. One thing was sure, Dad and Mom had known this man was a threat. They'd made our lives hell for a reason. I wished they'd warned us. We probably wouldn't have rebelled. We'd have seen them differently.

This bastard was the reason. He was the man who'd made our lives miserable.

I couldn't think straight. I twisted my wrists to loosen the surrounding rope in case I got my chance to bolt.

I wondered if Dad would come for me like this man suggested. Though Cassius wouldn't know about our strained relationship. Or that Mom looked down her nose at us. Maybe all this time, I'd been reading them both wrong. They'd been living in a bubble, too.

I had been too hard on my parents. They'd tried to love Archie and me but found themselves lacking from the trauma of losing their other children. They were grief-stricken. Unable to love to the same extent because their loss was too harrowing.

Still, something didn't add up.

As Cassius and his men broke in, my parents hadn't protected me when it mattered most. Shaking these thoughts away, born out of fear, I was at least reassured this man hadn't found Archie.

I dared to look out the back window to see if we were being followed. But I just saw the other SUVs following, transporting his men.

Maybe my parents would send a car after us. So they'd know where I was being taken. I watched out for landmarks. Anything that would help give away our location. That was if I ever figured out a way to contact them. I would have to figure out a way to escape. Something told me that would be impossible.

Maybe I could get my hands on a phone.

Panic rushed through me when Cassius leaned into my body. His fingers eased off the rope around my wrists, freeing my hands that throbbed and swelled.

Up ahead, tall iron gates with an elaborate design swung wide. We continued through, navigating along an endless driveway. An Italian renaissance mansion rose high with gothic flair, ivy clinging to the walls, unaware it had the choice to be free of this place.

The car pulled up into a circular driveway. Outside the front of the stone-pillared entrance, a man in combat gear stood as a sentry on the steps. He considered us with the same level of intimidation. The cars driven by Cassius's men parked behind ours.

Scarface got out of one of the SUVs. He opened my door and reached in for me.

"I've got her," Cassius told him.

The man stepped back and waited.

Reluctantly, I followed Cassius, spilling out of the car and looking up at the windows. Wondering how long I'd be here.

With a punishing grip on my arm, Cassius led me toward the front door.

My feet missed a step, and he caught me, pausing for a second and hugging me to his side. "You good?"

"Yes." It came out breathy.

He looked the way he felt, his body rock hard and toned. The physique of someone who worked out and kept his body finely tuned like the killing machine he was. I hated how he made me feel, his nearness causing an uneasy sensation of pleasure.

He led me inside.

Refusing to relent and show any weakness, I shoved away from him.

It didn't faze him.

We were walking through a vast foyer with pristine stone tile. The Italian design of old and new décor almost took away from the sting of being imprisoned here. My surroundings were breathtaking. The place was huge with high ceilings, and along the walls, tall bay windows let the light flood in. This classic opulence revealed more about Cassius. He either came from money or had acquired it—I didn't want to know how.

We continued up a sprawling staircase of marble with flamboyant handrails on either side. Cassius took a sharp right at the top of the stairs and continued along a hallway. His hand moved in my direction, gesturing for me to keep up.

This place was amazing.

You won't be here long.

I wondered how much Cassius would want for me. Whatever the price, I was sure my father would pay it.

A nagging fear my parents might abandon me chipped away at my bravery. Those thoughts melted into survival mode when Cassius led me into a room.

Keeping some distance between us, I looked around, taking in the bed with its generous blue duvet and the ornate Persian rug in the center of the hardwood floor. Other than that, it was a room that cared little for a person's comfort. Discreetly, I looked around for something that could break the windows.

I walked over to take a peek outside. A forest of trees obstructed my view. If I could make it out, I'd be able to disappear amongst them.

"This will be your room," Cassius said, like a concierge checking me in and not my captor.

"How long will I be here?" I said bitterly.

"Indefinitely."

Panicked, I tried to leave the room.

He was right behind me, and before I could escape, his hand reached out and slammed the door in my face.

His rock-hard chest pressed against my back. "You will join us for dinner at seven. Until then, stay in here."

"Please," I begged. "I haven't done anything wrong."

"Maybe not. But your father did, and that's good enough for me."

I spun around, facing him, adjusting to his body being so close to mine. His intimidation was bringing another rush of panic. I looked up at him, at his steely eyes that held no warmth. No kindness, no humanity, just a cruel man hiding behind a beautiful face.

I glanced at his full lips before braving to hold his stare. "What if my dad refuses to pay you?"

"We can have this conversation over dinner." He stepped back, reached for the handle, and pulled open the door. He left, closing it behind him with a slam.

I cursed him. Cursed this place. Cursed the fact my dad hadn't been honest with us. By not telling us anything, he'd put us at greater risk.

I pulled the door open and then froze in terror.

A sentry loomed large, guarding the way. The man gestured for me to go back in with a casual turn of his wrist. A man too big to fight.

I closed the door, turned, and leaned against it.

As if having an out-of-body experience, I strolled across the room, soon making it to the other side. Yanking the cord of the bedside lamp out of its socket, I carried the lamp back with me to the far side—toward the only wall with the green damask wallpaper—and hoisted the lamp high. With a violent thrust, I chucked it at the mirror.

A crash followed, then shattering glass as the pieces fell and scattered.

Staring down at the shards, I looked for one large enough to cut someone with and draw blood.

Then I'd use the distraction to my advantage and bolt into those woods.

Raising my gaze , I pivoted to see Cassius casually standing in the doorway with one hand tucked into his pant pocket, looking serene. He'd shrugged out of his jacket at some point. Rolled up the sleeves of his white shirt to reveal muscled and toned forearms. His stare flitted to the twinkling mirrored images that lay scattered in delicate slithers.

"Nice lamp."

He arched a brow. "It used to be."

"I hate this room."

"I've changed my mind." He widened his eyes with stark humor. "There are more pressing matters. If you behave like a good girl, I'll let you eat." His expression turned dark. "My office."

I took a step forward.

He pointed to the shards of the mirror. "After you get on your knees and clean up this fucking mess."

chapter
EIGHT

Cassius

PERCHED ON HER SEAT, ANYA LOOKED UP AT ME WITH PURE terror.

She was beautifully vulnerable.

A state I shouldn't have taken any pleasure in, but I did.

I wasn't a man used to soul-searching, but I did with her and found no guilt for stealing her away.

Triumph was the ultimate sentiment. And usually, sentimentality didn't factor into anything I did.

She took in the maps in frames. Glancing behind me to the far wall at the TV screen with flashing numbers and names of data that kept changing.

Her expression turned to intrigue as though trying to gauge why I'd need six clocks covering different time zones, including London, Paris, Hong Kong, and Johannesburg .

"If you insist on destroying your room," I told her, "I'll arrange other accommodations. A grave, perhaps?"

"I couldn't bear to look at myself in the mirror."

"Don't blame you." I didn't care to know why. "Just don't act out your spoiled revolt on my property." I waved my hand through the air. "Or I'll have to kill you."

"I'm worth too much."

Rounding the desk, I sat on the edge and fixed a glare on her. "Glad you're ready to talk."

She looked like she regretted her outburst. Her head bowed, hair tumbling over her face, limbs tight with tension as though ready to spring up and run.

She'd watched me push up and stroll over to the door to lock it. *There was no leaving.*

A sense of familiarity slithered up my spine because I knew what it was to be cornered. To be trapped and unable to escape. Instead of a Glassman doing that to me, I'd taken my power back and was on full assault. Ready to strike this woman down with the kind of words that would crush her spirit. Hating her all the more for this pang of something that could be construed as guilt. It wasn't, because I was dead inside and all the more dangerous for it.

And to think, all those years ago, her father had unwittingly set a trap for his daughter by creating me.

It's that kind of philosophical shit that can keep a man up at night.

I returned to the desk and slid the notepad before her. Then set the fountain pen beside it. "Passcodes to your social media. Write them down."

Soon, I'd know so much more about her. Most importantly, she would be the weak link into her father's world.

"I'm not allowed."

That made me suppress a smirk. "It's not a request."

"No, I'm not allowed to be on social media."

Lifting the pen, I offered it to her. "Or would you like me to help you remember?" I responded, not believing a word she uttered.

Glassmans weren't to be trusted.

"We were never allowed anything like that." She pleaded with innocent blue eyes. "Dad won't let us have them."

Interesting.

Maybe she wasn't lying after all.

He had been smart. He'd made sure she was safe and not vulnerable.

Let's try this. "Anya, what's your father's routine?"

Her face twisted in disgust that I'd even ask her.

Closing the space between us, I gripped her chin and tipped it. "Let's start with the morning. Does he exercise? Head straight to his office? Family breakfast?"

She squeezed her eyes shut, refusing to answer.

Her inhales became ragged as she sucked in long breaths. I was prepared to hold her like this for infinity until she talked.

"Anya, do I look like the kind of man who tolerates being ignored?"

"He's hardly there," she managed.

Her fingers wrapped around my wrist, but she didn't pull my hand away. Just held on tight as if holding on for something.

I let her go. "Hardly where?"

"Home."

"How often does he go away?"

Her lips trembled. "When are you going to let me go?"

"If you're good, soon," I lied.

"Please, let me call home."

"No."

"My parents are hardly there. I don't talk to my brother much."

What was she trying to trick me into believing? That this spoiled rich girl knew what it was to be lonely? Knew what it was to grieve a stolen life?

If we had anything in common, it would be that and only that—if it was true.

"I'm thirsty."

With a tight jaw, I reached back for that glass of water on my desk. The one I'd only taken a few sips from. "Here."

"Do you have something stronger?"

"Take the glass," I said sternly.

She took it from me and brought it to her lips, her hand shaking.

There was no time for this. I knew these games. My sister used to play them too. When I would send her to her room at night for bed, she'd always ask for another drink. Another story about our parents. Another snack. Even at her age, she'd clung to me as if I was all she had left in the world.

Because that's exactly what had happened—I'd been left to parent her.

And it had been this woman's father who had killed mine. His blood surged through her veins.

"Why have you brought me here?" She looked scared.

"You want to talk about you? We can do that."

Her pale throat rippled as she swallowed hard.

"You have his gold," she chided. "Why do you need me?"

"Because you have information I want."

"What kind of information? I promise, I know nothing."

"From my intel, you were at home. A lot. Which means you have access to your father's office. You see what he does in there."

"Why am I being blamed for something he's done?"

"Answer the question."

"Dad shuts the door. He's doesn't do much in there as far as I can tell. He has an office elsewhere. He's obsessed with his work."

"And what does he do?" I wanted to see if she knew, carefully studying her face for clues to her insight.

"He deals in foreign sales."

"And the commodity?"

"I'm not telling you one more thing until you let me call home."

"That's not going to happen."

She leaned forward, her head cocking to the side. "Who are you anyway? Really? You take me from my house. Steal from my father. You threaten me . . ."

Reaching for the hair on her nape, I scrunched it up and yanked her head back, leaning in to glare down at her.

"I'm someone you should be scared of."

I let that sink in before taking a step back.

She was quiet for a minute, but then her back straightened as if she was trying to make herself appear taller. Stronger.

"And yet . . ." she smirked. "I have no clue who you are. If you were such a bad man, wouldn't I know your name?"

"I run this city."

"Pretty sure it's my father who does that." Her brow quirked up. "You don't even sound like you're from here. You sound like some Ivy League northerner."

"Appearances can be deceiving. Look at you. Where's your accent?" I said pointedly. "Oh, that's right. Your father has hidden you away in your castle all this time."

"Cage," I thought she muttered under breath, but I couldn't be sure.

"Just talk and this will be over, because if you don't, you won't like the outcome.

"You want me to tremble in fear and tell you something. Well, I hate to break it you, I don't know shit."

"You think you have no need to be afraid, but that's where you're wrong. I'm the one person you should be afraid of, and you know why?"

"No. But I bet you're going to tell me."

"Because I have nothing left to lose . . ." I let my words settle in.

She tried to act like they didn't affect her, but I watched her. Watched as her jaw went rigid and trembled slightly. *Good.*

"We're done. You may go now."

I held her stare, triumphant at having caught a living, breathing Glassman in my snare. But then she surprised me as she smiled broadly.

"The next thing I break in this house will be bigger than a mirror."

"So much as touch one more item, and I will break you. Do you understand?"

"Yes." Her voice came out breathy.

"Do you remember how to get back to your room, or do you need me to arrange an escort?"

"Fuck you."

"That's what I thought. Now get the hell out." I watched her run from the room.

I felt my intrigue rise.

What was this woman capable of?

chapter
NINE

Cassius

I T WAS DONE.

My first strike against the Glassmans felt fucking fantastic. Anya had left my office looking like she was filled with terror. Seeing her fear felt like a victory.

How many times had I imagined this? Played it out in my mind in every detail. What I hadn't expected was bringing one of them here. Toying with one of them.

Back in my study, after sending Anya to her room, I calmed my thoughts and got back to work.

Ensuring that Calvetti Fleet, my father's business, continued to thrive.

With me at the helm, I'd turned this company into a multibillion-dollar empire.

It had been a grueling six months, with all our tankers being fitted with environmentally friendly double hulls. I'd soon be able to go after the sweet spot of the tanker cycle. Lloyds had been right about predicting my company would become the most influential in the industry. All I had to do was outwork the competition.

Dad was here, in the décor and furnishings of this office. I'd honored his memory and changed little. Wanting to keep his memory alive. From the photos of him and Mom on the walls to the family captured in snapshots from earlier years.

Time had stopped in this room—paralyzed by this need to remember.

Remember what *he'd* stolen.

Sitting before my iMac, scanning my emails, sending off a few, and answering urgent questions that Cassandra Harding, my CEO, couldn't answer. I let her micromanage when I was busy with other more pressing details.

Like now—having a Glassman beneath my roof.

Which was understandably distracting.

Not to mention she was extraordinarily beautiful. A decadent gift I'd exploit to wreak hell on her father.

After he'd torn his hair out in frustration and her mom broke down from losing her daughter. It was a decent start.

Searching my contacts, I hunted down the best person to offload the gold to and then turn it into liquid cash. The bullion deal would need some finagling. After all, it was engraved with its unique marking and would be easy to track. They'd have to melt it down and reconstitute it. But it was possible. The value would drop, but it would be worth the trouble.

Ridley pushed open the door—so much for stealing a few hours of peace. He wore that gray suit he had tailored for him on Bracken Street. The one he liked to wear when he saw his best clients.

He was also wearing his familiar pissed-off expression. The bastard got hazard pay. What more did he want?

"I'm busy," I snapped.

"It will just take a second."

I continued typing. "No."

"Did you kill him?"

He was obviously referring to the man who'd tipped me off to the fact Glassman was spending more time in the Garden District. The same man who'd gatecrashed my sister's wedding.

"We were going to let the police handle him, remember?" he said.

"Oh, that's what you meant."

He snapped his hand up, not wanting to hear any more.

"Thanks for stopping by." I threw in a wave.

"Were you in the Garden District this morning?"

I feigned having to think about it.

"There's a rumor," he began slowly, "I know it's not true. Because it would be fucking reckless."

"You have to admit, I wear reckless so damn well."

"You kidnapped Anya Glassman?"

Sitting back, I studied him, relishing his discomfort with the idea. He looked horrified. "Glassman will come after her."

"That's the plan."

"Right, because that makes perfect sense to set a trap for a psychopathic arms dealer!"

"Enjoy the show. Should be fun. I'll even provide popcorn if you're lucky."

"This is nothing but an old grudge, Cas."

"I don't need to explain myself to you. You know what he did. You know why he deserves his life to be taken apart piece by piece."

"Abhorrent, I agree, but—"

"Why are you here? As you can see"—I gestured around the room. "I'm busy. Tell me what you want so I can go about my day."

"What do I want? I'd like to stay alive if you don't mind."

"Then go."

"Your sister deserves better."

"When this is over, she'll be able to feel safe for the first time in her life."

"He'll put a bullet through your brain."

Considering he'd threatened to do that to me years ago, it was old news. "I have his gold."

"Where did you find it?"

I ignored that. "At least fifty million."

"What were you thinking?"

"Honestly, I was thinking that's a lot of fucking gold. So I took it."

He dragged his fingers through his hair. "Don't tell me anymore."

I suppressed a smirk at Ridley's reaction as I pushed up from my chair. "Glassman won't find her until I want him to."

"He knows you have her."

"That was the point."

"Where is she?"

"Why?"

"I want to see she's still alive."

"She is."

"I'm not leaving until I see her." He pointed a finger at me. "You've gone too far this time."

"That's not strictly true."

"If she's hurt. . ."

"She's fine." *For now.*

"I don't trust you."

"For God's sake." I gestured for him to follow. "Come on."

We headed out and into the hallway. When we made it to the foyer, he gave me a quizzical look. Then stood back, waiting for me in the center.

I walked back his way. "I'm showing you out," I said. "I'll be in touch."

"I'm not leaving knowing an innocent woman is locked up here."

"She's not innocent." I gave a gesture of that's just how it was.

"She's eighteen, Cas."

"Old enough to know about her father."

"Look, I know what that man did to you was. . . that he. . ." Ridley looked away, not wanting to say it. "Your father wouldn't want you to be this man."

"Had my father given Glassman what he wanted, my parents would still be alive."

"Your father did the right thing. You know that in your heart."

"What heart?"

Ridley huffed in frustration. "What are you going to do with her?"

"You don't want to know. Right? As my attorney."

He swallowed back his words. "It's her father you want."

"This works for now."

"Maybe it's time to consider forgiveness?"

"He robbed me of my father, Ridley."

He shook his head in disbelief. "Don't be this man. The man they say you are."

"And what is that?"

He mouthed the word monster but was polite enough not to say it out loud.

A blur of movement came from above.

A chair flew over the balcony and barely missed Ridley's head before it crashed to the ground behind him, smashing to smithereens. He raised his eyes from the crook of his arm where he'd shielded his face. Turned to stare at the chair. Then snapped a glare upward.

Anya peered down over the balcony at us.

"What the fuck?" Ridley looked horrified.

"We didn't lock her door," I said flatly. "I'm not a complete monster."

"You've got to contain her!"

"Go home," I told him. "Forget you ever saw her."

"I'm not leaving her here."

"You seem to forget. I'm the man who pays your ridiculous salary. Step outside and take a breath."

"Your mom wouldn't want this for you."

"She's not here. And tell me . . . why isn't she here?"

Ridley's shoulders slumped, and he peered up toward the balcony. "If anything happens to her, I'll never forgive you."

"Forgiveness?" I rested a hand on his shoulder. "You think I give a fuck about forgiveness? That word hasn't been in my vocabulary since your father failed to listen that day. The day he sent me away without warning my father. Their blood is on your family's hands too."

"Don't you think I'm haunted by that every day of my life?"

"Apparently not haunted enough. Since you're still giving me this shit right now."

"Cas," he whispered.

"I'll call you if and when you're needed." I headed up the staircase toward Anya.

chapter
TEN

Anya

CASSIUS GLARED UP AT ME FROM THE FOYER.
I'd barely missed his friend with the chair. The tall man with the slicked-back hair, cunning features, and that Louisiana accent. Cassius looked annoyed. They exchanged a few words below as though I hadn't just thrown a piece of furniture over the balcony at them.

Cassius's foot landed on the first step of the staircase.

Not waiting to see if he took a second, I scurried back into the bedroom and slammed the door behind me. Rushing over to the other side of the room, I flung myself onto the bed and braced for when he came in.

Cassius strolled in casually, his expression dangerously calm.

A shudder of regret stretched through me as I realized I wasn't safe where I was sitting and moved to try to get away. He caught hold of my ankle and dragged me back toward him. I kicked out with my other foot at his chest. He grabbed my leg and twisted it, flipping me over.

He grabbed my feet to still me. Struggling, I pulled one free.

With a swipe of his hand, he knocked my foot away from his face. The mattress dipped as he clambered onto it and reached for my hands. Clasping my wrists with an ironclad hold and leveraging both my arms up until he'd captured them above my head and pinned them to the mattress.

Looming over me, his heady cologne reminded me of dark fantasies turned real.

"What the fuck was that?" he growled, his body close to mine, heat and tension radiating off him.

"Let me go."

"If that chair had hit him. . ."

"Better luck next time." Snapping my eyes away, I refused to show how much he scared me and continued to squirm against him. "You have no idea who you're dealing with."

He looked amused. "You?"

"My father."

He let me go as though struck by some invisible force. His expression turned dark, reflecting hate and fury in his gaze.

Before he could respond, I used the opportunity of his moment of distraction and scrambled off the bed and back on my feet. "He will find you. And when he does. . ."

Cassius rounded the bed and stalked toward me with a dangerous stride, closing in fast. My back struck the wall behind me.

He slammed his palms against the wall on either side of my head. "You're going to be here for a while. Learn to be courteous."

"Courteous?" I scoffed.

"You're right. We're both fooling ourselves if we think this is going to be painless."

Even as he spoke those words, my eyes lowered to his lips as if they might say something else, something to comfort and bring solace.

His body pressed against mine, his firm chest against my breasts.

My chin tipped up in rebellion. "What are you going to do to me?"

He leaned in and dragged his mouth along my jawline, hovering over my lips. "I've yet to decide."

"You're playing with fire."

He smirked. "And you're sinking into the ice, Anya."

"What did my dad do to make you so angry?"

He went to say something, and then stopped himself.

"Whatever it was, you deserved it," I said coldly.

His expression changed at my comment, making him look even more sinister. "The danger is real. Act accordingly."

"You make it sound like I'm the one in the wrong," I responded with a calm voice, trying desperately not to show any fear.

"You have no idea how wrong you are. How every second you breathe is a goddamn privilege."

"You think you scare me? People have tried to intimidate me. And failed. No one can."

He stepped back. "Until you met me."

"Did he cut you out of a business deal? Is that it?"

He gave a smile, but it warped out of shape in disbelief. His eyes closed for a beat before he muttered, "You have no idea who your father is?"

"He can be stern. But he's fair."

"Your father is not the man you think he is."

Dread settled in my stomach.

His eyes blazed with hate. "Your father showed me what kind of man he is when I watched him kill innocent people."

"He would never do something like that," I said bitterly.

Stephen could be stern and sometimes volatile. Yes, he did use his fists, but kill? I refused to believe it.

"A man is known by his actions." I retorted.

"Back to the chair."

"It slipped from my grip."

"Is that so?"

"Yes."

"I watched you throw it."

"And what are you going to do about it?" I smirked.

Cassius towered over me. "Don't question me. You won't like the consequences."

Our bodies were so close that I swore he could feel my heart beating in my chest. A shudder ran through me as another plan came to mind.

Before I could think twice, I reached up and cupped his face with my palm. Then I used the rest of my false bravado to lean in until I was almost kissing him.

Daring him to press his mouth against mine. This was where my power lay.

This was what I could use against him.

Lure him in, then convince him to let me go.

I bit my lip, detesting this man with every cell of my body, but there was something else present, weaving its way through me at the close proximity of our bodies.

Something I didn't want to think about or admit. Shuddering against this rising need to make contact with him, to feel his touch like this, to have his body pressed to mine. I needed to fight this visceral reaction I was having to him.

His formidable eyes and sensual mouth claimed my focus. I raised my chin, pride shuddering through me at my will to survive this. To survive him. Because I could see in that glint in his eyes, I'd captured his attention. His focus never strayed from mine.

"You and I, we're not so different," I said huskily.

"And how is that?"

"We want the same thing."

"Anya," he said, his tone imperceptible.

He felt it too, this heat surging between us, this strange chemistry of captor and captive fighting for authority.

All I had to do was seduce him.

Endure the pain of being taken. Manipulate this man into seeing me differently. I was innocent, and if I could get him to see this, to believe that I had nothing to do with any of it, I might live through this.

Trying to steady the tremble of my hand, I lowered it to his groin and cupped him there, feeling him swelling in my palm. Keeping the shock of it out of my eyes as his length grew against my touch.

His nose brushed my temple. "You like it rough?"

"Yes?" I breathed.

Doubt crept in, and suddenly, I wasn't so sure I could follow through.

"Is that so?" His voice was heady with want and desire, making my body tremble.

Oh, God.

There was a slickness between my thighs, an arousal I couldn't fathom. My fingers curled around his impressive girth. "You want me. I can tell."

He grabbed my wrist to stop my hand. "Really, Anya?" Leaning in, he nestled into my nape, his breath warm on my throat, his commanding presence dominated every second that followed. It was easy to be drawn into his darkness, into the way he was able to control this moment. "Do you really think seducing me will work?"

I pulled away.

He gave an amused smirk, mocking me.

"I was aiming for you with the chair!" I snapped.

"Now that's a start. We can always do with more honesty around here."

"You know what we could do with more of? Decency." I pushed away from him.

"Try to remember where you had your hand ten seconds ago."

"I'm trying to remember what it is to not be here in this terrible place."

"We're done talking." He took hold of my forearm and pulled me across the room.

His touch felt electric against my skin. Like a live wire sending shocking voltage into my flesh. The kind you cling to because you can't help yourself.

I followed him out of the bedroom and down the sweeping staircase. My arousal shrank like a wilting flower. Those whispers of want and need faded with each step I took beside this evil man.

Precariously, I tried to keep up and not fall. We passed the same chair I'd thrown over the balcony. Evidence of what I was capable of. We continued onward, along a west hallway and through a door.

Down a spiraling stone staircase.

"We never use this part of the house because it's prone to flooding." He led me on. "It's beneath sea level. Which is never a good thing."

"Where are you taking me?" I asked as my eyes adjusted to the darkness, and I realized we were passing jail cells.

A chill ran down my spine.

"This house was built on an old Spanish fort," he said. "This is all that's left of it."

"Why are you showing it to me?"

He ignored me. "The things they did back then."

"I don't like it."

"I believe that's the point."

Nearing one of the cells, he gave it a yank and opened the door. "In."

"No."

"You threw a chair at my friend. This is a preferential punishment than the other one I have in mind."

I folded my arms across my chest, trying to hide the fact my heart was trying to beat itself out of my chest wall. "Well, you've got me intrigued."

He made a gesture for me to go on in. "I'm not sure how you've survived this far. Clearly, all grit and stupidity."

Head down, I took the few short steps into the dank room. Pivoting to face Cassius, I saw the shadows dance over his face.

I looked around and was revolted by where he was leaving me.

Rough blankets were strewn across a stained mattress.

A toilet without a seat.

A tipped-over rusty cup.

"I won't stay in here," I said. "I can't. . I would rather die."

"A fate worse than death?" He slammed the cell door shut and then started to lock it. "Guaranteed."

Once he secured me in, he held the keys up in his hand, and did the worst thing imaginable, he threw them across the hallway out of my reach. They landed with a loud clank.

Ass.

I ran toward the bars and gripped them, knuckles white. "You can't leave me in here."

He tucked his hands casually into his pockets. "Bet that bedroom we just left looks like a palace now?"

"You should be ashamed of yourself," I called after him.

Cassius was already walking away.

chapter
ELEVEN

Anya

A DOOR SLAMMED DOWN THE CORRIDOR, THROWING ME into pitch darkness.

My hands wrapped around the metal bars, and my neck strained to see if he was seriously leaving. Seconds felt like hours. Time moving too slowly.

I could feel my chest tightening with a heavy feeling of panic as I waited.

That brief moment of connection had dissolved into dust.

Even after I'd coaxed him on.

Even after I'd yearned for more.

The way he'd touched me had left me reeling. Like a magnet I had struggled to pull away from.

Unable to understand these twisting feelings, I stepped back as though trying to put distance between us, despite him already being gone.

Cassius could never have known the truth. That not only had I never been intimate with a man, but it was also even rarer to feel the brush of affection by my parents. I'd grown accustomed to it. Numb, but now a part of me was stirring from Cassius's touch.

I'd go mad if he made me stay in here.

Slumping onto the thin mattress, I felt like my flesh was crawling with confusion. Why was I intrigued by the man who'd removed all control? The man dishing out one punishment after another.

His presence. . . I both hate and crave it at the same time.

Eventually resigned to the realization that he wasn't coming back anytime soon, and that he'd refused to talk more, I lay on my side. Not wanting to take a closer look at what it was I was lying on, I drew my legs up and rolled into the fetal position.

Cassius, the man with the deep brown eyes that contradicted the depth I'd seen in him. A glimpse of kindness when he'd looked down at me that first time when I'd hidden in my closet.

Back home, in the Garden District, felt miles away, and yet it wasn't that far.

I wouldn't survive this place if I couldn't contain my impulses.

Still, rebelling against my captor felt so damn sweet. Like it riled him up but also stirred something in him. Maybe because he was clearly rebellious and saw that in me. Or maybe he just liked to fight in all its sordid forms.

There came an inexplicable familiarity with this stranger.

"Your father showed me what kind of man he is."

What did he mean by that? For a man to kidnap a woman, something terrible must have triggered it. The kind of hostility that would leave a deep scar. Enough to have him come after us like this.

Curling into a tight ball, I refused to believe a man could make my body feel alive yet tortured. The way it felt when he pressed his body to mine. Like it was right and wrong all at the same time.

Dragging the scratchy blanket over myself, I tried to block out the sound of silence. The way it highlighted every sigh. Every panic-drenched breath. Every whimper.

I dozed off, grateful to disappear from this hell.

Familiar nightmares twisted reality into terrible pieces as my mind tried to make sense of what I saw. Always the same hallway. The same voice calling to me from the darkness. *"Don't go down the hall."*

But I did. Just as I'd been ordered by our school teacher.

We assembled with the others. Those who, like us, had been selected to gather in the lunch room. Girls lined up in the back of the room. Dark circles beneath our eyes. Our clothes hanging off us like dolls. My hair in knots that would eventually take hours to comb through. We'd clung to each other, reassured we'd stay together.

All of us waited for the elegant visitor to pick one of the prettier girls. Like they always did. The plump middle-aged woman walked around scrutinizing each one of us. Finally, a nod from her to say she was done. She pointed at the one she wanted.

Me.

Stirring, the dream began to fade, but this time I was able to hold onto a thread of it. A memory wrapped in a nightmare.

Then a sinking feeling hit me when I remembered where I was.

In hell.

My sob echoed in the darkness.

I was still lying in a cell.

My stomach growled at the lack of food. When would Cassius come back?

A voice in the darkness broke through my thoughts. . .

"Anya, wake up." A man called from the void.

The sound of metal keys echoed through the air.

Then I was blinded by a light.

I blinked into the brightness, raising my hand to protect my eyes, which had not yet adjusted to the shock of a flashlight sweeping around me and illuminating this small space. On the other side of the bars stood the man I'd almost hit with that chair.

"Hurry up," he whispered.

A clank of keys.

"I'm going to get you out of here. Quick, before anyone wakes up."

I was on my feet and moving fast toward the door. "What time is it?"

"Three."

"In the morning?"

He slid a key in the lock, and it made a rusty scrape before he eased open my cell door. Grinding metal of the door opening. His gray suit was creased; he looked like he'd slept in his car.

"Why should I trust you?" I snapped.

He looked annoyed. "Do you have any choice?"

"What's your name?"

"I'm just a friend."

Hurrying through the cell door, I followed him, retracing my steps from where Cassius had led me down last night. The chill of the dungeons lifting as we made our way up a stone stairway. That memory of him telling me if the place flooded, it would be bad. Bastard. I had a revolving door of reasons to hate him.

But *this*, this could be my way out.

The stranger led me around corners and down hallways.

"Why are you helping me?"

"Shush." He tapped at a security panel, giving a nod that it was done. "This is the right thing to do."

"You're getting me out of here, right?"

"Yes, we don't have much time."

Staying was insane but going with this man, equally as risky.

The cool warmth of the early morning hit us. He scurried toward a waiting sports car. It was a gamble going with him, but there was no choice. Not really. We climbed into the front seat, both of us shutting our respective doors quietly. Trembling fingers reaching for my seat belt.

"No." He pointed at my feet. "Down. There's a guard on the front gate."

Shit.

"Are you taking me home?"

"Of course." His frown deepened. "Don't tell your dad where this place is."

I heard a sudden deafening crash as the windshield shattered. Glass scattered over my head. I turned my face away and squeezed

my eyes shut as I attempted to shield my head with my hands from
the sprinkle of shards landing on me.

The man threw himself over me and reached for the door handle and flung it open. "Out. Get out!"

Shoving the door the rest of the way, I spilled out onto my
knees, then sprang up, heading for the line of trees that was about
fifty feet away. My heart pounded in my ears. Glancing back, I saw
that man—my rescuer—running behind me.

"Go." He gestured.

Another shot ran out.

He fell flat on his face and struggled to get up, his hands and
face covered in mud.

I went back for him.

He frantically moved his arms. "No! Tell Glassman he let you go."

Really, because that's not what this looks like.

More bullets flew through the air. I ducked, making for cover.
The same woods I'd viewed from the window. Mouth dry with thirst,
I was panic-stricken. I considered raising my hands and surrender-
ing, but adrenaline drove me on.

My hem snagged on foliage, stopping me.

I yanked at the material, and it ripped with a terrible rending
sound. My legs were scratched by twigs as I hurried on between the
towering oak trees. I lost a shoe. Went back for it and then changed
my mind, kicking off the other. Barefoot, I sprinted into the denseness, ignoring the stabs of pain in my soles.

Running my fingers through my hair, I shook out the rest of
the glass splinters that had landed on me.

No. . .

An eight-foot brick wall stopped me in my tracks. A few feet to
my right rose another towering oak tree with an enormous width.
It had to be at least four hundred years old. One of its branches
stretched wide, reaching over the other side of the wall.

Quickly, I leaped onto a low hanging branch and made my way
up the trunk, careful not to slip, bark digging into my soles, climbing

higher and higher over thick branches, brushing leaves aside as my focus remained on making it over the other side.

I paused just long enough to peer back through the woods—seeing no one.

My bare thighs dragged along the unforgiving ruggedness as I scooted along a thick branch that bent low over the brick but not low enough. The drop was at least six feet. The road was clear. If I made it over, I could flag down a passing car. Or run to the other side and use the woodland as a shield making my way toward a house or car or a passer-by.

Lowering myself farther over the branch and hanging on, my arms strained as they took my full weight. Dangling. Building the courage to let go. Sweaty palms losing their strength.

I slipped off.

Screaming at the shock of landing. Agony jamming my ankles, losing my balance, and tumbling onto my back with a thud, winded.

Impossible to move.

I stared skyward through the oak leaves into the dawn.

Get up.

Get home.

Eventually, I braved shifting my arms and legs. Sitting up, I examined myself. Once I knew I was fine, I let a sigh of relief.

It took me a moment to catch my breath, but then I was up, struggling to my feet and hobbling off, whimpering at the agony of bruised bones.

The hoot of an owl.

Then silence again.

I squinted to try to see beyond the turn of the road. Seeing nothing, I continued on, hurrying faster to put distance between me and this place. Adrenaline causing me to shiver uncontrollably.

Then I saw something.

In the distance, the silhouette of a man. It looked a lot like Cassius.

Rubbing the distortion from my eyes to see better.

Fuck.

I bolted back in the direction I'd come from, trying to use the shield of the wall. I stopped abruptly when Cassius was standing before me. He had cut me off.

My chest tightened and my breaths were short as I again pivoted away from him.

"They will shoot you on sight," he called after me. "Better it be me that takes you in."

Caught between wanting to risk it and not wanting to feel a bullet, I froze. The hairs on my nape prickling, proving he was closing in behind me. He didn't need to say anything. His presence sent a paralyzing shock through me.

"What did I say to you about running?" his voice was low.

I turned to face him. "You'd kill me."

He came to stand before me. "Give me one good reason not to."

Raising my chin high. "Because the only person who hates Stephen Glassman more than you is me."

His brow furrowed as though with curiosity.

"Kill me now, and you won't discover his weak spot."

With a tilt of his head, he was seemingly resigned to that answer. He closed the gap between us and lifted me into his arms. "Don't fight me," he said.

Shaken and powerless, I reached behind his neck to hold on. Again, that closeness as his hands firmly clutched me to his chest. Nestling into his nape and breathing him in as though the man who was recapturing me was the only one who could save me.

He carried me toward a parked BMW.

He set me down beside it and opened the passenger door. "In you go." He set me down in the front seat and closed the door behind me.

He took long strides around the front of the car, walking with the kind of purpose that threatened to eat up all the darkness of this place. His fingers were hypnotically trailing across the hood of the car as he strode past it.

After watching him climb in beside me, I lifted my legs onto the seat and hugged them. "What happened to that man?"

Cassius started the engine. "You mean my fucking lawyer?"

"Your lawyer?"

He hit the gas and we accelerated, shoving me back into the seat.

From the way the tension flexed in Cassius's jaw, he blamed me for it.

"Tell me he's okay." I breathed.

"As far as mistakes go, that was your worst yet, Anya."

Throat tight, my body rigid with terror, I looked out at the endless woodland, already plotting my next escape.

Cassius gestured to the man who was guarding the gate. More men walked the property in twos. It was a miracle I'd ever gotten out. I doubted I'd get a second chance.

The staff in the foyer scattered when Cassius arrived back with me. He'd picked me up again to carry me in. I knew this way. Recognized the paintings on the walls, the damask wallpaper, and that familiar door at the end—he was carrying me back to the dungeons.

Burying my face in the crook of his neck, I didn't want to see. Didn't want to believe this was happening. That I'd failed to escape and my dash at freedom had resulted in a man's death. Guilt wedged in my throat. What was to stop this man from killing me?

I squeezed back tears of frustration, angry with myself for failing. I'd been so close to bolting across the street. Hiding in the woodland. That stupid fall had ruined my chance.

Too bruised and shaken to fight back. It felt useless anyway. He was too strong, too commanding in the way he ruled this estate. Too cunning with knowing every inch of this place, no doubt. Obviously ruling the men around us who'd watched on from afar as he carried me back in.

Cassius set me down outside the cell and gestured for me to go in. He assumed that confident pose as though expecting me to just walk in willingly.

"Why do you hate your father?" he asked.

I refused to share the truth. That he'd never acted like a father. That Stephen was often distant or worse, he avoided my brother and me as though we were an inconvenience. I hated him all over again because Dad had failed to protect me from him. The man who could kill me on a whim.

Seemingly annoyed that I refused to speak, Cassius again gestured for me to go in.

Holding my head high, I refused to move.

He strolled into the cell ahead of me, walking over to the nightstand and lifting a glass of water. "You must be thirsty."

Still, I refused to take one step inside that awful room ever again.

"Your brother Archie. . ." he said darkly.

"You leave him alone!"

"Give me a reason."

Head down, I scurried in and joined Cassius in the cell.

He handed over the glass of water. "Apparently, he and your parents made it to the safe room. Unlike you."

"You didn't find him?" It sounded triumphant.

"Not yet."

"Promise me you'll leave him alone."

"Do you promise not to disrupt my sleep with failed attempts at leaving?"

I brought the cold water to my lips, a rush of relief hit me with each swallow.

"Archie's innocent." *Just like me.*

Cassius made his way out, though this time he didn't lock the cell door.

"How much money are you asking for me?"

His brows knitted together. "I'm not holding you for ransom."

"Then why am I here?"

"I'm waiting for your father to come for you."

"He won't."

"What makes you so certain?"

I couldn't say it because anything else I gave him made me even more vulnerable.

"Then we'll lure him out some other way." Cassius left me standing there, stunned at his arrogance.

I was right back where I'd started. Tears stung my eyes as I tried to keep the blurry shadows at bay.

chapter
TWELVE

Cassius

THE WELL-GROWN GRASS BEHIND THE HOUSE SERVED AS a pathway toward what had once been our family chapel. More recently, this part of the property was rarely visited. No one else was permitted to enter this place. Not even my sister.

Because that was where I'd carried my mother's body after those men had left.

Even now, years later, I could still feel the weight of her in my arms.

The memory never left.

Sofia had not seen what I'd done to the chapel a decade ago. I'd hung a padlock from the thick doorway to ensure no one did.

Turning, I looked back to glance at the house where Anya lay sleeping in the dungeon. It had felt right placing her there for the night. But even as this anger ebbed for her trying to escape, I felt a pang of guilt.

Maybe because the house felt different.

There was no denying I found myself intrigued with my captive. Where there should be annoyance for the time wasted dealing with her, there was fascination. There was a sense of her value be-yond what I already knew.

Capturing her again just now had stirred my diabolical side. Maybe that was why I'd dedicated myself to maintaining the chapel as a teenager. I'd been trying to suppress some aspect of me I'd sensed rising out of the boy. The same cruelty that had me bringing Anya back this morning and punishing her with solitude.

Having her here brought a surge of devious pleasure. Her at-tempted escape was futile. Actually, it had been intriguing to see how far she'd get. I'd followed her until she'd made it as far as the road. Applauding her courage, even though I knew she'd fail.

Once in my arms again, she'd flung her hands around my neck and held onto me as though I was her savior. Her fragrance, a sub-tle vanilla and light—if light had a perfume—filled my senses. Breathing her in like I'd been rescuing my lost love and not the girl I was destined to kill.

I'd placed her back in the only room that she deserved. At least it felt good to tell myself that. The old me needed to know I was up for the job.

I'd walked away from her open cell with my willpower in check. But I'd wanted to strip her bare and do filthy things to her on the dirt floor. Yet something told me to curtail this need for revenge and play it out slowly.

Make her suffering a sacred thing.

She had to know what kind of man her father was. You couldn't live under the same roof and not see his nature. There would have been phone calls overheard. Conversations with his men. There had to be evidence that revealed his illegal activities. He was a goddamn arms dealer, for Christ's sake. She had enough insight to be useful for a while longer.

Understandably, the press refused to cover what that man really did—mainly because any journalist wanting to stay alive stayed away from any stories around that man. There were rumors, of course, of his ruthlessness, but I was beginning to suspect Anya had even been sheltered from those, too. To protect her or him, it was hard to tell.

I'd dreamed up so many scenarios of revenge, but this, this was the sweetest. Taking his daughter was the final step before my coup de grâce. Finally taking him down and his business, too. Ending his reign as a man who lorded over the weapons market in the States.

I rested my palm on the door of the chapel, taking a few moments before entering. Recalling how, as a devout Catholic boy, I'd once found this setting comforting.

After removing the padlock, I gripped the door handle.

Not yet...

Within the chapel lay the physical representation of my soul. The destruction of what I'd done to the inside sharpening my sensibilities.

Pulling open the doors, I was greeted by the echoey emptiness. Moonlight flooding in through the upper stained glass windows cast shards of muted moonlight over the chaos.

As I moved in farther, my soles crunched broken glass and dust filled my lungs. The faint scent of incense that had once burned here hung in the air. Candlewax, too. A reminder of what this place had been, a refuge, a simple place to say grace.

It crushed me all over again to see the place my mom had once cherished in ruins because of me. Once more, eviscerating my heart. Slicing away all doubts over this pursuit.

A decade ago, Stephen had left his mark.

What had followed that night was me leaving mine.

The chapel's state of annihilation remained exactly the same as that day. In what was meant to be a sacred place. Because I'd come here to beg God to undo what he'd done. Yet all that happened was an irrevocable decimation.

My mother's faith in her creator couldn't protect her. Just beyond the outer doors was where she'd died from her wound. The landmark of where my soul was given over to the devil—by my own will, no less.

That day, fourteen years ago, I'd vowed to see Stephen suffer like he'd made us suffer.

After he and his men had left.

After my parents' bodies had been taken to the morgue.

After my sister had been discovered in a catatonic state in the maze and transported to the hospital.

Something inside me had snapped, and I'd returned hours later to this chapel.

I'd wrecked one sacred artifact at a time. Tearing the baldachin off the altar and ripping it to shreds. Pulling at the gold-braided material and destroying it.

In anguish, I'd finished what Stephen had started in defiling our home. Engulfed in darkness, I'd gone wild in here and made a prayer of it.

Those same feelings of futility finding me still.

Even now, torn-up material lay amongst the spoils of a war that had been ravaged and raged against my creator. Scattered evidence of what I'd done. A maniacal act.

In here, alone, the night everything changed, I'd gone quietly mad. Wielding a sledgehammer. Trying and failing to dismantle the pews. Doing what I could to leave no place for anyone to sit and worship.

God no longer deserved that.

I'd moved on to the stone carvings of saints. Smashing my mother's favorite, St. Mary Magdalene. Then all the rest, imported from Italy those years ago when she'd felt safe here. Never imagining that just outside this place would be the site where she'd take her final breath.

My soul had been decimated that day. The consequences played out in this chapel by a young man who'd lost his faith in everything. No part of me was recognizable from the young man I'd once been.

I was as good as dead inside.

All those years ago, I had promised to kill every Glassman in that family. Yet, I'd brought that girl back as though second-guessing my own will.

"Lord, it's been fourteen years since my last confession." I opened my palms to show I still didn't care about any of that. "But that's not what this is."

You know it, and I know it.

It's a fucking miracle you're even hearing from me. Fourteen years since you tore my life apart. I never asked you for anything. All I did was give. I gave you me.

My fucking soul.

What you gave in return was worse than any nightmare. You dragged up hell from the depths and sent all that darkness to live permanently inside me. You made this my life. Since the day you let him kill my parents, you ceased to deserve my loyalty.

Have you come for the last piece of my soul by placing Stephen's daughter in my world? Challenged me to do the right thing? You kill indiscriminately and expect me not to do the same. Yet I am made in your image, Father.

This is what I offer you.

A front-row seat while I destroy her. We both know you're into that.

There, on the floor, remained my mother's rosary. A useless trinket. I stepped over it and moved toward what had once been an altar.

"Would you like your sacrifice to be here?" I raised my hand as though trying to hear. "Still silent after all these years. I'll handle it myself then. Handle her."

Making my way back down the corridor, I retraced my steps toward the dungeons.

It felt like the walls were closing in. The silence was a testament to the depths of this structure.

Down here, no one will hear you scream.

I was surprised to find the cell empty—the place I'd left a sleeping beauty.

The sound of running water led me to her.

Nudging open the door, I peered inside.

She was standing naked beneath an antique shower head. One in a long line of showers that afforded no privacy. A remnant of when these had been military barracks. She didn't see me, not at first.

I remained at the threshold.

She was a beautiful creature. A lithe nymph bathing beneath the spray. Her hands ran over her slender frame as though trying to make the most of the lack of soap. Glancing left, I saw her discarded clothes sitting in a puddle of water. With nowhere to hang them up in here, they'd become victim to the ancient drainage system. Putting them back on would leave her cold. I doubted she'd redress in soaking wet clothes. There was nothing left for her to wrap herself in other than that old blanket. For some reason, I didn't like the thought of her shivering.

There were no luxuries here. Nothing to make her feel welcome.

Anya tilted her face up into the water. Then opened her eyes. She froze, glaring at me with concern. Her innocence was emphasized by her nakedness or perhaps it was because she suddenly became self-aware and cupped her palms over her breasts.

"Come here," I ordered.

Hesitant at first, she left the shield of the pouring water and closed the gap between us, peering up at me. If she was ashamed of her nakedness, she didn't show it. Though she'd tried to seduce me before. So her willfully revealing no embarrassment shouldn't be a surprise.

Something told me God was laughing at me. Laughing at my sudden change of heart because me caring about her comfort wasn't the work of a monster—but even monsters had their moments, I mused. A chink in their armor where light shone through. Or maybe it was merely a prelude to sin. The way an animal plays with its prey before that fatal strike.

Either way, being here with her felt so damn good, my flesh ignited by her innocence. By the way she relented and came and stood before me. Her big eyes peering up in trust.

To the far left was an old cabinet and I vaguely remembered there being old towels in there—not ideal but they'd do.

I lifted one out and stretched the fabric wide. With a nod, encouraging her to step into it.

She looked at me suspiciously and then stepped into the center of the towel. "What's happening now?"

"I'm drying you off."

"Why?"

"What do you mean 'why'?"

She let me rub her body with the towel, remaining still, raising her arms for me and even relaxing a little. Anya felt pert and yet soft, her body yielding to the strokes of the towel.

"No one's ever done this."

"Hasn't anyone ever taken care of you before?"

Her eyes widened as she realized what this was. Or maybe what this wasn't.

That ancient chapel had done its best to remind me what kind of monster I was. This was what I had hungered for—her fear, her vulnerability. Yet something inside was cracking.

"I don't want it to hurt," she whispered.

"It's just a towel." I tugged it tight around her and tucked it in. My hands found their way to her face, and I held her.

It would be easy to lean in and kiss her.

Reassure her that she was safe. That she was safe from the ghosts of this place.

But I didn't. Instead, I'd wrapped her up in a towel.

Keeping her safe from me.

"Hold me." She leaned in and wrapped her arms around my body.

With my arms by my side, I peered down at her. She was holding on for dear life.

Fuck it. Wrapping my arms around her, I relented to what she seemed to need in this moment. This affection felt alien to me. This closeness far away from the man I was or even had been. She'd run away, I should be punishing her for it, not this.

"I like it," she confessed. "I've never been held like this before."

"Not by your mother?" I made it cruel.

"No." She peered up at me. "They never hugged us."

"Never?"

She shook her head, causing water to drip off her locks.

I was failing to do what I'd promised all those years ago. Maybe because some part of me found her more useful than I'd first admitted to myself. What else could this rumination be? But a subconscious realization she was worth more to me alive.

I brushed a wet strand behind her ear. "You may return to your bedroom," I said coldly. "Don't disappoint me again."

"I'll be good now."

Tipping her chin, I went to kiss her, forgetting myself, then pulled back before our lips touched—before I'd given her any part of me she didn't deserve.

Turning sharply, I headed for the exit, hating this distasteful glimpse of affection I had to shake.

Fuck. Anya had manipulated me. She knew how to be equally cruel.

She was a snake, capable of slithering up and biting me.

But then another thought hit me. I could turn her plan around on her.

Use her lust. Lure her in.

Bend her to my will.

And she would give me what I wanted.

Her father.

chapter
THIRTEEN

Anya

CASSIUS WAS WALKING OUT. LEAVING ME WITH THE fallout of these swirling emotions.

Leaving nothing but the sound of rain.

My tears spilled.

Not rain. The shower. A run-down bathroom. In a deserted house. In the middle of nowhere.

And I'm fine.

Just fine.

The towel he'd wrapped around me dropping like it was too much to bear—because he'd been the one to wrap me in it. Showing me the kind of affection I'd craved all my life.

Stepping over the towel that had pooled around my ankles. I was unsteady on bare feet and staggered back.

My body hit the tile and caused a shudder. Water gushed over me again. Eyelashes blinking through droplets as the empty room came back into focus.

Cassius had left me here.

The stark realization that everything that had gone on before hadn't been normal. This, being kept prisoner, paled in comparison to the life I'd come from. What did that say about me?

Sliding down the wall, I hugged my knees and replayed the last few minutes. I'd looked into Cassius's soul and seen unbound pain beyond that steely glare. Minutes ago, he'd been on the edge. Whatever he'd intended to do—something bad—he'd changed his mind.

After admitting to him that I'd never been hugged, he'd turned away sharply, not speaking another word, and left.

Images of my past came back into focus, bringing that familiar futility. Because I was finding out things about my father that made all of this make sense. And I didn't want it to make sense.

I'd never found peace. Never once discovered a sense of balance at home. Never found love in any of its forms. I'd given up on happiness. It had never come my way. It was merely acceptance that it wasn't for me. A surrendering of sorts. Letting the days slip by. I'd learned that if I didn't expect too much, it was easier.

After twenty minutes, the water ran cold and chilled my flesh; goosebumps kissed my skin.

Pushing to my feet and raising my chin high, I knew none of this reflected who or what I was. All that had gone before had happened to me and not because of me.

I refused to end up broken.

Refused to give up hope of ever getting out of here.

Looking over at where my clothes lay drenched, I realized I had made another mistake in a long line of them. Water from the shower had snaked toward my clothes and underwear, and they were useless to wear.

Chilled to the bone, I returned to where the towel had fallen and wrapped it around my body. It smelled a little musty, but at least it was clean.

I left my clothes where they lay and walked the length of the shower, out along the narrow hallway, and headed off to find something dry to wear.

Squaring my shoulders, I prepared myself to face off with Cassius if he scolded me for exploring.

He had sent me to my room, but I wasn't ready to go there yet.

Attempting to leave this house again was clearly off the table.

Staying here and persuading Cassius that I wasn't his enemy was my only option. I was determined for it to be on my terms.

Once I saw a member of staff, I'd befriend them. Then I'd give them a message to take to the outside world. Maybe they'd feel bad for me.

Making my way up the staircase. Following the turn of the hallway, glancing inside room after room and finding them all empty until. . .

I found his.

This was not what I'd imagined.

The room was simple enough with framed photos of New Orleans on the walls, from a nighttime shot of the French Quarter to another of the ceiling of the Orpheum Theater. Though there wasn't a single shot with a person in them.

On his bedside table, he had an interesting selection of books. The kind I might want to read. Well, before I knew he liked them, that is. A football rested on a shelf, and it looked like one of the players had signed it in gold ink along the middle.

A tall lamp had been left on—maybe that meant he was forgetful? And there they were, photos of his parents and one of a pretty woman beside them. She had the same eyes as Cassius and the way she stood next to him, casually and with a big, relaxed smile, made me think he had a sister. These few snapshots of his life were more clues to add to the others.

Stepping into his closet and running my hand along his shirts and pants, my hand swept over the material as if that alone would reveal more of who this man was.

Discarding that musty towel, leaving it where it fell, I pulled a shirt off a hanger and slid into it. Buttoning it up and lifting the sleeve to my nose to take a sniff—it smelled fresh. Moving on to his chest of drawers and finding a pair of boxer shorts and sliding into them. It would do for now. I'd always walked around home bare-foot—something my father scolded me for—so it wasn't too uncomfortable to walk around without shoes here. Though when I explored some more, I found a pair of socks in another drawer, so I pulled a pair on. They didn't fit right, but if I dragged them all the way up, they'd do. At some point, I'd ask Cassius for clothes and shoes.

Inside his bathroom, I towel dried my hair. Sliding his comb through my knotted locks to even them out; having not used shampoo, my hair felt wiry. A small leaf came loose in my hand to remind me I'd run through woods. I let it flitter to the ground.

A brand-new toothbrush sat in his medicine cabinet. I used it and placed it back where I'd found it.

I ambled off to look for a phone, still unsure where I was exactly, but maybe if I was able to hunt down a landline and call my father's number, it could be traced? Mom and Dad would be frantic. I knew they'd be doing everything in their power to get me home. Maybe this might even make them realize how much they'd missed me.

Running my hand along the stone wall, I felt the past in this house, as though those who once lived and died here haunted its hallways. This city was known for its history, and it made me wonder about this house, too.

Plants hung here and there, and more plants rose high in regal pots to brighten the interior. Continuing on, I was careful to walk on the stone floor and not slip.

I halted abruptly.

The twang of strings came from down the hallway. The strum of uneven notes. I could keep on going but avoiding the inevitable would just delay it. I'd have to face off with Cassius at some point. If it was even him.

Nudging the door open, I peeked inside.

It was Cassius, and he sat across the vast space in an alcove, holding a guitar. His fingers were trailing along the strings. His focus on the window and what lay beyond—a well-tended garden. As I stepped in farther, I could see what looked like a giant hedged maze. Someone took care of all this land. Someone who might be able to get a message out for me.

The notes stopped, and long fingers paused on guitar strings. He'd sensed me. Or maybe heard my footsteps.

"Is it possible to get lost in it?" I asked softly.

He snapped his head to look my way.

I wasn't going to let his steely stare unsettle me. "The maze?" I clarified.

"I suppose you could get lost in there."

"How long have you lived here?"

He pushed to his feet, but he didn't answer.

I made a gesture to say I'd borrowed his clothes. "Mine were wet."

Dark ember eyes shimmied over me, recognizing his shirt.

"I needed something to wear."

"Already arranged."

"Oh, okay. Well, I'll give this right back as soon as I have something else to wear."

It was the way he studied me, the way his narrowed eyes took me in. From my newly washed hair to my feet, he seemed as close to fascinated with another person as anyone could be.

"Have you heard from my father?" I held my breath.

"You have access to the west side of the house. I'll remain in the east."

"I'm not good with that. I mean, I get turned around easily. You'll have to say left and right."

His brow furrowed as though mulling this over.

"I'm good at other things," I defended myself.

His back straightened as he pointed. "East." His arm swung in the other direction. "West."

Cassius was as stubborn as he was mean.

He lay his guitar on a couch and continued toward the door. "Let's keep our distance."

"It sounds terrible," I called after him.

His back stiffened. Then with long strides and a straight back, he headed in my direction. His casual T-shirt and jeans did nothing to deflect from his intimidation.

He paused beside me.

My stomach fluttered.

His fingers were close to brushing mine. The curl of his hand was dangerous. He knew it. I knew it.

A part of me felt like if we touched, it would set the world on fire with how wrong it would be.

"Your guitar," I made my point. "Sounds like crap."

"I was tuning it up."

That made me feel guilty for a nanosecond until I remembered I'd been kidnapped. "Did you kill your lawyer?"

"Go investigate the maze. With any luck, you'll get lost in there." He moved away from me, heading back out of the room.

Guess I was dismissed.

"I'm allowed out there then?" I said, and he turned to look over his shoulder at me.

"I don't expect us to get along. What I do expect is for you to realize I hold all the power."

"Which way's the kitchen?"

"You're hungry?"

"Yes, I haven't eaten since yesterday."

He pressed his fingers to his temple. "There's food in the kitchen. Help yourself to any of it."

"I'm allowed to eat then?"

His hand rested on the door handle. "Head south. I sent the chef home. You'll have to take care of yourself."

"Didn't want your chef to see what you're up to?"

"Actually, I'm keeping him safe from you."

That was a cheap shot. "Cassius, what exactly did my dad do to you?"

He raised his arms to say look at me, this is what he did to me. This.

Then he walked out.

Despite him trying to direct me, it was still easy to get lost in this place. Trailing along the hallways and now and again peeking into rooms just in case there was a phone he might have forgotten was in there.

Recognizing a series of black and white photos that we'd passed by when he'd carried me back into the house, I retraced my steps until I reached the door we'd come in, surprised to find it open.

Outside, taking in the warm afternoon breeze and only now grasping the scope of this property. The woodlands stretched beyond the left side of the home. This, the route I'd taken when I'd bolted. All the cars were gone now. Even the lawyer's vehicle with its smashed window was gone.

Right over there on the grass, twenty feet away, was where I'd witnessed him being shot at. The grass was soft as I trudged over to the scene of the crime. The place where he had landed face-first after the second gunshot had rung out through the air. I knelt to examine the blades of grass for any droplets of blood.

A pair of shoes came into view, and I followed them up—

Gasping, I shot to my feet.

"We meet again." It was the lawyer.

"You're okay?" A rush of relief swirled through me at seeing my hero still alive.

He squinted when he said, "Still have ringing in my ears."

"They shot you?"

"More of a warning. Cassius's men are headstrong." He was calm. Too calm, and it felt wrong to stand here and talk when hours ago he'd literally tried to smuggle me out in the early morning.

My throat tightened with trepidation. "Did he hurt you?"

"Only my pride," he muttered.

"You were allowed to leave?"

"Perk of the job," he said more to himself. "How are you doing? Settling in?"

"I'm not a guest," I snapped. "I don't want to be here."

"It's temporary."

"Last time I saw you, you were trying to save me."

"Let's just take one day at a time."

"Did you tell my dad I'm here?"

"Listen." He glanced toward the house. "It's complicated."

Which sounded like a resounding no.

"You need clothes." He frowned at the shirt I was wearing.

"What's your name?"

"Ridley."

"You need to get me out of here, Ridley."

He went to speak and then looked toward the house—Cassius was standing there in the doorway watching us both. Cassius turned and went back into the house. Ridley gave me a gentlemanly nod and followed him inside.

Snapping my attention back to the woods. The same pathway up ahead I'd taken in the early hours when I'd bolted.

My feet were already taking me in that direction. Heart pounding and my mouth dry, the soles of my feet were tortured by bracken once again. Pushing foliage out of my face as I burrowed further in. I was grateful it wasn't swampland.

Grateful, too, that this time there was no glass to brush out of my hair. Ridley was clearly being paid a shitload of money to just pretend what had happened was no big deal. He could have been killed. Instead, he'd just strolled inside that house like it was a lazy Sunday and the man inside wasn't a kidnapper.

There, ahead, was that tall tree I'd climbed, and it welcomed me with its vast branches that stretched wide. My palms crashed against the bark as I edged once more to the low-hanging branches. I'd soon find my footing again.

Pausing, chest tight with the realization if Cassius caught me again, I'd probably be locked in the cell or worse. I'd certainly not be allowed to roam the house. Thirst and hunger confused my thoughts that railed on making no sense.

Trying to think clearly, see things from a different perspective. *You're wasting time—precious time that you need.*

Again, my foot came up on the low-hanging branch.

If I escaped, I'd be returning to my old life of being imprisoned back in that grand manor in the Garden District. Cassius would come for us and maybe this time even hurt Archie. I'd never forgive myself if I led him home only for him to kill my brother. Keeping him safe was more important than anything.

Keeping them all safe.

If I stayed and was brave enough to befriend this man, maybe I could convince him my father regretted any mistake he'd made that had hurt him. Surely seeing how much Dad hurt this man, he would. And maybe, if I got to know Cassius well, I'd be able to stop him from ever hurting anyone else. Bide my time until I was rescued.

And maybe, just maybe, I'd earn my freedom.

Resting my forehead against the scratch of bark, I breathed through this plan, praying it was a choice I wouldn't regret.

Retracing my steps, feeling battered from hunger and the sting of nature's flooring, I made it all the way to the clearing. There, standing on the doorstep and leaning back on the open door was Cassius. His beautiful dark eyes were unreadable. Strong arms crossed over his chest as though judging me for staying as much as he'd judged me for trying to leave.

With my head held high, I strolled toward him and continued on into the house, refusing to look him in the eye.

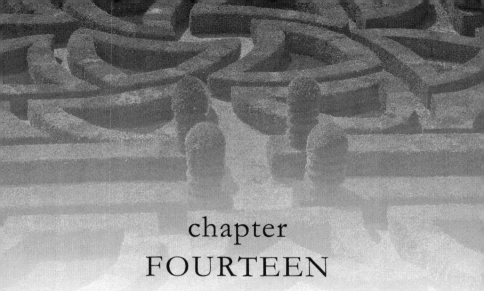

chapter
FOURTEEN

Anya

THE EVENING AIR WAS THICK AND RICH WITH THE SCENT of woodland. Dusk brought with it the birdsong only reserved for this late hour. Cricket frogs, though unseen, joining the chorus.

Exploring the property was the only thing keeping me sane.

I'd not seen Cassius since yesterday.

We'd both been avoiding each other. Or so it seemed.

Running my hand along the wall, I tried to find another way in. With its stained glass windows and modest steeple, this had to be a chapel.

"What are you doing?" a voice snapped from behind me.

I jolted with surprise, my heart pounding at the scare. Fascination must have flashed over my face to see Cassius wearing a Brioni suit, all tall, dark, and devastatingly handsome.

I tried to pretend I wasn't affected by him.

"I'm trying to get in here. Only there's a padlock."

"What are padlocks generally used for?"

"To keep people out."

He gave a look that told me that's what this was. "I was look-ing for you."

"It's not like there are that many places to hide around here."

He glanced back at the maze. "Well, clearly, you didn't look hard enough."

"Where is everyone?"

"I let the rest of the staff go. Thought it best you and I got to know each other better without interruption over dinner."

Which meant there was no one here who could get a message out for me. Frustration welled as I mulled this over. "What about your security guards?"

"Gone."

"Everyone?"

"I've kept two men to guard the property. They have strict in-structions not to interact with you."

"In case they find out I'm here against my will?"

"In case you mess up, and they have to shoot you."

I ignored that cruel barb. "Why do you keep this place locked?"

"Because that's where I sacrifice young virgins on the altar." Without a drip of sarcasm. "Interruptions can ruin a good ritual."

I stormed away from him, pissed off that he thought saying something like that to me would be considered funny. I mean, he could be a devil worshiper for all I knew.

Sprinting into the house, I hurried up the staircase toward my bedroom. Hurrying along the hallway to outrun him.

Not just him but also these foreign feelings swirling like wild birds set free in my chest, trying to fight this sense of belonging, this crippling want. This need to be near a man I was destined to hate. And why the hell did he think it necessary to dress up like that? All gorgeous and refined and ridiculously seductive.

And if I was honest, provoking Cassius had become a dark pleasure. I savored his jaw flexing in frustration, his intrigue—or something else, fascination for me, perhaps. The way he brushed his thumb across his lips as though buying time to think. The way his eyes sparkled when near me and then changed to reflect no emotion at all—he was very good at hiding himself.

I'd learned firsthand how the adults in my family ruled, though. They weren't intimidated by anyone. They always got what they wanted one way or another. Never seeming to let feelings get in the way. Love was a weakness never to be shown.

All I knew was unraveling. Surviving this, surviving *him* was down to me. Turning to look back, I felt a rush of pride I'd outrun him.

Continuing around the corner, I crashed into Cassius's chest, slamming against his hard abs, knocking the air out of me, and leaving me breathless.

When I moved sideways to get by him, he blocked me, forcing me to step backward until I hit the wall.

He pinned me there, placing his hands on either side of my head on the wall to block me in. "You know that was a joke, right?"

"Which one?"

He narrowed his sights on me, seemingly annoyed.

The air crackled with tension. A rush of electricity surging through my body that shivered with the contact of my palms pressing against his chest. The way he dragged his teeth over his bottom lip was dangerously alluring. I stared too long at his mouth, my face flushing with embarrassment. I wanted to press my lips to his. This need raw and this desire so brutal that I had to squeeze my eyes shut.

"You didn't let me add that I hadn't cleaned up from the last virgin sacrifice." He laughed, and small dimples appeared in his cheeks.

The kissable kind. "Fuck off."

"Excuse me."

I'm sure Cassius was usually impressed with his Brioni suits—like the one he was wearing now. Finely tailored to highlight his broad shoulders. I'm sure he usually dazzled everyone when he entered a room. Or even when he dragged his fingers through his lush hair in that pissed-off fashion as though this was the only way to keep calm. But here, with me, he was nothing but my captor. One with a stupid sense of humor. He rested a fingertip on my chin and tipped my gaze to his.

"What did you just say?"

"Don't remember." I turned my face away.

Again, he nudged me to look at him.

"Did you tell me to fuck off?" He hovered a pointed finger near my nose.

"What are you going to do about it?"

His lip curled at the edge. "Use your imagination."

"Nice of you to dress up for dinner," I teased. "But you're wasting your time. I'm not joining you."

"Don't make me dress you, Anya."

"You wouldn't—"

He took me by the arm and led me into the room that was meant to be mine. Guiding me across the hardwood floors of the bedroom. Letting go of my arm and opening the closet. I stood there partly amused at his bossiness and partly intrigued by what he might choose.

On the wall was a blank space from where that mirror had hung. The frame was now gone, and we both looked at it as though recalling how I had smashed the glass.

He reached for a hanger and pulled out a lemon-colored dress. Shoving it against my chest. "This one."

Hugging it to my chest, I watched him take long strides toward the door. Without turning around, he walked out.

The dress was pretty enough, but I was too old for frilled sleeves. An idea swarmed around my mind. Reaching all the way to the back of the closet, I pulled out the sparkly halter-neck dress I'd found abandoned in one of the many bedrooms. I'd tucked it out of sight. Like a raven hiding a shiny object, I'd claimed it. Though I'd not expected to wear it, not really. It had been more out of curiosity for finding another clue about who this man was and the people he knew. It had made me wonder if the woman this belonged to might visit.

Within a minute, I had stripped off my clothes and was looking at my reflection wearing the dress in the dark glass of the window.

The clingy material highlighted my curves and pushed my breasts up. A little loose around the hips, but it still stunned with its glamorous style.

The dress probably belonged to an old girlfriend, and it was going to be super awkward when he saw me in it. He'd no doubt be furious and change his mind about making me have dinner with him. I'd take pleasure in seeing him shrink in embarrassment when he saw what I was wearing. He'd realize I knew about his secret lover.

After brushing my hair, I hoisted the waves up and clipped them to create a sophisticated style that showed off my neck. Rummaging through the makeup bag I'd also found in the same room as the dress, I set to work applying a kind of war paint—a dazzling application of natural foundation, eyeliner, mascara, and bright red lipstick.

Checking my reflection in the window on the way out of the room, I was surprised to see so little of the old Anya because a curvaceous, sexy woman was staring back. Gone were the innocent eyes that were now shielded behind long black lashes and my mouth a bright red pout.

I made my way to the top of the stairwell and saw Cassius waiting for me below in the foyer. Straightening my back to elicit pride, I descended with my hand sweeping the banister on the way down.

Cassius looked up and fixed his intense focus on me with each step I took. My confidence soared as though shielded by the splendor of this dress.

He drank me in. Tucking his hands into his pockets and standing straight, blinking as though processing the woman before him.

When I made it to the last step, I clutched the handrail and waited for his reaction.

Only there was none. He merely stood there as though I wasn't. Seeing through me, calmly observing. If he was waiting for my move, he wasn't going to see it. As though both of us played this dark game of who would crack first under pressure.

I became breathless when he stepped closer. Peering up at his beautiful and yet haunting eyes, the way they crinkled with fascination. The way he emanated a stark energy that seemed impossible to contain. My core rippling with an uneasy sensation. Letting out a shaky exhale.

He reached into his jacket pocket and removed a white handkerchief, pressing it to my mouth and wiping off my lipstick. Bringing the material to his own lips, he moistened it, then returned it to my mouth to continue wiping away my bright red rebellion. The way his touch caressed my lips felt forbidden.

A ghost of a smile appeared curling at the edges of his mouth, shattering the illusion. "You'll do."

With his hand around my upper arm, I was being led toward the door. Anticipation welled in my chest that we were going out, beyond these walls to where my chances of escape increased with every passing second. The heat of the evening embracing us as we stepped into the courtyard, met by the chanting cicadas that hummed loudly around us.

Heart hammering with the hope that soon others would see me, I climbed in and then dipped my head as I slid into the passenger seat of his SUV. My captor slid in beside me on the driver's side.

"Where are we going?" I asked, pulling on my seat belt.

He gripped the steering wheel. "I thought it might be nice to dine out tonight."

There was so much to this man I hardly knew. Though what I had gathered in the short time we were together was that each decision, each action carried with it an alternative motive. This wasn't just dinner; this was something else entirely. I'd go along with it, too, because freedom lay on the other side of those walls, and tonight, he was the one taking me beyond them.

When he flashed me one of his endearing smiles, it threw me all over again. He was too relaxed, too confident to show any concern about losing me tonight. Maybe, just maybe, he was letting me go, setting me free. For some reason, that unsettled me. That tonight might be the last time I'd see him. It made no sense as I clung heavily to my deepest fear. Cassius was the first man who'd ever seen me— looked beyond the woman I was and actually seen me.

He drove the car through the tall double gate that had slowly swung wide before us.

I imagined what it would feel like if he slid his hand over and took mine in his. If he showed a flash of affection, how it would affect the evening moving forward. His touch softened the edges of all the hurts that had gone before.

Digging my fingernails into the seat to steady myself, annoyed I'd actually gone there, played with the impossible idea of us.

It didn't matter how much I fought against it. I wanted to know how his lips would feel like pressed to mine. What it would be like to be kissed by him, tongues swirling, being held against him.

I cursed him for it. "How do you sleep at night?"

He scratched the back of his neck. "Fine. Thanks for asking." His mockery had me gritting my teeth.

"Are you taking me home?"

"No, Anya, I'm not."

We were heading fast into the city, lights brightening the night sky, and pedestrians mixing with locals and vibrant tourists. People were flooding the streets and bringing alive the city I hardly knew.

"Who was she?" I turned in my seat to look at him. "Another kidnap victim?"

"What are you talking about?" He glanced over.

"Whoever owned my dress."

He smirked. "The one you stole?"

"Borrowed."

He agreed with a nod. "All in the details."

"It'll be awkward if it belonged to your mom."

He shot back, "You're not the only woman in my life, Anya."

My chest tightened with this revelation. He had a lover, a woman who kept her clothes and toiletries at his place. I'd be naïve to think a man this handsome didn't have a girlfriend. A lover he got to spend those lonely nights with.

"Let's hope she's not going where we are," I said. "That would be awkward."

"I imagine it would."

"What's her name?" I pushed.

"Sofia." He took his eyes off the road just long enough to study me. "She's my sister. The dress you found belongs to her."

Relief came with a flash of heat to my cheeks. He glanced over and caught my embarrassment. "Where's she now?"

"Far away."

"Bet you wouldn't like someone kidnapping her."

"How about you play nice tonight?"

"Yes, let's try to enjoy ourselves." My sarcasm practically dripped all over the floor.

The car turned onto Royal Street, and after a minute or so of driving down the busy road, we pulled up outside the front of Hotel Monteleone.

Cassius gestured to a valet as he opened the door. He got out and closed it behind him with a slam. With seconds to escape, I pulled on my door handle, ready to leap to freedom before he could make it around to my side. My shaky fingers slipped from the lock, and I was sure he'd heard my failed attempt to bolt.

Trying to hide this burst of adrenaline, I averted my gaze when he approached my side. I caught Cassius handing over cash to the valet and sharing words with the young-looking man.

He'd lost his mind thinking this was acceptable behavior—I could scream or cry out and other guests would run to help me. My chance was finally here. It was all in the timing.

Cassius opened my door with a click of his fob. Stepping elegantly out of the car with my hand in his, I joined him on the curbside. He pulled me into a hug and with his free hand, he threw his keys to the valet.

Cassius's mouth neared my ear, and he whispered, "Whatever you think this is, it isn't."

"What is that supposed to mean?"

"Don't talk to anyone. Don't try to signal to anyone."

I shot a glare in his direction. It wasn't unusual for my parents to dine here, so there was a slim chance they'd be here tonight. Though what was more likely was they remained home wracked with guilt and sorrow for my loss, trying to keep Archie safe, too.

He curled his fingers against my cheek, and his tone softened. "You look beautiful."

Those words had never been spoken to me before. What was I supposed to say? That I found him just as attractive. That being here tonight was a refreshing break from being locked up.

We made our way through the entrance as though arriving at a luxury hotel together as a couple was an ordinary event. Leaving behind the enduring heat and welcomed by the air conditioner that cooled my skin. He gave a nod to the concierge as we glided our way through the cozy foyer. Glancing left and right, I tried to get the attention of anyone who might look our way. Even after his threat.

He pulled me in tighter. "You'll be glad to hear life in the Garden District has returned to normal."

My flesh chilled with what he was insinuating, and my back stiffened as he guided me onward toward the dining room. The place where so many of our family dinners had been endured when my parents had brought Archie and me to this restaurant.

"What are you saying?"

"Your brother is living his best life. Back to playing video games and being a teenager without a care in the world. Seems a little strange, don't you think?"

No, he wouldn't have forgotten me. I refused to believe my brother was unaffected by my absence. Or maybe this was Cassius's way of getting a rise out of me.

Swallowing my fear, I allowed him to guide me as a lover would.

"What was it you told me about your parents spending little time at home?" he chided. "Care to elaborate on who exactly is watching over Archie?"

Not only was he spying on my family, but he also had access to Archie. If things had returned to normal, my brother would be vulnerable again. Alone in that big house without me to protect him. Surely after what had happened, our home was heavily guarded.

"Understand what I'm saying?" Cassius shook me back into the moment.

Fine hairs prickled on my forearms as his insinuation burrowed into my soul. "Cassius." My breath left me.

"Archie spends his time playing volleyball in the garden."

"I'll do anything. Please, don't hurt him."

He gave a ghost of a smile. "Do as I tell you."

"I will." And I meant it.

"See, this isn't so bad, is it?"

A bitter realization. "Anyway, no one will recognize me."

The dashing man beside me, with his arm tight around my waist, nudged me up against green damask wallpaper. His fingers trailed my scalp, and with a tug, he freed my dark locks. They spilled over my shoulders, proving he didn't care if others recognized me or not.

The maître d' led us to a table all the way across the full dining room. Chatter and the clatter of knives and forks on plates echoed around us. Soft piano music playing from another part of the hotel found its way to entertain those who didn't care about paying too much for an entree.

Rigid with tension, I held Cassius's hand as we navigated around the white linen-covered tables to find our corner table. I went to sit, and he stood behind my chair to ease it in for me, appearing as the ultimate gentleman.

He sat beside me and gave the order to the waiter, a man with a crew cut whose eyes avoided mine. "Champagne."

I stole the chance to look around to see if I recognized anyone. Maybe if I'd worn the yellow dress, I would be more likely to spark a familiar glance. This chintzy halter neck was a spectacular misfire. It made me mingle easily with the elite crowd who hardly looked our way.

When crew cut returned for our order, Cassius gave him back the menu and chose. "A dozen oysters. On the half-shell."

I leaned forward and whispered, "You didn't ask if I'm allergic to seafood."

He frowned. "Are you?"

"No."

"Didn't think so. It certainly didn't come up in my report." He flicked the napkin and laid it over his lap.

"You planned this?"

"Your father is evasive. It wouldn't surprise me if he just disappears."

He wouldn't leave me here, not with this man, not like this.

There was one thing that would bring attention our way. I'd witnessed it too many times. The raised voices of my parents arguing that brought long, painful stares our way. Disapproving glances from those who overheard. The last time we'd visited here, they'd argued about a trip out of state that Mom had wanted to take.

Maybe all this would change everything.

Bring us closer.

Remind us how precious our family was before this man invaded our lives.

"What kind of man drags a woman out like this?" I muttered, testing the waters. "To have her taste freedom but not let her have it."

He slid his knife to the left as though my words didn't faze him.

"Did you hear me?" I hissed.

"Unfortunately for you." He smirked. "Your ploy won't work, Anya. I don't argue. I debate. And I always win."

"You have such a high opinion of yourself." I reached into my purse, pulled out the red lipstick, and reapplied it while using the gold compact mirror. I ran my tongue sensually over my lips.

"Do you know why women wear lipstick?" I asked.

He rested the tip of his tongue in the corner of his mouth because he knew where I was going with this.

"Because a woman's mouth reflects another part of her anatomy," I chided.

"Thank you for explaining that so succinctly, Anya." He suppressed a smile. "I'm envisioning it."

My face flushed as I tucked the lipstick and compact back in the purse. Buying time so I wouldn't see him looking this way.

"You don't need makeup. You're naturally ravishing."

I wanted to believe him. I'd spent too long dressed down in drab clothes with nowhere to go.

Searching his face, I tried to see the sincerity in his usually closed-off demeanor.

His arched brow hinted he was pleased with my reaction. The flush of my cheeks. The silencing of my voice, him controlling the moment with a strike of victory.

"Anya, you're stunning."

I felt a fluttering in my chest that moved low into my belly.

Yes, he was evil, but he was still the first man to show any interest in me or even compliment me. I had been hidden away. Rarely allowed to mingle with others. Forbidden to spend any time with strangers. "I'm not used to. . ."

"The truth?" His frown deepened as he considered that, making me regret saying it.

Giving him anything of my old life was a bad idea because his words resonated in my heart like a string on a violin being plucked for the very first time.

Silence reigned over our table when the waiter set down a bottle of champagne nestled in a silver cooler. He uncorked it to prove he'd done this too many times to count. Then poured it into two flutes, all the while glancing at me and then Cassius. Perhaps sensing the tension, because after our glasses were filled to the brim, he withdrew, heading off to talk with other diners.

"Do you ever feel threatened by your father?" he added softly.

"No, he's not like you."

He let out a long sigh. "You have no idea how true that statement is."

"How many of your victims have you brought here for dinner?"

"Victim is such a passive word. Wouldn't you rather call yourself a survivor?"

"That all depends on if I survive."

"I know this is difficult for you, but have I not treated you well?" He reached for his champagne flute.

"Ask me this again after you've let me go."

He sipped the golden bubbles in his glass. "Trust me, I'm counting the hours until you're out of my life."

"What do you hope to achieve? We've established it's not money. What do you want?"

"I want you to open up to me."

"Make me." I let that tease linger.

"Careful," he said darkly.

"I could scream."

"But you won't."

"You're sure about that?"

"Yes, because I know how much you love your brother."

A silver tray of oysters was brought over and set down between us. Cassius eased a couple onto his plate.

"Your sister has lovely taste in clothes. I bet I'd like her. Why don't we invite her over for dinner?" It was worth a try.

He looked thoughtful. "She's not in town."

"Where does she live?"

"Try an oyster." He lifted one of the half-shells off the platter and lay it on my plate.

The shell was pretty, and it seemed sad to just throw it away afterward.

"When was the last time you talked with your parents?" I ran a fingertip around the shell. "When was the last time you saw your mom?"

His brow furrowed as he recalled. "Fourteen years ago. It was a Tuesday, and it had rained that morning. She was lying in my arms, barely able to talk. You've never really experienced fear until you watched someone struggling for their next breath, unable to take it. She bled out from a bullet wound and died in my arms." He lifted the oyster shell to his mouth and swallowed it with ease. "Unless you count the time afterward when I saw her lying on a metal slab in the morgue."

"Cassius." My voice was quiet, body still, too afraid to move.

He pointed at the remaining oysters. "Want another?"

My flesh chilled with a terrible realization—a hunch so raw I refused to believe it. "Who did that to her?"

"Make sure you squeeze some lemon first. It complements the taste."

Unable to move, or think, or even take a full breath, awash with fear.

He lifted one of the half-shells and brought it to my lips. Opening my mouth, I let him slide in the mollusk as though guilt wouldn't let me refuse him anything. I swallowed it with difficulty, my throat still tight. Cassius reached up and curled his finger to catch a teardrop on my cheek.

He handed me the flute of champagne. "Here."

I took the glass from him but was unable to drink. I placed it down and reached for my napkin and dabbed my mouth. Then used the corner to wipe away another tear.

Cassius offered me another oyster.

I raised my hand in refusal, watching him take another shell and savor the food as though he'd not just confessed the worst day of his existence. He ate as though his heart had not been broken.

As though his soul had not been mortally injured.

He wiped his hands on a napkin and pushed it aside.

"You're going to kill me, aren't you?" I hadn't meant to say it out loud.

He reached over, and his fingers trailed through my locks and then clutched them at my nape. His chestnut irises flashed with searing passion.

The people slipped away. The thrum of noise dimming. All that mattered was this moment. This connection between us blocked out every other sensation. This sense that no matter what had gone before, there was a sliver of possibility he'd come to change his mind about me.

Yet. . .

He hadn't denied it, hadn't told me that no way would he ever hurt me or that the gesture of his affection was meant as something else.

I pulled away.

"Up," he said, throwing cash onto the table. "Quickly."

We were moving fast. He'd wrapped his arm around my waist, directing me away from our table and shoving me through the kitchen door. Both of us were barely bumping into staff, who threw frustrated glances our way as we continued.

Glancing back through the window of the kitchen door, I saw my father peering in at us, his face aghast.

Stephen shoved the door open.

He was following, rounding the stark metal counters as he chased us.

We were out of there and moving fast along a hallway. I tried to dig my heels in, but with Cassius's strength, it was impossible to resist the gravity of his pull.

He stopped in front of a closet, and then after opening the door, pulled me inside and shut it behind us. He maneuvered behind me, his chest pressed to my back, his palm firmly against my mouth to prevent me from crying out. I bit down on his palm, but he just cupped my mouth harder.

A stunned shiver coursed through me. A rush from the way he wrapped his left arm tight around my chest, unwittingly squeezing my nipples and sending a shock of pleasure into my breasts. Heady sensations caused me to falter, and I leaned back into him.

Dad had been so close to catching us and rescuing me. My heartbeat thrummed faster, as though me slowing down in here just made it worse.

The waft of Cassius's cologne caused me to waver, riding the pleasurable feeling between my thighs.

It didn't make any sense—outside this door was probably the man who raised me, the man who called me daughter, yet in here, it felt more real.

This man was more alluring than anything or anyone I'd ever experienced.

The thought made me wobble on my feet. Reaching behind me

for balance, I clutched Cassius's thigh, digging my fingernails into hard muscle, feeling the shifting tension in his leg.

In my lower back, his stiffness nudged me, causing my breath to hitch, and a fantasy I was in no place to want, played out in my head.

Clothes off. Skin to skin. Our naked flesh pressed together.

"This isn't hiding." His voice broke through my desires. Like a bucket of cold water being dumped on my head. "It's a taunt. Delivered straight to your father, and we both know he's too much of a pussy to rescue you."

My tongue swept over his hand to rebel against him, to silence anything more he would say. I felt the shift of him behind me as he eased his grip and used the moment to spin me around to face him.

His dark expression met mine. Searching his face, I tried to speak, but I couldn't. I was confused. Hot and needy.

What did it mean that I didn't call for help.

I could scream.

I should scream, but that undeterminable look in his eyes stopped me. An unfathomable moment that stole my breath away and weaved doubt in my mind, spun what was happening between us into a complex web.

Cassius had shared that story of his mother like it was nothing—yet it was clearly everything, a clue to why he'd stolen me away.

He pinched my jaw and brought his lips toward mine, and I could have sworn he was going to kiss me. His mouth was so close that the scent of the champagne on his breath was on my lips. My body came alive again as sparks of white-hot heat made me weaken, causing me to shudder with want.

"Obey me," he said, his tone gruff.

His dominance snapped through this thread of desire like a sharp object.

I clutched his forearm. "That's why you kept your eyes on your watch."

His smirk was as cruel as it was inviting. "Let's go home."

He peeked out and checked that the way was clear. As we scurried along toward the rear of the hotel, it crossed my mind that no one else was searching for us. There weren't swarms of people who should have been alerted to the fact I'd been observed literally having dinner with my captor.

As we rushed out into the heated night air and moved quickly toward his SUV, those words exchanged with the valet at the beginning of the evening made sense. He'd planned all of this, including escaping out the back. The valet had parked his car a few feet from the rear door.

Back in Cassius's SUV, I brought up my legs and hugged them, angry with myself for not trying harder to escape.

Though as the car pulled away from the hotel, I had to question if I really wanted to be found.

It was impossible to pretend what had just threaded itself between us in the closet hadn't happened. A vivid connection. The intensity of two people needing the other to survive while hidden away together for those strained seconds.

Me protecting him from my father, because that's what it had felt like—because surely Dad would have killed him on sight. And perhaps Cassius was guarding me against something unknown, something sinister. Our dinner conversation revolved in my mind with all its perilous undertones.

As he navigated his SUV out of the city, we left behind the bright lights of the business district until all that was left was moonlight guiding us and the fluorescent glow of headlights ahead.

I couldn't look Cassius in the eye. Couldn't have him see this doubt and confusion. Regret crashed against what I should have done. I should have tried to get away from him. But that delay, that split-second decision having entrapped me all over again because I'd not called out for my father. In that moment, I'd chosen to stay with *him*, with Cassius, the man who drove us back toward his home in silence.

The man who'd revealed the darkest part of himself tonight. Delving deeper would be just as treacherous.

It was better we never talked of it ever again.

chapter
FIFTEEN

Cassius

WITH EACH PASSING SECOND, MY IMPATIENCE GREW.
By the time I had finished looking over the information tracking a tanker that was scheduled to leave the port of New York, I was itching to leave. Despite my best intentions, I needed to know what *she* was doing.

My thoughts were annoying, dragging me back to the Hotel Monteleone, and our dinner there last night.

The thrill of the chase.

Baiting the enemy.

That jolt of excitement blasted through my veins as my well-thought-out plan played out.

I'd held Anya in my arms in that small closet, so tight it had to have hurt with my hand cupping her mouth.

There was an unfamiliar expression on her face that I still couldn't define because after what I'd done to her, I didn't deserve her compassion.

Didn't fucking want it, either.

I had the desire to say fuck-it and cross the divide between us in that suffocating space and kiss her, and it appeared she wanted the same thing.

Call it by any other name but it was manipulation on her part—a guile of biblical proportions because it made no sense with her father outside that door looking for her. She could have screamed— and she hadn't.

It didn't matter how much I threw myself into my work, her name bounced around my brain like a pinball in a machine. I'd chosen to work in the city today. Here in the Orleans Tower, with its gym and the other amenities I took advantage of, making sure I could focus away from home. Usually, the view of the city brought me back to more important issues, but not today. Even as I glanced out at the horizon, all thoughts led me back to Anya.

I couldn't go to her yet. No, I had to bide my time.

Dangle her from the hook a little longer.

"What do you think?" Ridley asked, and I swiveled my seat toward the direction in which his voice came from. He had been working at the other table in my office and had shaken me from my musing.

With her in my life now, it was easy to get lost in thought.

I tried to scour my brain and remember what Ridley had asked me, but nothing came to mind. How could it? I hadn't heard a word he'd said because I was too busy wondering what a certain captive was doing.

Without answering, I stood, pushing up from my chair. The wood scratched against the floor as I shoved it back with force and urgency. The sound bounced off the walls, echoing through the room like a freight train.

The moment I heard it, I knew I had made a mistake. Ridley would pry, and then as if on cue, he did.

"Where are you going?" he asked.

My steps halted, but I didn't turn to look at him. There was no need to answer him, but I did anyway.

"I have a pressing matter I need to attend to," I responded vaguely.

"Is the pressing matter a certain woman . . . ?" He trailed off for emphasis.

I wouldn't dignify that with a response. That wasn't something I was ready to admit, so instead, I kept walking, and as I made my way through the door, I thought I heard him chuckle behind me.

Asshole.

It didn't take me long to arrive home. I was eager to see Anya and the speed with which my car took each twist and turn reflected that. The longer she was here, the harder it was to remember why I took her.

But just as the whys escaped me, it would all come rushing back. I could smell the blood in my nostrils all over again, the coppery tang of death, and it hit me in the heart why she was here and what I hoped to accomplish.

As much as she affected me, I needed to stay the course. All that being said, I could still play with my prey.

It would be fun to torment her, but even more fun to torment him. To have Stephen Glassman know I had her in my possession was a heady aphrodisiac.

When I arrived back at my estate, I didn't bother pulling my car around back. I stopped in the front circular drive and stepped out of my car. I headed straight for the front door, placed my finger on the keypad, and stepped inside when it clicked open.

Ever since my parents had died, I'd had the entire estate locked down. It was more secure than Fort Knox. Biometric entries, infrared scanning. If I didn't want anyone in, they couldn't gain entry, and if I didn't want anyone to leave . . .

Well, Anya knew the answer to that question.

My need to search her out had me taking the stairs two at a time, and when I swung open the door, I was met with a well-made bed and silence.

Fuck.

Where was she?

I exited the room as fast as I entered and went in search of her.

I continued to search the house, the bathrooms, the living room, the sunroom, but I found absolutely nothing.

My footsteps echoed in the hall against the silence.

Where could she be? I made my way to the far corner of the house to my surveillance room. Inside there sat two of my men, each one behind a computer staring at the images of the property.

"Where is she?"

There was no reason to clarify who I was talking about.

Robert looked up from his monitor and started to hit buttons on the computer dashboard on the desk. The fact that he didn't know off the top of his head grated at my nerves.

But at that moment, his ability to do his job properly wasn't my number one importance. Finding Anya was.

What if Ridley had kept me busy at the office while one of his staff rescued Anya? What if she was taken by someone else?

No.

She was here somewhere. They just needed to do their goddamn job and find her.

"Pull up all the footage for today," I barked out, and within a few seconds, the day played by on the monitors overhead.

"There!" I shouted, pointing at the screen. "When was that recorded?"

"An hour ago," answered Robert.

There on the screen, clear as day, was Anya. With her head held high, back straight and proud, she was walking out the back door of the house.

"Pull up the images from outside," I ordered, and I waited for the new footage. With the pride she had in her stance, I wondered if maybe she might've tried that tree again.

She wouldn't have gotten very far. It wasn't possible to leave the grounds without my permission. Not with my men stationed outside the perimeter of the property, but if anybody could escape, it would be her. She had proven herself to be resourceful.

"There." I pointed at where she was walking.

In the image, she was taking the path toward the maze.

Was she lost? Or was she going there on purpose?

Not a good idea.

Once inside, if you lost your bearings, it could be hard to find your way out.

It was constructed that way. When I took possession of the property as my own, I made tweaks, let hedges grow out, but that was neither here nor there at the moment.

I couldn't have Anya lost in the maze and starving to death.

If I was being honest with myself, a part of me still didn't want to see her hurt, even after what her father had done to us.

It was an odd thing to come to realize. I shrugged off the thoughts running rampant in my mind and set off for the maze.

When I stepped outside, I was surprised by the temperature. It had dropped.

The sun was about to set, and I needed to find her before that happened. Although I knew the maze backward and forwards, it still wouldn't make finding her easy.

I stayed on my path, entering the dark shrubbery. Once within the maze, the natural light from the sky flickered out. It reminded me of when a candle was burning and about to be snuffed. It was dusk in the maze with just enough light to make my way.

The farther I submerged myself in the labyrinth, the more concerned I grew. I couldn't pinpoint what this feeling was at first. Alarm coursed through me, and it felt like an empty void in my stomach gnawing at my gut.

Fear.

I was afraid for her.

Suddenly, as I made my way to almost the center, the clawing feeling had grown. It had a life of its own. My throat tightening with trepidation, I was terrified of what I would find.

The revelation of my concern was not something I could think about. The only thought was where she was and that she was safe, but it became harder to stem my roiling thoughts with each minute that passed. There was no reason she would be gone that long. I turned the corner and my feet stopped, and my eyes grew wide—

There she was.

Anya.

Dressed in a flimsy yellow dress, thin straps over her delicate shoulders. Feet adorably bare.

She looked like a nymph.

Tempting.

Taunting.

Something about her made me want to reach out and pull her in my arms. Her loose hair drifted as she stepped on the tips of her toes against a hedge.

I didn't make a sound as I watched her. She was reaching for something high in the tall shrubs.

Her right arm was stretched out far above her head. I watched her for a beat as she struggled to reach whatever she was trying to grab. Then her foot wobbled, and I knew she was going to fall.

I didn't wait for that to happen. I sprang into action, catching her in my arms before she hit the ground.

"What are you doing?" I scolded. "You could have hurt yourself if I wasn't here." My anger was misplaced, and I knew it. I wasn't angry with her. I was angry with myself for letting this woman make a dent in the wall I had erected around myself.

"One could ask you the same thing," she fired back.

She pushed my hands off her, righting her position.

My head cocked to the side, but I didn't speak. I just appraised her.

"You can't touch me like that. . ."

"I thought you wanted me to touch you . . ." I drawled out. Hints of seduction lingered in my voice.

"You thought wrong."

"I must be confused," I smirked. I didn't need to bring up the ploy. There was no point seeing as we both knew how that turned out. I won. I always did.

"If you must know, I was trying to help that bird."

"Bird?"

"The one stuck in the shrubs."

I moved past her, looking in that direction. "Where?"

"Shh, be quiet so you can hear."

Peering into the high shrubbery, I saw a flash of blue.

A blue finch was caught in the tightness of the leaves. Instinctively, I reached in, the backs of my hands were scratched as I forced them within the thin branches. Cupping the bird in my palm, I gently eased it out from the bushy twigs and held it out at chest level. It lay still in my hands, unmoving, the beat of its heart rapid against my fingers.

Anya came closer. "Is it hurt?"

"I don't think so."

"What should we do?"

Without a second thought, my hands fell open, and the bird seemed to think about its chance at freedom for a few seconds. It sprang into the air with a fluttering of wings as it took flight, up and out of the maze, flying toward the dark sky.

"You let it go?" she said wistfully.

I looked at her. "A beautiful creature should never be caged."

The realization struck us both at the same time—our eyes fixed on each other's as the moment settled into something more, something unfathomable.

She turned her back on me, reaching for my hand, and I waited, considering whether to take it. Whether to let her have this be what she wanted it to be.

It was nothing, really. Me guiding her out. Doing the right thing for a nanosecond before I could go back to the plan.

Remember the fucking plan.

I reiterated this thought as I wove my fingers through hers. Her touch was an annoying simmer beneath mine. A low current absorbed into my skin and deeper still into my tendons until it thrummed in the bones of my hand.

Anya and I walked out of the maze and I led us back toward the house, not willing to let her go just yet.

Just me protecting my asset.

That was what I told myself because anything else would be irrevocable.

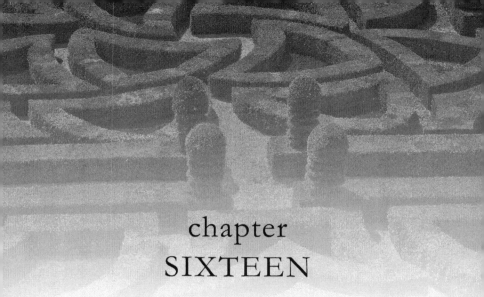

chapter
SIXTEEN

Anya

MAYBE I WAS THINKING TOO MUCH INTO THIS, THAT Cassius had stared straight into my eyes as he'd let that bird fly free. Because I was still here, even after he'd made that romantic statement about creatures not being caged. This, his place, was the ultimate in captivity.

In fact, lately, he was hardly ever here.

It was too quiet.

What was worse, the days melded together. It felt like I was living in an alternate universe. One where the day just kept repeating itself. But the worst part was that there was nothing for me to do.

I was bored.

And lonely.

A troubling thought that I didn't want to acknowledge was that I wished Cassius was here.

Even if he drove me crazy, at least I would have someone to talk to.

When I first got here, Cassius was around more, making sure I didn't get into trouble, but recently, probably because he had started to trust that I wouldn't do anything rash, he was more inclined to leave me alone in his house.

Well, not really alone.

I couldn't call this alone when there was security. I knew they weren't meant to hover, and they didn't. They did a great job of melding into the background, but the thing was, I grew up in a cage, so I knew where my jail keepers lurked.

The sound of my feet on marble echoed loudly. I was afraid I would alert someone, and they'd ban me to another part of the house. Being here wasn't that different than being in my parents' home. I was still invisible, and ever since Cassius had pulled back, more so.

With no clear direction in sight, I found my usual place in the kitchen. Without anyone being there, it felt eerily quiet.

My heart tugged in my chest as I remembered one of the few happy memories of a time before. Growing up, I never really had anyone, Archie sometimes, but more often than not, I was alone. The only person who spoke to me other than my homeschool teachers was the cook.

She was the only one who noticed me. Who paid attention to me. Who did anything special for me.

The need to bake weaved its way through my veins. The desire to feel at home, or whatever home was, rooted itself in my psyche.

Secure.

Settled.

Loved.

My happy memories were always with Maria, our Italian cook. Never with my mom or my father. She was the one who had been around when we were little. Filling the spaces our parents left by their lack of attention. We'd been too naïve to know that the moment a staff member showed any affection to us, they were let go.

I'd never forget that look in her eyes, the day she'd left us for good, as though Maria knew what really went on in that house and was powerless to help us. Maybe when I got free of this place, and free of home too, I'd seek her out and tell her what she'd meant to me. Tell her that when she'd left, the house had become cold and lonely all over again.

I shivered off the chill of the memory. There was no use thinking about that now. Too many staff members had passed through our doors to count. All of them eventually realized what they were dealing with—two children living beneath the roof of a tyrant.

I didn't know this kitchen, but it wasn't rocket science.

I made my way around the room, opening every cabinet and drawer. It didn't take me long to find all the essentials.

There was nothing like homemade cookies to make my heart feel full. Seeing as I would take any morsel of comfort, even milk and cookies at my captor's house.

Once I had everything I needed, I set out to get mixing. As I moved the spoon through the ingredients, I poured in every emotion. Pounded the dough until all the pent-up rage poured out of me. It felt good. It made me remember all those times I would be frustrated, and Maria would hand me ingredients and tell me to work out my issues—super cute considering I was thirteen years old.

By the end, she would instruct me to then pour love into it. I never really understood what that meant.

Maybe now it was starting to make sense. That if I couldn't talk to Cassius, maybe, just maybe, something like this would soothe his angst. It was clear that he carried pain within him. Baking and eating had often helped me, so why not him? Why not bring a piece of his childhood back?

As I separated the dough into little round balls, I couldn't help but think of Archie. The only person I had in this world. And he craved my baking.

The love I felt for him would never fade. We'd be reunited again soon, and I'd have so many things to tell him.

To cope, I had to nudge my little brother out of my head and focus on anything but the thought of him alone in that house. I had to focus on getting out of here and surviving this. I returned my attention to molding the dough into round balls.

Before I knew it, the cookies were in the oven, and I sat at the counter waiting.

It was strange that even with me in the kitchen, no one came in here to check on me. It made me wonder if they saw me walking in here and purposely avoided me. As if this was some sort of torture not allowing me to speak to anyone.

Isolating me.

It was obvious there was a man in security who was told to give me a wide berth and not engage. Cassius probably believed it was for the best. Maybe it was his way of breaking my spirit.

But as the smell of the best of home surrounded me, I knew he was wrong, I wouldn't snap. He didn't have the power to break me. If my father couldn't, no way could this man.

I spent the time it took for the cookies to bake, sitting and staring out the large windows that overlooked the property. Musing over the maze and wondering why anyone would create such a design in their own garden. The property was big enough, but it was unusual.

And that chapel held such a fascination; it didn't make any sense to be all locked up like that. Unless it was run down inside and dangerous, but it didn't look like that from the outside.

I hadn't spent much time outside, and the need to walk and explore was tempting.

I often felt like a caged bird. Needing the fresh air in the oxygen to spread my wings. This feeling had lingered for years. Even at my own home, I wasn't allowed to wander freely. It's a strange notion to come to the realization you've left one cage to find yourself in another.

A beep of an alarm brought me back to the present. The noise cut through the silence like a warm knife slicing through butter. I pushed up and made my way across the room with my oven mitts on my hands.

A burst of heat hit me as I opened the oven door. I pulled out the scorching hot tray, carrying it over to the counter where I rested them on a metal stand. Burning a hole in the expensive-looking marble probably wouldn't win points.

A whiff of richness.

Deliciously assaulted by the rich chocolatey aroma drenching the air. Like a hit of happiness that soaked into my brain. The warm feelings I got in my stomach were followed by a pang of hunger. Mouth watering, I grabbed a spatula and then shoveled a cookie onto a plate. It had risen perfectly and was begging to be eaten.

Reaching into the fridge to grab the milk, I heard footsteps behind me.

"Making yourself at home," *his* familiar husky tone said.

I refused to turn around and look at him. "Hardly," I mumbled underneath my breath.

"What was that?"

I pivoted, unprepared to look up at that astonishing man. *Damn*, he looked good in a tight T-shirt and ripped jeans. Like a rock star on tour—all he was missing was an electric guitar—all hard muscle and messy hair. I wasn't ready for these feelings to swirl as they always did when he was in close proximity.

I was not ready to be this close again.

The way he towered over me.

His cologne saturating my senses.

My knees weakened.

It was too much.

My flesh ignited as he closed the gap between us.

"Want a cookie?" I responded, my words making him look down at the plate in my hands. I continued to watch him, waiting for a smile, but instead, I was met with a look of disgust on his face.

"Trying to poison me?" he grunted.

A clever retort sat heavily on my tongue, but instead of saying it, I shut myself up by lifting the warm cookie and stuffing a giant bite in my mouth, dissolving into a hot mess of bliss. Chocolate chips played havoc with my tastebuds. I shuddered, my brain sending a silent message that the pleasure of this was probably nothing to the pleasure of him.

A long-drawn-out moan escaped my lips.

Flushing, as though he'd guessed my silent musing, I peered up at him.

He merely studied me, seemingly mesmerized by the way I licked the chocolate off my lips, sticky and thick. .

"I don't recall you asking for permission to cook," he said.

I took another bite and talked despite it. "If it wasn't so good, I would spit it on you, but I'd hate to waste a perfectly good cookie," I mumbled, mouth full. My mother would be disappointed with my poor manners.

"Unless you plan on eating all of them, they're going to waste. No one in this house will eat something you made."

His words stung, but regardless, I refused to let them bother me. Instead, I placed the plate of cookies down and took one of them with me before turning to look at him over my shoulder. "Your loss." I shrugged and stormed away—stopping in my tracks suddenly when I'd made it just outside the door.

I wanted milk.

Turning back, I was about to reenter the kitchen when my step halted.

There he was.

Cassius.

A cookie in hand. And a smile on his face. He was taking another bite, and as he did, he groaned as he chewed with an expression of pure unadulterated bliss. Looking wickedly seductive.

A smile crossed my face as I stepped back into the kitchen.

"Busted!" I said, smirking.

He set the cookie on the plate and walked away from it. "Checking for poison."

Watching him walk by me, I smiled at his boyish swagger and at the lowering of that wall of his, and the fact he had a chocolate chip on his very kissable lip.

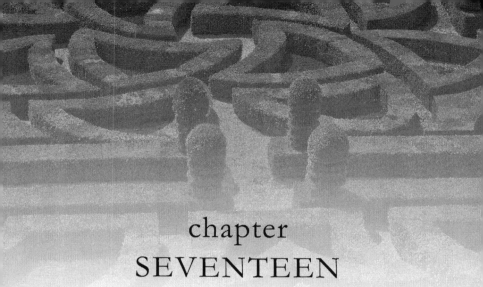

chapter
SEVENTEEN

Anya

TWO DAYS PASSED BEFORE I DECIDED TO BRAVE THE HOUSE in search of my captor. I had felt many different things after I'd found him eating the cookies I'd made.

One was confusion. How could he hide his enjoyment of it from me, and most of all, why?

What was the point?

Other than to torture me. Make me feel less. Not let me in.

I should be angry with him, but something stopped me. Maybe it was the sight of him standing there, looking like a normal man, eating what I'd baked. With nothing of the monster in him I'd believed him to be. That moment had humanized him. I'd witnessed him taking pleasure in something—as though I'd triggered a good memory. The boy glimpsing through the stark demeanor of a hurting man.

Cassius affected me in a way I didn't want to think about.

I tried to avoid him as much as possible. Borrowing books from his collection in his library and taking them back to my room. It was killing me to do this, but I wasn't ready to see him, and my conflicting feelings were getting the better of me.

I found myself creeping around the house.

Quietly taking the stairs down to the main floor, carefully treading the marble floor. I wanted to go unnoticed, not announce my approach.

I scanned the foyer. Maybe it was how big the house was, or maybe it was that no one was here, but it always felt empty.

There was something very creepy about this place. Almost like something sinister lurked around the corner. Secrets from what had made Cassius the man he was.

I couldn't put my finger on why, but the foreboding lingered.

When my foot hit the final step landing me on the main floor, I looked around again to see if anyone was here.

Like always, the foyer was empty.

I went in search of something. Someone. But I knew in my heart I was searching for *him*. Because as much as I knew I shouldn't speak with him, I couldn't help it.

A moth to a flame.

The great hall was empty. Heading out, I stopped in my tracks. Halfway down the hallway, Cassius's voice trailed from a room. His hushed tone proved he was talking low. Wanting to hear what he was saying but not wanting him to hear me, I removed my shoes and tiptoed toward the room the sound wafted out of.

Cassius wasn't alone.

Another voice carried with his, proving another man was with him. Moving closer, until I was right outside the door, which stood ajar, I tried to listen to the voices echoing from within.

I remained perfectly still, ears straining to listen.

I heard my name.

My heart leaping like it might explode. I didn't know why my body was having such a reaction; he was talking about me, and it threw me into a tailspin. Taking a deep inhale, forcing it in through my mouth, and willing the steadying breath to calm my body. Shaking, jaw tightening. Unsure of what I was so afraid of, but sensing it wasn't good. Whatever it was, my very survival might even depend on it.

That familiar southern drawl that belonged to Ridley.

I held my breath, bracing to hear Cassius talk with his lawyer.

Ridley's drawl was hushed. "Any contact with them?"

"You mean have they reached out?"

"Yes."

"No, they've gone radio silent. And they know where she is now."

"Well, that kind of fucks up your plan, right?" Ridley's tone cut through the quiet. "I can't believe her parents know she's here. Have known this whole time and have done nothing to get her back."

Unsteady, vision blurring as though trying to see through what they were saying, as though the words themselves formed images I couldn't comprehend because they made no sense.

Mom and Dad knew I was here. *They knew. All this time.*

And they'd done nothing to get me out of here. They had no way of knowing that Cassius wasn't torturing me. Or harming me in some way.

How can that be?

It was one thing not to come themselves but not to send help? It was impossible to comprehend. Impossible to believe.

"What do you think Glassman's game plan is?" asked the slick lawyer, seemingly amused from that rumble of a laugh.

My body stiffened.

Cassius's voice lowered. "If they haven't come yet, I don't think they will."

"How does this affect things?"

"It doesn't."

I imagined Cassius shrugging after saying it—as though my life was being reduced to an annoyance to be dealt with.

I couldn't hear anymore.

I needed to get away.

There was a plan in place, and as much as I wanted to know it, I couldn't bring myself to stay here one more second. The voices in my head screamed to run. Run as fast as I could. But where? How could I find a place where I could be alone?

I ran toward the back door, needing air to breathe. On the way through the dining room, something caught my eye.

A bar.

Fully stocked.

Before I could think twice, my hand reached out and swept up a bottle of alcohol with a swanky-looking silver and white label. I didn't even bother to check what I was taking. I ran, sprinting out of the house, desperate to suppress the truth—*they'd abandoned me.*

Warm musky air hit me as I tripped and righted myself. There was a dampness in the air that hung heavy with the threat of rain. I wondered how long until the storm came because that was what this felt like, an internal and external anguish swarming.

Running, I prayed for the sky to open and cleanse me. Cleanse these thoughts of rejection that plagued me. I'd always known my parents hadn't cared, but now, now the proof struck with the purest agony, like a stake in my heart that was irreparable and permanent.

I knew where I was going before I took my first step.

Cassius might find me, but it didn't matter. I'd given up caring. Given up the illusion of privacy.

Even as the hedges called to me, nature's cocoon welcomed within its tall winding hallways of green.

Tripping through the maze, desperate to become lost in my mind, too. Eventually finding a secluded corner. Huddling inside an alcove, not caring about the damp grass beneath, twisting the cap, tipping up the bottle to meet my mouth, and cringing against the burn of liquor as it filled my mouth.

Vodka.

Strong, but exactly what I needed.

Ridley's words haunted still. *"They're doing nothing to get her back."*

Bitter vodka filled my mouth like water, and I swallowed it down, swallowed the pain, impatient for the agony to ease or at the very least to get so drunk I passed out.

Craving oblivion.

Craving the hurt to go away.

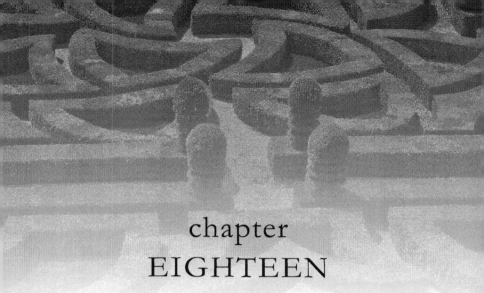

chapter
EIGHTEEN

Cassius

"Boss." The door swung open, and in stepped Robert.

I looked up at him from where I was sitting across the room. His brow was furrowed, and he held an iPad at his side.

Something wasn't right.

"Speak," I grunted, setting my drink on the table. The amber liquid slushed against the glass.

"We might have a problem," he muttered, looking at the floor.

Which did not bode well for him. If it had anything to do with Anya and the way he stared at the floor, wanting it to swallow him up, it did.

"A problem?" There was no mistaking the sarcastic edge.

"It's Anya."

"Have you fucked up again?" I hadn't seen her for days, and I liked it that way. She made me uneasy. Made me question my motives, and that wasn't good.

When I saw her in my kitchen baking . . .

It had given me a warmth in my body I didn't want to

acknowledge at the time. I had fired back at her, putting her in her place, a place she needed to stay. I couldn't sympathize with her. Couldn't let my thoughts run wild. Who knew what direction they would go to weaken my resolve.

Better she stayed far away and hidden.

No matter how much I tried to get her out of my head, she always lingered there despite my best efforts.

She was like a petrichor after rain. That earthy scent after the skies had opened—that freshness that wouldn't go away. I needed to purge her, but she was stubborn as fuck.

"What did she do now?" I grit out through clenched teeth.

"Took off out the back."

"And this is alarming because . . ." I led, annoyed to be interrupted for this. She was fine the last time and knew better than to try to escape.

"It's getting dark."

With that, I turned in my chair and looked out through the window.

The sky was turning a hazy shade of gray, but in the far distance, it touched the horizon in bright bursts of pink.

I waved him away. "She'll be fine."

"She was carrying something with her."

I swung back to look at Robert. My interest piqued. "What do you mean?"

Pushing up, I headed over to him, gesturing to look at what he obviously wanted to show me on the iPad.

With a few swipes of the screen, he brought up the surveillance video. There, on the screen, like a bad case of déjà vu, was Anya walking through the door leading to the garden again, but this time, her companion was a bottle of vodka.

Shit.

"So she wants to get drunk." I headed toward the door.

"Where are you going, sir?" he asked, perplexed.

"To recapture my prisoner."

"Want a flashlight in case it gets dark?"

"Don't need it." And I didn't. I knew the maze and my way around it with my eyes closed. Still, the moonlight was a welcome guide.

The sun was receding into the horizon. The dusky night sky hovered close. I followed the turns within the maze, each one bringing me closer to the center. I hated to think about the state I was going to find her in.

The sound of tears.

Jeez.

Standing above her, I could see she was already drunk. Slumped near the hedge where she'd discovered the bird. Her body turned away from me. It was the way her head slumped over and the way her chest wobbled as she lifted the bottle to her mouth and took a large gulp.

She took another swig of vodka. "You."

"Me," I responded, my mouth twisting into a smirk. "Why are you here?"

"I live here."

I blinked at her. "In this maze?"

"Yes. This is my new home," she slurred. "It's better than with them, but you *know* that. I hate that you know . . ."

I crouched to eye level. "Know what?"

"Know they don't care. They never did. The whole time I was nothing."

The pieces of the drunk puzzle that was Anya connected. She knew her parents knew she was here. And they'd done nothing to help her. Because they just didn't care.

She'd been eavesdropping again.

"Why didn't they come?" she hiccupped and swayed left.

I used the movement to my advantage and swiped the bottle from her.

"Hey, that's mine. . . "

I shrugged.

"Does that mean you're drinking with me?" Her eyes widened with mischief.

"No."

"Cuz you just can't handle your drink like me," she chided.

"Stand up. We're going back to the house."

"No."

I watched her waver. Whatever she was trying to do came over wrong because instead of bobbing side to side, her head gestured the *yes*.

"Don't make me pick you up."

Drunk and animated, her eyes went wide. "You wouldn't dare."

"Try me."

She rolled her eyes on a large and obnoxious huff.

"Fine." She pushed to her feet, and it looked painful to watch.

She stumbled forward, pushing my hand away and—and face-planting.

Feeling guilty for not catching her in time, I scooped her up in my arms and threw her over my shoulder, caveman style.

"Hey, put me down," she grumbled, her words slurring.

With her in my arms and the bottle in my free hand, I looked down at it.

Great.

She'd drank a lot more than I thought. No wonder she could barely walk.

"If I put you down, you'll fall. Then I'll just have to pick you back up. Be a good girl and make this easy on me."

"You have no right to tou—" Anya's eyes closed before she could finish the sentence.

"Touch you?"

"Yes."

"Hush."

"I'm sick of being good."

"Anya," I said sternly. "It's dark. You will die out here if I leave you behind. Now quiet."

I heard her grumble again, but she didn't fight. I imagined she was too drunk.

As we made it out of the maze, we were met by the light from the house illuminating the pathway back.

She'd stilled in my arms.

I opened the door, heading in with my find, and dropped the bottle back on the bar on the way in, carrying her on to my room. Once there, I pulled the duvet back and placed her in bed, not even bothering to undress her. Her shirt had risen though, her taut stomach muscles showing, the underside of her breast peeking out.

I hadn't noticed, but her shirt was wet with what I assumed was vodka, making the fabric wet around her nipple.

The girl needed to put on a decent shirt. One that covered her. *Fuck.*

"Anya. You need to change. . ."

"Don't want to. Just want to sleep."

I crossed the room and opened the cabinets, finding a tank top.

"Take off your shirt. I'll help you."

"You just want to see me naked," she slurred.

I shook my head. "Not like this."

"Then like how?" She giggled. "You want me."

"Anya . . ." I scolded. "Just take off your shirt. I'm not watching."

I turned and heard her drunken stumbling as she sat up, swearing.

When the noise stopped, I pivoted to look back down at her. Anya's eyes were closed. Her chest was barely covered by the tank top she'd failed to pull on properly. Her arms weren't even in the shirt. *Goddammit.*

I sat on the edge and helped her into it properly, touching her skin felt like it branded me. She was fire scorching my skin. She moaned erotically, and I swore I would combust from the sound.

"There. Done."

I needed to leave, but instead, I watched her from where I sat close beside her on the edge of the bed, making sure her breathing was safe.

"Don't leave. . ."

I halted and turned to face her. Her eyes were closed, but she wasn't asleep. "You always leave me."

For a moment, I thought she was talking to me.

"Archie." She was quiet again.

I moved closer to hear what she was saying.

Her voice a whisper. "Don't trust them . . ."

She was talking in her sleep.

"It's all there, Archie, in the Lafayette Cemetery. Didn't want to scare you with it." Her eyes flew open, and she looked at me. Fear in her eyes. Absolute terror. As though still caught in a nightmare, her body was shaking.

My legs hit the mattress, and it startled her.

A desperate sob escaped her. "Don't hurt me."

"Of course not," I whispered.

Was she talking to me or her ghosts?

Shame flooded through me. Seeing her like this, vulnerable and full of fear. My sickening plan had been to use her, exploit her. Now, I just knew I couldn't do one more thing to her. I wouldn't be that man.

I sat beside her and took her hand in mine. "You're safe now."

"Promise you won't leave me; I just want to close my eyes."

"I'll stay."

"You'll make sure I'm safe?"

"I'll make sure you're safe."

I held her hand to my mouth to kiss away the pain, hers as well as mine. This war had caused our lives to be interwoven, and one couldn't be free without the other.

I laid her hand down gently so as not to awaken her.

Pushing up, I headed over to the corner of the room to sit in that high-backed chair, keeping some distance so as not to startle her if she woke up, but close enough if she needed me.

Getting comfortable in the seat, I turned my attention back on her. That enduring sweetness in her features even more pronounced with her asleep, the way her eyelids blinked through what looked like a nightmare.

It made me wonder if she was dreaming about me.

chapter
NINETEEN

Anya

LANGUIDLY STRETCHING, I REACHED OUT TO FEEL THE soft linen—this wasn't my bed.

Lifting my head off the pillow, I peeked over the duvet and sensed Cassius before I saw him in the corner where he sat in an armchair.

His focus completely on the book he had open on his lap. Looking as fresh and as complicated as I usually found him. His finger curled over his lower lip, deep in thought. Twinkles of morning light flitted over him, a reflection from the shadowy outline of leaves coming from the oak tree outside the window.

Sun rays were flooding in too harshly, along with that shock of pain in my head reminding me I'd discovered his liquor cabinet—more precisely, his stash of vodka. I replayed all that had happened last night.

What I could remember, anyway. Me over his shoulder as he carried me to bed—his.

Peeking below the covers, reassured to see I was wearing a

tank top. With no memory of putting it on, I assumed Cassius had stripped me naked. Something told me he'd been decent about it.

The reason I'd tried to dive to the bottom of a bottle flashed into view as raw and agonizing as that moment I'd overheard Ridley telling Cassius my parents weren't coming for me.

No one was.

Grief intertwined with my insides. How would I ever come to terms with being hated so much by my own parents? A wall of grief hit me. A futility I'd tried to deny. This pain would never lift. It melded with each cell of my body bringing a new bitterness.

Dark and mysterious eyes were now on me.

"Good morning," said Cassius, half-amused and half-chastising.

"How long have you been there?"

He stretched his arms over his head and curved his spine, answering with, "A while."

Something told me he'd been here all night. The clues were easy to decipher. He was still wearing his clothes from yesterday, and his lush hair was messed up as though he'd spent the late hours running his fingers through it.

Glancing at the bedside table, I saw the gift laid out from the gods—two Tylenol and a tall glass of water. I reached for it and gladly swallowed them and the water, quenching my thirst, self-consciously wiping a few droplets off my chin.

He frowned his concern. "How do you feel?"

"Never better." I lied, looking around his room.

It made me wonder why he'd brought me here and not the sparse bedroom meant to be mine.

"Can I get you anything?"

I frowned his way. His kissable lips were vaguely annoying, as was his attempt at caring for someone other than himself. This new side was unsettling, or maybe this was the side I'd never seen before. Like another fragment of the complicated man revealing itself.

I'd rather get lost in his mesmerizing eyes than be reminded of last night.

He pushed to his feet. "Want breakfast?"

"French toast."

"Seriously?" he let out a chuckle.

"It's the ultimate cure."

"You think you're up for eating that?"

"I only had two drinks." I think.

Living in a gilded cage—and I didn't mean this one, I stole my rebellious moments where I could. Frequently sneaking gulps from my dad's liquor cabinet. I wasn't a stranger to booze. The usual suspects easily to go down were Bailey's, Godiva Chocolate, and a swig of Grand Marnier when shit got too much. *And shit was always too much.*

Cassius looked concerned.

Pushing myself up, I added, "You have the ingredients."

He strolled to the end of the bed, and his critical eyes bored down on me. "I'm surprised you aren't hanging over a toilet right now."

I shooed him backward with a wave of my hands to give me some room to get out of bed. Sitting on the edge and waking up a little more.

Cassius threw a robe on the bed for me to put on. "Use that."

"Nice of you to watch over me last night. Didn't need to."

He didn't look at me. "I'll see you downstairs."

Within minutes, I'd made it back to my bedroom. Freshening up in the bathroom and wiping away any evidence of a hangover from last night—or at least trying to. Picking up the hairbrush Cassius had left for me, and catching myself in the mirror, the realization again hit me—I'd been abandoned by my family.

I cringed at my reflection. I looked like hell.

Lips trembling, I tried to steady my rising panic. Refusing to crumble under this crushing pressure. No, it's a lie. Dad would want Cassius to believe they weren't coming while they hatched a secret plan.

Take the advantage. The element of surprise.

If I'd learned anything from seeing my father operate, it was that he was ruthless. He might look like he was cold, but deep down, he cared deeply for us.

Trusting them was all I had left.

I found my newly washed jeans and T-shirt and slid my feet into my Converse shoes. Heading out of the room with more questions than answers.

Within the kitchen, I again found Cassius with his head in a book. He'd seemingly been waiting for me.

He looked up at me. "You look presentable, at least."

Yawning, I said, "It's not like we're going out."

"Actually, we are."

Sometimes, like now, Cassius was hard to read. It took me a few seconds to work out that he wasn't joking.

"What? As some kind of punishment?" I bit out.

"Time will tell."

That wasn't scary at all.

"What are you reading?" I asked. "It must be good if you can't put it down."

He flipped the cover for me to read the title of *"Beyond Order."* Flipping it back to look at the cover himself. "Jordan B. Peterson. It's pretty good." He set it down on the kitchen counter.

Maybe I'd read it, too. His collection of books were a lot like this one, seemingly heavy and full of soul-searching.

"First, I need to give you something." He smirked as he reached inside a drawer. He was holding sunglasses and carried them over to me and slid them onto my face. "I'm not a complete asshole."

I rolled my eyes beneath the shades in a snarky—*that remains to be seen.*

"Careful," he chastised.

He gestured for me to follow him out of the house to where he'd parked his BMW.

"How many cars do you own?"

He glanced over. "Two. This and the SUV."

I shrugged. "We have three."

"Seeing as you live here now, you own nothing."

I tried to pull away.

He grabbed my arm. "Not so fast. Where do you think you're going?"

"Why did you say that?" I huffed.

"Isn't the answer obvious?"

"Not to me."

"I like to fuck with you."

With a jolt of my arm, I shifted him off me. "I'm not going."

He lowered his sunglasses. "I wasn't giving you a choice, Anya. Get in."

The glare of the sun hit me, and I squinted behind the shades.

The click of the doors locking echoed in my ears. A reminder that me trying to escape from this car wasn't going to happen.

Within minutes we were driving away from his home and heading fast toward the city. Peering out my side window, I couldn't help but obsess over everything I saw, as though soon I'd be locked away again and all of this would be out of reach. From the ancient oak trees with their branches stretching wide to the lush moss hanging off them, providing a dreamy view.

"How's your head?" he broke the silence.

"Oh, you care?"

"Believe it or not, yes."

"It's fine."

"Fine? Never a good word. Are you nauseated?"

"No."

"I'm impressed." He glanced over at me. "Most people can't move, let alone want to eat the next day after the way you acted last night."

"You have no right to lecture me."

"I'm the only person who's ever paid attention to you."

"That's not true." *It kind of was true.*

Though Archie was there for me when I needed him. We didn't always get along or see eye to eye, but as we'd gotten older, we'd grown closer. We also realized how much we needed each other. I wondered how much Dad and Mom had shared with him about where I'd gone.

"Other than your brother," he piped up as though reading my mind.

I kept my eyes on the road so as not to give away our secret. The one we'd been forbidden to share. The one that would give away that our bloodlines were different from our parents.

All I got out of Cassius after that were looks of disapproval and the occasional shake of his head.

We parked on Chartres Street and headed off on foot to walk through the French Quarter. I looked around to see if bolting was a good idea or even possible. He'd be faster than me, but if I ran into a store, I might just escape. Trying to judge how far I'd get before he caught me.

My stomach churned as I mulled over what my punishment was to prevent me from ever drinking again. We turned onto Decatur Street, and that was when he took my hand and held it tight.

Okay, this was super weird and totally unexpected...

We looked like we were going into Café Du Monde, a place I'd always wanted to visit but had never been allowed. It stung that as his prisoner, I was actually getting to go out more than ever before.

We settled at a corner table as though we were merely two friends having an early Sunday breakfast. At nine in the morning, the place was quiet with just a few tourists trickling in. I assumed as the day went on it became busier.

Within minutes, a waitress brought us our order of two mugs filled with café au lait and a plate full of white powdered beignets.

Cassius placed one on a plate and slid it my way. "Best hangover cure I know."

I lifted the small pastry and took a bite, and my eyes nearly rolled into the back of my head at the doughnut's consistency that melted on my tongue and the sudden buzz from its powdered sugar. "Oh, my God," I said, covering my half-filled mouth.

"Yeah, thought you'd like that."

"I can't believe I've never been here."

His expression turned contemplative as though curiosity was

mixed with sadness for me. As he sipped his coffee, he gave a nod of approval.

I brought another beignet to my mouth, taking a big bite and moaning at how good it tasted. Wanting to admit being at a café out in the open with others felt like normality. But this was not what life had been. I'd merely lived vicariously through our staff who'd told me of these little treasures nestled in the heart of the city.

Archie and I had tried to replicate days like this. There were many Sundays just like this one, where I'd made French toast for us for breakfast. Both of us bonding over the sweet taste of comfort food. We'd carved out these moments for each other—created our own traditions. Our own memories to cherish.

I missed him now. Not wanting to admit that and draw any more attention to my brother, I kept quiet about it.

"You're not going to eat yours?" I asked, chewing. "Why not?"

"Because the reason you're eating it is because you drank too much last night. And the reason you drank too much is because of me."

His admission made me stop mid-bite. He really was capable of thoughtfulness. It clashed with his sinister motives and fucked with my head.

Lowering my beignet, I set it on my plate. Then mentally retraced all the steps to what he was insinuating. They added up to something greater. "You can always let me go."

Cassius continued sipping coffee as though contemplating it. "I wasn't referring to our agreement."

"Agreement?"

"You staying with me."

"That sounds like I have a choice."

"You overheard my conversation with Ridley." He drew in a sharp breath. "Which means you were eavesdropping."

"I didn't. Fine, maybe I did. Maybe I just wanted to hear news from home."

"You got drunk because you were upset to hear your father isn't coming for you."

Somewhere in the kitchen, a plate crashed to the floor. The smash so loud I could feel it all the way in the depths of my soul. The scurrying of staff to go pick up whatever had smashed felt panicked.

Cassius didn't seem to notice. "No one is coming to rescue you."

"You don't know that."

His glare told me he did. If he found this strange, that they weren't coming, he didn't make a thing of it.

He turned to face me. "Last night, you mentioned visiting Lafayette Cemetery a while ago. Do you remember?"

Maybe what came next was him lecturing me on drinking. Then I realized with each thing I shared, I might give something about me away. Something I didn't want him to know about me—like I wasn't actually a Glassman, not in the sense that mattered. If my stock went down and I was useless to him . . .

I shook the thought from my mind and went with, "It's all a bit vague."

"What happened?"

"I was just visiting the cemetery. Like the tourists."

"Interesting."

"Not really. I went to pay my respects."

"Something upset you while you were there?" He leaned closer. "What was it?"

"It's normal for people to shed tears at those places."

"But not to come away scared. To warn their brother of danger."

I'd rather think about anything other than that place. The wall of names. One of them being mine. Reaching for my coffee, I took several long gulps. Remembering how I'd felt this morning made me set the glass down and nudge it away.

"You can talk to me," he said, his tone kind.

My back stiffened at his seeming ruse to soften me up. "You took a big risk bringing me here. People might recognize me from my photo and tell the police they've seen me with you."

"For that to happen, your photo would need to be released to the public."

I tried to swallow my searing doubt, this lump in my throat not resolving.

"As you've never been here before, I'm assuming you were kept hidden. Are you curious why?"

"How do you know I've not been here before."

"You've never tasted a beignet." He shrugged. "And the fact no one brought one home for you is a fucking travesty."

"It's just a doughnut."

"You don't know this city." He caressed his forehead as though massaging out the pain. "Anya, you've been protected all your life." It almost sounding soothing.

"From what?"

From him.

"If you're so precious, why wouldn't your father report you missing? I'll tell you. He doesn't want the FBI digging around his life. Doesn't that set off alarms with you?"

"I'm in just as much danger at your place, apparently."

"I can't deny it."

A jolt of panic shivered up my spine as I realized. "You have cameras?" When he didn't deny it, I added, "In my bedroom?"

"No, not there. Or your bathroom."

He'd replayed the footage of me outside his office door with my ear pressed against it as I'd listened to his conversation with Ridley. "You're spying on me?"

"They're for security." He shrugged. "It's good to get a heads-up when you're expecting someone."

"Like my father?"

"Only apparently, he's not coming."

A jolt of doubt had me reeling.

My dad wouldn't abandon me. He would search out where I was and demand my release. Or at least send someone to come get me and lower the risk to himself. That would make sense. I would forgive him that. I wouldn't want anyone else hurt because of this man.

Despite all these doubts, I had to manage what was right in front of me—him.

"I've only known you a short time," I began.

He seemed to guess where this was going, and his frown deepened.

"You seem reasonable. Other than the fact . . . you know."

"Your point."

"Whatever argument you have with my family is not with me. I'm caught in the middle. It's not fair. I believe you'll do the right thing."

"Which is?"

I nudged a beignet on a plate toward him. "You know."

He pushed the plate back my way. "Life's not fair. That's the first lesson you need to learn. Second, you leaving is nonnegotiable."

"But—"

"I haven't finished. The fact you're able to move freely in my home is a goddamn privilege."

"You can trust me—"

"Clearly, all evidence suggests—and I'm referring to that bottle of Chopin Reserve vodka you almost finished off last night—that you can't even trust yourself."

"Well, excuse me for trying to find ways to cope." I glanced down at my half-empty plate. "I just wanted to feel better." *I wanted to forget.*

"Do you?"

A stab of sorrow. "I don't want to eat alone. I'm done eating alone."

"You had Archie."

"Not anymore."

"What do you want?"

"I'm lonely." I hated admitting it.

He rolled his eyes and reached for the pastry on his plate. The one I'd pushed in front of him. He lifted it to his mouth and took a bite. A quirk of a smile lit up his face as he chewed. Using his napkin to wipe his mouth, he nodded to show his approval. "Usually, I don't like to have anything that . . ." He stopped himself from saying any more.

"You should never refuse yourself pleasure."

He quirked a brow. "What do you know of pleasure?"

Playfully, I shoved the rest of my beignet into my mouth to show him and smiled through the bliss of perfection melting on my tongue, beaming.

Cassius's expression softened as he reached out and wiped his thumb across my lips, using it to dust off a smudge of powder. Bringing it to his own mouth and sucking it clean of sugar.

"Isn't it good?" I said, still breathlessly watching him.

He conceded with a smirk.

His tongue flickered to lick his mouth clean, and it looked dangerously alluring. A sensual teasing he seemed oblivious to.

I dipped my middle finger into the sugar on my plate and suckled on it, wondering what other places in the city I might get to see.

Cassius zeroed in on me, and it made me uneasy. As though he was seeing me in a different way for the first time.

"In other circumstances, we might have been friends," I mused.

He gave a curious smile. "How exactly?"

"You could teach me things. Show me things I've never seen."

"What sort of things would you like to see?"

"Everything," I said breathlessly.

Our eyes locked.

I felt a tingle in my chest like a butterfly that was trapped within and was searching its way out; fluttering around my chest, making me giddy. Vaguely aware, his hand was reaching for my nape and was guiding me toward him, toward his mouth, soft and inviting.

After all this time of wondering what it would be like to kiss him, I could finally feel the pressure of his mouth on mine, gentle and coaxing.

Hesitant, I feared he'd pull away. Instead, he pressed harder until his tongue darted in, edging my mouth wider, our tongues battling, his more dominant and mine needy for his control, for him. Captured by his hand on my nape that was firm and masterful.

Yearning to be owned in these unfolding moments, I willingly fell into this silence between us, surrendering to what felt so right.

My racing heart was seemingly catching up with this passion I'd fallen into so naturally. A sudden fear it might end was mixed with a heady confusion that he was who I wanted to be with. *Him* who I craved. That all this time, I'd resisted my feelings toward him, refusing to allow my heart to go there.

His grip on my nape softened, and he leaned back and went to say something, stopping short of sharing his thoughts.

My cheeks grew warm as I glanced around to see if anyone had caught us, I couldn't look at him for a minute. Instead, I wrapped my fingers around my mug.

He looked intrigued. "You've never been kissed before."

"And you'll never get to kiss me again." I glowered.

If he was hurt, he wasn't showing it.

"I can see you already regret it," I tested his reaction.

His dark glare held mine and sent a shudder through me like he had physically shot me with a poisoned dart to stun me into silence.

Then he broke into a heart-stopping smile and it looked shockingly sexy on him. It made me wonder if I'd managed to break through his walls.

Until he unleashed the words, "Getting to know you is like putting your family beneath a magnifying glass."

"I want to leave," I said before I could stop myself.

He pushed to his feet. "Fine."

Cassius was shutting down on me, which was not something I wanted to happen.

"You're upset with me?" I reasoned. "Why?"

"Upset. No, that would mean I care. Spoiler alert. I don't." His words hit their intended mark, but I refused to show him that.

"You're trying to break me down." I glared up at him. "You can't."

He talked through gritted teeth. "I'm not trying to do anything to you. Other than contain your sorry ass."

"Listen, you asshole, if I can survive a Russian winter as a child with a thin coat, I can survive you." I snapped my mouth shut.

Oh, no. . .

I'd just given away I wasn't born in New Orleans.

Pushing myself up, I tried to hide the terror crawling beneath my skin, like a thousand ants burrowing into flesh. I refused to look him in the eyes.

He snapped his hand out toward me to demonstrate I was to take it. Instead of asking me about my outburst, Cassius just led me out of Café Du Monde, and we trekked back to the car.

I'd just handed him the mother of all clues. Coming to this café had probably been him trying to lower my defenses and getting me to talk. As though sensing my regret, his hand wrapped tighter around mine to prevent me from trying to run.

"Let's go home," he said. "I've wasted enough time."

chapter
TWENTY

Cassius

AFTER DISCARDING THE GOWN ON ANYA'S BED, I SET TWO
cream boxes beside it, then stepped back to watch her
reaction to what was clearly for Mardi Gras.

She was looking at me differently since I dropped my guard and
allowed a moment of weakness on my part.

I'd told myself our kiss at Café Du Monde meant nothing, but
ever since, I'd felt emotions I don't want to think about coming at
me too fast.

I'd fought and lost that battle.

I kissed her.

I pressed my lips to hers. Sunk into that delicious fucking feeling. Allowed my stone-heart to finally pump.

She deserved better.

The words crashed into me again and again.

A storm in the middle of a barren ocean, the kind that drags you
under. It confused the hell out of me, because she was his daughter.
His blood ran through her veins.

I'd made it my life's work to destroy each and every one of them until their bloodline was wiped from the earth. Destined to take my time and make each death count.

I was supposed to be starting with her . . .

This woman who stood before me.

This woman who was not just a beauty but also a weapon, bashing down my walls.

Anya stared back at me, an intensity in those shimmering blue eyes.

Curiosity got the better of her, and she stepped forward and peeked inside one of the boxes. She pulled out the masquerade mask. "We're going to Mardi Gras?"

"Yes."

The disguise was needed for us to disappear into the crowd. We'd be able to move about the revelers unnoticed until I decided otherwise.

We'd fade into the background after it happened.

Vanish into the night.

I would leave another scar on that family.

What I'd planned may be fucked up, but I was still going to do it.

She lifted the lid to the other box and found a pair of shoes to match the dress.

"Get dressed."

She ran her fingers over the gown. "You're seriously expecting me to put this on?"

I ignored that and headed for the door.

"I'm not wearing this."

Pivoting, I walked back toward her. "You will." I left no room for objection.

"After all you've done, you think my mom's still going to have a float at Mardi Gras?" She looked horrified. "Just carry on as normal? Like her daughter hasn't been kidnapped?"

"She is."

"How do you know? You're lying."

"One thing I'm not is a liar. Put it on."

"You broke our special tradition," she whispered to herself. "You've torn apart my family."

"That's the plan." And from what my team could tell, her family continued their lives like she'd not left in those devastating circumstances. A cruel consequence that Anya was slowly discovering.

"Each year, I help Mom decorate the float. Instead of doing that this year, I'm here."

"I know. Which is why I invited you."

"Fine." Defiance burned in her eyes as she pulled her T-shirt up and over her head and off. Unzipping her jeans, she slid them down her hips.

Gesturing my hand to stop her from going any further, I was fixed where I stood as though her defiance kept me hostage. "What are you doing?"

"Getting ready." She reached around behind her back and unclipped her bra strap, flinging it onto the bed. Her fingers hooked beneath her panties and peeled them off her hips, kicking them off her feet and across the room.

If this was the war she wanted, she'd get it. I'd faced off with more dangers than her. Yet even as I told myself this, I was riddled with doubt. Anya had a way of breaking down my defenses and chipping away at my desire to end her world.

She stood naked yet confident, still defiant, a nymph-like enchantress who captured my focus.

A shock of feeling in my gut, a roiling desire. "Meet me downstairs."

"Make me."

The air was thick with doubt, that suffocating heat from outside somehow finding its way inside. The sound of the fan the only noise piercing the silence that fell between us.

Whether it was her disobedience that spurred me on or my need to get her covered up, I headed over to the set of drawers. Resting my hand on a pair of matching silk underwear and pulling them out.

Turning to face her again, I threw them at her.

She caught them.

Then let the underwear slip from her hand to the ground.

I tried not to look at her round plump breasts or the way her nipples beaded—tried to keep my gaze on hers instead off lowering it to what was hidden beneath.

She was a shocking beauty. With porcelain skin.

The fucking universe was trying trap me.

The subtle sway of her hips where she rested her hands was too much. She had no idea what she did to me.

Her naïveté struck a nerve.

The temptation to throw her onto the bed and bury my dick inside her was enough to burn me up from the inside out.

No. I couldn't do that.

Despite what her father had done to me and my family. I wouldn't sink to that level.

Stepping forward, I showed Anya her nakedness wouldn't dissuade me.

Pressing my nose to her forehead and with a gravelly voice saying, "How much do you love Mardi Gras?"

With her body trembling, she responded like a deer caught in the headlights, stunned by my show of interest, her breathing becoming faster.

"I used to love it."

"You still can."

"Fuck you."

Running my thumb along her bare arm, I coaxed her further. "Be a good girl and get dressed."

"No."

She tipped her chin, a defiant glare carrying her desire straight to my dick. And she was so fucking naked, so fucking vulnerable, it hardened. Our bodies were only inches apart.

"I used to like it," she whispered.

My cock twitched in my pants. "What?"

"Mardi Gras."

"What did you love about it?"

She tipped her chin higher. "Everyone comes together to celebrate life."

"We can do that."

"I got to help decorate Mom's float." Sorrow welled in her eyes. "It was the only time she showed any interest in me."

She couldn't see my response. The way I closed my palms and clenched them all while sending a silent curse her mother's way.

Soon, she would see her daughter and know that I still had her.

Anya's hand was at my waist. She'd scrunched my shirt there and was holding onto it. That and her nakedness left Anya open to me.

Like a book wanting and needing to be read.

Needing to be understood.

This show of weakness sent a hum of pleasure through me.

This wasn't good.

I couldn't allow this woman into my world.

She was a Glassman, and I could never forget that fact.

Anya would never know the intel my team had gathered before I stole her away. It had stated her parents were hardly ever at home. That they were seen coming and going to that house in the Garden District and that their activity was highly suspicious. It was as though they had two lives. One in NOLA and another elsewhere. The question was, why?

"Mardi Gras is all I had to look forward to," Anya admitted softly.

My cruel intentions for later this evening bubbled beneath the surface.

The day was planned out to the last detail. All that was needed was Anya's compliance. Her putting on that dress and masquerade mask and being presented as a lamb to the slaughter.

"Get dressed now," I made it an order.

Her lips pouted as she again raised her sights and settled her focus on my lips. A seductive allure as though willing me to kiss her.

"Obey." Even as those words left my lips, I felt her nipples beading against my chest and her breathing becoming rapid, her unexpected response hypnotic.

"Tell me what you want from me," she whispered.

"This."

She swallowed hard. "This?"

I needed to get inside her thoughts. See her clearly so that manipulating her became second nature. Her compliance was essential.

Falling for her wasn't possible.

I'd rather cut out my own heart.

She dragged her teeth along her bottom lip. "I'm not going anywhere with you."

"And miss your chance to escape like you did at Café Du Monde?"

"Like you'd have let me go."

I grabbed the silk off the floor and knelt before her, easing her left foot and then her right into the lingerie. Lifting up the material along her calves and tugging it over her thighs, my fingers brushing against her soft flesh. Fitting it perfectly. Unwittingly, my thumb caressed her, and she shuddered beneath my touch. She reached out and rested her hands on my shoulders.

It would have been easy to lean in and touch her. Suck her through the thin material that separated us. Feel her shudder in ecstasy.

My will of steel was as reliable as it always was. She could have her fun teasing me, but I could never be seduced—my moral code might be broken but I would never take a Glassman to my bed.

I was a better man than her father.

Pushing to my feet and at the same time snagging her bra off the floor, I again towered over her. Sliding her arms through the straps , I brought it forward to cup her breasts with the material, feeling the softness and the plumpness of her breasts. Then I moved around her to secure the clasp behind her back.

Raising my stare over her shoulder, I saw the reflection of us in the new mirror that replaced the broken one. My fingers trailed along her shoulder to even out the left strap, then gave them both a tug to lift her breasts. Reaching around to ensure the cups fit snugly, I felt her nipples bead beneath the blue silk.

Our eyes met in the reflection.

I became stiff despite trying to resist this urge to touch her again. That deep-seated ache in my belly convinced me that taking her was my right.

I own her.

Could take her at will.

She turned to face me and peered up, her eyes settling on my lips, enticing me to lean in and satisfy her need to be kissed, kissed like we had back at the café. It had been me instigating it last time. Here, now, it was Anya begging with her eyes for another.

She was intoxicating.

"I'm sure you're capable of putting the rest on," I said firmly.

"Don't." Her words were barely a whisper.

I was already heading for the door and refused to look back.

A pang of arousal thrummed inside me, as I tried to put as much distance between us as possible.

I soon made it to my bedroom so I could change, too.

She wouldn't be the only one dressed in costume—I'd gone for a three-piece suit with a waistcoat and tails. My own masquerade mask was simpler than hers.

Waiting in the foyer, I counted the minutes until I saw her at the top of the staircase.

She began the slow descent, picking up her hem as she headed toward me, the masquerade mask in her other hand ready to wear. Her eyes were heavily highlighted as though to make up for the disguise she'd soon wear. Her lips were a defiant red that begged to be kissed.

She came down the stairs with the gown flowing around her feet.

Stunning was the only word to describe her.

If only this was a different time, a different place, if only she wasn't her.

The peacock design on the bodice twinkled beneath the foyer lights. It hugged her curves, showing off her body.

I pivoted. I didn't want her to see my reaction, whatever the hell that was.

There was a visceral need rushing through me to grab her and take her in my arms, and for a moment, the veil of hate had lifted, and I saw her differently.

I drank in her exotic features, those wide-set eyes that set her apart, and as my gaze stayed on her, I tried to decipher who she looked like more, which parent's genes dominated hers.

It struck me when looking closer. She had neither.

Yes, she had the same rich brown hair, the slender height, the same striking beauty, but now looking at her, that's where it ended.

Her eyes fluttered in wonder, taking in my costume and the mask I was wearing.

"Put it on," I demanded of her.

Not waiting to see her do it, I headed for the door.

Outside, sucking in a lung-full of fresh warm air, I tried to cleanse myself from these filthy thoughts of what I wanted to do to her.

My hate was twisting and morphing into something new. I didn't like the way it made me doubt every action I'd ever taken, doubt the decisions I'd made, the way I dealt with the nightmares as though there was an alternative.

As I left the house, I cursed the woman who followed for bewitching me.

Still, if I knew anything about this town, spells could be broken. Hearts shattered. Lives desecrated. All it took was time. The patience to see the inevitable strike at what was sacred.

Even the air seemed to still for her. I didn't need to turn to see she was behind me. The hair on my nape prickled, letting me know Anya wasn't resisting what the night had to offer.

I opened the passenger door to the BMW. "In."

Anya ducked her head and elegantly lifted her hem to climb inside.

There was no surprise she ignored me during the drive there. She was probably plotting her escape. Or maybe she was mulling over how much she'd miss her mother's float in the parade.

I, on the other hand, was questioning how she'd cope if she saw it.

I parked the BMW on Camp Street, and we headed out on foot.

As we turned onto Bourbon Street, the noise became almost deafening. People had amassed from all over New Orleans for the biggest night of the year—of course, this was a month of celebrations, but tonight, the city came alive.

Heaving crowds moved as one as they headed in one continuous throng along Bourbon Street. The aromas of sweets, barbecued food, and beer mingled with the multitudes, some drunk and some just lively with the thrill of night swarming the pavements.

Pulling Anya behind me, I held her hand tight in mine. We sank into the revelers, many of them, like us, costumed partygoers.

Saxophones, trumpets, and trombones played off one another in a harmonious rhythm, setting alight the night with that familiar backdrop of music, the upbeat notes eliciting vibrant dancing all around us. The air thick with a wet heat that cleaved to us.

Shouting over the hecklers, I said, "This way."

With my arm wrapped around Anya's waist to keep her close, we nudged our way through the marauding crowd toward the edge of the parade.

Multicolored floats were passing us by in a slow-moving, controlled procession. Those who rode them joyfully called out to those who'd gathered, throwing down beads to the frantic hands waving for them.

We stood side by side, watching more floats glide by. Unlike those around us, though, we stood silently watching as though merely witnesses.

"Is this your idea of fun?" snapped Anya.

She shouted something else, but it was lost in the din.

The bright flowers covering a float stood out from the others with their natural flair. Three women aboard the floating stage threw out colored beaded necklaces to the audience. One of the women looked middle-aged and was easily familiar.

Although I suspected she'd be here, seeing her celebrate today, seeing her ability to offer genuine smiles as though nothing was amiss in her life, sent a shockwave of disgust through me. Soon, Anya would see the tall brunette too, the strikingly stunning middle-aged woman from the suburbs—her mother.

The flowered float drew closer.

Anya's face was aghast. Her gasp was heard even over the noise. She shot a wary glance my way.

Pressed in tightly, we rocked against the multitude of bodies around us. My grip weakened around her waist, and Anya pulled away, moving forward and ducking beneath the tape that separated us from the floats.

She hurried toward the float and reached up. "Momma!"

This was why we were here. The reason I'd brought her out tonight, to dangle Anya before her mother. A savage attempt to cause nothing but pain to Victoria Glassman, to see her like she was now, frantic to reach her daughter.

Anya hurried alongside the float with her fingers close to touching her mother's. Her mom meeting her halfway, leaning over the balustrade, to brush her daughter's fingertips.

I stepped forward, ready to snatch Anya back into my arms.

A shoulder struck against me hard, knocking me backward. He was one of the revelers; he threw a wave to apologize and then disappeared from view.

Glancing back toward where I'd last saw Anya—seeing her scrambling to climb the float. My gut twisted that I'd let her get that close.

My focus gliding back to Victoria, who was imminently about to whisk up her daughter to safety. It was in Victoria's eyes that I first read doubt. Her expression was morphing into confusion, eyes darkening as her hand drew back.

Victoria straightened and flung a string of beads into the fray.

Turning away.

Turning her back on her daughter.

The flowered heavy float continuing on. . .

Confusion flashed across Anya's face, raw and endearing.

She seemed to be playing out in her mind what had just happened. From across the crowd, I watched as she started to search faces.

She was looking for someone.

She was looking for me.

Her eyes were wide.

Panic and fear filled them.

Buffered by the hordes of people, she couldn't see me anymore.

Glancing left, I watched her mother's float disappear from view behind another larger one.

When I looked back, Anya was gone.

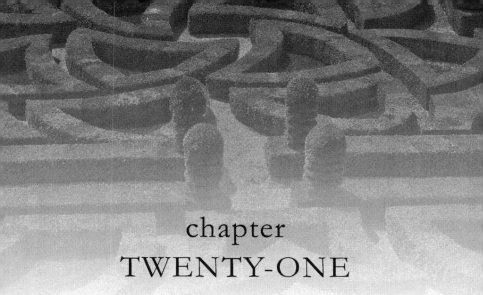

chapter
TWENTY-ONE

Anya

CHOKING ON A SOB, PUMMELED BY THE BODIES AROUND me, reluctantly moving with the sea of people as they swept me along, buffering.

Mom withdrew her hand.

Willingly let me go.

Her eyes turned dark as I witnessed her change of mind to save me. She hadn't seen Cassius because she'd not dragged her stare from mine. She couldn't have known he was there. She didn't demand the float be stopped. Or even try to scramble off it to get to me. A thing I would have done to save my daughter.

But I wasn't her daughter. I never had been. Because she'd never treated me like one. Her decision to let me go was unfathomable. She could see the fear in me. The desperation. Something had caused her to change her mind and I needed to know what it was.

Turning, shifting to face the other way against the sway of the crowd, I looked for Cassius in the swarm of bodies—he, too, was gone.

The freedom I'd craved now felt like a chokehold at my throat. Indecision flooded through me, causing a chill to surge into my veins, despite the crushing humidity.

"Cassius!" I yelled.

Desperate for him, terrified I'd lost him. Lost the one person with whom I'd ever felt a true connection. This didn't make any sense. Shouldn't I rush for freedom? Run toward Camp Street and onward past Lafayette Square; in forty minutes or less, I would make it all the way home to the Garden District.

Instead, I found myself shoving my way through the crowd, until I finally saw the corner of Bourbon Street. I ran to a storefront and shoved open the door.

It was empty.

Once inside, I took in the walls covered in tribal masks and gothic paintings, trinkets, and feathers, and voodoo dolls of all shapes and sizes. Religious statues were standing side by side with miniature skeletons.

And then I saw a person, but he didn't move—it was a lifelike mannequin wearing a demonic mask. It had looked so real, elicited such a visceral feeling, as though familiar.

I saw the image of my father behind that mask. The truth spilling like a million shards of glass cutting into my heart. All this time I'd feared the wrong man. The reason Cassius hated my father was now glaringly obvious—my father had killed someone he loved—that had to be it. A chill washed over me, the hair prickling on my forearms. He'd tried to tell me, but I didn't want to hear it. More importantly, I didn't want to believe it.

Tonight, with my mother's rejection, the veil finally lifted, and I saw everything differently, a sudden clarity. Deceit within my family home that begged to be known. Surviving it felt vital.

And poor Archie was still there.

Unable to catch my breath, unable to endure these profound representations of good and evil all around me—the power of darkness and light, I spun and yanked open the door, the jingling of a bell breaking the silence as I fled.

Out into the night.

Lifting my hem and sprinting onto Ann Street. With no money, I'd have to walk back to the Garden District. But that was the last place I wanted to go. I didn't trust what might happen to me when I got there. Trying to persuade Archie to run away with me last time had failed, and no doubt, it would fail again. I'd need time to find a way to free him from their clutches.

Turning around and around, I prayed I'd not lost Cassius forever. I'd never find my way back to him. His home was tucked away on the outskirts of the city, far from anywhere, and would be impossible to find.

And then I saw him . . .

Standing in the distance alone in the street. His silhouette was next to his parked BMW. Dressed in that familiar costume and eerily still wearing that masquerade mask. He remained like that, watching and waiting as though gauging what my decision might be—to come with him or to flee. There was too much space between him and me not to take a significant chance to lose him.

Home had never felt so far away. Not the French-style 1850s mansion on Third Street that had felt more like a prison than home, but the sprawling manor tucked away in the thickest woodland in a secret location. The home that belonged to Cassius. To find it again, I would need him.

I'd always needed him.

Cassius strolled toward the car and opened the door to the passenger seat. He strolled around the front and climbed in, leaving the passenger door open. He pulled off his masquerade mask, letting it hang on his chest by the ribbon, revealing his devastatingly handsome face, his tortured eyes full of conflict.

In that one gesture, he was giving me the space to decide whether to let him go or return home with him.

Was he really offering my freedom?

Looking back toward Bourbon Street, I felt my past slipping away. A dizzying chaos of the parade weaving in the opposite direction. Turning back toward the sports car, I felt the true gravity of him. The man who'd captured me entirely, and I didn't want to let this chance of chasing after something remarkable slip away.

My chest tightened with dread.

Like a slow gliding shark in still waters, a silver Lexus drove toward Cassius's BMW and pulled up beside it—my father's car.

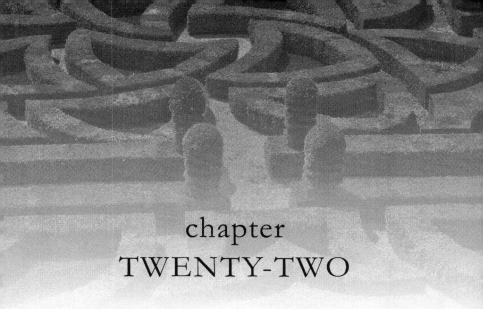

chapter
TWENTY-TWO

Cassius

PALMS FISTED IN MY LAP; LOOKING OUT FROM THE FRONT seat of the car, I chose not to look Anya's way.

It was easier.

Let her make the decision.

She needed to decide what she wanted.

I wanted her to want this.

Despite everything, despite it not making sense, I needed her.

Every cell in my body was filled with doubt that letting her go was the right thing—because it meant she'd be going back to that home—with them. The one where the Glassmans got to rule and wreak havoc.

If I gave any shits about this girl, despite the fact she was one of them, then letting her return to that house was a mistake.

She didn't know what I knew.

Didn't have any idea of who her father was and what he'd done. The catastrophic work he did that destroyed not only people but also nations.

A blinding fury at myself for letting her return to that family.

When I saw her safe, my chest squeezed with relief. She was looking back at me from beneath an awning. If she wanted to, she could run back to the parade and easily disappear into the throng, and I'd lose her forever.

She held my gaze for a beat, and then her eyes widened in horror. She gestured for me to turn around. To look at something, her motions sharp and insistent.

A silver Lexus pulled up beside me.

I knew that car.

Reacting fast, I ducked down in my seat and quickly slid out the door and onto the ground while using the car as a shield.

Bullets cascaded in a deafening crescendo of metal striking metal. Shattering steel and glass. The ear-piercing noise shut out the cheers of the crowd not that far away.

Taking the risk to peek above the car to look for Anya and not seeing her, my flesh chilled with the thought a stray bullet might hit her.

Or her dad might grab her.

Within reach, just beyond where I crouched, was a red door—a familiar entry into a jazz club I'd visited in the past.

If I can just make it there.

Launching myself toward it, bending low to avoid another spray of ammunition that flew over my head. I yanked the door open, I was met with loud music coming from a corner band, so loud they were only now becoming aware of gunshots outside.

Guests were rising from their tables, uneasy from what they thought they'd heard. Squeezing between the tables, I worked my way through the small audience who were rising to their feet.

My heart was pounding.

When I made it all the way through to the other side, a blur of movement came at me from the rear door of the club.

It was Anya.

She flung herself into my arms, and I clutched her to my chest, holding her tight.

"The car's circling." Panic drenched her words. "They're coming back."

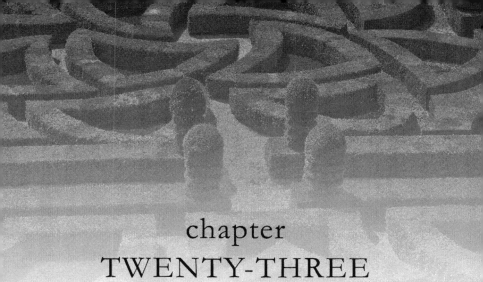

chapter
TWENTY-THREE

Anya

LIFTING MY HEAD FROM WHERE IT LAY ON HIS CHEST, feeling the beat of his frantic heart, I tried to get Cassius to listen. "We have to call the police."

"No." He was adamant.

He was here, with me, and my heart squeezed that I'd almost lost him. Gripping his shirt and refusing to put distance between us ever again.

With shaking hands, I swept them over his chest, checking for any injury. "Did you get hit?"

He grabbed my hands. "Anya, I'm fine."

"Okay, that's good. That's good."

He cupped my face with affection. "Are you all right?"

"Yes."

"You're in shock."

"Come on," I begged him to come with me, but he resisted. "We have to hide."

"Apparently, I don't have your father's blessing."

"Shut up. This is serious! He could have killed you."

Agonizing—the moment before everything came crashing down . . . my mother's hand pulling back—her rejection.

Agony caught in my throat as I replayed my mother's betrayal . Couldn't think of that now. Couldn't let myself crumble from the agony of her refusal to help me. We still had to survive that car coming back around.

Denial was easier to swallow, my throat tightening, grief-stricken. "My father isn't a murderer." *Even though I knew he was.*

Cassius hugged me tighter.

I buried my face against his chest again. "Was it really him?"

"We can't stay." He avoided my question. "Do you trust me?"

"Yes."

Together, we scurried toward the back of the club and down a slim hallway, the sudden confusion all around us conflicting with my own terror.

Cassius opened the door and checked the way was clear. With my hand still in his, we edged along the road, and now and again, glanced back down the street, looking out for the Lexus.

Carrying over the rooftops came the joyful notes of Mardi Gras clashing with what we'd been through.

The world was still turning as ours fell apart.

We headed that way. My heart hammering, mouth dry, clinging to Cassius as we sprinted back toward the parade. We merged with the crowd and disappeared into the swarming bodies. Cassius tugged off his jacket and let it slip to the ground, losing it quickly. We pushed our way into the center to shield us from the street.

"We can't go home yet," he said.

Moving deeper into the crowd, hand in hand so as not to lose each other, we let the movement of their swaying mass carry us past building after building until we broke out from the crowd to hurry down St. Charles Avenue.

The Pontchartrain Hotel welcomed us with old colonial décor and the chill of air-conditioning as we stepped inside the brightly lit foyer. Finally, I felt able to breathe. My tremors lessened.

To the concierge and probably the rest of the staff who greeted us on our way in, we would have looked like any other partying couple.

When we reached the check-in desk, the clerk advised us, "There's only one room left, sir. 'The Melpomene.'" He looked at us suspiciously, like two revelers suddenly needing a room for something elicit.

Cassius opened his wallet and brought out several hundred-dollar bills. "One night."

When the staff member refused to check us in without leaving a credit card on file, Cassius slid more cash across the desk. I wasn't sure if my father had the ability to track someone with their credit card, but he wasn't taking that chance.

The veil hiding who my father was had lifted. Clearly, Cassius believed he had the kind of connections who might tip him off. Which is why we took the room under the name Blacksmith and kept our masquerade masks on as we made our way through the hotel.

Within minutes, we'd taken the elevator to the top floor. I couldn't help but glance suspiciously at everyone we passed. Paranoia clung like vines suffocating everything in its wake.

"This is safe." Cassius tried to reassure me as he slid the key card into the door. "No one knows we're here."

Both of us explored the room. Checking out its luxury décor of rattan furniture, velvet drapery, and even a small fridge. Within the bathroom sat a claw-foot tub, and in different circumstances, I'd have run a bath and soaked my aching limbs.

"This was a good idea." I tried to sound calm, grateful even, but my heart was breaking, and I wasn't sure how much more I could take.

"It's a miracle we got a room this time of year."

It was a goddamn miracle we were still *alive*.

Cassius pointed at a portrait of Tennessee Williams. "Did you like *A Streetcar Named Desire?*"

"What?" I cursed him for trying to make it look like being here was anything but okay.

"Anya," he said, his words hinting he was trying to take my mind off what had just happened. "I've got this."

"I haven't seen any plays," I admitted.

"Not one?"

I shook my head.

He looked sad for me. "You'd like it."

How could he be so calm after everything? So reasonable and able to think on his feet. *Because this is what he expected* came the harsh truth of realization. He'd always known what kind of man my father was. What he was capable of.

"Cassius." I tugged on his sleeve. "You were almost killed."

His lip curled in a half-smile. "I would have been if you hadn't warned me."

"I should have done more."

"You were very brave."

"I never knew him. Never knew what kind of man he really is."

"Don't talk about him." He looked off, his mouth twisting in hate.

"How long will we stay here?"

"Overnight." He led me into the bedroom. "I'll sleep on the couch."

I walked toward the window. Pulling the curtain aside to peek out. Cassius tugged the curtains closed. "Not a good idea."

That brief glimpse beyond the window had shown the parade was still going on. People were joyfully celebrating Mardi Gras, dancing and laughing in the streets. And in here felt like an unlikely combination of a kidnapped girl who chose to stay with her captor. The man I was falling for.

Yet . . .

There was no other way of asking it. "You knew my mom would be there tonight?" He'd dangled me before her.

"I wanted to see the pain in her eyes, Anya."

"This has to stop. Now."

He gave a shrug that maybe I was right.

I studied his reaction. "You saw what happened?"

He strolled away from me and knelt before the fridge. Maybe he was thinking of the answer he'd give. Or maybe that was his way of ignoring the question. Opening the door, he pulled out two bottles of Perrier water and then offered one to me.

"No, thank you." I turned my back on him. "Can you help me out of this?"

He stood behind me and unzipped the gown and helped me climb out of it. There was no sense of vulnerability at all even though I'd stripped down to my underwear in front of him. Though I'd done worse before we'd left the house, having stood naked before him. It made me wonder if he found me attractive at all. He'd kissed me at Café Du Monde, surely that meant something. Meant our connection went deeper.

Maybe we'd even find our way to a place of trust.

I threw the dress onto a high-backed chair. He lifted one of the robes off the bed and helped me slide my arms into it. I sat there, pulling off my shoes, grateful to be able to take time to think clearly.

"What do you know about my dad?" I said.

Cassius gave a long sigh. "He's not the man you think he is."

"Clearly."

"I'm sorry you had to see that."

"Is Archie in danger?"

He began to walk away.

"I mean from them. My parents."

"Honestly, I don't know."

"I have to go to him. Tonight."

"No."

"We have to at least talk about it."

"It's too dangerous." He stood there, his expression conflicted, and then walked away, disappearing inside the bathroom.

My heart was breaking all over again. The thought that I was no longer in that house and Archie was there, vulnerable and alone, was terrifying. I had to get back to him. Somehow, I had to persuade Cassius to let me go rescue him. Maybe we could do it together.

The sound of the shower echoed. Sitting here alone, I wrapped my arms around myself for consolation, trying to deal with these feelings of abandonment, these awful truths.

Feeling powerless.

Maybe Cassius was rethinking everything. Maybe this was his way of letting me go without having to say it. Because it would be easy to walk out that door. The risk of keeping me prisoner was clearly dangerous.

I wondered if he regretted it. Regretted it all, the kidnapping, keeping me in his home, and tonight, especially when the walls of his consequences came crashing around him.

I could get dressed and leave. Try to get home. But I kept replaying my mom withdrawing her hand from me.

My father's car pulling up next to Cassius's. That terrifying sound of gunfire.

She wasn't my mom. Not really. She'd never seemed inclined to step into that role or build that kind of relationship. We'd never spent precious mother-daughter time together. There hadn't been bedtime stories. No shopping trips out to bond or time to truly get to know each other. We were strangers. I may have lived beneath the same roof, but I'd always been kept at arm's length. Now, as I mulled over what came next, I had to ask the hard question. What was the best decision for Archie's sake? Each choice carried undue risks and so many different outcomes.

I'd been wrong about everything. My life was now seen through a veil of deceit. My parents were not the people I believed them to be. There would come a time when I would have to accept that.

And where did Cassius stand amongst all of this? What was he not telling me?

The answer lay with him.

Unable to wait, I headed in his direction and turned the handle to the bathroom door.

My breath left me . . .

Cassius stood naked beneath the shower as a torrent of water cascaded off his tall and toned body, his dazzling physique kissed by tattoos upon wet, bare flesh, making him appear as a breathtaking work of art.

A thrum came low in my belly, lower still as arousal stirred between my thighs, a yearning to step inside the glass walls and press my body to his, feel his heat against me. Nuzzle into him. Breathe him in.

Eyes closed, his face turned into the stream of water, giving me more time to admire his impressive length curling downward. The shock of seeing it took my breath away. Having never seen a naked man up close before.

My cheeks flushed wildly as I backed away, hands reaching behind me for the door handle.

He opened his eyes.

I froze, pinned by his intense gaze.

Pressing a hand against the glass of the shower, he said, "Everything okay?"

"I have to ask you something."

His eyes twinkled with knowing. "Can it wait?"

"Yes. No."

"Let me grab a towel."

"Were you ever going to let me go?"

He froze, self-searching in his expression, a flinch of agony.

"I need to know." I needed to know what his intentions were for me.

"Go back to the bedroom. Wait for me."

"Tell me." Tell me now before I die a thousand deaths knowing that no one can be trusted. Not my father, not my mom, and most of all, not him.

"There's a Bollinger on ice. Open it."

Teeth clenched, I snapped, "I don't need it."

"I know."

My lips quivered at him, dragging out what should clearly be a no. That his plan for me might even be fatal.

He didn't say it.

Didn't deny it.

I ran from the room and headed toward the door. The exit was clearly marked, the one that would lead to the hallway. I'd take my chances out there, even in this bathrobe, where the world was cruel and uncertainty reigned, but at least I'd have a chance of surviving.

Cassius's hand came crashing down on the door, and he slammed it shut before I could fully open it.

He grabbed my shoulders and spun me around to face him. "We can't do this now." His naked body spotted with droplets of water, muscled forearms flexing as he pressed his hands on each side of my head to cage me in. "It's not safe out there. You have to trust me."

"Trust you?" I spat the words.

I knew it was a mistake to do this while hiding. When the enemy was out searching for us. His enemy. But what about the enemy within? The man who was just as much a hazard for me. Even as he stood before me dripping wet and totally naked, his primal stance of overpowering me was doing something to my head and causing ripples of sensations. It felt like our hearts were beating at the same time and in the same rhythm. That what passed between us intensified our bond.

These thoughts and feelings raging against what I knew to be right, to be true. That no matter how much I wanted to dress this up into something sacred, the harsh truth remained; I was his prisoner. Even as some part of me yearned for more of this captivity with him.

Maybe it was wiser to try to get home.

Surely my father would greet me with open arms. He'd never hurt me. Doubt settled in. Every breath taken as fragile as the last.

"My dad loves me," I said bitterly. "He doesn't kidnap young women like you do."

Cassius peered down at me, conflicted. "You were collateral."

Tears stung my eyes.

"Anya—"

"And now? What's your plan now? What do you plan to do to me?"

He broke my gaze, seemingly trying to search for the right

words. "I can't let you leave. I nearly did back at the parade. But that would have been a mistake."

"I hate you." Even as I cursed him, I craved him.

"You have every right."

Fury swept over me, and it refused to let go. Frustration for these roiling emotions, daggers of pain that felt like flung knives, forcing agony deeper and deeper until I couldn't bear it any longer. "Do you feel anything for me?"

His denial hurt worse than anything I'd felt before.

"Tell me."

He shook his head as though trying to shake off a thought. "You and I . . ."

"Because I'm his daughter?" Even as I said it, I couldn't share the truth, couldn't speak the words that would prove I was as deceitful as my family.

"My feelings are irrelevant, Anya."

"How can that be?" Frustrated with him, I raised onto my toes, leaning in and pressing my mouth to his. Kissing him hard. Punishing him with a bite to his lip, feeling his mouth open in response. He let out a sigh, breathing into my mouth. His hands reached for my wrists, and he held them tight and lifted them above my head.

His crushing kiss widening my lips so his tongue could enter. Battling with mine, forging a truce between us, then launching an attack of passion, a fight for the truth in a rousing and needy way, biting and nipping and clashing teeth.

He pulled back. "Bad idea."

"Why, because it's me?"

"Because I want it. And what I want usually turns out to be a mistake."

"What if this one time you did the right thing?" I'd tried to cure this longing for him, but nothing worked.

There was an endless need that tore into me.

Was he saying we'd never fall in love? We'd never get to that place of trust because there was too much distance between us? Too much had happened that could never be faced. Yet my heart clenched with the thought of not having him.

Tears pricked my eyes. "I want . . . this."

"You don't know what it is you're asking for."

"Yes, I do, Cassius. I see past the wall you've put up. I see the good in you. The fight. I see the pain. I'm trying to reach you. Meet me halfway."

"I don't do . . . feelings."

"Really, because I can see all this is hurting you."

"What do you want?"

"You."

"How can you be sure?"

"I'm still here, aren't I?"

His lips curled seductively, a coyness in his half-smile.

"I want you." And it had always been yes to *this*.

The promise of intimacy between us—stretching beyond the world outside and all that it had done to us.

He let go of my hands, allowing me to shrug out of the white robe. It slipped from my shoulders to the floor, leaving me standing before him in my bra and panties. I reached behind my back and unhooked my bra. Let that slip from my shoulders, too. I showed off my breasts, feeling empowered as he drank in my nakedness.

Glancing down to see his erection rising out of dark curls, regal and as intimidating as him.

He stepped forward and pressed his forehead to mine. "Everything will change between us."

"It already has." I breathed. "I know you feel this, too."

"I don't deserve you, Anya. A man like me—"

I cupped his cheek. "I forgive you."

"I'm not sure you can." He squeezed his eyes closed at the weight of those words. The impossible shifting of us toward something more. It would be a cruel future, one where we both knew what his intentions had been for me. We wouldn't survive it. Our past was too complicated. Too ruined. My body yearned for all that had gone before to be forgotten for these few hours ahead of us.

Tell him.

Tell him you're not a Glassman.

He lifted me up in his arms and carried me down the hallway toward the bed. Laying me on top of the duvet and helping me climb beneath it.

He pulled on one of the bathrobes to cover his nakedness. "Only you and I would ever understand where we've come from." He brought the duvet up and dragged it over me. "That's something we can hold on to."

"I know." It didn't make sense that he was tucking me into bed.

Not after all that sensual tension, not after my body was so alight with passion, I thought I might combust.

He gave a look of understanding. "After all you've been through tonight, us, being more at this moment, wouldn't be right."

I went to protest, but he held a fingertip to my mouth. "I promise to tell you everything tomorrow."

"I can't sleep."

He gave a nod of understanding and lay down beside me, with him above the duvet and me beneath it; I felt the warmth of his body spooning behind me.

"Let's catch our breath, Anya. I just want to savor this, okay? Let me have this one last night with you."

I glanced over my shoulder in protest.

"After I tell you what you want to know, this may never happen again."

With his words ruminating in the depths of my consciousness, I fought and lost the will to stay awake. Falling into sleep, begging my heart to be brave enough to hear the truth of what it would take for us to be more.

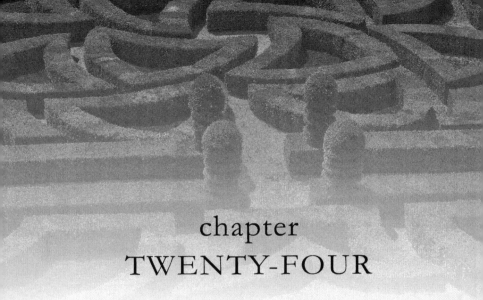

chapter
TWENTY-FOUR

Cassius

W E MOVED ALONG IN THE SMALL BOAT AMONGST THE towering brilliance of nature's cathedral, with its impressively tall cypress and tupelo trees rising all around us. Steering the small motorboat farther into the heart of Lake Martin, we took in the beauty of the swamp.

We'd spent the day at opposite sides of the property. With Anya in the library, needing solace from the scars from attending Mardi Gras, and me, staying in my office. Throwing myself into work. Though honestly, I was really trying to come to terms that this may be our last evening together.

Because I knew I was going to have to bring her here.

The place it all began. Where my story started. The reason I'd spent a lifetime trying to hold my very existence together.

We glided by hefty oaks adorned by Spanish moss draping over their sprawling branches, low enough to kiss the murky, brackish, untamed waters below.

"What are we doing out here?" Anya shook me from my musing.

"I wanted you to see this."

She'd sensed my melancholy. Offering a kind touch to bring me back to the present, back to her.

I needed to do this.

Needed her to hear it from me. The truth that would leave a scorched earth behind us because there was no other way than to walk through the ashes of the truth. She'd never look at me the same.

I would miss this short-lived affection between us. Those moments that shimmied and shined to hint that we could have been more.

Only here, in the dimness of the marshland, could this be done. Where no one could overhear. I needed solitude. A place where no one else could judge me, other than her.

A pelican swooped over the boat, and we watched it climb higher, sweeping up and out of the towering trees flying southward.

Despite the heat, my body chilled as the memories of this place swirled. The open space was closing in around us.

A cold sweat snaked down my spine as I replayed the moments that had unfolded here. This marsh not that far away from my home. The events that changed my world.

The consequences of that day playing out with a heady mixture of cruelty and greed.

Looking around us now, it was hard to remember the young man I'd been. Impossible to recall those feelings of innocence. Of trust. A part of me wanting to yell out into the dusk to reach the younger version of me.

Run!

Escape into the marshland. Don't listen to him—to Glassman. Don't carry his threat back to my family. *Don't let him have that power over you.*

A blue heron waded amongst the abundance of greenery. Beneath the water, unseen creatures lurked. The aliveness a symphony of song. Continuing through, I took pleasure in pointing out egrets and pelicans. Suppressing a lazy smile when Anya flinched—she'd seen the alligator not that far away, bathing on a leafy bank.

She wrapped her arms around herself in a hug. "Why have you brought me to the worst place on earth?"

I shot her a glare. "Don't be quick to judge. Swamps are critical. We need them. They protect us from storm surges. Filter waste. What you're seeing is the way nature purifies."

"If you say so."

"I do." I swept my hand across the water. "This place provides the balance we need to exist. It saves us, really. From ourselves."

As the deadliest predators upon this earth. Humans.

An evening song of crickets accompanied us as we went farther into the murkiness. The high-pitched cry of the male insects wooing their mates in an unceasing chirping.

Anya shivered in anticipation or perhaps it was that small voice inside warning danger was nearby. I couldn't blame her reluctance. She'd been brought here by a man like me and that alone should elicit fear.

She jumped when our boat knocked against something unseen. She reached out and gripped the sides of the boat, her focus on me as she tried to gauge my mood and guess what the hell we were doing here.

Turning off the engine, I let us drift with the slipstream. The scenery moved around us in a continuous portrait of the colors of life.

"Cassius?"

I wanted to make sure she was comfortable at least. "Warm enough?"

She nodded and hugged her knees. Dark locks of hair fell over her delicate features, making her look vulnerable. Even as I'd gotten to know her strength. Her ability to endure without hardening her heart. There would be a time when she came to see me as the man I really was. Soon, the truth would curl like a giant wave and crash against the sands of time that I'd somehow been able to hold back.

Until now.

Soon, she would be ruined forever because of it.

Just like all those years ago when my innocence shattered. It would be no different.

"I'm so sorry to be the one to tell you this," I said. "But your father is an arms dealer."

Horror flashed across her face, her eyes blinking as though to shut out the words. "You're sure?"

My expression gave her the answer she didn't want.

"Oh, God."

"Maybe knowing that will somehow help explain how you and I came to know each other."

"Why you took me?"

"Yes."

"What would an arms dealer want with your family?"

"More than we could deliver." I raised my hand to stop her questions. I would share everything with her soon.

Although I was hurting her, this felt like it was me who carried the burden of grief as if we were already, in some way, intrinsically connected by something more.

"It was here," I began quietly.

Anya's attention zeroed in on me, as did the stillness of the moment.

She nodded for me to go on, offering a kind smile to coax me into the inevitable.

"I was fourteen. I'd flown in from New York on my father's jet. Taking a break in my semester. Only it wasn't my father's men who collected me from the airport." The memory of that SUV gliding down the runway into view was a stark and real and agonizing memory filling me with regret for allowing myself to be ushered inside Stephen's car.

"When I refused to get in, Stephen gave the order for his men to encourage me to join him in the back seat." I tilted my head to impress upon the fact there had been no way to resist them. "Then he drove me to this place. This swamp. Brought me out on a boat. Just the two of us. Alone."

"Why?" She was breathless.

"He wanted my father to know he could get to him. Or at least his children. He wanted my dad to know my life had been in his hands."

A pair of reptilian eyes peeked above the water, glassy and sinister.

"Cassius?" Anya drew my focus back to her.

"We were in a boat very much like this one. I couldn't go anywhere. Knew well enough not to leap into the water and wade to the bank." Exhaling, I tried to say the words so deeply engrained in my soul. The catalyst of evil that had seeped into my DNA, weaving it into something new. Forming a double helix of evil, twisting throughout my being and changing me, mutating me on the cellular level into a monster.

The cruelty with which Stephen's message was spoken so calmly, so precisely. His threat began a war against my father. One that endured today, but with his son, with me.

"Stephen told me to advise my father that if he didn't allow him to place weapons on one of his ships docked in the New York Harbor—the *Santa Marina*, he would kill him. What he was trying to do was straight-up piracy. Apparently, my father had refused him once. My dad kept this from the rest of the family. Even Ridley's father didn't know. Dad had tried to handle it but clearly had failed to impress upon Stephen it wasn't going to happen. Dad had told him not on one of his fleet of ships. Not ever."

"What did my dad say?"

"Stephen warned that if I gave this message to anyone other than my dad, he would find me and kill my sister and me."

Anya's eyes widened with horror.

"When Stephen finally let me go, and his car dropped me off outside my home, I was badly shaken. I didn't want to tell my mom what happened because I didn't want to worry her. Plus, I knew she was with my sister, and probably didn't even realize I was home late. I tried to get to my dad to give him the message, but he was busy taking back-to-back meetings."

"Your dad wouldn't see you?"

"His men sent me away." More precisely, it had been Ridley's father who'd refused to let me in that room. A fact she didn't need to hear. His son had more than carried the burden of guilt for well over a decade. Perhaps the only reason he'd stayed around long enough to watch me throw my life away.

A mosquito launched its proboscis into my forearm. I slapped it dead. "They wouldn't let me see him. They told me he was too busy. I thought I had time. Thought that once the evening came around, his men would filter out like they always did, and my father would see me. And then I'd tell him what happened." Wiping away a streak of sweat off my neck, I willed myself to go on. "I should have fought my way into his office. Fought anyone who tried to stop me. Instead, I was the well-mannered son who asked for permission to speak with my own father." I cleared my throat. "I failed to warn him Stephen was coming."

Anya looked horrified.

"They swept through the house like a plague, killing everyone in their wake. My mother died in my arms in the garden."

"You saved your sister?" Her voice was distant.

"I should have saved them all. After Mom died and we knew we couldn't do anything more for her, we hid. In the only place they couldn't get to us."

"Where?"

"The maze."

Tears welled in her eyes.

"I don't want your sympathy, Anya. I want you to know why I hate him. Why I took you from him. Why I wanted him to suffer because I had you." My hands clenched into fists as I gathered the strength to say the rest.

"I'll never forgive him."

"I am beyond forgiveness, too."

"No, you're not."

I raised my hand to stop her. "You're about to hate me. Maybe even more than him."

"Never."

"After my parents' funeral, I followed him to your house in the Garden District. Stephen was alone. I didn't care for my life. I cornered him without his men close by. Told him what my intention was. I vowed to come after—" I bowed my head as I said the rest. "That I would find you. Bring you here. And kill you."

"Revenge?" she whispered it.

She knew no one could stop it. Not now. Not here. Should my threat go as planned, no one would hear her scream.

"I forgive you." Her words carried on the air.

My stare held hers. "You shouldn't."

"And yet, I do."

"Forgiving me isn't smart. I'm not a man who deserves it."

She leaned forward and pressed a finger to my mouth. "Stop. I do. I understand. I get why you did it."

"Anya," I snapped. "I was going to kill you."

"You weren't. I see that. I know you would never have hurt me. That's not who you are. And after what we did to you, I can understand."

"You've done nothing wrong. Other than being born in that family."

She hesitated, ready to form words but unable to say them. "I'm glad you told me."

Perspiration spotted her brow. She swiped it away with her hand.

"I've scared you."

"No, I'm just fucking hot."

A half-laugh escaped my lips. *You haven't lost her. Not yet.* My brain scavenged for signs she was trying to be brave. Trying to placate me. Before she left me for good.

Anya slapped my forearm. A jolt of pain. She held my gaze. "Mosquito."

"This was a bad idea, wasn't it?"

"We could have bought repellent."

"Then you would have guessed."

"Not in a million years." She sucked in a sob. "He's a monster."

"I'm the monster, Anya."

"No, you're the result of his cruelty. I pray God does something."

"Don't hold your breath."

Our boat shifted, turning a little before continuing. Anya gave a nervous glare my way.

Rolling my sleeve up, I scooted to the edge of the boat. "Probably a gator." I reached my hand into the water. "Let me check."

She leaped toward me. "No!" Her fingers latched onto my arm and yanked it away from the surface.

I shook the droplets off my hand. "I have this thought that won't go away."

"What?"

"If I die, all your problems will go away."

Anya fell on top of me, knocking me backward and landing on my chest. Rocking the boat. I shifted us both to get comfortable and welcomed this much-needed hug.

She clung to me. "You saved me from him."

Resting my head back on the edge, I peered toward the starlit sky and wrapped my arms around her as we drifted with the slow-moving tide.

"You're not the man I thought you were."

"Is that good or bad?"

"You should know by now nothing scares me. Not this place. Not my past. Nor the truth. I'm beyond all of that."

"I wasn't trying to scare you. Merely get across how an adolescent kid would have reacted to being brought all the way out here. And told all that."

"It was what happened after this place that changed you. You were so young."

"I can take you anywhere you want to go. I want you to know that. I can give you money. Get you out of New Orleans—"

"I'm not going anywhere."

"How can you still want to be with me?"

"How can I not?"

Her embrace, her resting her head on my chest, her stark beauty taking on a mythical status, as though the profoundness of her being was God taunting me with the happiness I would never deserve.

"I can't let you go. I should. But I can't," I whispered.

"Then don't."

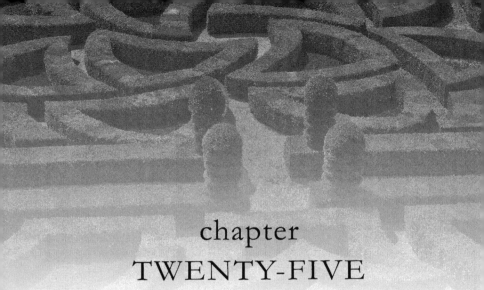

chapter
TWENTY-FIVE

Anya

ONCE CASSIUS HAD FALLEN ASLEEP, I CAME OUT HERE to the garden so he couldn't see me like this.

Tears were staining my cheeks. I tried not to think of that car pulling up beside Cassius or those bullets flying. The thought of him being killed and taken from me forever.

Everything he'd told me in the swamp last night revolved in my mind like a living nightmare that wouldn't cease.

The end of my innocence was marked with the realization my father was a murderer.

A fucking arms dealer.

Involved in the underworld of crime. And if I really admitted it to myself, after recalling the kind of men who'd visited him in the house, it had been obvious. From the money that flowed. The way he kept us out of sight. The fact he'd had children before us. It was terrifying to think of this man as my father.

A man involved with the worst kind of crime. He had the resources to destroy anyone who crossed him. *Anyone.*

The thought of Archie still in that house made my skin crawl. I had to get him out.

Only it would have to be strategic.

I'd brought out a blanket and wrapped it around my shoulders, needing the extra warmth to endure the late evening chill while I breathed in the freshest air. The garden sprawled before me as though it whispered that new memories were possible.

Happier times might even be possible.

Seeing what lay beyond in a new way. Instead of being imprisoned in this place, it felt like a refuge.

I reeled back, hit by the realization. I thought I'd been counting down the days until my escape, but sometime during my time here I'd started to enjoy each moment. Not living for yesterday. Or tomorrow. Just today. Cassius Calvetti—broken, twisted Cassius— taught me the most important lesson I'd ever learn.

To live.

Beyond me, the neatly trimmed maze was a contrast to the wild foliage that sprang up around it, tendrils of plants and flowers nearing its sides as though just as fascinated with its creation.

The ghost of Cassius's words from the early evening in the swamp stayed with me. More than just his touch. The way he'd made me feel last night in that modest hotel room at The Pontchartrain. Safe and nurtured.

Though even as we'd shared a rare intimacy, he'd refused to take me. Refused to bury himself deep inside me or even let me pleasure him. I'd merely become a wanton mess of a woman trying to fall asleep in his arms.

All that was left was for my imagination to fill in the spaces in-between the fantasy made half-real by him. Let my thoughts carry me to the moment he made love to me.

I should have told him I wasn't a Glassman. Maybe that was why he held back his affection. Maybe this was what prevented him from going there with me.

I'd almost shared the truth in that scary swamp and told him about my adoption. I'd wanted him to know I had felt pain too.

That we had more in common than he realized. I'd loved my adoptive parents, even after discovering their lost children. I'd felt their loss as though it was my own. Filled in the blanks of that story and entrusted them with how they'd handled their grief. Even as they came and went at home and gave us so little time, I'd found love for them.

Now, after Mardi Gras, all that was left of those feelings was a void. A crack so deep, it could never be mended. Not now, after I'd witnessed an attack on Cassius from that slow-moving car. My father might not have shot the weapon that almost killed Cassius, but he'd been in the car.

An owl hooted from a treetop. I'd once heard they could become vicious when protecting their young. I had glimpsed that kind of primal cruelty from my parents. Only when my mom had the chance to save me, she'd turned away. She'd given up on me. Or given me over.

But why?

More tears sprung from my eyes. Swiping them away, I willed myself to find the strength to find my way through this.

I felt him before I heard him.

Turning, I saw Cassius strolling across the lawn carrying two mugs.

"I thought I might find you out here." He offered one to me.

Accepting the mug from him, I watched the steam spiral and leaned in to sniff the drink. "Hot chocolate?"

"That okay?"

"I'd never figured you for that kind of guy."

"I'm full of surprises."

"You really are."

"I can switch it for something stronger?"

"It's perfect." I breathed in the aroma of the sweet cocoa.

He studied my face though was polite enough not to mention he could see I'd been crying.

I turned away, not wanting him to see me like this.

"There's a lot to process." His voice was soft and kind.

"Nothing you say will make me feel better. It won't change anything."

"I wish it was different. You deserve that, Anya."

"It still doesn't explain why he never came for me." I looked at him as if he had the answer. "Though I'm glad he didn't."

"Need some space?"

With a gentle shake of my head, I said, "Tell me about the maze?"

He looked that way with a sentimental smile. "I had this crazy idea about building one as a kid. My parents made it happen."

"Just like that?"

"They told me that if we had one, I'd have to take care of it. I did then, and I have since. I've honored that promise." He pointed at it. "Now that is one of the best things to ever happen to me."

I wondered if that was what held him here. "It's just a maze."

"It's everything it represents."

"A labyrinth you can get lost in?"

"So much more. Mazes go back all the way to Egypt. They were created to protect kings. In history, royalty entertained guests in them." He gestured I was right in some way. "For me, it was always a place that could be just mine. Somewhere to be introspective. Though I didn't realize it at the time. A place I could disappear."

It was a part of him. Something sacred that he couldn't abandon. Perhaps many of his cherished memories were in there.

"What do you think about in there?"

"Anything and everything. At least, I did."

"It's beautiful."

"As a kid, I read about how a maze was created to study the navigational skills of insects. Bees were observed in them. They found their way intuitively."

"How?"

"Apparently, bees see the world coming their way when they fly. They have a natural navigational instinct. It's fascinating, really."

Staring up, I took in the night sky.

"Humans can find their way with the stars, if they get lost, using celestial navigation."

"Following the North Star?"

"Absolutely. And, if you familiarize yourself with a few constellations, you can find your way." He pointed upward. "Just like the sun, stars travel from east to west. This is something my mom taught me; if you want to know which way you're facing, look for Mintaka." He pointed at the stars. "Can you see? There, on the right of Orion's Belt. It rises to true east and sets close to true west."

"Which one?"

"Orion the Hunter." Cassius came behind me, and with his free right hand, he took mine and guided it up, pointing it toward the sky. "See?"

Three bright stars were in a short, straight row.

Feeling his warmth against my body, I sank into the comfort of his touch, my flesh tingled where he was pressed tight. Leaning back, I rested my head on his chest. His lips touched the top of my head with affection.

He'd shared this so naturally as if it was easy for him to talk about this moment in his past with me.

"To be totally sure," he added, "look out for the brighter stars on either side of the belt stars, one is blue and the other reddish." He wrapped his arm around my waist and hugged me.

I ran my thumb along the sun inked on his wrist. "What does this one mean?"

"Something my mom used to say: 'Don't forget, Cas, the sun is also a star.'"

"What does it mean?"

"There are billions of stars, but only one of them is strong enough to be the sun. She used to call me her strength."

"That's beautiful."

"Still, I've not exactly been the son she imagined." He inhaled sharply. "All that celestial beauty also reminds us there's something greater out there orchestrating our lives."

"We were always destined to meet."

His breath was warm on my neck. "Destined to cross paths."

"Maybe more than that." Despite having my back to him, I felt his melancholy. "Would you want that?"

"I . . . will always protect you, Anya."

That was a *no*, that he didn't see us being anything more. Even after this closeness, we'd never move beyond what we were now.

"Cas." I said his name with the sanctity it deserved.

"I kidnapped you. That's hardly the foundation for a good relationship."

He tugged the blanket tighter and wrapped his arms around me in a possessive hug.

These quiet moments with him were what I held on to. His layers were peeling back and revealing his extraordinary depths.

He nodded toward the maze. "When Stephen came for me, I ran in there to hide."

An imaginary flash of movement before me as though I was seeing that event replay all over again—two young people disappearing within—being chased by men with guns. So vivid, so real as though I, too, was personally recalling that day in all its horror.

"You hid in the maze," I said wistfully.

"The maze hid us."

Which meant the maze was so much more than a sum of its parts. It was a profound representation of the way nature had protected him that day.

No wonder it was impossible to walk away from it. To leave this town and the memories of what came before.

Reaching for his hand, I said, "Take me in there."

He turned his back on it in a quiet refusal.

"Who looks after it then?"

Tending and trimming the hedges to maintain their precise design.

"I have a gardener. Well, I did before you. I only go in there now to find and rescue you." He winked.

That made me smile.

He looked over at the maze with affection, eyes conflicted with a flurry of emotions. Maybe some part of him was still trapped within. That young man still running along its leafy corridors, turning corners and stumbling around its sharp bends, maybe even unable to find his way out.

"You once asked if I trust you," I said softly.

"Yes."

"Do you trust me?"

"I believe I do, Anya."

Taking his drink off him, I placed our mugs on the stoop and rose to face him again. He looked at me with a curious arch of his brows.

Interlocking his fingers with mine, holding his hand tight, I led him toward the maze.

chapter
TWENTY-SIX

Anya

I PULLED CASSIUS FARTHER DOWN A HEDGED PASSAGEWAY TO where I believed the center of the maze to be. My free hand ran across the delicate leaves as we turned a corner. I was so ready for what was to follow that my body quivered in anticipation at the intimacy it craved, my nipples beading in anticipation for his touch.

His kiss.

His hand slipped from mine.

Glancing back, I was staring at nothing. Cassius was gone.

Wait.

Seconds ago, he was right behind me.

His voice came from the other side of the hedge. "The lanes that lead through the labyrinth are like the veins that lead through the heart. The more lost you become, the more love will depart."

"What does that mean?" Because I was lost.

And lost without him.

Heart hammering, I realized this was how Cassius had eluded my father. He'd moved about this labyrinth and defied him and his men. They'd had no idea there were moving parts to this place.

Walls that gave way to another side—because that was the only way Cassius had just disappeared into thin air. These leafy walls hid him now just as they had protected him that day.

Stepping back to where I last saw him, I gave the hedge a nudge, but my hands slid between the bush, scraping my palms.

A rustling came from behind me. But there was no one there—like an illusion. I turned and followed the rustling down the passageway.

Then nothing.

Silence.

I tried to shove another hedge to get to the other side, fingers buried deep in leaves. The pressure of a palm covering my mouth. I screamed into a hand, pivoting quickly.

Cassius stood behind me, laughing. A rush of delayed terror mixed with amusement at his playful smile.

"How did you do that?"

"It's a secret." He waggled his eyebrows.

I thumped his arm.

Swiftly, I was hoisted up with my legs on either side of his hips and pushed against the hedge behind me.

His mouth was close to mine. But no kiss came.

Caught in what felt forbidden, my arousal spiked. He let me down slowly. My feet touched the grass as I reclaimed my balance.

Turning on his heels, Cassius headed down the way we'd come.

"Where are you going?" I called after him.

"Back to the house."

"No you don't." I hurried after him and grabbed his arm. "Show me the place."

"Being in here . . ." he said the rest with his eyes.

"This is not a negotiation." Grabbing his hand, I pulled him back into the heart of the maze. Cassius relented and reached into one of the hedges. Seemingly feeling for a metal catch. The hedge opened ajar. Enough for us to slip through. He led the way, moving into the next space.

This was how Cassius had evaded Stephen all those years ago.

That man had stolen everything that was sacred in Cassius's life. He'd even stolen the joy of this maze. We could reclaim it, here, now, together. If only my guide felt ready to open his heart completely to this, to me, to all the possibilities that surrounded us.

"Ready?" Cassius reached into another hedge, and his hand disappeared into the leaves.

We entered what had to be the center with four walls of green shrubbery. A secret hideout. He didn't have to tell me this was the exact location where he'd sheltered all those years ago. Where he'd remained silent and waited for those evil men to give up and search elsewhere. That all those years ago it had saved his life.

Pulling the blanket off my shoulders, I laid it down in the center, tugging on the corners to make it a square. Cassius studied me carefully.

"You're not leaving," I said firmly.

His back stiffened. "Excuse me?"

"This is me kidnapping you."

He looked amused. "Sure you want to go there?"

"Play along." I motioned with a sweep of my hand.

He hesitated and went to say something, seemingly searching for the words his soul couldn't say. His expression was full of wonder.

I knelt onto the blanket and tapped the fabric. "Down."

He knew what this was. He also knew why I was doing it. Why it had to be here. Like this . . .

Cassius's long fingers caressed his jaw thoughtfully. There was conflict in his eyes as he weighed what was being asked.

"This is not a request," I said darkly.

He was at his most beautiful when his brows met, and his eyes softened, as though that final wall of his was coming down, the final wall of the maze.

The final puzzle was *him.*

Getting to know Cassius had been just as complex as this place, heading down one way and having to turn and find another pathway to get to this man's soul. Discovering his depths, pushing beyond his darkness and seeing what lay at the center, a light that reflected so much love but had been hidden for too long.

Whether he saw it as a game or just did it to placate me, I didn't care. He finally relented and lay on the blanket, his feet hanging off the end because he was so tall.

Leaning over him, my fingers trailed down his buttoned shirt, undoing one at a time, tugging the material open to reveal the fine hairs on his chest. Tracing a path over his toned chest, I admired the curves and the tautness of him. Tugging at his shirt, I helped him shrug out of the sleeves, leaving him bare-chested.

His hand came down on mine. "Careful, I might fall for you ."

My skin tingled with his touch. "Do you want to?"

He exhaled sharply. "Anya."

His hold slipped from mine in a way to say he was surrendering.

He kicked off his shoes, one and then the other. Helping peel off his socks, I threw him a shy smile.

Moving onto his zipper, I lowered it and dragged his pants down over his hips, taking my time to strip him naked as I pulled down his boxers. A tall, exquisite form of a man lay exposed before me.

"Aren't you going to take off yours?" he asked curiously.

"This isn't about me."

This wasn't revenge for what he'd almost done to me in The Pontchartrain Hotel. This was him being totally vulnerable to me. This was me showing him how I felt about him. This was what I had needed more than the air itself. This yearning would destroy me if I couldn't have him like this.

My craving for him intensified.

I traced a pattern with my fingertip over each tattoo, the compass design on his chest, the heart that had to mean family, and that sun on his wrist—the first tattoo I'd glimpsed when he'd knelt before me that time while I had hidden in the closet.

Now look at us, all fear gone and understanding left in its place.

"What does this one mean?" I asked of the compass.

He shrugged. "At the time, it was meant to represent not losing my way with myself. But clearly . . ."

"I found you," I said wistfully.

"Actually, I found you."

"No, I'm talking about the real Cassius, the one . . ."

His expression softened revealing he knew what I'd been about to confess, a word that terrified me, and surely scared him, too. Maybe showing him how I felt was safer for now.

Tenderly, I kissed along his jawline up to his mouth, softly at first and then nipping. He opened his lips further, and I used his movement to my advantage, dominating with pressure and making it mine. Tongues lashing each other's, searching, claiming, a frenzied attack that turned tender.

Lavishing him with affection, I pulled my mouth away and made a new path with my lips.

Across his arms.

Down his chest.

"Are you ever going to let me go?" He moaned.

"Never."

"You don't have to do this," he whispered.

"You need this."

He reached up and stroked my face showing just how much this was true. In the reflection of that look we shared was proof he cared for me. The way his lips curled into a smile at how much he was enjoying this, savoring me, savoring *us*.

Gripping his wrist, I directed his hand back to his side. "Stay still."

"So, it's like that?" He smirked and rested his hands behind his head, leisurely watching.

I trailed downward, pausing at his groin, nervous about what came next, nervous I'd get it wrong.

"It's okay." His words gave me permission to stop.

Instead, I planted a passing peck there, teasing.

"Here." He rested his hand on mine and together we wrapped our fingers around his wide girth, gripping it, with him guiding me, moving it up and down slowly. "Take me in your mouth," he whispered.

I lapped at the tip, running my fingers around the edge, then took him all the way into my mouth, running my tongue along his hardness until he hit the back of my throat.

"Fuck . . ." His hips tipped a little.

"Is this right?"

"Yes." He smiled a little and pointed beneath where I held him firmly. "Here, too."

While pumping his erection, I dipped my head and sucked his balls, my lips sliding off them and then capturing each one with my mouth, encompassing them, my hand steady on his width, gliding from his girth to his tip in steady strokes.

"I want to see you." He tugged on my sweater.

"When I say."

He let out a frustrated groan, and it morphed into a primal noise of pleasure when I returned my focus to suck his erection. Stretching my lips wide, I accommodated his iron hardness, silky to the touch, a shiny bead of liquid at the tip.

He studied me studying him.

A sticky slickness formed between my thighs, my arousal at fever pitch, this need so great I couldn't deny either of us what came next. Me ripping off my own clothes, hurrying to feel his naked skin against mine.

"Come here," he demanded.

Climbing on top of him, I straddled his thighs, sinking low until my slickness ran along his hardness, rocking back and forth while my thighs trembled.

"I have to touch you," he said, his hand reaching up to caress my exposed breast, his fingers pinching my nipple, eliciting a bliss that traversed all the way down.

A long moan escaped me.

Rising up, holding his stiffness between my thighs, I sank down until the tip pressed a little inside, slicked but unable to go any further. I knew it would be like this, tight at first, fearful of the discomfort, but my body yearned for him to be in me as strongly as a lost soul thirsts for sustenance in a desert.

Cassius seemed to know my struggle as he reached forward and gently applied a fingertip to that small bud between my thighs, circling, flicking faster, until my insides coiled, my body giving up the fight as he pushed his way in, deeper still, filling me completely.

"Don't move," he said.

A flood of pleasure swept away my trepidation. Perhaps it was the way his left hand cupped my breast and his right flickered me down there in delicious circles, but it was easy to surrender to this, to *him*, easy to sink a little lower and rise up just as guarded, riding him, pleasure shuddering into my body and building and building until my jaw was slack and I was staring into his eyes mesmerized at just how incredible this felt.

It had taken all my will, all these acts of kindness, but I finally had him. Like this, making love beneath the stars, safe and surrounded by nature. Shielded from the breeze of the evening, we were hidden and safe in the shade of the tall walls surrounding us.

Head thrown back, a moan of pleasure tore from me as I came and came, a blinding ecstasy possessing my being. Pure and raw and vital as the sensations owned each breath that I had to steal back. Wracked by nothing but the sensations of him.

I slumped onto his chest, and he wrapped his arms around me, his lips pressing my head with endless kisses. He remained buried deep, and it felt delicious.

Lifting my head slightly, I realized, "You didn't finish?"

"Well." He made a gesture.

"Oh . . ." I said as I pulled off him, and then slid back down and gripped him again. My arousal spiked again, exhilarated that my first time had been with him, here, in the sacred place.

"I want us to start again," he said. "A do-over."

"Pretend this is our beginning?" He nodded at my question. "Okay."

"Listen, I can't promise it will be easy, but I'll try."

"And I promise when you're an ass that I'll never forget what you told me about the sun."

"*You* are the sun."

Lost for words, knowing the profoundness of his meaning, too overwhelmed with how far we'd come, I continued on, retracing his length with a gentle touch. Yearning for the peace we both wanted.

Finally, as I continued, he shuddered against me, one hand over his eyes, covering his face as he came, a blissful expression as I seduced his release from him.

"Anya," he cried out.

I had ravished Cassius.

Showering him with affection endlessly, taming his inner demons, or at least doing everything I could to try, soothing the part of him that had once been hurt beyond repair—but now showed promise of healing.

His head crashed onto the grass, and he stared up at the stars, pointing at them. "Orion's Belt."

"It's shining over your home," I said wistfully.

Starting again with kisses, tenderly trailing my affection on his neck, I continued to ravish him. This was the way to show how much I loved him—even if saying it would never happen. The only way to have him see all the possibilities of what we could become.

chapter
TWENTY-SEVEN

Anya

WAKING UP SNUGGLED AGAINST CASSIUS'S WARM BODY in *his* bed felt like I'd slipped into heaven unseen, wanting to stay here like this just watching him sleep.

Dawn was breaking, and although there was so much to learn about Cassius, one thing I'd gotten to see was that first thing in the morning, he loved waking up to fresh coffee. This was how I wanted to spend my days with him, making him happy and nurturing him in all the ways he might have lost out on having a family over the years.

I crept out from underneath the blankets, trying to be as quiet as I could, but apparently, it wasn't enough.

"Where are you going?" His voice was rough and husky with sleep.

I turned back and looked at his sleepy form with his eyes barely open, and a part of me wanted to climb back in and let him have his way with me all over again. Like last night, when we'd moved from the maze to his bedroom, with him carrying me in his arms like he was saving me all over again.

"We're sleeping in until noon," he murmured.

However, as tempting as it was, I whispered, "I'll be right back. Don't get up."

After a brief visit to the bathroom to pee and freshen up, I threw on a pair of leggings and a T-shirt, and once my socks and sneakers were on, I headed downstairs.

As usual, no one was here. It was as if Cassius told them that if I was walking around the house, they needed to be scarce.

Within a minute, I'd brought out the coffee and began my search for the filters, going from cupboard to cupboard and then drawer to drawer.

I paused sharply when I saw a metal key tucked in the corner of one of them. The kind that was the right size for a padlock. There was only one place here that had one of those that I knew of. I reached for it, the need for answers was too strong to ignore. I mean, what would be the harm? He wouldn't need to know I'd slipped out of the house with this.

As soon as I got back, I'd set the coffee maker to begin, happy with the thought Cassius would wake to the scent drifting through the house. But not yet. I wanted him to sleep in for a while first.

Over the last month, I'd spent a great deal of time exploring the property, including the wonderous maze. But there were places I hadn't seen yet, and now that I had Cassius's trust, it was a perfect time to explore.

The early morning sun was the perfect backdrop for my leisurely walk as I breathed in the fresh air and took in the beauty I'd not allowed myself to enjoy.

Striding through the grass in the opposite direction of the swamp, I refused to get too close because all of those creepy creatures lurked in there. I had allowed myself a glimpse a few nights ago when Cassius had taken me out on that small boat. That was enough adventure for one lifetime.

Had my father's men done something in there? There'd be more guilt to swallow if he had.

Later, I'd discuss with Cassius about rescuing Archie. When he was in one of his more agreeable moods. Which I was finding him in more and more.

Following the pathway through the trees, I used the modest steeple for a guide. Careful with each step up the wooden steps toward the door. A heavy feeling was weaving its way through me.

Something inside told me I shouldn't go in.

But a bigger something, something I couldn't put my finger on told me I should brave my fear and see what hid behind the grand entrance to the private chapel. This place felt important like a big part of the missing pieces of the puzzle. Like maybe in this building was a part of the broken man I had come to care for.

Cassius had forbidden me to see what lay within. Which made it all the more intriguing. But that was when I'd first arrived in this house.

I eased the key into the lock, proud of myself to see it fit.

With things different between us, this wouldn't be frowned upon, surely.

So instead of waiting for permission, I followed the saying, 'it's easier asking for forgiveness.' And we were closer now, more trusting.

The door was heavier than expected. The wood, thick and aged. Time had done nothing to soften the hard lines.

Just inside, I took in the dark and dusty sight. The scent of mildew and mustiness hit me, and something else.

Death.

I took the steps down even though they threatened to crack and crumble beneath my feet. They didn't look safe. They led to a torn and faded red carpet that was covered with slippery green moss.

Braving to go farther into the dilapidated chapel, it reminded me of the place time had forgotten. Dust particles danced high before the faded stained glass windows.

I glanced at the banister surrounding the altar at the front. It looked even worse in its faded and rotting state with half the spindles missing. Walking down the center, I looked from left to right—

Someone had done this.

More damage had been wreaked than just the hand of nature.

Though nature had woven herself into every corner, every crevice, and every surface. The air smelled as though all living creatures, including rodents and bugs, that had once scurried in had been unable to find their way out.

No life could live here.

This place reminded me of an aging photograph.

A tomb draped in cobwebs.

Tiny streams of light fought against the dirt, allowing little visibility.

An eerie silence surrounded the stale air.

Each step I took creaked.

Why had this place been left to rot?

Moving over to one of the statues, I peered up at what had once been a marble sculpture of Mary Magdalene. Swiping a layer of soot off her feet, it left a dark smudge on my palm.

This place was filthy. The saint who'd once had a prominent position must have meant something to someone once. Maybe Cassius's mom had placed her here.

Beside my footprints were the fresh prints of a man's shoe, proving someone had been here recently. Standing where I stood. Perhaps he, too, had looked up at the saint with equal awe—or maybe with sadness that she'd been so badly neglected.

There were so many questions. I didn't know where to start to make sense of any of this. One thing was for sure, this had once been a family sanctuary, and it had carried weight and meaning. And if I guessed correctly, my father's men had done this.

Leaving Cassius to abandon it. Or maybe he came in here from time to time to stoke his fury and keep his hate constant.

This was a crypt of devastating memories.

A warm sense of purpose overtook me. I could make this place a secret project. While Cassius was at work, I'd sneak in here and clean up this place. It would give me something of value to do.

There had to be something to use to clean it.

I looked around, and at the back of the chapel, I found a closet door and opened it cautiously, terrified something might scurry out at me. Inside laid a discarded, beaten-up broom. Reaching in, I grabbed it and brought it out, giving it a try. I wiped a streak of dust off the floor and made my way along.

This would take months. Still, there'd be more cleaning products in the house. I'd make it a wonderful surprise for him. Maybe even bring him in blindfolded and watch his reaction to all my work.

The door creaked on its hinges.

"What the fuck are you doing?" Cassius's voice bellowed from across the way, cutting through the silence like a serrated knife aiming for bone.

I went to answer, but he cut me off.

"I warned you never to come in here!" His rage was palpable.

He'd paused on the threshold, his eyes wide as they watched where I'd attempted to sweep, as though it was me who'd made all this mess. "What are you doing?"

"I'm trying to make it beaut—"

"You had no right." He swept his hands through the air. "No fucking right." He pivoted fast, heading out and slamming the door on the way with a bang.

The walls shuddered, dust powdering up. The building creaked and strained as though the building itself had come alive with monstrous memories.

Dread drenched the air.

I stood still.

Shocked and bruised at his outrage.

But even as I trembled, I knew. Knew I had to find him. Had to search for him.

A part of me warned that I should let him calm down first, but I hated the thought that I'd done anything to bring him pain.

Being with Cassius and understanding him was like learning to speak a language you never heard before. One you rarely interpreted. The only way to truly understand him was to coax a meaning to all of this out of him.

Leaving the dust and the mayhem, I retraced my steps. Too upset to glance back.

It took me a while to find him as I wandered back through the house.

Music carried.

The notes squirmed and twisted with the base of an electric guitar. Not his, but something familiar, something like Archie had listened to, with its raw lyrics and dangerous drums. The singer screeched his agony.

Drawing me closer.

I found Cassius in a room I'd never seen before. Down a hallway and hidden. I hadn't discovered it yet. Maybe a place he didn't want me in, but I couldn't stop myself.

I needed to see him.

I'm the moth, and he's the flame.

I needed to stare into his eyes where he can't lie. Where he can't hide, and I could see the truth.

I pushed the door open, unseen.

He was holding out an electric guitar. Staring at it. The lyrics of the song morphed into something worse, ramping up the torturous tension. Notes wrapped themselves around me. "Closer" by Nine Inch Nails.

And I knew his pain. Felt *his* pain.

His agony was suffocating.

Tears burned behind my eyes, but I refused to let them fall.

Our eyes collided. I was like a deer caught in headlights.

The moment happened slowly . . .

The guitar was flying through the air.

Smashing against the wall.

Broken into smithereens as slivers of wood and wires and plastic shards went flying.

Time stood still.

If hate had a name, it would be the look Cassius was giving me. It tore me in two. He ripped me into shreds with a fitful glare.

He squeezed his eyes shut. His face contorted with confusion. "I'm in the house. This is now. I'm in the present moment. The past has no hold. The future isn't here yet." He was talking to himself, trying to coax his clear and present panic away. "Just breathe. That's all that's expected."

"That's all," I whispered. "Just breathe, Cassius." I tried to comfort him, but he was like a wild animal after an attack, like a creature unsafe and too close to run from.

A sob escaped my lips. My chest heaved as I tried to draw in a breath. Coldness edged its way over me and through me, causing my skin to chill like ice. It shattered me into nothingness as I became the abyss of whose eyes I was staring into—his.

"Anya . . ." His voice broke.

A look consumed his eyes. One I hadn't seen before. Almost like . . . remorse. His chest heaved with regret, heaving with a thousand emotions tearing him apart.

"I'm—I'm sorry." He looked lost.

And at that moment, I was reminded that his father had died here, and out there, in the garden, his mom had passed away at the hands of my father. He'd stayed here ever since, even as a grieving young man to endure the loss.

Quickly, he closed the gap between us almost seeming calm. All of his rage was gone. His hands lifted in a motion of defeat.

Yet, like a scared animal, I was still afraid, and my soul was crushed by his words and actions. "Don't—" The emotions I had held back released in a rush, my hands trembling from the emotions swirling inside of me.

He was beside me quickly, taking me into his arms, holding me in a tight embrace. "I didn't mean it. I didn't mean to scare you."

Kiss upon kiss was placed on my forehead.

And then a kiss on my nose.

A press of his lips to mine.

My jaw trembled.

"I didn't mean to scream," he said softer.

"Why did you?" I heaved a sob.

And then another.

I turned to look away at the floor, but he placed a fingertip under my jaw. Our eyes locked, and I could see the agony.

"You tried to clean it?" He swallowed his apology.

I didn't speak, just stared up at his beautiful, sad face.

"It was inside that chapel I lost the last part of me."

Reaching up, I cupped his face, tracing his lines, trying to show him the love and tenderness I had never seen. "I'm sorry." I leaned forward, placing my lips on his jaw. "I'm sorry," I kissed him again. "I'm so sorry."

He held me away. "It's not your fault."

"No, but it's why I'm here."

"It is."

"And I want to be here. With you. Help me help you purge your pain."

"Nothing can."

"What happened back there?"

He looked off, eyes full of anguish. "You can't go in there."

"Cassius, you have to tell me why. You have to open up to me."

Torment twisted his face into a kind of pain I'd never seen him wear before. "I can't."

"Please, tell me." I moved toward him and held his hand, coaxing.

"You will hate me as much as I hate myself."

"Not possible," I said quietly.

"He wasn't dead." Cassius swallowed. "My father."

"What do you mean?"

"When I held my mom as she lay dying, she told me Dad was dead. That he'd been killed back in the house. She really believed that. But he wasn't gone."

"What do you mean?"

"He was held at gunpoint, but they hadn't killed him yet. After Stephen left the maze, after he'd given up looking for me, he went back for him. My dad. He escorted him at gunpoint into the chapel. He shot him with a silencer in the head. That's why we didn't hear it. Left his body behind the altar. I didn't see my father lying there. Even after I carried my mom back to the chapel. Not at first."

"How do you know he escorted him at gunpoint?"

"Stephen told me himself, when I went to face off with him. A few weeks after he'd killed my parents. Stephen boasted my father had begged him not to harm us. He told me that my father asked him to take his life instead of ours." Cassius reached out for something and leaned on the wall to prove this was all too much. "While I was cowering in the maze, my father was still alive. I could have saved him."

"Your mom thought he was dead."

"It was my job to know."

"You couldn't have known. You were saving your sister."

"I could have saved them both." He drew in a sharp breath. "I'll never forgive myself."

"You're not looking at it the right way, Cassius."

"How do you mean?"

"Your father saved you. This was his legacy. Even when his life was threatened, he didn't tell Stephen about the secret place within the maze. He didn't give up his children. He was your father right until the end. It was his job to protect you. And he did."

"He was the best father." His tears welled and fell down his face.

"He really was."

"I've never told anyone this." He pressed his hand to his heart as though trying to hold that beating muscle together himself, trying to prevent it from breaking apart irrevocably.

"I want to know," I soothed. "So we can be here for each other."

He swiped away a tear. "I broke my favorite guitar."

"I'll get you another. Or maybe I'll punish you by buying drums instead."

"You'd be punishing yourself."

"True."

"I'm sorry for everything."

"I'm offering a lifetime of forgiveness." I swiped a stray tear off his face. "If you're willing to forgive me, too. For being that man's . . . daughter."

"You can't choose your parents."

Tell him, tell him now . . . That I wasn't from that monster.

"You're nothing like him." He tucked a strand of hair behind my ear.

He was in no state for me to bring all of that up now. Maybe he'd come to forgive me for waiting so long to share this. He wasn't ready to hear it now. And anyway, I didn't want Stephen to take up one more second or thought of our time. He'd already drawn enough oxygen from the room.

"What do you want?" I lulled him. "What can I get you to make you feel better?"

"Just you."

"I want to take away your pain."

"What do you need?"

"You know what I need, Cassius. Something tells me you need it, too."

He gave a nod of understanding.

"Fuck me," I coaxed him.

He scrunched a lock of my hair behind my nape. "Anya."

"Use me. Kiss me. Give it to me. Let me help you feel better. Let me heal you."

"What if I hurt you?"

"Hurt me. Take it all. All of me."

He looked at me warily.

And then his mouth crashed against mine.

chapter
TWENTY-EIGHT

Anya

CASSIUS CARRIED ME OUT OF THE MUSIC ROOM IN HIS ARMS. There came a flood of relief that we'd both made it out of there in one piece emotionally. I'd glimpsed him at his worst, yet, somehow, I'd found the strength to soothe him. To bring him down from the heights of fury. Because I'd glimpsed his pain in all its raw cruelty. Coming back from all he'd experienced was nearly impossible. Yet every journey had a first step, a beginning, and we would just have to find ours.

He'd shared with me his most shameful secret. And I knew, knew with all my heart it had been the catalyst for all that had followed in his life. What had motivated him to harm my family. That the fallout of what Stephen had done had almost verged on irreparable damage—*almost*.

With me snuggling up against his chest as he carried me, nestling my face into his nape, I breathed him in. He carried me all the way to the room he'd first put me in when I'd arrived in this vast home.

I gave him a quizzical glance as he laid me on the bed. "Why are we in here?" I asked with a jolt of uncertainty.

He gave a nod as though all this was already thought out. "Trust me."

"I do, but . . ."

"Be right back." He stepped away and headed for the door.

"Where are you going?"

"Give me a second."

Sitting up, curious why he'd left me here, I considered climbing off the bed and leaving this room. Unable to shake the discomfort of lying here with all the stark memories that slithered and sloped in the corners.

The space where that broken mirror had hung on the wall, a terrible reminder of what I'd done to it when I'd first arrived.

I didn't like this room at all—in fact, I'd gotten chills each time I'd passed by it.

Cassius flew back in with a smile on his face. He held up a foil packet. Of course, a condom. He threw it onto the side table.

He closed the space between us and pressed a fingertip to my lips. "I'm starting in reverse. All the places I hurt you in this house, I'm going to make you feel good. So all you remember are the good times."

"Seriously?"

He nodded. "Go with me on this, okay, like I did with you in the maze."

"What happens now?" I asked wistfully.

His brow furrowed as his thoughts spun around his beautiful mind. He grabbed the back of my head with an iron grip. "I've wanted you from the first time I saw you."

"But I thought—"

"Don't say it. Let me make it up to you. Ask your forgiveness the only way I can." He gave a ghost of a smile.

His palm brushed over my throat and glided toward my left breast, and my nipple beaded beneath the contact of the pinch of his hand, causing arousal in my core. His hand moving downward still, sweeping over my abdomen, exploring.

I lifted my T-shirt and eased out of my jeans with his help, both of us scrambling to undress.

Shirts flew.

His pants and my bra came off next.

Reaching low, I eased my panties off my hips and nudged them down my thighs, and he helped with them the rest of the way until my underwear was off.

He stole a glance. Dragging his teeth along his bottom lip, he studied me there. My sex throbbed in anticipation of his touch. I let my thighs fall apart, inviting his teasing.

With us both naked, he lay on top of me with his warm body heating my skin.

His fingers trailed downward, and the sensation made my thighs tremble, my mind scrambling to grasp how we'd gone from arguing to this—me aroused and surrendering with each inhale, thighs spreading in invitation.

Cassius seemed to sense my responses before they happened, the way he commanded my body with each touch, the way he set me alight. The more his fingers explored, the more my body reacted to having him caress me the way he did. He knew how to touch me, with equal parts firm and gentle strokes. I imagined he also knew how to find the exact spot that would bring the most pleasure.

His lips trailed along my collarbone and tickled my skin as he buried his face in my neck and nuzzled, kissing me tenderly there, sending shivers.

I brought my hand up to cup my breast, the tingles too much to bear. His hands pressed over mine. I slipped my hand away and let his rest there, flushed with the pang of pressure as it beaded beneath his palm. He circled a pointed fingertip and it sent shudders of arousal sharp and vivid into my core.

"You like this?" he teased.

I nodded. I loved it, every second, every touch, every caress, being leisurely stroked and nurtured as though this was my first time. Only my first time was in the maze when I'd done something similar to him. And he'd let me. Now, I was seeing how a real man makes love, with the skill of an artist who knows how to carve marble. How to trace the natural curves and rivulets, brushing this way and that, chipping away all resistance.

My skin the form he'd mastered as he teased and flirted with his fingers, seducing and lulling, sparking the brightest passion.

I couldn't speak another word—couldn't let them escape my lips because he'd stolen my breath away—he'd taken one of my nipples into his mouth and was sucking, using his tongue to thrum against the sensitive tissue. One breast and then the other, his tongue was darting between them, flicking before nipping with his teeth and sending an erotic pleasure between my thighs.

He leaned up and reached for my hand, kissing my fingers tenderly, and worked along my wrist, forearm, and then leaned in to run his tongue beneath my armpit, continuing on between my breasts and downward, downward still, until he reached my abdomen when he ran his tongue along my public bone and lower toward my core.

Our eyes met as he said, "Relax."

With a nod, I told him I would and felt myself sink deeper into this bliss he wanted to give me.

The sensations he elicited were delicate at first. He flicked slowly, circling, and then frantic as he devoured me like a delicious flower, blossoming beneath the thrill.

I opened my legs wider for him.

"My Anya." His voice was husky, his breath warm.

His mouth possessed me there, playing, teasing, and flicking, hungrily eating my secret place, causing my back to arch and needing a release more than anything.

Spellbound . . .

Each time he lowered his defenses and let me in had felt like a victory. This, now, here, felt like destiny.

He continued ravaging me with affection between my thighs until I was soaking wet. His raw craving revealed in his obsessive owning of my body, kissing and licking along my flesh like he was mapping me out to return to later. Memorize the way I responded to each sublime touch that led to him possessing me.

Lifting my head off the pillow and glancing down, seeing his rock hardness rising up like a threat—the kind I would beg for if he made me. It was so engorged, revealing he was just as turned on.

Gently and slowly, he slid one finger into me, watching my reaction and judging how deep to go. Moving in and out slowly at first, and then grinding out a perfect rhythm, bringing a never-ending bliss.

Shaking my head, whipping my hair from side to side, proving I was wanton for more. Unable to hide this rising desire.

All air in my lungs snatched away.

My orgasm detonated into a million pieces, his flicking tongue possessing me, possessing every conscious thought. Writhing and squirming beneath the way he obliterated everything except these sensations bursting through me, surging like a life force that could turn time forward and back, turning me inside out and somehow, someway, moving me onward into a different future.

Claiming me as *his*.

I reveled in his power and exulted in his brilliant control. His ability to take all that pain and weave it into something sacred, something that would sustain us.

As I came down to earth, he slowed the rhythm, seemingly respectful of how sensitive my flesh felt after his minstrations.

Shuddering still, I turned my eyes on him as he withdrew his fingers. This roiling passion for him and for a life with him, made my heart soar.

My lungs were still trying to drag in air.

I knew he'd wanted me to feel safe here in this room, feel cared for and protected. To undo all that had gone before. In so many ways, it was happening.

He moved away, but before I could protest, I saw him stretching for the bedside table. He grabbed up the condom and tore it open, rolling the sheath over his impressive length and throwing the packet playfully over the bed.

Cassius climbed on top of me, using his elbows to hold up the weight of his body.

He eased into me slowly.

He was studying my reaction to gauge how much I could take.

When he tipped his hips ever so slightly, that familiar blinding pain hit me between my legs. But even still, I widened my thighs and coaxed him on, needing more of him.

With a nod, I let him know I was ready for more, more him, more of this, more of everything he was willing to give.

He thrust into me, slow and sure, forceful and with passion. His length began a steady glide in and out, slick against my arousal, driving me toward the edge again. My mouth gaped with the pleasure as a rush of fullness and bliss exploded inside me.

Pouting through these delicious sensations. A luscious intensifying of fiery passion burning within. He leaned low and pressed his mouth to mine, his tongue searching my mouth as he took me harder still. Battling with mine as I fought to say with a kiss what my words had failed to say, that I wanted this, needed this, needed him.

Cassius was giving me the intimacy I'd craved in those lonely nights when I'd first arrived here. A passion awakening alongside these untapped emotions surging with greater intensity. Like my heart was opening, full and wanting of the love he offered, even as it was jagged and broken and fragile.

A ghost of a smile touched his lips. "Tell me what you need."

My lips parted in a teasing pout. "Harder."

His eyes studied mine as he ground his hips and thrust deeper. "Like this?"

"It feels . . ." I breathed. He pounded me with an intense beat. "Oh, yes, don't stop. Not ever."

His hand slid low between us, and he beat out a stunning rhythm on that small bud that responded to his touch.

A soft moan escaped, revealing my rising pleasure. Shuddering in response to the way he was playing with me, his fingers flicking to a beat that felt like a dark spell being cast on my sex.

My throaty groan met by his triumphant stare.

Looking down, I followed his line of sight and zeroed in on where all that pleasure was focused, the place where my body was on fire with want.

He, too, looked down at where he was entering me. "Fuck."

My nipples were so hard they panged with desire. When he raised his gaze, he caught their pebbling, too, and dragged his teeth over his bottom lip. "God, you're so beautiful."

My arousal continued to build at his touch. At his thrusts, hot and heavy with a demanding tempo. My thighs trembled as his hips rocked and pumped.

Staring into his eyes, revealing how turned on he made me. How far to the edge he was pushing me. Keeping me revved so near to falling into an abyss.

Refusing to break eye contact, I defiantly held my own as I held onto my power so that he could see I was strong enough to hold us both up.

A long throaty groan of desire escaped my throat. Never wanting this feverish pleasuring to cease.

His thumb's circling stilled. "Anya."

"Yes?"

"Come for me."

Heady from his command, jaw gaping, and mind free-falling, unable to fight this orgasm, fight my feelings for him, struggling for air, my pelvis begging for deeper penetration that came with each pummel. Our lips hovering so close his breath merged with mine.

His left hand grabbed my throat. "Like this?"

"Yes."

Feeling like his possession of me was complete.

His voice was husky. "Because you're mine now."

"I was always yours." *And I always would be.*

His thrusts were relentless as the intensity grew, capturing me in its thrall.

Effortlessly, I chased after my climax, this blinding pleasure holding me in a spiral, sustaining the ecstasy, stealing what felt like my last breath. Seemingly dragging me along through an erotic wilderness, swept up into a dream, I was too gone, shuddering through erotic sensations that made us one.

His completely.

Just as he was now mine.

chapter
TWENTY-NINE

Cassius

ANYA LAY FAST ASLEEP WITH HER HEAD RESTING ON MY chest. Locks of her soft hair spilling like still water over me. It felt like a drug when she touched me. Being in her presence was enough to calm me.

As she rested, I allowed my thoughts to carry me back to the carnage of the hours before.

To the room where it all started for us. Had I purged the darkness living inside of me? If anyone could help me, it would be Anya.

Her eyelids blinked open.

"I'm sorry." I said the words that I'd been dying to tell her as she slept.

She stretched languidly. "You already apologized."

"I know." I let out a regretful sigh. "It doesn't excuse what happened."

"You were angry. You were hurt."

I pulled her in and pressed my lips to her forehead. "I was, but that wasn't you. I wasn't angry with you. You can't condemn the daughter for sins of the father."

"But isn't that why you brought me here?"

"I do feel like I saved you from him. Even if that wasn't my intention." Because my intention was catastrophic. Living with this would never be easy. "You." I looked into her eyes. "You've changed me."

She stared up like she wanted to believe me but wasn't sure.

"You asked me to tell you, so I will. I want to show you ... me." I eased myself from beneath her and swung my legs off the bed and got up. Getting dressed, I gestured for her to do the same.

Then I took her small hand in mine. "Do you trust me?"

"I do."

"Come with me."

"Where?"

"We have to go back."

Her eyes widened in concern as she interpreted my meaning. After a few seconds, she agreed with a nod.

Together, hand in hand, I walked us back to the place where it all ended for me. Where my life as a young man changed irrevocably. Where I became the man I was now.

Together, we went back to the chapel.

We walked along the well-worn pathway to the place that had once brought joy but had morphed into a prison for my soul, where it was destined to be trapped forever—*before her.*

Before this beautiful woman came into my life. Agreeably, I had brought her here, but she wanted to stay, which felt like an unseen miracle.

Anya, this young woman who carefully stepped over the threshold with me to the most haunted location on the property, one where the ghosts continued to savage me day in and day out, cleaving to my being as though I was the only vessel for their revenge.

The place was desolate and, at the same time, filled with chaos. Debris was strewn across the aisle, with not one patch free of disarray, paying tribute to all the sins cast amongst the crumbling walls.

I leaned back against one of the pews. The only one not touched by a sledgehammer. By my hand, no less.

Folding my arms across my chest, I said, "You were going to try to clean this place up?"

She nodded. "Seems silly now."

"No, it was more than I could ever have asked for. More than I deserve."

"Don't say that."

"I'm sorry to bring you back in here but I think it's the right place to do this."

"Do what?"

"Tell you what really happened that day."

Whispers of memories scurried out of the shadows.

She nodded, encouraging me to go on and turning to look for a place to sit on a half-destroyed pew. She gave a shy glance my way as though knowing she was drawing attention to what I'd done to the seat all those years ago. There was enough there for her to get comfortable.

"You're the best thing to ever happen to this place," I whispered.

"Oh, Cassius, we can rebuild. If it's something you want to do." Unsure if I'd ever be capable of that, I drew in a deep, cleansing breath. "This was the chapel of the estate. Passed down from generation to generation. A part of our family history." I smirked. "A good old Catholic, Italian family. During the plague of the 1920s, when it was unsafe to attend church, my ancestors built this so they could pray safely." I drew in a sharp breath. "It meant so much to my mom."

Anya fixed her attention on me, never wavering.

"Anyway, I wasn't supposed to run the business. I wasn't supposed to be involved. I never wanted that for myself. I wanted to give myself to something different."

"Like what?"

"I loved music, but I loved science, too. Mom used to joke I'd make a great doctor because I was always fascinated by science. I never got a choice."

She looked around as though trying to tie all the pieces together. "Why do you hate this place?" A tremor in her tone.

Those same old emotions coming at me like a freight train—

Throwing me into the fray, as though I'm back there again. Looking beyond the pews, seeing a blurry image—me, as though having an out-of-body experience and witnessing it all over again. My former, younger self was standing at the altar.

"My father."

I moved away from Anya and started to pace. "As you know, I found my mother laying where we left her. She'd been dead for hours. I picked her up and carried her in here and lay her over there, near that pew. That's when I saw him." I gestured to where my father's body had been discovered. "Dad had been shot in the head. All that time that I had been hiding in the maze like a pussy, my father was alive."

"Cassius, you were fourteen."

"I don't give a fuck. I could have saved him. I *should* saved him. Instead, he was brought in here and killed. He died alone."

Anya's eyes were filled with sorrow. "I'm so sorry."

"Then I went back for my sister and brought Sofia to sit with me in here to wait for the police."

"Why didn't they arrest Stephen?"

"There weren't any witnesses left alive to testify to seeing him here. Only Sofia, and she couldn't speak. She couldn't testify it was him. As I'd been hiding in the maze and merely heard gunshots, I was an unreliable witness. Even after telling the detectives what had transpired out on the swamp only hours before."

"Why didn't they believe you?"

"Stephen had witnesses who put him at another part of the city."

"They lied for him?"

"Most people would. If they wanted to live."

"After everyone had gone. After the police, the medics whose only job was to take the bodies away, I came back here."

"Where was Sofia?"

"Hospital."

"You were alone here?"

"I refused to leave."

"What about your friend Ridley?"

"His father kept him away. The only reason his dad survived was he left minutes before Stephen and his men got here. He'd stopped me from seeing my dad. From warning him."

"He passed on that guilt to Ridley?"

"After Ridley graduated law school, he came to work for me. I assumed he felt obligated to do what he could to protect me after his father had inadvertently gotten mine killed. Though I've told Ridley I'm not sure anyone could have stopped Glassman."

She looked around, aghast when she realized it had been me who'd done all this damage.

"I came back to the chapel trying to make sense of it, but I couldn't find anything. Couldn't find any meaning behind it. So, I made it make sense. In my own head, anyway. I found a sledgehammer and—" I scanned the chapel to say the rest.

"Even the statue?" she said breathlessly. "To find meaning?"

"I tried and failed to, so I punished God. Tore down his house. He broke me, so I broke his sacred home. Tore it to shreds. Allowed this place to die. Because at that moment, I couldn't have faith. Couldn't find anything to believe in. My only goal from that day out was to avenge their death. And since then, I haven't . . ."

"You haven't what?"

"I haven't been able to leave this chapel."

"What do you mean?"

"In my mind, I wake up here every day. In my dreams, I'm standing over there before St. Mary Magdalene. My nightmares are all here. Each waking hour I'm in here. A part of me never leaves." Shaking my head, I admitted my truth. "What you see here around us, is me."

She took a few seconds to process my words, trying to make sense of the way I'd annihilated everything that had been sacred.

"No," she soothed. "This is just a building. A structure. Where terrible things happened. This is not you. You're more than this. You're remarkable and profound and have so much to offer."

"I can't find my way out," I admitted it, *finally*.

She took my hand and led me toward the door.

The bright afternoon light met us on the other side, spilling over us, casting a brightness that I soaked into my bones as though for the first time. A shift within, a sense that perhaps, just perhaps, I'd be able to separate from what clung to me in that place, in the hidden corners, in the center, and lower still in the floorboards deep underground.

Together, we made our way back along the pathway, putting distance between ourselves and the chapel, and for the first time when I stopped to look back, it looked different.

"What if it never lets me go?" My throat tightened.

"It's you who must let that place go, Cassius. Your faith never died in the chapel." Anya squeezed my hand. "It was always inside you, waiting for you to draw on it again."

My fingers traced the sun inked on my wrist as though the sign had always been with me.

She nodded. "The answer was always there."

Together, in silence, we drew our faces up to let the sunbeams warm us as we continued back toward the house, forever changed.

chapter
THIRTY

Anya

ASSIUS HAD TURNED OFF ALL THE CAMERAS IN THE house—telling me he wanted us to have a certain amount of privacy from now on. They'd remain on the outskirts of the perimeter, carefully monitored by two of his men. We'd be able to have more freedom to do many things we didn't want others to see.

I made myself busy during the days that followed, searching out every single room and making sure I knew every part of this house, just as I was getting to know Cassius better. He'd gone to the office for a few hours, leaving me to spend more time in the chapel tidying up, but he'd at least admitted to himself we'd need a crew to help with the major structures and furnishings. We probably had a year of work ahead of us.

Taking a break, I'd come into the kitchen to grab a chicken salad for lunch. Standing by the counter, I poured hot water into a mug to make tea.

Peering out the window, I watched a familiar car pull up the driveway and park. Ridley, the slick lawyer, was swaggering out of it toward the house.

By the time I made my way to the front door, he'd entered and gone off somewhere. It didn't sit right with me knowing he was here and Cassius wasn't. But I'd been reassured countless times we could trust him, and he was an old family friend—so I held on to that fact with the kind of faith only reserved for the brave.

Eventually, I found him. And there he was, sitting behind a desk in a swanky office. Comfortable enough to throw his feet up on the desk and use the landline to make a call. Ridley raised a pointed finger to warn me to stay quiet as he finished up.

Standing before him, I folded my arms across my chest and waited impatiently. Taking in the sophistication of the private space. The ornate ceiling. The crown molding. The elegant glass desk in the middle.

It all screamed feminine. A stark difference to Cassius's office, which was understated and masculine. Other than the powerful man who resided within it when he was here, it was void of emotion.

This office screamed of years of use . . .

A sinking feeling weaved its way through me, followed by a protective one.

I took a step forward, hand on my hip. "Does he know you're in here?"

It didn't take a rocket scientist to know this had probably belonged to Cassius's mother.

"I don't think he would like—" I started to say.

Ridley lifted his hand up to silence me. "You don't need to worry about Cassius. . ."

"Don't I?"

He placed the phone down. "Not where it involves me."

I raised an eyebrow, challenging him to tell me more.

"How are you, Anya?"

"What are you doing in here?"

"Hello to you, too." He smirked.

"Does he know you're on the estate?"

"Excuse me?" He pushed up and sat on the edge of the desk.

"Look, I know we had a rough start, me failing to get you out and all that."

"You did the right thing."

"Well, not so sure about that now." He shook his head slightly. "Anyway, Cassius tells me things are good between you two."

"What else has he told you?" I gave him a suspicious glance.

"Look, I've known this family for a long time. My father was his dad's attorney. By the way you're looking at me, I can come to the conclusion that you don't trust me."

"I feel protective toward him."

"Considering everything you've been through, that's admirable. I want you to know I'm not the enemy. Neither is Cas."

"I know."

"It must be hard to trust anyone after what you've been through."

I shook that off. "Cassius told me how much you did for him after his parents died. How grateful he is."

"Well, he's like a brother to me."

"I know what really happened. To his family." I stepped closer. "About the part your dad played in that."

"Not sure I like your tone."

"I felt comfortable enough to be honest."

"Seeing as you're shooting daggers, I know you know the truth. The day Cassius tried to speak with his father, it was mine who sent him away."

"I'm sure he meant well."

He shrugged. "I've spent every day of my life trying to make it up to him. The guilt eats at me every single fucking day. Sometimes, we make mistakes. Sometimes people don't forgive."

"But he doesn't blame you."

"Only himself."

"What do you do for Cassius exactly?"

"I try to keep him on the straight and narrow." He shrugged. "I look the other way."

"But you've done bad things for him?"

"I make a call now and again."

"As bad as what my father does?"

He went to speak and then seemed to think better of it.

"I'm nothing like my father."

"I heard that. And we're grateful you're not in league with your parents, which I would like to say, is a relief, because I don't know you, Anya, but the little I do, I'm glad you see things as they are and not as you hope them to be."

"How do you mean?"

"We're not out of the woods yet."

"Because you don't want to have to kill me?" I tested a theory. "In case I don't do right by Cassius."

He let out a laugh.

"What's funny?"

"I'm his lawyer. I don't do any of the killing." Just when the words settled heavily in my stomach, he winked at me.

That was a threat—raw and real and without any lines blurred. He'd made it clear that fucking up wasn't an option. Not for me, anyway.

The room became bathed in a deathly silence. Awkward and heavy and desperate for one of us to break it.

"Anya, you obviously came in here to find me, so please tell me how I can help you."

Just do it, I scolded myself. *Ask him.*

This isn't like you to act shy. . .

"I need your help."

"With . . .?"

"I need to get a message to my brother."

He hesitated. "What would you want me to tell him?"

"That I'm okay. That I'm going to rescue him from that house." I just wasn't sure when.

"Cassius can't know."

"I'm not sure that's such a good idea."

"If you can find a way without Stephen or my mom finding out. Maybe get a staff member to deliver it. The gardener would do it. I can give you their names."

He raised his hand. "Stephen would shoot me on sight."

"If you were careful. . ."

"And then Cassius would gut me like a fucking fish."

"I don't think he would."

"That's because you don't know him."

"He's changed."

"I'm sure you're a great influence. But you can't take the monster out of the man once it's moved all its furniture in."

"What the hell does that mean?"

"It means, watch yourself around him, Anya. He's got a dark side."

"I know."

"I don't think you do, sweetheart."

"Don't patronize me. Don't call me that."

"How does Anya Glassman sound? Is there a better ring to it?"

He didn't need to hit so low. "I'm nothing like my father."

"Time will tell."

"There are more secrets about me than you could ever learn in a lifetime," I blurted out.

Again, that quiet.

That slow twisting of his mouth into a smirk. "Go. Do something. You cook, I hear? Go bake some cookies . . . or . . ."

Pursing my lips, I held back on the tirade I was on the verge of spewing—that he may consider me untrustworthy, but I wasn't the one who got his father shot in the head like Ridley's untrustworthy dad. Yet Cassius had found it in his heart to let his son into his life.

Or maybe he was just keeping his enemies close.

I turned to go, pausing by the door. "Oh, by the way, we need to buy Cassius a new guitar."

Ridley looked surprised. "A guitar? Cassius already has one."

"About that . . . he kind of doesn't. Anymore—" I bit my lower lip.

"What did you do?" he gritted out.

I shook my head. "It wasn't me. Not really. Well. . . "

He let out a long, drawn-out sigh. "Explain."

And I did, I told him all about the music room, about how I found him holding it and how he threw it when he saw me standing there, as though I was the reason for all that fury. In so many ways, I suppose I was.

I didn't tell him about the chapel.

Or what happened within.

Because that was just ours. And there was no reason for anyone else to hear Cassius's confession. Or to know all that had unfolded since between us. All the passion, all the healing, and all the love that flowed between us. Because those sacred moments had to remain pure, just between us, and not shared with anyone else.

This was me protecting Cassius the best way I knew how.

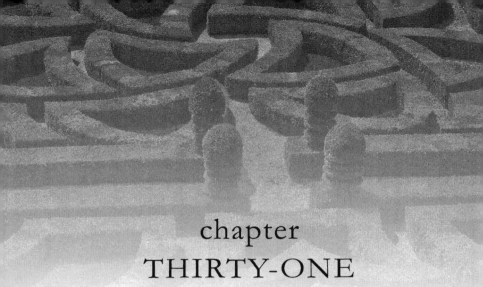

chapter
THIRTY-ONE

Cassius

"I HAVE SOMETHING TO SHOW YOU!" ANYA GREETED ME at the door, her face lit up with excitement.

"And I have something to give you." Without giving her a chance to protest, I grabbed her by the waist, flung her over my shoulder, and carried her through the house.

Work, well, that was something I'd tried to do this afternoon, but after fighting these roiling desires and this fantasy that wouldn't let up, I'd just come home early to be with her. This, this was as dark as any obsession went—me trying to unravel all the damage I'd done by reenacting all the different versions of it. As if we'd have lived through different circumstances in other lives. This was me trying to put all the broken pieces back together.

"What's happening?" She laughed, her joy palpable.

The days and hours that unfolded since the first time in the maze had left me wanting to do nothing but worship her.

"Wait, where are we going?" Her tone turned nervous.

Understandably, as I was carrying her down the stairs that led to the dungeon. With her still over my shoulder, I headed toward the last cell in a long line of prisons. Putting her down, I watched her reaction.

Which was predictably horrified. "What is this?"

Without giving her time to react, I nudged her backward into the cell, towering over her, lifting her hands above her head, and pressing them into the brick. Caging her in, I used the force of my will to overpower her.

I could have sworn her heartbeat thundered against my chest like a trapped sparrow. But this was me baring my soul, and if she was to love all of me, she'd have to love my darkness, too. If we were to endure in a relationship, she'd have to accept every piece of me.

Taking her mouth, kissing her like this moment was all we had, pillaging, swirling my tongue, savoring her taste, obsessively controlling, fucking her mouth with mine until her moan proved she was relenting to my passionate attack.

Her breaths were short and sharp as she recovered when I broke away.

Lowering to my knees, I glanced up at her, watching her reaction to the way I unzipped her jeans and tugged them down her hips.

"I won't have to stay in here?" she whispered, eyes wide with uncertainty.

"No, but you will have to remain very still. Understand?"

"I'll try."

"It's not a request," I demanded.

Her exhale sharp and sudden, she darted her gaze around the cell as she understood what this was. She frantically nodded, almost begging for it.

"I'm glad we understand each other."

She shifted her thighs farther apart.

Which was all I needed by way of invitation. I dived into her, burying my face between her thighs, devouring her. I consumed everything she willingly gave as she tipped her hips forward, demanding more as I fucked her with my tongue.

"Oh, God," she moaned.

Her long, drawn-out sighs and whispers echoed as she came hard, shuddering against me.

Pushing to my feet, I leaned in and kissed her again, sharing her taste with her.

Eventually, I pulled away and rested my forehead against hers in the silence, letting this moment convey what I wanted her to know. "I put you down here. In the cold and the dark. Anya, I'm so—"

"Stop. I've already forgiven you. That was then, and this is now." She smiled so wide it almost shattered my heart with its intensity.

Helping her, I pulled up her panties and jeans to redress her.

Taking her hand, I led her out of there.

"Does this place really flood?" she asked as she kept up with my long strides.

A grimace was my answer, considering I had fucking locked her cell gate for a night.

"Clearly, I have issues," I mumbled.

"Hadn't noticed."

I bowed before her. "I'm the king of fucked up. Welcome to my world."

"Okay, shut up and listen for a second."

"This is how you win me over?" I smirked.

"I came with you to see your surprise. Which was entertaining if you're into . . . that. Now you have to come with me to see mine."

"Am I going to like it?"

"I think so."

I gave her an amused look because that wasn't exactly delivered with certainty. Though I was eager to find out what she'd done with her free time.

"Sooo . . ." I led.

And she smiled, a fucking heart-stopping smile that I felt in my bones.

"I'm not telling," she beamed back, teasing.

She appeared to be rather pleased with herself. That was fine. She could act smug; I knew I would get it out of her eventually. Most likely when I had my head buried between her legs again and she was begging me to take her. From that look on her face, she could read I was ready to take her now.

She moved restlessly as though she regretted her decision to taunt the beast. She let out a long, drawn-out, overdramatic sigh. "I'll show you. But you have to follow me."

"Follow you, now that's intriguing."

Her cheeks turned a bright red, no doubt sordid memories of the wicked things we did around the house, playing through her mind.

"No, we're not going to the maze." Her lip pulled up ever so slightly when she thought I was no longer looking; she'd allowed herself a smile.

I wanted to laugh, and the feeling was still foreign to me. But I was starting to learn when I was with Anya, I was prone to feelings I wasn't used to. She had a way of bringing them out in me.

Together, we walked through the house, and I let her lead the way. When she stopped in front of my music room, I hesitated. Memories were flashing through my mind after what had once transpired in there. I'd almost brought down the fucking house last time.

"I'm going with no thank you." I went to pull away.

"Just go in." She tsked at me.

I grunted, not wanting to go back in and see all that destruction, but I followed her anyway. I was learning that as much as I didn't want to admit it, I would probably follow her anywhere.

The space was now clean.

Still, I couldn't understand why she'd want to come in here so soon after I lost my shit. Then again, if she was using the same logic as I had been, we would make a new memory.

This was me getting a taste of my own medicine, and it was sweet and daring yet bitter to swallow. "What are we doing here?" My mood was tainted from a guilty residue that clung, nevertheless.

Anya had a way of working herself inside you. Getting into the darkest parts and bravely throwing in light. She was an untamed fire, and I desired the feel of the heat.

Finally breaking our eye contact, I scanned the room.

Then I saw it. A brand-new Gibson custom guitar.

"What's this?" Not the smartest question ever poised.

"You need me to tell you what a guitar is?"

I lifted my hands and scrubbed at my eyes. "That's not what I meant. And you know it."

"So, then what did you mean?"

"Goddammit, Anya! You know exactly what I meant. Why?"

"Why did I do this?"

Because I'd sworn never to pick up another instrument again after what I'd done to the last—in front of her.

She stepped up to me. Placing her hands on my chest, she rose up and placed a kiss on my lips. "I want you to play."

"Why?"

"I know what it means to you . . ."

"And what is that?"

"It's your escape. Your happiness. Your peace."

That last word made me shudder, and no reply was worthy after that. I merely pulled her closer, sealing my mouth over hers and saying everything I wanted to say like this, showing her everything I wanted to express but couldn't.

Our kiss was cut short when my phone rang in my pocket.

A sudden start as I recalled who I'd invited over for dinner. My sister, because having her meet Anya felt like the beginning of normality. The kind I'd not known I'd secretly craved and never believed possible.

I tucked my phone back into my pocket. "There's someone I want you to meet."

"Here?"

"I invited my sister over."

She paused, worrying her lip. "You want me to meet her?"

"I do."

"She knows about me?" She looked nervous. "Why . . . after what my father did?"

"Because unlike me, she never judged you for the actions of your father. Come on. Let's go, she's waiting."

My voice came out more forceful than I'd wanted. The truth was, the more we spoke about it, the longer I thought of my original plan to harm Anya, and the more I felt like an asshole. More than this, I felt remorse like it had been encased in my DNA.

"The guitar's incredible," I told her.

"Ridley might have helped."

"I kind of guessed." I tried to suppress a frown. "When did you two talk?"

"Yesterday."

I took her hand in mine and pulled her down the hallway.

"I should change," Anya said, looking nervous, "before I meet her."

"You're perfect," I told her.

"You sure?"

"Very." I arched a playful brow. "Never been surer in my life."

We found Sofia in the parlor facing the vastness of the property behind the house—the view of the maze clear from here. Their green hedges neatly trimmed. The structure preserved after all these years yet it had taken on a new meaning.

To Sofia, the way her shoulders remained tight with tension as she stared off at it in a worrisome trance, it still represented her worst days. She'd run from the pain and I, well I'd run directly into it and made a home from the debris of our lives.

However, Sofia had handled it differently, doing everything in her power to never be here more than she had to. Only when necessary. When she turned eighteen, she'd insisted on getting an apartment in the city, and that was where she lived until she met the man who'd become her husband. She was happy now, and that had meant everything.

Anya's hand pulled out of mine.

Reluctant to have her revert to a time when she fought me, I answered her gesture with my own. Bracketing my arm around her shoulder and then leading us closer to where my sister was standing.

Sofia pivoted to look at us—her eyes wide as she assessed Anya.

And then there it was.

The biggest smile reaching her bright eyes—and in all honesty, I couldn't recall the last time she'd shown any conceivable joy like this since she was a girl. Sofia crossed the space between us, bursting with love and affection.

My beautiful sister, the woman who'd grown out of the child who I'd kept alive all those years ago. It made my chest ache, but before I could think more about that, I trampled the rising feelings.

I smiled. Not as wide, but a smile, nonetheless. "Sofia, I want you to meet Anya."

Still, I didn't drop my arm, but then when my sister reached out to pull her into a hug, I was left with no choice but to let Anya go.

Sofia hugged her as if they were long-lost friends. Not enemies, but I guess in Sofia's sheltered life, they weren't. Not really. I'd ensured my vendetta was mine alone and never touched her.

"You're Anya?" The question was heavy with the weight of its meaning—that she was Stephen's daughter.

"I'm so sorry for everything my father did to you." Anya's eyes filled with tears. "I don't know how to make it up to you."

Sofia raised her chin high. "You're proof there's such a thing as balance in life."

"I don't know about that," she replied softly.

Sofia swapped a knowing nod with me. "Let's sit. I want to hear everything about you. The woman who stole my brother's heart." Her pearls of laugher reverberated through the air, soft and full of relief.

This was the Anya effect—bringing calmness to an otherwise dire situation.

I imagined this was what Anya was like in her other life. The one before this. Recalling what she'd admitted to me about her home life. That it had been lonely. At the time, I'd not understood. But now, looking at how relaxed she was and how much she enjoyed this company, I realized she'd never had this.

No.

That wasn't strictly true.

She had Archie.

I remembered everything she ever told me about him. The way

her eyes had sparkled when she shared those affectionate stories of him—how they fought but also how they helped each other survive the worst of the years. Her expression glittered with love for her brother.

And I knew exactly what I needed to do.

Find a way to give her *this* again. Her sibling relationship that meant so much. Somehow, I had to find a way to get her to see her brother.

Or maybe even bring Archie here.

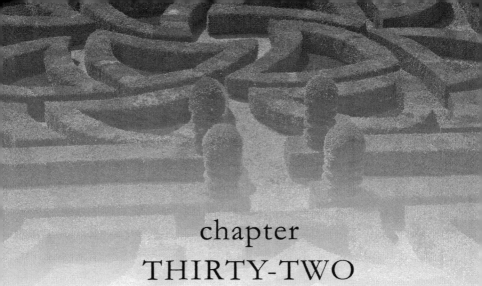

chapter
THIRTY-TWO

Anya

AFTER A WEEK, I BECAME EVEN MORE RESTLESS.
I tried to stay busy by baking, mostly, and preparing almost too much food for us. Making sure the staff were always well-stocked up with cookies. Finding myself overwhelmed with the work I'd set for myself in the chapel—he wasn't ready yet to bring others in to help. More than anything, I missed Cassius when he wasn't here.

The thought that Archie was still living under the same roof as an arms dealer, that cruel man who'd once called himself my father, gnawed at my nerves. I wondered if he missed me.

The sound of a car pulling up in the driveway filled me with excitement, and I hurried to greet him, heady with the thrill of seeing Cassius. Like a magnet, drawn to see him as soon as he stepped in the door.

Only it wasn't Cassius who'd entered the foyer. . .

I was looking up at the man who meant so much to him. Ridley was standing there as though he'd come to see me.

"Anya." He glanced down the hallway as though checking we were still alone. He led me down another hallway. "How are you?"

"Fine." Straightening my back, I exuded confidence. "You?"

His face bore a rainbow of expressions from conflict to warmth. "Your father visited me."

"What? When?"

"In my office. Yesterday."

My throat constricted with panic as though my father was here. He shook his head. "We can't tell Cassius."

"We must."

"No, listen." Ridley shifted uncomfortably. "Stephen informed me the only reason he didn't rescue you is because he was concerned Cassius might act impulsively."

Impulsive? Like his men shooting at another car in the middle of Mardi Gras? Trying to kill the man I . . . *loved*. It hit me then like a ton of bricks.

I loved Cassius.

I'm not sure when it happened, but it did.

But what did that mean for us, for the situation?

I couldn't think about that. I needed to think about what Ridley had just told me. If he knew Stephen had acted impulsively, it made me wonder if Ridley even knew about that.

I wasn't going to be the one to tell him. Maybe Cassius trusted this man, and maybe he didn't. It was crucial for me not to reveal anything that would put us in any more danger.

"Did you tell my dad I want to stay here?" I bit out.

"To be honest, Stephen's the kind of man you listen to. You don't interject."

"I saw my mom at Mardi Gras," I said. "Did he mention that?"

"No, what happened?"

"She turned away from me."

"Maybe you were wrong about that."

I ignored that scathing comment. "Did he mention Archie?"

He tucked his hands in his pockets. "Your brother wants you home."

"You talked to him? What did he say?"

"I didn't get to speak with him personally, no." He looked nervous.

"What's wrong?"

"Anya." He studied the floor with concern. "Archie's not doing so well."

His words cut into me like shards of glass cutting through my body, and I felt guilty that I'd left him there.

"Quite frankly, Anya, your brother is having psychological issues."

My heart stuttered with trepidation. "Tell him I love him. Tell him I'm coming for him."

"Don't share this, understand? What I'm about to tell you."

A cold shiver rose through me, like a snake slithering up my spine and heading for my throat, threatening to wrap itself around my neck and choke me. This man was meant to be Cassius's friend. This man was meant to be my friend, too.

He gave a hesitant sigh. "Your father mentioned the rift with Cassius's father was long over. That he had no argument with Cassius." Ridley pressed his hand to his chest in earnest.

"I witnessed my father try to kill Cassius."

"I think they thought he'd hurt you, Anya. They didn't see you and suspected the worst. But now they know you're still alive."

"Where is this going?"

"My job has always been to protect Cas."

"I know."

Ridley shuffled closer. "Don't tell Cassius we talked. His life may depend on it."

Reluctantly, I gave a nod, needing to hear where this was going. "Can you get a message to Archie?"

He waved that off. "Listen, whatever you think of Cassius, he's a good man. He's made some shitty decisions. You being one of them."

"I know why he brought me here."

"It's all been one confusing situation."

"Stephen killed his parents." Astonishment dripped from my accusation. "In cold blood."

"That rift happened a long time ago."

"Stephen never went to prison for it."

"I know this has all been hard for you."

He was changing the subject, and it infuriated me.

"You're a lawyer. You didn't think to prosecute the man who killed your father's client?"

"You're very naïve, Anya."

Affronted, I folded my arms, compelled to walk away. "What's your point?"

"They will kill him."

Cassius. He meant Cassius. . .

Ridley stepped back as though aware the space between us was too intense to sustain. "*If you don't go home . . .*"

"He told you that. Stephen?"

Ridley gave a sharp nod. "I can't stop it."

"They've already tried."

"Your father will let him live, Anya. But he must return you home first. Safely."

"Cassius won't let me go."

"Then you have to leave of your own volition."

"I don't want to go back."

Surprise flashed over his troubled features. "Maybe there's been an element of brainwashing. I'm sure Cas didn't mean to—" He searched for the words.

"You have to tell him they're coming."

"You love him, don't you?" Ridley didn't wait for my answer. "If you really care about him, you must go home."

Shaking my head, I silently pleaded with him not to say this, these terrible words that would mean me abandoning the man I loved.

We both heard it at the same time—a car pulling up in the driveway, the familiar sound of wheels rolling on gravel. Cassius was home.

Ridley fixed a glare on me. "Leave with me now."

"No."

"Obviously, Cassius will come after you. If he turns up at your home, though, he'll be shot on sight. It's imperative you make him see you don't feel the same way about him."

"And lie to him?" I bit out.

"If nothing else, Anya, do it for your brother. He's not well. He needs you."

"What do you mean not well?"

Ridley's expression turned tortured. "I didn't want to scare you, but his complexion is pale. He may be having some kind of breakdown."

"I need to talk with him."

"Apparently, neither of you were allowed phones."

"Bring Archie here. He'll be safe."

"Only if I want to be six feet under." He sounded affronted. "Leave, or they'll kill him. If you don't go back, no one and nothing will stop your father's rage."

"I never really knew my dad." My heart broke as Ridley's threat closed in.

"Take it from me, you don't want to." He waved that off. "Just do it until your brother is better, perhaps. I'm sure he'd do the same for you if the circumstances were reversed."

"You're willingly sending me back!" I inhaled sharply. "After everything you know about that man?"

"You're his child, Anya. You'll be safer than anyone. His family comes first in all he does. Stephen promised that if you come home now, he won't harm Cassius. It will be over." He gestured his frustration. "I'm Cassius's counsel. I do what I feel is best for him."

An arctic chill sliced into my bones. "Cassius won't let me go."

"Well then, you'll have to find a way. Or his death will be your fault. His blood on your hands." He stepped back and headed down the hallway, leaving a blast of terror in his wake.

"Wait," I called after him. "Can you promise Cassius will be safe?"

He pivoted to look back at me. "I've kept him alive all these years, haven't I?"

I wasn't so sure that was true—more likely it was despite this man that Cassius had remained alive.

"I'll wait ten minutes." His voice was a hushed whisper. "Cassius trusts you not to leave. He told me himself. We'll get a head start because of it. I'll take you home. Be strong, okay?"

Trembling, I gave a nod. But even as I agreed to go with him, I doubted I could go through with it—through with leaving this place, leaving the one man I'd fallen so in love with.

Yet if saving his life meant I had to leave him, I'd have to find the strength to do it.

Leaning on the wall, trying to stay upright and not crumble, I inhaled through my panic as I tried to think this through. I could just leave. Not tell Cassius. Only he would come for me with no explanation.

He'd die trying to save me.

I had to find another way to break it off. And I knew, knew with all my heart there was only one way through this, and that was to crash into hell and make a life for myself there.

My heart shattered into pieces as though it was already done.

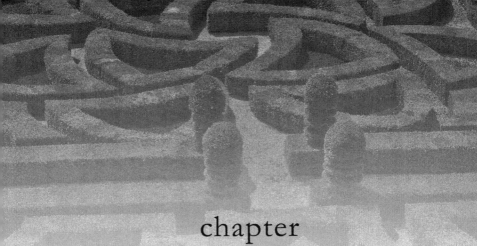

chapter
THIRTY-THREE

Anya

WHAT IF I WAS MAKING THE WORST MISTAKE OF MY life?

How would I know?

I was never going to survive this.

Pressing my palm to my chest, I replayed Ridley's rant about how Cassius's life was threatened, his words haunting my every step toward him. Finding him in the kitchen, his face lit up when he saw me as he happily shoved one of my cookies into his mouth.

He looked relaxed and seemingly more beautiful than the last time I'd set eyes on him.

Contentment.

Knowing I would be the one to shatter it sent a strike of pain into my beating heart—threatening to stop if I went through with this.

Maybe we could take our chance. Maybe we could leave here and go abroad.

Archie won't survive it.

By the time we tried to rescue my brother, it might be too late for him. Ridley was right about one thing; Archie would never abandon me. I might be the only person who could save him.

If my father had sent an olive branch for me to grasp, and I refused it, and Cassius was killed, I'd never forgive myself. I'd have to live with that forever.

He was just so beautiful in his boyish mischief, taking another cookie, coming around the kitchen island to hug me. "Coffee?" He smiled.

His body warm and comforting against mine as he pulled me in close.

"Sure, thanks," I said, even as I knew I wouldn't drink it.

Ridley told me he would wait for ten minutes. I was certain I had eaten through half that time already.

"How was your day?" I asked.

Cassius waved it off. "Business. Boring shit. Yours?"

The force of his intrigue hit as he turned his steely focus on me. "You okay?"

"I'm worried about Archie."

He set an empty mug down and came toward me. "Let me deal with it. That's what I do."

"What if . . . what if something happens to him? I'd never forgive myself."

He licked his lips free of a crumb from the corner of his mouth. "I'm handling it."

"And you're not going to tell me how?"

"Let me worry about all this." He shrugged. "Protecting you is my priority. And anyone you care about." He came at me and lifted me right off the floor and set me easily on the edge of the countertop. We were the same height. His fingers tangled through my locks. "I have news. Ridley checked on your brother. Archie's fine."

I flinched. He noticed.

Perhaps one of them was lying, and it scared me that I didn't know if it was Cassius.

He brought me in for a hug and I fell against his firm chest.

I breathed in his essence, his soft cologne soothing, comforting, an aroma I couldn't live without. But I was going to have to learn how to. My chest constricted so tight I had to inhale sharply just to draw enough oxygen.

"It's going to be all right. I promise," he soothed.

I wanted to believe it.

I needed his assurances. Needed him to guess what was wrong and tell me that I was doing the wrong thing.

All earthly elements for human survival were seemingly drawn out of the room. Oxygen, argon, nitrogen and even gravity itself were gone.

"How would you like to go to New York? We can fly out tonight."

"I would love that," I said, my voice shaky.

He dragged his teeth across his bottom lip seductively. Nudging me back, his firm hands shifted the hem of my dress up my thighs and revealed my panties.

"Don't." I shivered. "No."

"No?"

"I have to tell you something."

Don't say it. Don't say it. Don't say it.

There'll be no way back. No way back for either of you.

"I thought you liked it."

"I don't want to be with you." Squeezing my eyes shut, I hated myself for saying it, hated the words as though they hadn't spilled from my own mouth.

He stepped back, looking confused. His intense focus tried to read the truth from the woman who'd just shot an arrow into his beating heart.

If you love him, you'll let him go.

This is was the only way to save him.

I slid off the counter. "I told you I wanted to be with you because you scared me."

His face contorted in quiet agony.

"I can't hold it in anymore."

"You're lying." He looked out of the window as though trying to decode what had happened before he'd come home.

"I'm going to my room." I went to leave. "I don't want to see you ever again."

"You can't leave," he said bitterly.

"I am."

His brows knitted together. "Did Ridley say something?"

"That's right. Throw the blame onto anyone but you." Clutching my belly, I tried to hide this ache, this anguish, the hurt that felt like I was birthing grief itself.

"We need to talk," he said softly.

"We've done enough of that ever since I was brought here against my will, don't you think?"

"Where are you going?"

I spun around. "If you really care about me, you'll let me have some time alone." I stormed out along the hallway, heart wrenching in anguish, my body shaking so bad I felt shell-shocked.

I was traumatized, just like anyone who'd suffered a terrible ordeal—but I cared more about what I was doing to Cassius.

This is the only way.

Not stopping, refusing to look back, refusing to have any excuse to return to him and beg his forgiveness—fearing I'd not survive seeing what was in his eyes, I scurried out the front door and sprinted toward the Lexus parked not that far away.

Climbing inside the passenger seat, I gave a nod to Ridley that I was ready to leave.

You'll never be ready.

A part of me would always be trapped here in the shadows of the agony that I'd left behind. The futility I'd caused.

You're just like the others, I scorned myself.

"What did you say to him?" asked Ridley.

"Drive. Just drive." Tears sprang, and I couldn't stop them.

"You did the right thing."

"Why did you tell him Archie was fine?"

"We don't need him being heroic."

We accelerated fast and I was shoved back into the seat with a violent propulsion. Thrust so hard that going in the wrong direction was impossible to fight. This was the only way to save him.

Cassius, forgive me.

Forgive the world just one more time.

As my thoughts left him in that dark place, they turned toward the cruelest future. One where I knew what my parents thought about me. A loveless home that felt more sinister than ever. The ominous tendrils of that Garden District house drew me closer.

In saving Archie, I'd lost myself.

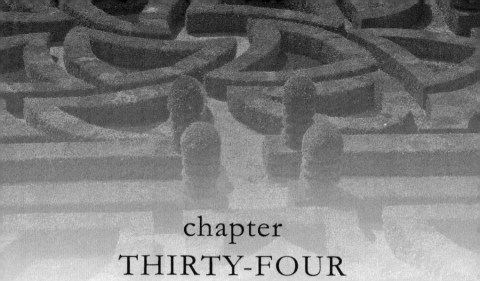

chapter
THIRTY-FOUR

Cassius

WAITING ON THE DOORSTEP, I FELT A WARPED SENSE of reality as I watched Ridley's Lexus navigate up the driveway toward the estate.

Possessed by fury, I stormed toward his parked car. Not even waiting for him to get out. I yanked the door open and pulled him out by the scruff of his shirt.

"What did you do?"

"Cassius, please." He cowered.

I slammed him back against the car. "Where is she?"

"Calm down."

Letting go of him, I stepped back. "Tell me you didn't take her back!"

"I tried to intercede between you and Glassman."

"What the fuck!"

"He's going to kill you, Cassius," he snapped. "Are you so blind you can't see it?"

"For the gold—"

"His fucking daughter."

"He doesn't love her."

"You don't know that."

"She's been a prisoner in that house her whole life."

He reacted to that with a sly glare.

"And how long was she a prisoner in yours? Five weeks."

"Don't you dare judge me."

"He's still her father. I had to take her back." He pointed a finger at me. "I risked my life trying to placate him."

"You betrayed me."

"It's over, Cassius. She's gone." He motioned to clarify. "Anya's home. With her brother."

"I shouldn't have let her leave."

"Right, because that's totally normal."

"Glassman killed my parents. And you just wander up to Stephen's front door for a chat."

"He called me. He came to me."

"And you took the meeting?"

"You were gonna kill her." His face contorted into disgust. "Think about that. And she knew. She might have forgiven you, but she knew what you'd planned for her. What did you expect to happen? You both wander off into the sunset together?"

She changed me. She saved me.

"You don't know anything. What we have."

"Move on. Put this mistake behind you. Glassman understands why you did what you did. But the issue with your father wasn't between you and him. He had no grudge with you. Now that she's back, he'll let this go."

"He shot at me during Mardi Gras, Ridley. Did he tell you that?"

"He was trying to protect Anya."

"And you believe him?"

"We have no choice."

"He took me out to the swamp. I was a teenager. He threatened to kill my parents. And he made good on that promise."

"For your sister's sake then. Move on."

"Don't twist this into something it's not."

"I'm not going to stand by and see you kill yourself. I promised my father on his deathbed I would take care of you. Don't make me break that vow."

"I never needed taking care of."

"This fight with Glassman must end."

"You believed him? Believed his lies?"

"For your sake, yes."

"What did she say in the car?"

"Anya?"

"Yes! Anya!" I yelled.

He gestured for me to calm. "She was happy to be going home. She wanted to see her brother. He's everything to her. You know that."

Happy to go? A lie infested with something sinister.

"She was relieved it was over," he added.

"She said that?"

"Go away for a while. Get out of town. For God's sake, sell this place. There's nothing for you here."

"This is my home."

"You always hated it here. You told me that once."

"Things change," I said bitterly. "Once again, you and your family fucked mine."

"An illusion, Cassius. She was scared. She'd have told you anything. Her life was under threat by you."

"She understood why I had to . . ."

"Kidnap her?"

This wasn't working. Nothing I told him could twist this macabre perspective into something good. Only Anya herself could have done that, and she'd chosen not to. "She went back for Archie's sake," I reasoned.

"Tell yourself what you need to, but for God's sake, don't try to find her."

"You can't stop me."

"Actually, I can. If you to try to contact her, I'll arrange for a restraining order against you."

"So that's how it's going to be?"

"If that's what it takes to keep you alive."

"Get the fuck out," I snapped.

"I'm trying to save your life."

"You drove her to her death."

"You're delusional."

"He shot at me, Ridley! The night of Mardi Gras. Emptied an assault weapon into my fucking car. She could have been in it."

"At some point, one of you must back down."

"Her mother doesn't want her. I saw that with my own eyes. Saw her reject Anya. Didn't even try to save her."

"Save her from who, exactly?" he said coldly.

A low blow delivered with the coldness of a man who'd gone on with his life as if he hadn't witnessed the desecration of my family.

"Why did you stay, Ridley?"

"I've treated you like a brother." He turned to get in his car. "Yes, my father turned you away when he shouldn't have that day. I've had to live with that."

"That wasn't you."

"Still, I've put your happiness above my own so I could at least find some peace in all this."

"Then let me have her."

"Your father should have let Glassman put those weapons on his ship to transport them. It was once, Cassius. Once. Then everyone would have gone on with their lives, and no one would have been hurt."

Heart palpitations made my head spin. "It wouldn't have been just the one time. Glassman would have demanded my father do it again and again. And you know what he would have had over him, the fact he did it the first time. My father was a good man. He fought for what was right. He died for us."

He looked defeated. "I'm just trying to prevent any more deaths."

"You may have just done the opposite."

He broke his focus from me and turned toward his car. "You know where I am should you need legal counsel."

"I'm firing you."

"With all I know about you?"

"Yeah. Wanna test me on that theory, go ahead."

He climbed in and revved the engine.

Running my fingers through my hair in frustration, I wanted to hate him, but the years he'd been there were too deeply engrained even as he betrayed me now. He'd never been a brother to me, but he'd been close. Close enough for me not to kill him now.

He sped off down the driveway.

Leaving behind the mess he'd wrought.

My heart hammered, and my mouth was dry from grief. What he'd done was unforgivable. Anya was in danger. How could he not see that?

I stormed back into the house.

The last hour had melted into a shit show. Right after everything had started to feel so damn good for the first time in forever.

How could I stay in this place and go on with my life knowing she'd gone back to them? With every breath, I sensed things weren't good for her. During her time here she'd unwittingly dropped so many clues into her life as a Glassman. One thing was sure, her life had been lonely.

The disgust I felt consumed me. Disgust that she was spawned by those people. Letting her go wasn't an option. Not when I knew what that man was capable of.

They'd neglected her before, and they'd neglect her again. She could leave, of course, was certainly old enough to. If Glassman was willing to let her.

Replaying our time in the kitchen just now, I tried to piece together our last conversation. Tried to understand what had made her change her mind about us.

Rage blinded me to the truth.

What if I'm wrong?

What if she really hated me all this time, and I'd manipulated her into staying. All that burning passion between us was nothing but an illusion I'd wanted to believe was true.

Ridley was right about one thing. I had intended on killing her, and she knew it. I was no better than her father.

Let her go.

Only after I know she's safe.

Blinking, taking in my surroundings, I was back in the center of the maze, looking around with only a vague idea of how I'd come to be standing here again. As though drawn to this small, sacred space surrounded by tall hedges, a little unruly.

Unruly like her.

In here I could think. In here, my mind stilled just long enough for me to break the pieces of the last hour into decipherable constructs.

Every moment with her had been more precious than any day before it. She'd brought light to my darkness. Hope to futility. Every scene in this maze replaying as I refused to let them go.

Us in here. In the center of the maze.

I wasn't giving up on her. I was going to come for her. I knew she'd gone back for Archie. Sacrificed her own happiness for his safety. Because that was who she was.

And that, in and of itself, proved she wasn't a Glassman.

Not stained with his blood running through her veins because she was nothing like them. She was kind, and patient, and forgiving, not bitter and cruel. Even after everything I'd done to her, she found a place in her heart for me.

Leaving me—she had done that to protect me.

It was all I had to hold on to so that I didn't spiral into madness.

Ridley gave away her motive to return. Glassman had threatened he'd kill me if she didn't go back.

So she went back.

She hated her father, always had, and her returning to that house was a testament to her bravery. To the beauty of her soul.

Retracing my steps that I knew so well, I headed back into the house and strolled into my office.

As soon as I entered the room, my phone rang. Fishing it out of my pocket, I glanced at the screen, hoping it was Anya.

It was Ridley again. What the fuck did this bastard want?

"Why are you calling me," I growled into the phone.

"Don't hang up," he responded. "I'm sorry about before, but this isn't about—"

"Like I give a fuck about apologies. We've been over this—"

"Listen to me. This isn't about us. Archie is here."

"Anya's brother? Is he hurt?" Why weren't they together?

Over the line I could hear him walking to another part of his office, probably for privacy. "He's shaking. He's desperate to talk with you."

"Fuck. Let me speak with him." I listened as the phone was handed over to Archie. "Hey, buddy, you okay?" I asked him.

"H-hello." Archie sounded painfully young.

My fingers scrubbed at my brow, trying to forget the fact I had once threatened his life.

"Archie. What's going on?"

"Mr. Montebello tells me I can trust you. He says you're the only one who can help my sister. I saw Anya arrive home. But I was already out of the house. I ran away. I can't go back. He'll kill me." His voice sounded strained.

Even Glassman's own children hated that man. The terror in his tone was palpable.

"You can trust me, Archie. Is she still at home?"

"Yes. You have to get her out—"

"I'm working on it. Everything is going to be okay, Archie. He wouldn't hurt her, right? He's your dad."

"That's just it. He doesn't love her. She's in so much danger. Get her out of that house. You don't understand. She found out the truth at the cemetery . . ."

His words resonated, taking me back to something Anya had unwillingly shared with me in her drunken rant.

Something about secrets. . .

Something about finding their family mausoleum and what she had discovered within.

How had I not seen it?

Like lightning striking, it hit me. It all came together. Every piece of the puzzle I had missed. Every comment Anya had ever made. In her drunken state, she'd unwittingly shared her memory of a Russian winter while with me at Café Du Monde.

She'd been born abroad.

The Glassman family had only ever lived in NOLA.

"Archie," I said, keeping my tone even. "You're both adopted?"

Quiet reached out from the other side of the line.

"Still there, buddy?" I coaxed.

His voice was weak with worry. "She told you?"

Closing my eyes for a beat, letting that truth sink in with the profoundness of its meaning.

What I'd unwittingly set in motion.

They had taken her as a child. From the kind of place where there would be no records to mark her birth?

My hands shook with anger.

It finally made sense.

Anya was the replacement.

A girl taken. Abused by her father. Kept prisoner for one reason alone.

To defy me.

All those years ago in Lafayette Cemetery, Glassman had taken my threat to kill his children seriously.

He had taken my revenge away at his own hands.

He had killed his own children, so I couldn't.

Anya being in danger was my fault, because now that I knew, who knows what he would do to her. "I promise I'll get her back," I reassured him, hearing Archie's sigh of relief. "You're safe with Mr. Montebello, okay. Can you hand him the phone back?"

A shuffle on the line and then I heard Ridley's voice. "I'll take care of him."

My fingers tightened around my phone.

The tension still thick between us.

"I'm so sorry, Cas. For what I've done. I'll make it right. I'll keep Archie safe—"

"Bring Archie here. It's safer. We both know that." My calm tone eased the strain. "I have better security. Don't fuck up again."

"I won't."

Hanging up, I paced as though that was key to setting all the pieces together and seeing a way to get her out of this alive.

Making it right was all I had left in this world.

Grabbing my car keys, I stormed out of the house and leaped into my car, following another clue.

I needed to see if I was right.

The drive was a blur. Each second felt like it meant something, that it counted toward the distance between us.

Parking outside the cemetery, I hurried within its towering stone walls and searched for the Glassman tomb, striding past those buried long ago, respectful of the dead as I trudged through the graveyard.

I soon found the gray-white, free-standing mausoleum, "Glassman" carved into the alcove above the stone archway. The wooden door with Stephen's coat of arms stamped above the entryway with the filth of his last name.

What secrets do you hold within?

What had Anya seen that day that had startled her so badly? Her alcohol-laced rambling was more than relevant now as I headed up the short steps to open the door to the chamber.

Using my shoulder, again, and again, and again, until the way was laid open—and I was standing in the doorway. Either side of where I stepped, there was splintered wood from the broken-down door, which hung off its hinges.

I walked into the shadows of the dead.

There, to my right, lay ten marble gravestones. A lineage of Glassmans set to rest in tombs.

The last one set my flesh to ice.

I tasted bitterness, a poisonous realization that what I was looking at was a marked tombstone with Anya's name etched on the front in gray rippling marble.

Nausea threatened to spill.

Raging forward with this fight to see it through, I knew what lay within. In a blur, a frenzy, I rested my hands on the stone lid and, with sheer force, shoved and shoved again until the stone moved, grating its resistance and proving futile to my strength.

I peered in.

I was drenched in a cold sweat as my eyes adjusted to the darkness of what served as a grave. Looking up, I broke my glare, trying to make sense of what I was seeing inside.

Around me, dust particles danced and settled and sparkled, set alight by the fading rays peeking through the window.

Nausea welled again. I was close to choking. My gut burned my insides out. My heart squeezed tight with the horror of it.

"Monster."

My words echoed as I left.

chapter
THIRTY-FIVE

Anya

LEANING ON THE WALL, I DRAGGED MY FINGERNAILS against painted brick while trying to catch my breath from where I had searched for Archie. I was still waiting to go into my father's office.

His office door was closed.

One of his men who guarded it told me, "It won't be much longer."

Because me coming home after a kidnapping and waiting outside to be greeted by a loving parent was perfectly normal.

They'd even given up pretending.

Maybe Archie was in there with Dad. Maybe that's why I hadn't found him in his room. Or the kitchen. Or even the garden.

I'd come back for Archie. For Cassius, too, and every breath I inhaled in this house felt wretched. Swallowing this dread, preparing not to show fear with what I knew about the man on the other side

The door flung open.

There he stood. My father. He filled the doorway with his intimidating presence. "Anya." He held his arms out.

Feigning I was the good daughter, I stepped toward him and leaned in for a hug. I inhaled that scent of him, the rich cologne and stale cigar smoke causing bile to rise in the back of my throat.

"My poor, sweet child," he tried to soothe me. "Thank goodness you're home."

"Dad."

He held my shoulders and nudged me back to better look at me. "We have a doctor coming to examine you."

"I don't need that."

"This is non-negotiable." His lips thinned. "I'm afraid your mother isn't able to be here to greet you. She's dealing with another issue. She wanted to be here."

Issue? What could be more important than this?

He waved it off and turned to his office. "Want to come in?"

Looking past his doorway and into the treacherous organization of his office, I shook my head. It felt like just yesterday when I'd witnessed Cassius's men ripping up his carpet and digging a hole in the floor to get to a safe. Now, all evidence of that was gone. The carpet re-laid in a green pattern of something a psychotic brain might like. No sign of anything askew.

I fixed my focus back to my father. "Where's Archie?"

"He went to stay with a friend."

Wait.

"Who?"

"He'll be back tomorrow."

"How is he?"

Because the last I heard, he was close to breaking.

"He'll be fine. Hungry? Shall I arrange for food? How about pasta? You love pasta."

"I couldn't eat anything right now."

Dad shooed away the guard and waited until he was out of ear-shot. "Did he hurt you? Cassius? Did he . . ."

"No," I responded quickly, suspecting he was insinuating I'd been taken by force.

"We have a lot of questions."

"What kind?"

"I want you to write down everything you can remember about his house. The security system. Was there a code? Draw a map of the property."

But he'd already been there once. The night he'd killed Cassius's parents, so either he was faking interest, or he was checking to see if anything had changed on the estate.

My flesh crawled. "Why, Dad?"

"It's good to have."

"You're not going there, are you?"

Stephen hesitated. "Would that be a problem for you?"

He knew. He had to know that Cassius and I had become lovers. Maybe Ridley had betrayed us. Maybe it had been because I'd stayed with him after he'd almost gotten shot after Mardi Gras. Whatever the reason, my father might know more about what we'd become.

Or maybe I was overthinking it.

"I'll try to remember everything I saw." I made it convincing.

"I heard you went to Café Du Monde with him?"

"Yes."

"There was no chance to escape there?" He sounded suspicious. "No one to signal to?"

Again, I shook my head no.

"And tell me, Anya, back at the Hotel Monteleone, you saw me there? Trying to rescue you from him. But you ran?"

Cassius had strong-armed me then, but I didn't want to say it and put Cassius in any more danger than he already was. "I didn't see you."

"Right, that's what I thought. I just want you to know we were doing everything we could to get you out of there."

"I know."

He scratched the back of his neck. "Want to sit with me while I work?"

"No, I think I'm going to wash up."

"Let the doctor see you first. I want him to . . ." He twirled his finger. "He may need to take evidence off your body. You understand?"

"Why?"

"It's standard procedure."

"But . . . you didn't go to the police?" It came out before I could stop it.

"Cassius threatened that if we did, he'd kill you, Anya."

"He told you that?"

"I don't underestimate what you've been through. We've all been incredibly worried. Archie wasn't doing well at all. We've tried to keep him busy. That's why him being with friends is so important."

"Who is he with?"

"Your mother knows the other boy."

"I saw Mom at Mardi Gras." I watched Dad's reaction.

"She's been incredibly worried, obviously."

I'd pushed my father enough. If he suspected I knew what he did for a living, I might become a victim of his wrath. Just thinking that this man bought and sold weapons sent a shiver through me. The deaths he'd caused . . .

"Anya?" He tipped up my chin.

I had no choice but to play along. "Thank you for persuading Ridley to bring me home."

"It was either that, or he'd suffer the consequences."

Which made me feel guilty for being hard on him. Dad had threatened his life. Ridley had little choice in the matter but to bring me back.

"I'm going to my room for a bit."

"My door is always open for you, sweetheart," said Stephen. "Even if it's closed." He threw in a wink.

Heading off, I felt his stare on my back until I was out of sight.

chapter
THIRTY-SIX

Cassius

IF YOU WANT TO TALK ABOUT RECKLESSNESS, SEE ME COMING to the Garden District in daylight. See me standing on the doorstep of the man who wanted me dead. The man who'd murdered my parents. Decimated my life. Threatened to end my sister. The man who'd stolen Anya back.

Stephen answered the door like this was a regular home and him opening the door was a usual encounter.

He knew I'd come.

Stephen glowered. "You've got some nerve."

My fists clenched, my fury simmering. "I know what you're planning to do."

"You kidnapped my fucking daughter."

"Where is she?"

"My daughter will need years of therapy after what you did."

"Only, she's not your daughter, is she?"

His eyes glazed over. "It's best you leave now."

"You replaced your children. Now that's some sick shit."

His mouth twitched. "Proof?"

"Let Anya go."

"Stay away, and she'll remain safe."

I moved to get into the house, but he blocked me. Farther down, several of his men guarded the hallway. I'd never get past them.

"Anya!" I called out.

He pressed his hand to my chest. "Try it. Blood will be spilled and not just yours."

Jesus, he really was evil enough to threaten her life.

"You can have your gold," I said. "There's got to be at least thirty million. I'll personally bring it back. Give me Anya and you get the gold."

"You'll bring back my gold for my daughter?" He smirked. "You've got some balls."

Looking past him, I tried to see if Anya was in there. "She's not your daughter, though, is she? Archie isn't your son, either."

"The truth is, I do want my gold back. It is, after all—" He yelled the rest, "My fucking gold!" He calmed down quickly like a psychopath with spittle on his lip. "Let's negotiate. Your life for the gold."

"I want to speak with her."

"Go have a meal, Cassius, as it's going to be your last. Make it count."

"You don't love her."

His brows arched. "I did buy her for a fair price."

"In Russia, right?" I watched his reaction.

"Stay away from my family."

"I'm coming for them."

His eyes widened with this dark promise.

Because he knew that I knew.

Just beyond him, two men headed for us. Big men with big attitudes who could mess everything up if I didn't use caution.

"If you want your gold, keep your dogs at bay," I said through clenched teeth.

"Are you going to beg for your life like your father did?"

I should have punched him for that. Still, there was more damage to be done to him if I kept my cool and kept walking. I ignored this burning desire to kill Stephen in cold blood and his men along with him.

He called after me. "You're a dead man walking." Anya would be dead, too. I knew that in the very marrow of my bones. Walking away meant that I might keep her alive until I could get back to her.

Driving away from the house at breakneck speed, I pulled over and parked at the edge of the Garden District. I vaguely watched a tram go by with a few passengers inside. Tourists, maybe.

Fishing out my phone, I placed Stephen's address into the search engine. Ascot Residential came up as the realtor who'd sold the Glassmans their property on Fifth Street. The house had cost them a few million fourteen years ago.

Another property came up.

A house within driving distance.

Interesting.

Maybe this was the answer I had been searching for.

She'd offered up each clue for me, and all I'd had to do was listen and decipher them.

The truth was glaring in all its cruel reality. Stephen hadn't expected me to take this long to take revenge. He'd played out his sick plan and seen an end to it.

Ascot Residential had its realtor's office on Magazine Street.

An easy drive.

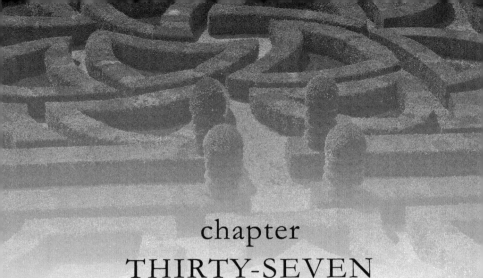

chapter
THIRTY-SEVEN

Anya

Mom's voice echoed against the walls from downstairs.

I didn't care about seeing her, but maybe she'd brought Archie back. Bitterness shuddered through me in a mixture of anger and regret. Anger for the turmoil she'd caused in not protecting us from my father, and regret for ever trusting her.

Gripping the banister, I descended the stairway, ready to face off with her.

That was a lie.

I'd never be ready to face off with the woman who'd rejected me when I'd needed her the most. A pivotal moment at Mardi Gras when she'd pulled back her hand and let me fall into the abyss causing gut-wrenching agony to settle and swirl and harden my heart.

Or maybe she'd done me a favor.

She should be bolting up the staircase to meet me halfway. Screaming my name with relief her daughter was home safe. Doing something, anything to prove she loved me, and whatever happened at Mardi Gras was a misunderstanding.

She didn't realize her actions pushed me even more in the direction of loving Cassius. The only person I trusted in all of this. The only time I'd ever felt truly loved and cherished was with him. As soon as I knew Archie was safe, I'd leave.

Hushed voices came from the kitchen. Boldly, I nudged the door open and peered in, scanning the room for Archie.

Mom looked different somehow. Her hair coiffed to perfection as always, and that Chanel suit pristine. Her sickly rich perfume wafted across the kitchen. Dad's jaw was tight with the usual tension as he watched my reaction, perhaps gauging my loyalty to them. If this was baptism by fire to survive these people, then I'd have to endure the heat and continue faking my loyalty.

Maybe they'd suspect with Archie not here, there was no reason for me to stay. Finding my brother was all that mattered. He was vulnerable and needed me. Every decision felt like it made a difference to whether we survived this.

"Here she is." Mom walked toward me with open arms.

Entering the kitchen, I fell into her hug, pressing my cheek against her chest, feigning I was the good daughter who needed them. Wrapping my arms around her, I acted like she was all that mattered in life. They were all that mattered. Playing into their game, I hoped to convince them I was oblivious to what they were.

"I've been frantic," she said breathlessly.

"Mom."

"My poor baby," she cooed.

The sickly scent of Dark Dahlia enveloped me, that familiar perfume bringing back every memory screeching like a car crash in my mind.

"I couldn't sleep until you were home." She planted a kiss on the top of my head.

My cheek pressed against the scratchy fabric of her jacket.

She held me at arm's length. "We did everything we could."

"I know," I said, trying to be cheerful.

"You've suffered a terrible ordeal."

"He didn't hurt me," I offered.

"When you're feeling up to it, you can tell us everything."

"Maybe we should take you to the hospital?" Stephen's compassion was almost convincing. "We don't want to force you."

I lied with a smile. "He let me come back to you."

"Your father made it happen." Mom's tone was full of pride. "He reached out to his contacts and got you home safe."

Really? Because I kind of think I came back of my own volition.

"Are you hungry?" she asked kindly. "What can I make you? We can order in if you'd like."

"Can I talk to Archie?" I made the request sound casual.

"Of course." She shrugged. "Let's set up a call."

"When is he coming home?"

"When we feel it's safe."

"It's safe for me." I subdued the taint of sarcasm.

"I'll let you two catch up." Stephen strolled by us. "Glad to have you home, pumpkin."

We both watched him walk out with the stride of a man who seemingly held all this together with his sheer will.

With him gone, I felt braver as I turned back to Mom. "Where were you?"

Her lips quivered as though suppressing tension. "There's been a lot to do. Your father and I worked relentlessly to get you home."

"You never called the police?"

"Cassius threatened that if we did . . ." She delivered the rest with a pained expression.

Don't go there.

Don't do this now.

Don't risk it.

Yet, the questions burned bright. I couldn't go on pretending the distance between us hadn't always been there. Maybe some part of me wanted to believe these people really did love me and wanted to deny they were masters at gaslighting, spewing lies, twisting reality, and wearing me down.

A sob caught in my throat. "Why didn't you take my hand?"

The corner of her lip twitched. "At Mardi Gras?"

Yes, at fucking Mardi Gras.

Back when I'd wanted to be saved and believed what was ahead of me with her was safer than the man waiting for me in the crowd.

Not forgetting all I knew about Cassius was crucial. Holding those threads of truth that threatened to fade. Wiped out if these two had anything to do with it.

She gave a dramatic sigh. "I thought if I took your hand, he was going to shoot you in the back."

Ice surged through my veins.

Because that could have been the plan all along, and maybe, just maybe, I'd not seen it because of the turmoil of every passing second.

Her tears welled, and she was overcome with emotion. "Letting you go was the only way to save you."

Bringing myself back from the brink, I whispered, "You did the right thing."

She swiped a tear. "I was confused and scared. If anything happened to you, I would have been the one to blame."

Hugging her again, I wrapped my arms around her and tried to comfort her.

"Are you sure he didn't touch you?" she said coldly.

Shaking my head, I didn't look at her. I tried to hide my eyes that might reveal how much I loved that man and how much I missed him. Giving him up and coming back here had been the hardest thing I'd ever done.

"Why did he take me?" I looked up at her now, wanting to see the lies spinning behind her façade.

"Why does any man do such a thing? For money, of course."

"He has money."

"Well, that may be true, but he wanted your father's gold."

"He took me, too."

"Let me get you something to eat."

"I'm not hungry." I followed her across the kitchen, annoyed at her fussing, the way she opened the fridge and peered in as though trying to keep busy.

"When will Archie be home?"

"He's not as strong as you." She let that sit as an excuse.

"Mom?" I laid the word down as an accusation. The *what the hell are you not telling me* kind.

She shut the fridge door. Her head bowed, eyes down.

"What?" Dread circled my feet as though the ground might open and swallow me whole.

"We can play these games, sweetheart," she said coldly. "Or we can be honest with each other."

Swallowing, I waited for her to continue.

"We saw you with him at Mardi Gras." Her hand snapped up to silence me. "After your father retaliated."

Cold slithered up my spine as she faced me.

"You were observed running away. Disappearing into the crowd with him. You went willingly."

"You pulled your hand away," I said bitterly.

"I've already told you—"

"Am I allowed to leave this house now?"

"The risk is even greater."

"You can't keep me a prisoner anymore."

"How dare you!"

"I won't go back to living like that."

"Like what? Like a princess? Given everything you could possibly need? Toys, games, clothes."

"You never let us out of the house."

"I'm sorry we couldn't protect you from that monster. God knows we tried."

"Let me speak to Archie." I held out my hand. "Call him. Get him on the line."

"We know, darling." She smirked. "And we know you know."

"About?"

"What your father does for a living."

A chill washed over me, my flesh crawling with dread. Maybe she was bluffing. It was hard to tell with her.

"I don't care about any of that," I managed.

She stepped forward. "And the last thing we want is you sharing that knowledge with anyone else."

"I would never . . ."

"Archie shared with us a small detail about you both. That you know you're adopted."

And he'd been rewarded with a black and blue eye for it.

"You never told us," I muttered. "Why?"

"To protect you."

"How many times did I tell you I had memories of a different time? Of snow. Of a building that was the Kremlin, for God's sake. You told me I'd dreamed it."

"I never wanted you to feel we didn't love you."

"Where are my real parents?"

"Dead."

"Dead?"

My heart squeezed for the loss even though I'd never known them. All those ruminations about getting to meet them, about finally being reunited with my family.

"Anya, I didn't want this to be so raw. You've pushed my hand."

My throat tightened at the way she'd delivered it so cruelly. My past wrapped up into a few words that meant nothing. Not to her, anyway. Not delivered with kindness, no stories of my birth mother and how she'd tried to do anything but give me up.

"What did you do to him?" I whispered it. "To Archie?"

She dragged in a deep breath. "Archie was fishing for clues. Did he tell you what he found?"

Oh, God.

"What did you do to him?"

"Daddy sat him down and encouraged him to share everything that was on his mind."

They were fucking psychopaths.

Through gritted teeth, I said, "If you hurt him . . ."

"He's my son. I love him."

"But he's not, is he?" This wave couldn't be tamed. "I meant not your firstborn."

"You don't know the full story."

"You mean about the other children? The ones before us."

"We were heartbroken. We were wrong to try to use you to replace them." She leaned on the kitchen counter. "Try to understand."

"How did they die?"

"By Cassius's hand."

Horror stretched through me. "No, he didn't."

He wouldn't.

"He got to you, sweetheart. I was scared he would. And he did. He made you believe all sorts of things. I can see that now."

My legs buckled, but I didn't want any help from her.

"When he saw that Stephen and I had built another life for ourselves with new, beautiful children, he wanted to rip that away from us too."

"He was fourteen," I said.

"And capable of so much cruelty."

Hugging myself, I didn't know who to believe anymore, didn't know which way to turn, or what to do next.

"I went to Lafayette Cemetery," I admitted. "I saw their tombs."

"You shouldn't have gone without me." She offered a kind smile. "I didn't tell you because I knew it would scare you. Knowing that our first children were murdered. That it could happen to you. I didn't want you to live with that."

"You should have told us."

"Come with me. We can put flowers on their tombs. Put this all behind us."

"Why would I go there?" *With you.*

"Because they were your brother and sister."

"How did they die?"

She glanced toward the door. "We can't have your father overhear us talking about this."

"The garden then."

"I need to walk. Come with me. I'll tell you everything about what Cassius did to us. How he destroyed our family."

"Mom?" No, I refused to believe it.

"It's not your fault. That man twisted what you believe."

Confusion warped my thoughts as I tried to decipher the lies from the truth.

"I was young when I married your father. Your age. Just as trusting. Wanting to see the best in people." She softened. "I love you. I'd do anything for you."

"But when Archie asked about our adoption, Dad punished him for it?"

"Your father's not good with his emotions. His biggest flaw. But if I can forgive him, so can you."

"I can't."

"I need you, Anya. I need to make it all up to you. I should never have let your hand go. I hate myself for it."

If I went to the cemetery and saw all of this through a different lens—saw that Cassius had a hand in harming children—I'd never recover.

And anyway, I didn't believe it. Because love had a way of shining the truth where lies liked to hide.

Shaking my head, I told her I didn't want to go.

"I'll tell Archie to meet us there," she whispered.

chapter
THIRTY-EIGHT

Anya

ALL I COULD THINK ABOUT AS I WALKED ARM IN ARM with Mom through the Lafayette Cemetery, was if Cassius saw me he would be heartbroken.

Because this looked like I'd gone back to them. Yet there was still hope for us and maybe, just maybe, he'd know it was all part of the plan to get back to him.

The insanity continued. Mom acted like the perfect parent, going on a late afternoon stroll with me, her well-behaved daughter.

The graveyard was a short walk from home. It took mere minutes for us to get here. I was grateful there were no tourists to shuffle by. No one to pretend to smile at.

Maybe when we got there, I'd be brave enough to ask her about why she'd given us the same names as her other children. That conversation loomed closer, and though uncomfortable, it couldn't go unsaid. I wondered if she knew I'd managed to get inside the mausoleum.

We were closer to it now, and that same old trepidation picked up its pace, causing my heart to race. Seeing a coffin with your name on it does something to you. It makes you question life. Makes you nervous to take a wrong step.

It makes you question everything.

Marveling at my ability to keep up the pretense, I squeezed Mom's arm to comfort her. I acted like all those years of neglect meant nothing. That I had shed all that loneliness and forgave her absence.

She seemed to fall for it, too.

As though my love for Cassius could fade that easily. I *had* come back for him, hadn't I? Surely, he would still have some love left for me. I missed him badly, my feelings not fading but growing more intense.

When I saw others walking around the graves, I looked to see if they were Archie. Mom knew that saying he'd meet us here would be all she'd have to say.

She swapped a comforting smile with me when we turned the corner. Her eyes left mine to fix on the entrance, turning panic-stricken.

Blinking against the sunset that glared its rays over the Glassman name.

She hurried ahead through the door of the mausoleum, frantic. I followed her, my hands trembling at the mess. The door was off its hinges. The worst kind of vandalism.

Inside was that familiar stuffiness of dust and dimness, the air heavy with a musty scent.

My hand cupped my mouth when I saw it—

The cover to the tomb was shoved away from its seal. The one with my name carved into its marble base.

A deathly scream tore from Victoria as she peered inside. Joining her, I braved to see what she was looking at. Within the stone base was nothing. No evidence of disruption. Just a cavern where a coffin should be.

Victoria fished inside her coat pocket for her phone.

"Where's her coffin?" I cringed, even as it made no sense.

With shaking fingers, Victoria traced the number on her phone. "Stephen, pick up. Stephen!"

"What's going on?"

"He knows!" she yelled. "He knows they're alive." Her eyes were wide with dread.

Alive?

She glared at the screen. "What do you mean you already know?" she screamed into it. "When did he come to the house?"

"Cassius came to the house?" My heart set off at a rapid beat.

"He couldn't have found them!" She let out a primal scream.

Throat tight and chest constricting, I drew in a breath but was unable to fill my lungs. I didn't understand what was going on. Mom had weaved so many lies I struggled to unravel them.

Just twenty minutes ago, she'd tried to make me believe Cassius had harmed them. Yet, all this time, their children were alive, living somewhere else. All the pieces swarmed together in a hornet's nest of lies.

The last piece of her scheming was too grueling to comprehend. Or endure. It cut into me. That primal shriek of panic of a mother's love.

Staggering back, I was blinded by the horror of having lived with these people all my life. Crouching against another tomb, I tried to breathe.

"*I went to see Stephen and threatened his children.*" Cassius had told me what he'd done all those years ago.

They had hidden them. Hidden their firstborn children from him.

"You told him about this place?" She threw her phone down.

The screen smashed.

"What's going on, Mom?"

"What have you done?" She towered over me. "You told Cassius about the tomb. You led him here."

Guilt savaged me like a wild animal lunging at my throat at the vague memory of my drunken rant he would have overheard.

Disgusted, I managed to ask, "Your other children are alive?"

"You'd never understand."

She'd believed Cassius would make good on his promise to kill her children. Only he'd murder their decoys—us—which would have left them safe.

She'd placed us in harm's way.

He was never meant to fall in love with me.

"Cassius won't know where they are." I glowered. "You've kept them hidden. How would he find them after all this time?" I said with a bitterness I felt deep down to my bones.

"Stupid girl. He never knew to look for them."

My stare shot to the empty tomb, the unspoken words hanging between us. *But now he would.*

"He would never hurt them . . ."

She bent low to sweep up her phone. "Your father just told me Cassius came to the house. He knows where they live." *No*, I refused to believe one more lie. "Cassius will see his threat through with them."

Pushing to my feet, I hated the seconds that dragged by in confusion, so I relented and followed her out. Looking at her differently, I threw daggers into her back because I was sickened by her. By them both.

We hurriedly returned to the house, though I didn't bother going in. Both of us climbed into Mom's Mercedes-Benz, and she drove us out of the Garden District at breakneck speed. I didn't know exactly where we were going, but I knew it was to them. She didn't have to say anything. The way she weaved in and out of traffic, she was scared.

"And you're supposed to be the adults," I muttered, dragging on my seat belt.

"You dare to judge me," she seethed.

"Yes, actually, I do."

"You have no idea what I have been through. What your father wanted to do . . ."

"Then tell me."

"You'd never understand. You've never lived. You've been kept safe. Away from anything that would ever upset you."

"Mom, we've been literally kept prisoner. You never let us out. You're hardly home. You knew what kind of man Dad was and you didn't stop him from hurting us."

"He hurt me, too. You didn't see it because I tried to protect you from his violence."

"Protect us? You did nothing."

"He wanted to kill them."

My throat tightened with terror. "What?"

"Stephen refused to let them die at the hands of that man, so he was going to kill them himself."

An ice-cold chill slithered up my spine, my mind trying to grasp what she was saying.

She looked pale. "Kill his own children. *My* children." Her shrill voice rang through the air as she continued, "I didn't let him though." Her head shook back and forth. "No. I couldn't let my babies die. I came up with another plan. And he agreed." Her hands formed into a prayer.

"We were the decoy."

"I couldn't let them die. You're not a mother, Anya. You wouldn't understand."

"It's fucked up. You see that right?"

She stared off at nothing. "And what was it all for. . .*that man* is going to kill them anyways."

I didn't voice my own fears, but I knew Cassius, and that knowledge scared me more than anything. I'd left him full of anger and bitterness. I'd left him broken all over again.

Broken enough to kill?

I tried to hold it together and not show any fear in case she fed off it. But as more time passed, my jaw rattled with fear for those children, and my knee bounced up and down that it was taking so long to get there.

I was a mess.

Like someone had stabbed my heart with adrenaline, it pumped rapidly, feeling like it was going to beat out of my chest. If I thought it could explode, it would. I felt dizzy as she sped up, taking turns way too fast.

I wasn't sure how long we drove. Less than an hour. But eventually, she stomped on the brake, causing the seat belt to slice me in two—or that was what it felt like because it yanked my neck with such force. I watched as she scrambled to undo her seat belt and get out.

The towering bronze gate looked secure. Mom exited, throwing the car door wide open and running toward a pedestrian entrance at the side. She rummaged around in her handbag for a key—a key for that lock. Before she could use it, the tall gate swung open.

Terror flashed over Victoria's face as she went on through.

I knew where we were even without her telling me. This was fourteen years of truth pouring out. The past that had been hidden glaringly presented in all its ugliness.

I was going to meet the children we had replaced. Though they wouldn't be kids any longer, I mused darkly. Like me, they'd aged and grown into young adults. They'd lived a life of seclusion, just like us. Yes, I was the decoy, but I imagined they, too, had suffered.

Surely, they had because they'd not been allowed to flourish beyond these walls. Or maybe they had the lives we'd so desperately wanted. All those years when Mom and Dad weren't around, this was where they'd come.

Soon, I'd be able to ask these questions myself. Soon, I'd see what they looked like. Would she look like me? Would she hate me even though I had no part in this?

The sun had set over the vast estate. It was bigger than the home I grew up in, but it was obvious the real Anya and Archie lacked for nothing. The grounds of the property were deserted. The woodland surrounding it provided the kind of cover a family in hiding might need.

And I knew without a shadow of a doubt that something was terribly wrong.

Don't do that to yourself.

Don't carry the blame.

Yet, I did as if I was the cause of all this turmoil.

The home I grew up in was a fortress. I found it hard to believe Stephen didn't provide the same level of security for his blood. Following the woman I had once thought of as my mother, I watched as her skin paled and terror reflected in her eyes as she came to the same conclusion as me.

Something had happened here . . .

But what?

The surrounding air was heavy, and when I inhaled deeply, I thought I could smell copper. The scent of blood. Or maybe it was the acrid scent of dread. Afraid to walk another step. Afraid to open the door. Afraid to see what lurked behind the walls.

Would there be carnage?

With a sharp inhale, I summoned every bit of strength I had, ready to take a step forward. But first, I threw a glance at my mother.

"Are you coming?"

Our gazes locked.

Fear festered in her eyes, and her hands shook as doubt swept across her eyes.

"I can go in alone if you want," I whispered.

Cassius wouldn't hurt me. If he was still here, he could hurt her. Without a doubt, he would try.

"Maybe it'd be safer if I go in alone." I tried to convince myself.

She squared her shoulders, making the trepidation go away as fast as it presented itself. "They're my children."

Right, because if you want to just stab a knife into my heart while you're at it—go ahead. My mom had already done so much damage, she'd be hard-pressed to have anything left to destroy.

With a nod, I looked up at the imposing door, then reached out and turned the handle.

I wasn't sure what I was expecting, but when it opened with no resistance, I felt like I'd gotten punched in the stomach. A part of me hoped we weren't too late and wished with all my heart this nervous feeling weaving its way inside was unwarranted, but as the door creaked open, I knew deep in my gut Cassius had been here.

Together, we headed in.

It was bathed in darkness like I was walking into a crime scene. Our footsteps echoed as we progressed farther inside, bouncing off the walls and breaking the silence. The fine hairs on my forearms prickled.

It was warm. Somewhere in the house, a window or door had been left open, allowing the musky Louisiana air to filter in.

Too thick to breathe. Or maybe it was fear that made inhaling a struggle.

"This way," she said.

I followed, wary of each step she took because I didn't trust anything she did. As we walked through the foyer, I took it all in.

They'd lived in luxury. Enough gold and silver décor to clash like a bad headache. It aged this place up by giving it a twisted, regal flair like a madman had done his worst in trying to pretty up the place.

We climbed a vast staircase.

"Anya," she called out into the void. "Archie!"

I startled, but then realized she was calling out to *them*.

My chest ached with the harsh reality that she was calling to her real children. My name wasn't my own. Not even stolen but given away to a girl who was meant to die because of it—me. That was what this woman had planned. Spending one more second with her felt sacrilegious, like insanity weaving around my body.

Jesus. They'd even gone with the family portraits on the walls as though no one would see their warped minds. The photo of them all as one happy family was sickening to look at. She was pretty, the other Anya, brunette like me and with the sweetest face. Archie wore glasses and looked so damn innocent it made my heart break for him. My jealousy melted into sympathy.

Please be alive.

We found the same thing in each room as we searched.

Nothing.

Not one person in this place.

The only sign anyone had ever lived here was the half-eaten sandwich we found on a blue china plate in the kitchen. Life, that was what had happened here. Two children who mirrored the ones in the Garden District, but these were the precious ones.

There was no way to tell how long that food had lain discarded. Where were they?

"The security room," my mother said.

I looked over at her. "There's a security room?"

"Of course."

She clarified in her answer that security for them differed from security for us. The security I had was to lock me in. To keep up the façade that I mattered. In truth, this was what mattered. This place and the people residing within.

I was scared for them.

This was what it felt like to die inside yet live on. To know your entire life had been filled with deceit.

Silently, she led me to the security room.

On the floor, lying with his hands tied behind his back was a man I had never seen before. His eyes were closed, his pallor gray from the strain. I wondered if he was dead or unconscious, but when my mother ran toward him and ripped the tape off his mouth, his eyes opened.

"Where are they?" She shook him.

Confusion marred his face.

Running forward, I worked at the binds at his wrists until he was free from the tape. He righted himself, sitting up but not meeting our stares.

"He took them." His voice was low, defeated. "We tried to stop him."

"Who?"

"Calvetti."

No, I refused to believe it, but I knew he'd been here. I could feel his presence even if I couldn't see him. Feel his pain dripping off the walls.

"Where are the others?" Victoria yelled. "The other guards."

"Your children sent them away this morning."

"They have names!" She slapped him across the face, and he flinched.

Cassius has them.

My choked sob echoed through the room. My soul thinned into glass that Cassius was hammering into pieces, a continuous pounding away at me until I was nothing but shattered and useless on the floor.

Was he really fulfilling his threat to my father all those years ago? Was he really going to kill them?

Or maybe he already had.

My knees buckled, and I slumped to the floor.

What have you done?

chapter
THIRTY-NINE

Anya

EVEN THOUGH MOM WAS IN SHOCK, SHE WANTED TO drive us back.

The security guard refused to let her, insisting he drive Mom's Mercedes to take us home after he saw the state we were both in.

She'd seemingly lost everything—her children. She certainly didn't come off as a woman who'd brought all of this on herself. She played the victim so damn well.

I was worried about the guard, too, and all he'd been through, but the man wouldn't take *no* for an answer. Feeling responsible for losing the children seemed to motivate him. Perhaps fear of what my father might do if he didn't put it right. It wasn't his guilt to bear, though.

Mom sat in the passenger seat in silence while I was in the back.

Her feelings for me evident by the way she refused to even look my way. She blamed me for Cassius finding them. But of course, she did. Nothing I could have told her would have changed her mind.

Keeping my mouth shut, keeping my screams at bay, I remained silent during the entire ride home. I didn't trust myself to speak to her. I couldn't trust the emotions rising. Hurt and confusion bled out like an open wound refusing to clot.

I wanted to tell the driver to pull over and let me out, but I had to stay and see this through. I had to make sure Archie was safe.

Cassius's hate for Stephen Glassman had once fueled his bloodlust. The thought of all the damage I'd done by leaving him made me feel like I was drowning. I could have prevented this—had I known. That was just it. I'd gone in blind to Cassius's estate and only now saw more than I ever had. A veil lifted to pull back all the lies I'd been living under. All that time, Cassius had been the one saving me, even if he hadn't intended that at first.

Eventually, the car came to a stop, and I realized we were home. *Home?*

I could no longer call this place that. I no longer belonged, but then again, I never had.

And with the children dead or at least exposed, there was no need for me. No need for a decoy for protection.

Before this, before Lafayette Cemetery, I'd believed saving Archie was possible. I had to stay until I knew where he was. It was no small thing to fake my way for a few more hours.

As I climbed out of the Mercedes into the night air, it felt almost comforting. As if the sky void of light purposely reflected these swirling emotions. A vacant feeling. Trepidation of walking back into the prison I'd once called home.

Dad stood on the front step to greet us. "Get in!"

He was talking to both of us. Not just me but Mom, too. His guards stood behind him, silently threatening us to follow his order.

If he blamed me for losing his children, he didn't say it.

The sound of my mother's sobs was heart-wrenching. She went on ahead, but her wails became muffled in my ears like I was stuck underwater, drowning, and worse still, like I was okay with not breaking free.

Letting the darkness devour me felt reasonable.

Dazed, I made my way into the house and then ran up to my room for refuge.

The one I grew up in. The room Cassius had discovered me in. Then swept me out of here too quickly for me to catch my breath. Yet all I could think about was him.

On the desk, I found the name "Anya" written in my handwriting on a notepad to now be a screaming mess of a lie. I'd never been allowed to be me. I'd been kept here all that time. They would probably keep Archie and me apart for the rest of our lives. Grabbing the paper and balling it up, I threw it across the room.

That wasn't me. But then who was I?

It didn't matter now.

Lying on my bed, I withered into a ball, not deserving the warmth of a blanket. Because I should have come back for Archie sooner. Sobbing even as my heart couldn't take the aching anymore. Even after my soul bled out.

Even after there were no tears left.

My vision cleared as I looked at the wall. At the cutout from *Teen Vogue* I'd hung there all those years ago. The image of a small girl locked in a cage and not allowed to leave a mansion of horrors. Those stars in the frame had been my only escape. As I continued to reminisce about the art I'd felt drawn to, I was reminded of that night when I'd made love beneath the stars.

Of finding a home.

And I knew . . .

We were all wrong about Cassius.

Maybe he had taken the Glassman children from that house, but he would never kill them.

No.

Even when he believed me to be the biological child, he had never hurt me.

Those children were still alive.

Scrambling out of my room, I ran through the door and down the hall. My breathing was heavy and faltering as I took the stairs at breakneck speed, almost tripping. Desperate to get to a phone. When I barged into my father's office, I was grateful to find it empty.

The landline was the only phone that didn't require a code, so

I lifted the receiver and dialed Cassius's number with a shaky hand, needing to speak with him.

"Hello," a familiar lilt answered.

"Cassius?"

"It's Ridley. Anya?" He sounded confused.

"You have his phone?"

"He wanted to make sure you could speak with one of us. But . . . I thought Cassius would be with you by now?"

"Is he coming here? I'm in the Garden District." *The place you dropped me off.*

"No, that wasn't the plan."

"I need to speak with him." Needed to tell Cassius I knew with all my heart he would never hurt the Glassman's children. I needed to tell him I loved him. That I believed in him.

"He's not with me."

"Does he have the children?" I swallowed my dread.

"What children?"

"Can you tell him to call me if I give you this number?" I pleaded.

My emotions were scrambled and then burst like a dam breaking with nothing to hold it back.

The line went silent.

"Are you there? Ridley?"

"I don't understand." He let out a frustrated sigh. "Aren't you meeting him? That's what he told me."

"Meeting him where?" I whispered, my trepidation heavy.

"The swamp . . . at the other end of the estate."

"His place? Why does he think that?"

"That's where you told him you'd meet. He said you texted him from your father's phone. He gave me his cell just in case, because he wouldn't have service there. That way if you needed to speak with him . . ." He inhaled sharply. "Anya. You're the one who texted him, right?"

The phone dropped from my hand.

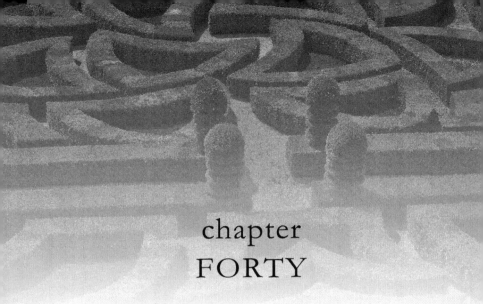

chapter
FORTY

Cassius

AFTER GRABBING THE DUFFEL BAG FROM THE BACK OF MY car, I pulled the door shut.

The gold was heavy to carry.

The thick night air was sticky, sweat causing the back of my shirt to cling.

Leaving the car sheltered by a towering oak tree, I headed for the edge of the swamp.

The only illumination came from my flashlight as I held it out before me to lead the way. The ground scattered with creatures. Now and again, the fake fluorescence reflected their glassy stares.

It wouldn't be long now.

I'd finally have Anya back.

This was where I'd brought her.

This dense swamp where I'd confessed all I'd done. Lain myself open and cut myself wide to let in the light, making myself vulnerable.

I allowed her to know everything because I'd needed her to grasp the extent of all I had done. More importantly, why.

Even now, I doubted she'd be able to love all those parts of me I couldn't love myself.

Maybe it was the hour, but the terrain felt jarring this time. Even as I respected the marshland. Even as I knew it well and braved what lurked.

As my shoes crunched over the thick moss, it no longer transported me back to my youth. *No*, in my mind, I could only see Anya's face.

Those memories of what had happened before all those years ago, fading. What had once held a visceral revulsion with this stank smell that had made me gag now held no power over me.

Though I still had to fight against the foliage to get to the location I'd agreed to meet her in the text she'd sent:

"Cassius, I need to see you. Where's the gold?"
"I hid it in the swamp," I'd answered.
"Meet me there."
"Where we met before? At the edge where Stephen once took me. The place I showed you?"
"I remember."

Anya had changed the way I felt about this place.

Now I could see the beauty of the marshland. In turn, I'd hoped to change her mind about it, too. Maybe even lift some of the fear off this place.

She wasn't here, however. My body didn't need her here to remember how she'd made me feel.

How she'd comforted me.

How she'd helped me.

She changed me completely that night.

A night much like this—with all the familiarity of a Louisiana aura. The landscape was draping the trees in endless moss. I knew this marshland well because I had played here as a boy. Over there, I'd fished for largemouth bass. Harkening back to the days a teenager had once found adventure here—but all that had been snatched away.

The squawk of a bird drew me back to why I was here. The call of a heron, maybe?

Retracing my steps, I headed toward the boat we'd left that day. The same one we'd promised to come back to soon.

The same place Stephen had brought me all those years ago. I found the small motorboat where we'd tethered it to a cypress tree. The clearing up ahead was a good place to wait.

Unzipping the duffel bag, I revealed what lay within the fabric, then flung it unceremoniously into the base of the boat. It creaked against the weight of the bars.

Checking my watch for the millionth time.

Scanning the swampland with that glare of my torchlight. Over the bracken, over the dark, murky waters, the shine of Spanish moss reflecting. The glint of silver eyes, the sound of scurrying, of hiding away.

Anya, it's going to be okay.

I needed her to listen while I explained how I had changed. How I would give up this bloodlust for her. I would do anything for Anya.

Time slowed.

The soft melody of the swamp my only company. Insects buzzing and the water rippling, the creaking of the boat. An insect bite on my forearm was easy enough to ignore.

We could live a new life. One in which the past no longer haunted us. It would be an opportunity to carve out a fresh beginning.

Lost in my own thoughts, I was eager for this to be over.

The familiar crunch of the wet grassland breaking beneath steps sounded, emanating from the movement of heavy soles.

His steps.

I turned quickly, and as expected, Stephen stepped out into the opening with his gun drawn. His flashlight in his other hand. I raised my arm to shield my eyes from the glare. Both of us lowering our flashlights in a temporary showdown.

"What the hell are you doing?" he snapped, his voice breaking above the marsh song. "I'm meeting someone."

"Back there!" He pointed toward where I'd parked. "You were meant to meet her back there."

"You should have been clearer when you pretended to be her texting."

A slow, steady smile rose on his smug face.

I had made peace with dying long ago. When surrounded by so much death, it's easy to familiarize yourself with it. It's grooves and fissures, its easy nature, the way it lulls and seduces. The way it selfishly takes and takes and takes.

This, on the day of my death, all the sweeter for knowing I'd saved Anya. And her brother, too.

"You don't look surprised to see me," he sneered.

"Nice night for an evening stroll," I said casually.

"Well, I'm happy you joined me. Seems we have a lot to discuss." His eyes scanned the landscape. He looked scared but then again, he preferred the city.

"We have a lot to talk about," I began.

"Not really. All we have to talk about is you dying."

"And your gold."

"Fuck the gold."

My head shook back and forth as I tsked. "Come now, you wouldn't even still be talking to me if you didn't care about the gold, now would you?"

I had him. I could see it from the way his eye twitched and his greedy mouth gaped like one of those crawfish I'd once caught— before placing it back and letting it live.

Because killing had never been my thing. Never been what or who I was, even as I'd tried to convince myself it was something I could do. But to kill to save another life, maybe I did have that in me.

He glowered. "Where are my children?"

"Is Anya still alive?" My throat constricted on that question.

"Yes, for now."

"What do you want?" I asked firmly.

"Do you even have my gold out here?"

"You know I do." I gestured to the boat.

"What the fuck is it doing in there?"

"It was heavy."

He raised his gun on me. "Tell me where they are."

I scratched my head as though trying to recall.

"You were never man enough. You didn't kill them."

"Guess you'll never know." I gave a ghost of a smile. If he wanted to play this game, that was exactly what we'd do. I had all night.

I had whatever time remained until he pulled that trigger and left me for the swamp.

"Tell me where Anya and Archie are," he said, uncertainty flashing in his eyes.

He'd always been impatient.

"Which ones?" I chided.

A click proved he'd cocked his gun.

Didn't budge though, instead, I offered up. "I'm not afraid to die. You don't scare me, Glassman."

His frown deepened as he turned his flashlight into the thicket. "Maybe not, but maybe this will persuade you." He pointed his weapon into the denseness.

I followed the direction of where his gun pointed until it collided with Anya's wide eyes.

"Anya," I bit out.

She stepped into the light. "I came to warn you."

A swell of emotions hit me in the chest. All that I could offer her was a comforting smile, my eyes conveying *I'll get you out of here.*

Glassman raised the gun at Anya's head. "Tell me where they are."

"She's in front of you." I turned my attention back to Glassman. "You're pointing a gun at her. Your daughter."

He hissed. "I'll let her live. I want my gold first."

"Dad." Anya stepped toward him.

"Wait," I warned her.

Glassman sneered her way. "I'm not your father."

She seemed unshaken. "Did you ever care?"

"Only for what you could do for me."

"I was merely part of a plan? What was going to happen to me once they were safe?"

He shrugged.

She took a step closer to him, recklessly brave. "Why?"

"Why what?"

"Why the ruse? Why the caskets? Why all of this?"

He kept his gun on her. "Who cares?"

"I care," she snapped.

"We planned to merely fake their deaths, at first. Hide them away. But then your mother couldn't see a future where she couldn't have them back in our lives. Have her family back home."

"So, Archie and I became a bait and switch?" she asked.

Stephen's head bobbed up and down in agreement.

"But you didn't expect Cassius to wait so long to come to you?" She glowered at him. "I want to hear it from you," she added, her eyes darting over to me.

"The plan seemed reasonable. Once we dealt with him—" He waved his gun at me. "Once we got our children home. No one had seen you or your brother. No one would be the wiser."

"You locked us in a cage, just so you could switch us out when Cassius died," Anya bit out.

"Well, if you put it like that." His eyelids were heavy.

"Why the caskets?" she asked.

"Contingency. If he ever found out you weren't the real Anya, we would lead him to the caskets at Lafayette. He'd believe them dead. It would be over either way. I didn't expect the fucker to open it!"

"Did you ever, even for a minute, care?"

He seemed to think about it.

I charged Stephen. Throwing my body weight into him. Knocking him back. Wrestling to grab his weapon. A shot rang out. The sharp sound reverberated through stale air. Glassman lay winded, struggling to catch his breath.

Pushing to my feet, I felt a stark burning in my side. I looked down at my ripped shirt at my waist where he'd hit me. Adrenaline pumped too hard through my system for me to feel any true pain, but I pressed my hand to my side.

"Cassius!" Anya ran to me.

"Run," I demanded. "Run!" I yelled again.

"I won't leave you."

"At least hide," I begged her.

Stephen's gun was raised at me again, which was better than having it aimed at Anya. She hurried over to me, but I stepped in front of Anya to shield her.

"Again, we're back in the swamp." He smirked. "I'll finish what I should have done all those years ago. If only your father would have just done what I asked and allowed my guns on his ships. But no, your father was a self-righteous fool, and you're no better."

"Maybe so, but I still have your gold."

"Give it to me."

"Want your gold? Go get your fucking gold." My heel gave the edge of the boat a kick, and it jerked away from the shoreline.

"Idiot!" he cursed, scanning the surface warily.

The boat drifted off . . .

He went for it, wading into the murky waters until he was chest-deep before I could say another word. He closed in on the boat, threw his flashlight ahead of him, and scrambled to climb into it, shoving the oar aside.

I pivoted fast, grabbed Anya's hand, and pulled her behind the towering trees.

"Dad," she cried out.

His arms reached over the edge as he stretched to pull himself up and into it. The boat rocked against the weight of him.

A splash came from something unseen.

"Help him," she said on a sob.

I sprinted to the edge, but Anya caught my hand and held me back, gesturing to that swirl in the water to our left.

That churning now calm.

"Jesus." My glare snapping back to where Glassman was chest-deep. "Get out! Get out of there!"

Glassman reached for one of the gold bars, his face contorted into triumph. The boat tipped as he pulled on the side of it to clamber up—capsizing it.

He surfaced, this time trying to climb onto the upside-down boat, struggling to make it.

Glancing at Anya, I turned my focus back on the man who was frantically trying to pull himself out of the water while his hands kept slipping off the base.

And then he wasn't there.

There was splashing. Violent thrashing. Water circling.

Grabbing Anya, I turned her the other way, not allowing her to see the horror of it.

Not that far away, a heron watched on with cold indifference, uniquely mastered by nature.

Gliding my flashlight over the swamp, those grey murky waters, I stared at the ripples expanding and then calming.

A circle of bubbles lifted to the surface.

A gator.

An eerie stillness followed.

The upside-down boat drifted into the darkness.

A chorus continued as though the creatures didn't even care.

Anya leaned against me, and I wrapped my arm around her, pulling her close and closer still, knowing the swamp had taken him.

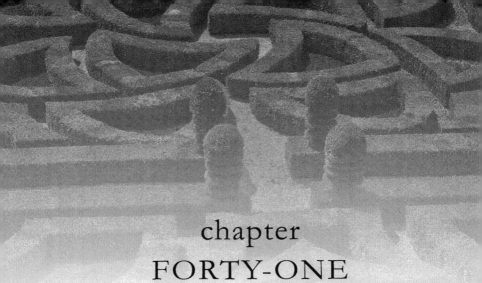

chapter
FORTY-ONE

Anya

D RENCHED IN TERROR, I CLUNG TO CASSIUS AS WE STOOD
on the bank looking out at the surface of the water, glassy
and now still.

I didn't know how to feel and didn't know what to think anymore as my eyes scanned the surface of the green water.

Unsure of these feelings. The loss heavy even as his cruelty left
shadows within me. He'd planned on letting me die—ironically at
the hands of the man who stood beside me.

The man who'd ended up saving me instead.

"It was quick, right?" I asked, even now conflicted at the horror
of that kind of death.

"It was, Anya."

Even after all Stephen had done, my heart searched for
understanding.

"Where are they?" I whispered.

Cassius grimaced in pain.

And I then realized. "You were shot? Are you okay?"

Pressing his hand to his side, he reassured me. "Flesh wound. A graze, really."

"Let me see." I tugged at his shirt and pulled it up. By some miracle, the bullet had left only a superficial wound. "We need to get you to a hospital."

He frowned. "I'm fine, I'm more concerned about you."

"Cassius, you have to tell me where they are."

"Stop." He stepped into me, his arm reaching out, his fingers touching my jaw and tipping my face up. "They're fine. I'll take you to them, but first I need to do this."

He cupped my face, and his lips touched mine. He breathed life back into me with a brutal kiss. Like he thought he would never kiss me again.

Against my mouth, he whispered, "I love you. I love you so fucking much it scares me. I thought—"

I stopped him with my own mouth then. There was no need to talk about what-ifs. We had both lived through this and had survived because of each other.

His arms wrapped tight around me, and we lost ourselves in this embrace for a moment. Our kiss spoke of all the pain we had been through but had come out stronger, having endured this together.

"I love you too," I responded against his lips. After our mouths pulled apart, my eyes stung a bit but I felt a surge of so much emotion for this man standing in front of me. "I am unequivocally in love with you Cassius."

Neither of us moved for a beat, letting the moment wash over us. Then, when we were sure this was real, Cassius pulled back. "I know what you need."

"To see Archie."

"He's at the house."

Relief washed over me that he was safe.

"And the others," he whispered.

Words stuck on my tongue as the reality set in. I was going to meet the real Anya. The real Archie. I was going to see them.

"If they are back in the world," I whispered, pushing the fears out of my mouth, "who does that make me?"

"It makes you Anya. It makes you mine. It makes you the strongest woman I know."

Interlocking our fingers, we walked back the way we'd come, nudging the moss out of our way.

"I'll come back for the car," he said.

In a daze, he maneuvered me forward with a gentle arm until we were back on his estate, back on familiar property.

A place I considered home.

We walked past the maze and swapped a knowing smile with each other.

Ridley was heading our way to meet us and beside him, walked Archie. My brother took off in a run toward us, trying to get to me, opening his arms and slamming into my chest in the biggest hug he'd ever given me.

"What happened?" He crushed his face against me.

"It's over."

"Dad—Stephen, he was going to hurt you—"

I nodded. "Yes, he's dead. We're free."

"We're free? We can go out and things?"

"We can go out."

Archie looked as dazed and confused as me. Lost. Like he had stumbled out of the maze behind us, disoriented from the hell he had escaped.

"Dad told me you were at a friend's house," I asked him.

"No, I overheard Dad arguing with Ridley about you—" He glanced Ridley's way—"so I looked up his number and went to his office."

"You ran away?" My voice was wistful, proud of his bravery.

"I came looking for you." Archie fell into my arms again and hugged me like he'd never let go. "He told me Cassius was protecting you."

"What do you need?" I asked him. "What can I get you?"

"Just seeing you're safe is all I need."

"You're the best brother."

Archie looked nervously toward the door.

"What's wrong?"

"Do you want to clean up first?" asked Cassius.

"What?" And then I realized what he was insinuating and looked toward the house. "They're in there?"

"Yes," he replied warmly.

Cassius stepped toward Archie and placed a supportive hand on his shoulders. "You'll always have a place with us."

I watched Cassius as he kindly reassured my brother.

With us, he was telling him he could live with us—if he wanted.

I knew Cassius loved me, but still, I wasn't sure what that meant. I had hoped, but as my heart thumped rapidly in my chest, I was scared of what he really meant.

He turned and pulled me into a hug and kissed the top of my head. "I'll fight for the rest of my life to make you happy, Anya."

Tears welled in my eyes, and I bit back a sob.

"Thank you," I mouthed, the words lodged in my throat.

"Ready?" He gestured toward the house.

Taking a deep, cleansing breath, I walked that way with him and drew on Cassius's strength as he led me inside the house. We made our way toward where Glassman's children were waiting.

Grief stuck in my throat for what we'd have to tell them.

Turning the corner, we entered the room.

The hairs on my nape prickled.

She looked like me. We could be sisters with a similar height and similar features. The only difference was in her eyes. Not the color. No, that was the same. But it was also what reflected in her gaze. She looked jaded, like me. Seemingly hurt by life.

The same pain shimmered in her brother's eyes. As I watched them studying us studying them, I suspected they were thinking the same. That our lives were interwoven in all its complex and dangerous beauty.

The Glassmans had sheltered them, too. The children were also victims of them, even after living in all that luxury. But they'd been tortured in their own way.

The fallout of those years had yet to unravel.

None of us would ever be the same.

I would tell them my story. They would tell me theirs. And afterward, we would make our own way in the world. Because that was what we'd always craved, the freedom to make our own choices.

Knowing Archie was safe meant breathing without fear was possible again.

I had survived. Fallen in love.

Found myself.

Found *him*.

And that was all that mattered.

EPILOGUE

6 years later . . .
Cassius

BRIGHT RAYS OF SUNLIGHT BEAMED IN THROUGH THE center of the maze. This secret space in the middle held sacred memories. No one knew how to get in here. No one other than Anya and myself. It had become our secluded sanctuary.

Life had settled tremendously since I was a teenager and hid here with my sister. This space had once haunted my dreams—now, all that had softened, and I saw it differently. A place that had sheltered me when I needed it.

The place Anya and I had made love for the first time—all that affection pushed out the ghosts of my past.

I'd never thought this possible before her, but now, there was one more person who was learning the path in here.

It might take her years to figure the maze out, but for now, my daughter wobbled around it with the same awe Anya had once had when she'd entered here.

That moment of me letting the bird go free all those years ago would represent so much to us. The memories meant so much. I'd wanted to come in here to replay it, somehow send a message back to the man who'd once stood here, me, and reassure him all would be well.

Recalling opening my palms and letting that small bird fly free . . .

I couldn't help but smile as I wandered back through the maze, marveling at how well I knew its pathways, forwards and backwards, and its leafy corridors that led me out into the garden.

I paused for a beat to soak in the sun.

No longer searching for vengeance. My life absorbed with trying to make sure the girls in my life were happy.

Back then, when all those walls came crashing down. After Glassman had died in the swamp. After Victoria had left New Orleans. Even after her children had stayed. I had begun a new life.

Alone.

Content.

Anya and I weren't married right away.

What I knew with a stark realization was that after the life she had endured, she needed to make her own choices. And because I loved her, I gave that to her. Although I fought against the urge to demand she live with me right away, I didn't.

I gave her time.

Anya and Archie had rented a house near Tulane University. She'd always wanted to study English, and it was there, in this prestigious institute, that she did. She wanted to see what being independent was.

I threw myself into the business, though more recently I had found a CEO who could take our company to the next level so I could pursue studying music, reading more, and rebuilding the chapel. I wanted no part of it to be recognizable. I'd wanted more time with Anya.

For a year, we were a normal couple.

It took everything I had inside me not to become a caveman and demand she come home, but I bit back that impulse and instead, waited for her to come to me.

And she did, eventually.

It only took a year. The longest year of my life, if I'm going to be honest.

Once she finished a normal college freshman year experience, she made me teach her how to drive. Then, after she'd garnered full independence, she felt ready for her and Archie to move in with me full-time and she would commute to Tulane.

Under my roof, I coaxed her to marry me, and she said *yes*. I didn't give her much choice.

"What are you smirking at over there?" I heard my wife say from across the clearing of grass.

I stepped farther out onto the stretch of green in the middle of the maze and headed toward them. Toward Anya, who was standing with our daughter, cheering with each step she took. "Hurry up, she's about to launch!"

"Taking her first steps?" I hurried closer.

"Wait. She's changed her mind. Don't hold your breath."

"She's ready," I said.

She laughed. "Don't pressure her."

"Like I pressured you? Pretended to give you a choice? But you were always going to be my wife."

She laughed out loud while rolling her eyes. "I knew how hard it was for you to back down and not act all caveman on my ass. That's why I love you so much."

"I thought you loved me for all the wicked things I do to you. . ." I trailed off, teasing her.

Her cheeks became bright red.

After everything we'd been through, the fact Anya still blushed was probably one of my favorite things about her.

No matter how awful her life had once been, there is still a sweet and innocent quality about her.

"Stop looking at me like that," she giggled, "I'm trying to get our daughter to walk."

"Here, let me help." I moved to sit opposite them, lowering to my knees, lifting my hands up to encourage her to come my way.

"Come to me, Grace. Come on." She carried my mom's name,

and in so many ways, she was like her—the same beauty, same kindness, an easy grace to her.

When Anya had suggested it, she'd moved me to tears.

"Dada," Grace cooed, and then on shaky feet . . . she toddled over to me.

Joy rushed in as we watched her brave steps forward. When she made it the few feet between us, Anya clapped her hands in joy as our daughter wrapped her arms around my neck.

Grace hugged me. "Dada."

"I'll never get used to that." Squeezing my eyes shut, I breathed through this happiness coming too hard and too fast.

I planted a kiss on her cheek. "I'm so proud of you."

I felt Anya behind me before I saw her. I could always sense her presence. Like we were inextricably connected and always had been. She was my way through the maze of life, too.

Anya and Grace were everything I needed.

All I wanted.

Together, they took all my broken pieces and sealed them back together, making me whole again. Making me content.

And the new version of me felt younger and carefree. Like the shadows of the past were no longer hovering. Lifted away, evaporated into a bright, new horizon.

Because of them, I became the man I should have been had my life not changed so abruptly. When all had seemed lost. All hope gone. She'd found me amidst my pain.

Because of them, I was given a second chance at life. I was given the family I had always needed and desired and I would never let anything or anyone ever harm them again.

They would always be safe with me.

I was finally complete.

With them, I had found happiness.

Now.

And forever.

THE END

If you want a little more of these characters, we wrote a FREE
bonus scene for Cassius and Anya, got to
https://shor.by/RavishingBonus
in your phone or computer browser.

Talk To Cassius:
Want more Cassius? Message him here on Facebook:
https://shor.by/ChatwithCassius

also from author
VANESSA FEWINGS

PANDORA'S PLEASURE

MAXIMUM DARE

PERVADE LONDON and PERVADE MONTEGO BAY

PERFUME GIRL

THE ENTHRALL SESSIONS:

ENTHRALL, ENTHRALL HER, ENTHRALL HIM,
CAMERON'S CONTROL, CAMERON'S CONTRACT,
RICHARD'S REIGN, ENTHRALL SECRETS, and
ENTHRALL CLIMAX

&

THE ICON TRILOGY from Harlequin:
THE CHASE, THE GAME, and THE PRIZE

vanessafewings.com

also from author
AVA HARRISON

ACKNOWLEDGMENTS

Thank you to our friends and family for putting up with us (Looking at you Brad and Eric)

Thank you to everyone that helped with The Ravishing.

Jenny Sims.

Debbie Kuhn.

Jaime Ryter.

Champagne Book Design

Hang Le

Wong Sim

Lucas Bloms

Thank you to Connor Crais, Vanessa Edwin, Kim Gilmour and Lyric for bringing The Ravishing to life on audio.

Thank you to Viviana Izzo for all your help with our audio promo!

Special thanks to Greys Promotions.

Thank you to our AMAZING ARC TEAMS! You guys rock!

Thank you to our team.

Karen Hulseman, Lauren Luman, Lupita Gonzalez, Suzi Vanderham, Kelly Allenby, Lulu Dumonceaux, Jill Glass, Gel Mariano. Parker S. Huntington, Leigh Shen and Mia Asher.

Thanks to all the bloggers! Thanks for your excitement and love of books!

Last but certainly not least...Thank you to the readers!

Thank you so much for taking this journey with us.

ABOUT THE
AUTHORS

USA Today Bestselling Author **Vanessa Fewings** writes both contemporary romance and dark erotic suspense novels. She can be found on her Facebook Fan Page and in The Romance Lounge, Instagram, Twitter and Goodreads.

She enjoys connecting with fans all around the world.

Ava Harrison is a *USA Today* and Amazon bestselling author. When she's not journaling her life, you can find her window shopping, cooking dinner for her family, or curled up on her couch reading a book.

Connect with Ava

Book + Main: bookandmainbites.com/avaharrison

Facebook Author Page: www.facebook.com/avaharrisonauthor

Facebook Reader Group: www.facebook.com/
groups/778471848896125

Goodreads: www.goodreads.com/author/show/13857011.
Ava_Harrison

Instagram @AvaHarrisonAuthor

Book Bub: www.bookbub.com/authors/ava-harrison

Amazon: www.amazon.com/Ava-Harrison/e/B00Y41M4KU

Text 'Harrison' to 313131 to get a text when I have a new release!